KAREN ROBARDS

Guilty

HODDER

First published in Great Britain in 2008 by Hodder & Stoughton
An Hachette UK company

This paperback edition published in 2020

1

A CIP catalogue record for this title is available from the British Library

Paperback ISBN 978 1 529 34900 9
eBook ISBN 978 1 848 94332 2

Typeset in Plantin Light by Palimpsest Book Production Ltd, Falkirk, Stirlingshire

Printed and bound in Great Britain by Clays Ltd, Elcograf S.p.A.

Hodder & Stoughton policy is to use papers that are natural, renewable
and recyclable products and made from wood grown in sustainable forests.
The logging and manufacturing processes are expected to conform to the
environmental regulations of the country of origin.

Hodder & Stoughton Ltd
Carmelite House
50 Victoria Embankment
London EC4Y 0DZ

www.hodder.co.uk

Christopher, this book is dedicated to you in honor of your June 2008 high school graduation.

We are so proud of you!

Love always, Mom

Acknowledgements

I want to thank my husband, Doug, and sons, Peter, Chris and Jack, for hanging in there one more time; my fantastic editor, Christine Pepe, for her patience and keen eye for detail; my agent, Robert Gottlieb, who always works so hard for me; Leslie Gelbman and Kara Welsh and the rest of the gang at Signet; Stephanie Sorensen, who does such a good job with publicity; and Ivan Held and the rest of the Putnam family, whose support I greatly appreciate.

1

'Where the sweet hell do you think you're going?' Just after midnight on a steamy Friday in Baltimore, fifteen-year-old Katrina Kominski was halfway down the fire escape of the run-down brick apartment building where she had lived for the past seven months when the bellow from above froze her in her tracks.

Busted, she thought, because what she was doing was sneaking out after being grounded for the weekend.

Clutching the peeling black metal rail and casting a scared glance up, she discovered her foster mother leaning out the fourth-floor window above her, fat cheeks jiggling, pink curlers bobbing, tent-size pink housecoat zipped up to her cowlike neck. Behind her she could see two of the other girls – Mrs. Coleman took in only girls; right now she had five in the three-bedroom apartment – crowding around. Twelve-year-old LaTonya looked scared. Sixteen-year-old Natalie looked smug.

Jealous witch had probably told.

'Out,' she yelled back. The response was pure bravado, because down below her friends were watching. Inside, where no one could see, her stomach knotted in fear. Her heart pounded.

Should she go back, or . . . ?

'Come on, Kat!' Jason Winter – the to-die-for-cute boy she was crazy about – yelled up to her. She looked down in terrible indecision. He was at the wheel of his beat-up blue Camaro, which was idling in the alley below. It was crammed with kids; her best friend, Leah Oscar, had her head stuck out the rear window on the driver's side, yelling 'Come on' to her along with Jason, while making urgent get-down-here-yesterday motions. A kid with black, curly hair – Mario Castellanos, one of Jason's good friends – had his head out the front passenger window, his hands cupped around his mouth as he yelled insults at Mrs. Coleman, who was now raining abuse down on Kat's head.

'Look out!' Leah shrieked, pointing at something above Kat. Jason yelled something, too, and a couple of the other kids stuck their heads out the car windows as they screamed warnings, but Kat was already looking up again, and what she saw sent her heart leaping into her throat.

Marty Jones, Mrs. Coleman's live-in boyfriend, had taken Mrs. Coleman's place and was halfway out the window. Last time she'd seen him – about half an hour ago, when she had supposedly gone to bed in the small room she shared with Natalie and LaTonya

– he'd been zonked out on the couch. Now here he came after her, barefoot, wearing his gray work pants and a wife-beater, which looked disgusting on his huge, hulking, hairy body. Like Mrs. Coleman, he was maybe in his mid-forties. Unlike Mrs. Coleman, he didn't even pretend to like the girls she fostered for a living.

Except in a creepy way. Like, he'd told Kat to call him Marty instead of Mr. Jones. And he was always trying to get her to sit on the couch next to him while he watched TV. And a couple of days ago he'd popped the lock on the bathroom door – he'd sworn it had been unlocked, but she knew better – and 'accidentally' walked in on her when she was in the shower. And . . . well, there were lots of ands.

Kat hated him. He'd been eyeing her since she had arrived from the group home where she had been sent after the last foster-care placement hadn't worked out. Being a skinny, cute, blue-eyed blonde was not a good thing when the world you lived in was full of predatory men like Marty Jones. Over the last couple of years, Kat had learned to recognize them at a glance, and to keep as far away from them as possible.

Only it was getting harder and harder to keep away from Marty.

'You better get your ass back up here right now!' Almost through the window now, Marty saw her looking up at him and shook his head threateningly at her. He held a baseball bat in one hand. As their eyes met through the open metalwork of the stairs,

Kat's stomach plummeted toward her red Dr. Scholl's sandals. Time to face the truth: Marty scared the bejesus out of her. 'Right now! You hear me, girl?'

Oh, yeah. She did. And even as the weight of him emerging onto the top of the fire escape made the whole thing shiver warningly, she ran, hanging on to the rail, clattering down the remaining steps to the encouraging screams of her friends, heart pounding, sweating bullets all the way.

If he caught her . . .

'Hurry, Kat!' 'He's coming, he's coming!' 'Fat old fart, you gonna knock them stairs right off the building you don't get off them!' 'Kat, you gotta *move*!' 'Jump for it!'

'You better not run from me!' Marty yelled after her. 'When I catch you, I'll . . .'

What he would do Kat never heard, because she jumped down the last two steps just then to land hard on her wooden soles on the cracked asphalt of the alley, and hands reached out of the Camaro's door, which had opened in anticipation of her imminent arrival, to drag her inside. She half leaped and half was pulled in on top of a shifting mass of teenage bodies. The door was still partially open when, tires squealing, the Camaro peeled rubber out of there. It slammed shut, though whether from the force of the forward motion or because somebody reached out and grabbed it she couldn't have said. As she struggled to sit up, Kat caught glimpses of long rows of brick walls broken up by cheap aluminum-framed windows and zigzagging fire escapes, and overflowing dumpsters and piles of trash that hadn't quite made it into the dumpsters, and an odd person or two slinking through the dark as the headlights flashed over them.

'That was so cool!' 'Man, he almost caught her!' 'Is that fat guy your dad?' 'I thought he was gonna knock the whole fire escape down.' 'You think they're gonna call the cops?'

'No, they won't call the cops,' Kat replied to the last thing she heard as she wiggled her butt down between Leah and her boyfriend, Roger Friedkin, while Donna Bianco was squashed against the far window. With the four of them wedged into the backseat and Jason and Mario up front, the car was hot despite all the windows being rolled down, which was due to a broken air conditioner. It was too humid for jeans, which she was wearing because she didn't possess any shorts, but she had teamed them with a red tank she'd 'borrowed' from LaTonya so she wasn't actually dying or anything. 'If they did, the social workers would come and take me away, and they don't want that. They need the money. I heard them talking about it.'

'You gonna be okay when you go back there, Kitty-cat?' Jason asked with the quiet concern that had first made her lose her heart to him. His eyes – blue as the waters of Chesapeake Bay – looked into hers through the rearview mirror. Her stomach fluttered in response.

She nodded.

'That fat old fart's gonna whup your ass, Kitty-cat,' Mario chortled, turning so that he could look at her. He smirked at her. 'I bet he's gonna like it, too.'

'Shut the hell up, why don't you?' Jason punched his friend in the arm.

'Ow!' Mario, glaring, covered the spot with his hand.

'It's okay,' Kat said to Jason. Then she looked at Mario. 'Why don't you go jerk off somewhere?'

Mario gave her an ugly look in return, but something, probably the thought of incurring Jason's further displeasure, kept his big mouth shut.

Too late to erase the image he'd implanted in her mind, though.

The thought of what her reception was going to be like when she returned to the apartment was already enough to make Kat want to puke. Realizing that she'd given Marty an excuse to lay his hands on her terrified her. Mario was right, although she hated him for saying it. If she went back, Marty would do something to hurt her and enjoy every minute of it. And she was as sure as it was possible to be that Mrs. Coleman wouldn't object.

Her fists clenched. Her mouth dried up. Tears pricked at the backs of her eyes, although she'd die before she'd let any fall.

I'll worry about it later.

'Hey, how about we get us some beer?' Mario yelled. He had to yell, because they were on the expressway now, speeding toward D.C., and with the wind rushing in through the open windows and the radio blaring and several conversations going on at once it was the only way to be heard. The big halogen lamps lighting the road from high overhead made it almost as bright as day inside the car. The Camaro was speeding, weaving in and out as it passed other cars and light trucks and a couple of big eighteen-wheelers that rattled like marbles in a tin can as the Camaro shot by.

'Yeah!' 'Beer! Woo-hoo!' 'I could use a beer!' 'None of that light stuff. I like my beer *heavy*!' 'Let's get us some beer!'

Kat hated beer, but she said nothing.

The Camaro swerved suddenly, and Kat clutched reflexively at Leah's arm. From the blur outside the window she knew that they were off the expressway and flying down an exit ramp. Jason stomped the brake at the intersection at the bottom of the ramp and everybody was flung violently forward, with the four in the backseat nearly thrown onto the floor.

As they picked themselves up and wedged themselves back into place, they all started laughing like what had just happened was the funniest thing ever.

Kat, too, because they were her friends.

As Jason swung the Camaro out onto a nearly deserted four-lane road crowded with closed retail establishments, Mario banged his fist on the dashboard and turned to look at the rest of them. 'Anybody got any *dinero*?'

'I got a dollar and . . . look at that, twenty-two cents.'
'I got a buck.' 'I got seventy-five cents.'

'I . . . don't have any money,' Kat said, when all eyes were on her after everyone else in the backseat had turned out their pockets. 'I'm not thirsty anyway.'

'That's okay.' Jason looked at her through the mirror again. 'I'll spring for yours.'

And he smiled at her.

The hard little knot in Kat's stomach eased.

That late at night, even McDonald's twin arches were turned off. The only things still open were gas stations and convenience stores. A Quik-Pik on the next corner was all lit up, and Kat assumed that was Jason's destination.

'Does somebody have an ID?' she asked, meaning a fake one, as the Camaro, still traveling too fast, bumped into the parking lot and slid to a stop beside one of the gas pumps. The parking lot was deserted. Through the glass windows, Kat could see a solitary clerk behind the cash register. It was a woman. She looked Hispanic, and young.

'I do, but it don't matter.' Mario grinned at her. 'I can pass for twenty-one easy.'

'His ID's good, though,' Justin said. 'Way better than mine.'

Everybody piled out of the car and started walking toward the store.

'I gotta pee,' Leah announced cheerfully, and looked at Kat. 'You wanna come to the bathroom with me?'

'Yeah,' Kat agreed, and the two of them broke off

to head around the side of the building where a battered sign announced *Restrooms*. They had both finished and Kat was washing her hands while Leah, peering around her into the mirror, fluffed her hair, when they heard a series of staccato sounds from outside.

Crack! Crack! Crack!

'What the hell?' Leah gasped, whirling to look at the door, which had no lock.

'It's a gun.' Kat knew what gunfire sounded like. Mrs. Coleman's government-subsidized apartment was actually one of the nicer places in which she had lived. The seven years she had spent with her mother were a blur of crack houses and abandoned buildings and the occasional homeless shelter. After that, she'd been passed around among relatives and friends until one day a social worker had come and taken her away. During that time, the sound of gunfire had been a nightly occurrence. For years she had slept huddled in corners listening to it, praying that a bullet wouldn't find its way through the walls and into her flesh.

'Oh, shit.' Leah ran for the door. Kat was right behind her, slowed a little by her cumbersome footwear. What they saw as they burst around the corner of the building was the rest of the gang bolting toward the Camaro like something bad was chasing them. They were screaming at one another, fighting about something, but Kat was too far away to understand the words. All she knew was that Jason looked scared to death – and Mario was holding a gun.

Her breathing suspended. Her gut clenched.

There was a man between her and Leah and the car. An older man, stocky and gray-haired, in what looked like a blue uniform. He was on his knees with his back to them. Leah flew past him without giving him so much as a glance. As Kat ran up behind him, he groaned and kind of toppled over on his side, then rolled onto his back. She saw that he was clutching his chest – and then she saw why and stopped in her tracks.

Bright blood bubbled up between his fingers, which were pale and pudgy, spilling over them, pouring on the black asphalt that glistened faintly in the store's reflected light. In a single lightning glance, she saw that there was a badge on his chest, gleaming silver, with a cheap plastic name tag below it. She wasn't close enough to read the name.

He's been shot. She remembered the gun in Mario's hands, and a chill ran through her.

He saw her. She could tell he did, because his eyes flickered.

'Help . . . me.'

Oh, God. She dropped to her knees beside him, bent over him, looking at him in horror, frantic to do something, anything, moving his hands aside so that she could see the wound. Then her hands came down one on top of the other as she pressed desperately against the hole, trying to stem the flow of blood. It was warm. And slimy. There was a smell. A sickening, raw-meat kind of smell.

'Hurts,' he muttered. And closed his eyes.

'Kat, come on!' The voice – Leah's – shrieked out at her as the Camaro screamed to a stop just a few feet away.

'Come on! Come on!' They were all shouting at her, but she couldn't move. Couldn't have gone to them if she had wanted to. She could feel the man's – his name was David Brady, she could read his name tag now – life slipping away, feel the energy leaving him as if his soul were rising around her. All she could do was stare at the car and feel the dying man's life ebbing, and her own heart thudding, and then the Camaro sped off with a squeal of rubber and she was left alone.

Really alone, because David Brady was dead now. His life force was gone.

She stayed beside him until she heard the sirens. Then she jumped to her feet and fled into the darkness, with David Brady's blood still dripping from her hands.

2

Thirteen years later ...

Something's wrong. The thought hit Tom Braga with all the explosive force of a bullet to the brain.

His gut clenched. His pulse speeded up. As his breath caught, he continued to listen to the empty silence on the other end of the phone with building intensity. He didn't know how he knew it for sure, but he did. They were speaking on cell phones, he and his younger brother, Tom from his unmarked car, which was at that moment slicing through the downpour en route to Philadelphia's modern Criminal Justice Center, where he was scheduled to be in court at nine – that would be in about three minutes – Charlie from wherever the hell he was. They were both cops, he a homicide detective, Charlie a sheriff's deputy. On this rainy Monday morning, they were both on duty. And unless he was totally going around the bend, Charlie was in trouble.

'Yo, bro, you still there?' Tom gripped the phone so hard its edges dug into his palm, but his voice stayed deceptively casual. They'd been talking about

Mom's weekly Sunday dinner, which Tom had missed for the third time in a row yesterday because he was tired of being ragged on all the time about being thirty-five and single and because sometimes his congregated family, nineteen strong, was enough to drive him nuts. In the middle of rubbing Tom's nose in the glories of the chicken parmigiana, which Charlie knew was his brother's particular favorite, twenty-eight-year-old Charlie had grunted as if in surprise, then simply stopped talking in the middle of a sentence. And Tom had started getting this really bad vibe.

'Yeah,' Charlie replied, to Tom's instant relief. Until he realized that his excitable brother's voice was absolutely flat, and he could hear Charlie breathing hard. 'Um, look, I gotta go.'

'Okay, well, you tell your sweet little wife Marcia hello for me, hear?' Tom's tone was hearty. Cold sweat prickled to life at his hairline. 'Tell her I'm looking forward to that homemade lasagna she promised me.'

'I'll do that,' Charlie said, and his phone went dead.

With that answer ringing in his ears, Tom practically ran through the red light he was rushing up on. Slamming on the brakes hard enough to make the department-issue black Taurus fishtail on the wet street, he managed to stop just in time to avoid barreling out into the middle of the busy intersection. Despite the fact that he was way too close to it, he was all but blind to the traffic that began rolling past just inches from his front bumper. The steady procession of headlights made the gloomy day seem even darker than it really was. Rain sluiced down over his windshield, pounding on the roof and hood with big, fat drops that hit with a quick *rat-a-tat* and splattered on impact. The windshield wipers were working hard on high. The radio played easy listening.

He was oblivious to all of it.

Charlie's wife was named Terry. And fixing peanut-butter sandwiches for their two little hooligans was about as good as her kitchen skills got.

'Jesus.' It was both prayer and expletive.

Taking a deep breath, Tom called on years of experience to separate mind from emotion, and did what he had been trained to do in emergency situations: What came next. Unwanted, an image of Charlie as he'd last seen him flashed into his head. Black-haired, lean and good-looking, as all the Braga siblings were, Charlie had been sitting in a plastic blow-up kiddie pool in his tiny backyard about three weekends back, clad only in trunks, happily yelling for help while his four-year-old twins dumped bucket after bucket of hose-cold water over his head. Seeing his brother's laughing face in his mind's eye didn't help, so Tom did his best to banish it as he punched buttons on his cell phone. His hand was steady. His thoughts were clear. His pulse raced like a thoroughbred pounding for the finish line.

An infinity seemed to pass as he listened to the ringing on the other end.

Pick up, pick up, damn you to hell, Bruce Johnson, pick up.

'Johnson here.'

'Tom Braga.' Tom identified himself to Charlie's supervisor. The cold sweat that had started at his hairline had by now spread to his whole body. Adrenaline rushed through his veins like speed. There was a tightness to his voice that he could hear himself, yet at the same time he felt very focused, very calm. 'Where's Charlie?'

'Charlie?' Johnson paused. Tom could picture him kicked back in his chair, coffee and a newspaper on his desk, an island of good-natured calm in the center of never-ending chaos. The Philly sheriff's office was large, with numerous departments and hundreds of deputies and support staff, but he and Johnson had grown up together in tough South Philly and in consequence knew each other well. The big, burly sergeant was a favorite with Tom's whole family. 'Let me check.'

He covered the mouthpiece – not well – and yelled, 'Anybody know where Charlie Braga is this morning?'

Hurry, Tom thought, gritting his teeth. Then, having realized what he was doing, he deliberately relaxed his jaw.

Seconds later Johnson was back on the line. 'He took a witness from the jail over to the Justice Center. Wasn't that long ago, so he should still be there. Any particular reason why you're interested?'

The Justice Center. Tom could see it, a little more than a block away on the right. It was a tall stone rectangle topped by a dome, with vertical lines of windows glowing yellow through the rain.

The light was green and the intersection in front of him was clear. He registered that and at about the same time became aware of impatient horns honking behind him. A split second later he stomped on the gas. The rear tires of the Taurus sent up plumes of water as the vehicle responded.

'I was talking to him on the phone right before I called you.' Tom's voice was steady despite the fact that the bad feeling he'd had was getting worse. He was rushing toward the building now, anxiously scanning as much of it as he could see while weaving in and out of traffic in an effort to get where he was going fast. Cars were parallel parked all along Filbert Street, the narrow, pre-Revolutionary War era avenue out in front of the Justice Center. People hurried along the sidewalk, past the building, and up and down the wide stone steps leading to the main entrance. A sea of umbrellas and splashing feet were about all he could see of the pedestrians. From outside the revolving doors, he got a glimpse of the security checkpoint with its guards and metal detectors. Nothing looked out of place. There was no sign of trouble. But his gut was telling him otherwise, and one thing he'd learned during his thirteen years as a cop was to never go against his gut.

'He gave me a signal, like.' Even as he scanned the area, Tom continued talking to Johnson. 'Something's wrong. You need to alert whoever else you've got over there that something's possibly going down. Get some backup to Charlie's location, stat. And tell them to keep it quiet. No sirens, nothing like that. I just got a real creepy feeling.'

Johnson snorted. 'I'm supposed to send in the troops because you've got a creepy feeling?'

'Yeah.'

'Will do,' Johnson said. He was enough of a professional not to take chances when it was a matter of another officer's safety – and not to question another cop's instincts. He covered the mouthpiece again, and Tom could hear him giving the necessary orders.

'Where in the Justice Center?' Tom yelled into the phone. Yelling was necessary to get Johnson's attention again. Tom was in front of the Justice Center now, cruising past the long row of bumper-to-bumper parked cars, where there was, he discovered with a quick glance up the block, no longer an available place to park. Not that it was going to make any difference. Ignoring the cars piling up in honking indignation behind him, he double-parked beside a big silver Suburban.

'Subbasement,' Johnson replied. 'Probably.'

Shit.

The subbasement was a badly lit and ventilated rabbit warren two stories underground. Holding cells for prisoners needed in court that day, administrative offices, the courtroom for arraignments, anterooms for lawyers and court officials and bail bondsmen – all that and more were located down there. The place teemed with activity from seven A.M. on as the accused, the convicted, the acquitted, and everything and everyone connected with their cases rotated in and out.

Charlie could've found all kinds of trouble down there.

'I'm on the scene,' Tom said grimly, and disconnected.

Jumping out, head bent, into the pouring rain that began instantly soaking his short, thick black hair and court-ready attire of navy sport jacket, white shirt, red tie, and gray slacks, he slammed the door and took off at a sprint toward the building. As he ran, he reached beneath his jacket to unsnap the safety strap on his Glock.

If he was lucky, he wouldn't need it. But then, he'd never been very lucky.

3

Being a prosecutor is not for sissies, Kate White thought grimly as the backs of the elegant Stuart Weitzman pumps she had bought on eBay for ten dollars rubbed against her increasingly tender heels with every purposeful step she took. The pay was lousy, the perks were nonexistent, and the people – well, all she could say was that there were a few good apples mixed in with all the rotten ones. A very few.

'Get a move on, would you? If we're late he'll hang us out to dry,' Bryan Chen muttered behind her. A small, compact Asian-American, the forty-two-year-old veteran assistant district attorney was definitely one of the good apples. Four months before, he'd taken her under his wing when she had graduated from law school at age twenty-eight and joined the prosecutor's office. It was the first step on a career ladder that she was determined would take her to the (lucrative) pinnacle of one of Philadelphia's stellar super-firms. Bryan, on the other hand, had been an assistant DA for going on sixteen years now and seemed perfectly content to make a career of it. Of course, he didn't have a hundred thousand dollars in student loans to pay off and a young son for whom he was the only source of support, either.

She personally wanted more, for herself and for Ben, her sweet-faced nine-year-old, than to live for years on end in a tiny leased house on a diet of pasta and peanut butter at the end of every pay period.

And she meant to get it.

'We're not late,' she replied, with more confidence than she felt.

Pushing through the heavy mahogany doors of Courtroom 207 in the Criminal Justice Center, she was relieved to see that she was right. The 'he' Bryan had been referring to – Circuit Court Judge Michael Moran, a humorless appointee who was presiding over today's circus – was nowhere in sight, although the courtroom deputy stood in front of the bench with an anticipatory eye on the door that led to the judge's chambers, obviously expecting His Honor to appear at any second.

Hurry. Must not get on wrong side of notoriously cranky judge before trial even starts, she thought as she strode – big, long strides that killed her feet – down the aisle. Her shoes were wet and the highly polished terrazzo underfoot was slippery, making speed a dangerous proposition. But under the circumstances she felt she had no choice. The defense was already in place, and the courtroom galleries were full. The only thing missing was the judge – and the prosecution. Still, cutting their arrival dangerously close to the wire wouldn't cost them a thing as long as they were in place before the judge came out.

In other words, what he didn't know couldn't hurt them.

The deputy kept watching the door to chambers. Meanwhile, the bench remained unoccupied. Silvery rivulets of rain streamed down the pair of tall windows that flanked the bench, making the courtroom seem unusually closed off. It had been officially autumn for more than a week, but today's cold rain was the first real indication they'd had that the seasons had changed. The downpour was also why they were late – every available parking spot near the Justice Center was taken, which meant they'd had to park in a garage on the next block – and why unruly strands of her normally sleek, shoulder-length blond hair were escaping from her once-neat bun to wave around her face. She could only hope the mascara she'd hurriedly swiped on – it was waterproof but cheap, so you never knew – was still framing her blue eyes and not making inky rivers down her smooth, ivory-pale cheeks. Looking like a sad clown was not the way to win the kind of notice she wanted.

Despite the danger inherent in charging full-tilt toward the counsel tables without keeping her mind totally in the moment, Kate multitasked. Juggling umbrella and briefcase, she ran her fingers beneath her lower lashes in the hope of doing away with any errant black streaks, then brushed down the front of her once-pricey black skirt suit with quick little whisking motions that just seemed to make the wet spots bigger, and plucked the damp front of her white

Hanes T-shirt away from her chest so that it wouldn't cling too closely. At the same time she absorbed all of it, the large, high-ceilinged room with its mahogany-paneled walls, the bent heads of the public defender and his client close together as they conferred over a yellow legal pad, the steady murmur of conversation and rustle of movement from the packed gallery, the musty smell of too many damp bodies jammed in together, with a quick surge of satisfaction. This was her world, the world she had fashioned for herself out of nothing but her own determination. The knowledge that she belonged in it now, that she was one of the good guys, brought a small smile to her lips. Walking a little taller, she was instantly brought back to earth by the stabbing of the thrice-damned shoes into her heels. The price on the pointy-toed pumps had been right, they were black and real leather and definitely added to the professional aura of her secondhand suit, but Jesus, they *hurt*. It was all she could do not to limp.

Beggars can't be choosers, as the last – and least lamented – of her foster mothers used to say. This month she had paid the rent *and* the utilities *and* the babysitter *and* the minimum on her Visa bill and student loans *and* put gas in the car *and* bought Ben a new pair of sneakers. Now, with six days to go before the first of October – she was paid semimonthly, on the first and the fifteenth – she was scarily close to dead broke. That was pretty much how it went every month, which meant there was little – as in practically zero – in the budget for work clothes. The thing that made it difficult was that to achieve her goal, she had to look like a professional. A *successful* professional. Ergo, she turned to eBay when necessary. But like everything else in life, getting the right clothes on the cheap came with a price, and today the price was apparently going to be hamburger heels.

The minute hand on the large, round clock that hung over the door to the hall through which prisoners were brought into the courtroom moved incrementally. It was now officially nine o'clock.

To hell with her shoes. They had to *move*.

'Look out, here he comes.' Bryan practically shoved her through the low, swinging door that separated the gallery from the well just as the stone-faced deputy turned to face the crowded courtroom and drew himself up to his full height.

'All rise,' he boomed, fixing Kate and Bryan with a warning stare as they scrambled into place behind the counsel table at the last possible second. Everyone else stood, too, so that they were all on their feet together and focused forward as the door to chambers was pulled open from the inside. 'Court is now in session. The Honorable Judge Michael Moran presiding.'

While Judge Moran – 'Moran the Moron,' as he was known to the assistant DAs – strode out, his black robe flapping around his portly frame, his round, ruddy face beneath its short thicket of iron-gray hair already tired and cross-looking at nine o'clock in the morning, a steaming coffee cup in his hand, Kate quietly dropped her umbrella to the floor, slid her briefcase onto the table, and struggled to catch her breath. Instead of watching the judge assume the God position behind the polished mahogany bench, she shifted her attention sideways to the jury box, which was to her right. It held fourteen people, twelve jurors and two alternates, skewing older, white, and female, which was just the way she had wanted it. This was at its heart an armed-robbery case, nothing unusual for Philly, but the defendant, Julio 'Little Julie' Soto, a twenty-three-year-old street punk, had beaten up the woman behind the convenience-store counter badly enough so that she had spent five days in the hospital. That degree of violence, in Kate's estimation, was uncalled for and the mark of a dangerous man. She had refused to plea-bargain. The Commonwealth – that was her – was asking for a sentence of not less than twenty years.

Not surprisingly, the defendant had opted to exercise his constitutional right to a jury trial. Not that it would help him in any way. She had the goods on him, from eyewitnesses to fingerprints to tape from a security camera, and unless he was next in line for a miracle, he was going away for a long time.

'Good morning,' Judge Moran said to the courtroom in general. His tone was sour. Kate presumed he didn't like rainy Mondays any more than anybody else. To the left of the bench, the court reporter, Sally Toner, a plump, fiftyish blonde, was seated in front of her computer. Her fingers flew over the keys as she recorded the judge's greeting, as she would everything else that was said in the courtroom that day.

'Good morning, Your Honor,' Kate and opposing counsel chorused faux-cheerfully in reply. Synchronized small talk was a skill largely left untaught by law schools, but most lawyers managed to pick it up anyway. Over time Kate was sure it became as automatic as sucking up to the judge.

Judge Moran nodded and settled into his tall leather chair, carefully positioning his coffee in front of him and accepting a sheaf of papers handed to him by the deputy. That was everyone else's cue to sit, too, which Kate did with relief, surreptitiously easing her feet a little way out of her shoes. The deputy turned back to the courtroom with his usual bit, announcing that they were assembled there in that courtroom on that morning in the case of the Commonwealth of Pennsylvania vs. Julio Juan Soto, blah, blah, blah, blah. Kate tuned him out.

First chance I get, I'm sticking Band-Aids on my poor heels. She always kept some in her briefcase.

Since she was wearing hose, that would require a trip to the ladies' room, which would have to wait for a break.

Rats.

Pulling her notes from her briefcase, she discreetly checked her reflection in the small mirror she kept clipped to one of the inside pockets. What little makeup she wore seemed to have survived the deluge more or less intact, she was relieved to see. Just as she had feared, though, her hair was well on its way to working free of its bun – she quickly pushed the pins holding it in tighter – and her nose was shiny. Otherwise, she was good to go. She wasn't gorgeous by any means, but she was attractive, with a square-jawed, high-cheekboned face punctuated by intelligent blue eyes and a wide, soft-lipped mouth. Her nose, which was a little too long, was her worst feature, in her opinion. The fact that it was, at the moment, glassily reflecting the fluorescent lights overhead didn't help. Under the cover of setting her briefcase on the floor, she managed to swipe her nose with a blotting tissue from the packet she kept in there along with various other emergency items, then straightened just as the deputy ended his spiel.

Judge Moran's attention, she was glad to see, was still focused on the papers in front of him. Beside her, Bryan had pulled a yellow legal pad and pen from his own briefcase and was doodling away. This was nominally his case, but she had done all the preparation and would be trying it. After the trial was over, unless she did something horribly wrong and got fired, she would be handling cases on her own from then on out, no longer tucked under Bryan's wing. Her bar exam results had come in just days before: She had passed with flying colors. Except for the official swearing in, she was now a full-fledged member of the Pennsylvania bar, and no longer required supervision to work as a prosecutor.

She, Kate White, was a real, honest-to-God lawyer.

Just saying the words to herself gave her a thrill. Who woulda thunk it? Nobody she had ever known once upon a time, that's for sure. Sometimes she had trouble believing it herself.

'Mr. Curry?' Moran looked up from the papers at last and frowned in the direction of the defense. 'What's this?'

Kate's antenna went up. 'Mr. Curry' was the public defender, Ed Curry, who had been opposing counsel on several of the cases Kate had worked, enough so that she thought she knew how he operated by now. Average height, thin, balding, mid-forties, dressed today in a rumpled gray suit with a white shirt and navy tie, Curry wasn't given to springing surprises in court. Straightforward and unimaginative, with an air of impatience, he did a competent job for his clients in the meager time he was able to allot to each of them.

Curry stood. 'Your Honor, I apologize, but our office just received the information on this witness late Friday. Over the weekend, I talked to the man in jail, and I found him to be cred—'

'Witness? What witness?' Kate jammed her feet back into the torturous shoes and shot upright, accidentally sending her wheeled chair flying back toward the bar. Bryan grabbed it, stopping it before it crashed. Judge Moran sent her a quelling glance. Curry's gaze shifted her way for a split second, and then he quickly refocused on the judge. He looked uncharacteristically ill at ease. *As well he should*, Kate thought. Springing a surprise witness on the opening day of a trial was one of those Lawyer 101 no-no's that even newbies like herself knew not to do. A quick check showed her that the jurors had brightened with interest. *Not good.* Whatever was up, she didn't want the jury hearing about it until after she did. She needed details on what was going down and time to assess its impact on her case, to say nothing of coming up with a way to neutralize any potential negative fallout before the jury got so much as a whiff of whatever it was. 'Your Honor, permission to approach the bench.'

'Permission granted. You, too, Mr. Curry.'

Kate whisked out from behind the counsel table and marched toward the bench, her screaming heels be damned. Body language was worth a lot in a courtroom, and sometimes you just had to make the opposition aware that you weren't going to take their crap. Otherwise, the bullies – and there were lots of them in the legal profession – would gleefully kick your ass.

Refusing to look at her – *Hah, he knows he's out of line* – Curry walked forward, too. As soon as he joined her in front of the bench, Kate pounced.

'Your Honor, opposing counsel knows very well that it's too late to introduce a new witness. Discovery was closed weeks ago. I—'

'Spare me the lecture, Ms. White.' Judge Moran held up his hand for silence. 'You can rest assured that I'm well aware of the appropriate timetable here.'

Kate clamped her jaws shut, crossed her arms over

her chest, and glared, hopefully presenting a picture of five feet six inches – no, five-nine with the shoes – of slender, eloquent indignation for the benefit of the jury. The jury couldn't hear what they were saying – the conversation was being conducted in low tones for just that reason – but she hoped that at least they could read her body language loud and clear: *The defense is trying to pull a fast one. Don't be fooled.*

'In case it somehow escaped your notice, you interrupted Mr. Curry,' Moran continued. He looked at the public defender. 'Mr. Curry, I presume you were about to tell me just why it is that this is the first we've heard about this witness. And I warn you, if I find that you've deliberately withheld information from the prosecution . . .'

Curry shook his head vigorously. He, too, knew Moran's reputation for firing off contempt citations at lawyers like parking tickets, and nobody wanted a contempt citation with its accompanying time in jail until somebody could get the offending attorney off the hook. It cost the unlucky recipient too much time, money, and aggravation.

'Nothing like that, Your Honor. As I was saying, the witness just got in contact with our office on Friday. He's in custody himself, and claims he was unaware of the facts of the case until then. His evidence is compelling, and it provides my client with a full alibi. You may be sure that I wouldn't have brought it to your attention otherwise.'

'Bull—' Kate caught herself in time, swallowed the

inevitable ending as Moran turned a warning gaze on her, and hastily substituted the judge-friendlier '—ocks, Your Honor. The evidence against the defendant is overwhelming, as Mr. Curry knows. This witness cannot possibly provide a credible alibi for his client because we already have eyewitnesses, a security videotape, and forensic evidence placing Mr. Soto at the scene. There is no way your client' – and here she shot a hard-eyed look at the public defender – 'isn't guilty as sin.'

'Ms. White, I realize you're just out of school so we all have to cut you some slack, but for future reference that's usually up to the jury to decide,' Curry said. As Moran's focus shifted to Kate, Curry gave her a snarky smile.

'That's right,' Moran said before Kate could reply. He nodded gravely, and Kate saw just how he had earned his nickname: The man clearly didn't know when he was being had. She also realized that Curry knew Moran far better than she did, and was using that knowledge to his advantage. It didn't matter if his tactics were blatantly out of order. All that mattered was how they played to this particular judge on this particular day. Now Moran was frowning at her. 'Remember, Ms. White, we are here to find out the truth, whatever that may be. Potentially exculpatory testimony cannot be ruled out simply because the timing is inconvenient for the prosecution.'

Moran's lecture had the patronizing tone of a professor to a student, and Kate's hackles rose even higher. She pursed her lips. The defense's tactics were becoming as clear as glass to her: Curry knew he couldn't win today in court, so he was trying to delay. Delay was a defense attorney's best friend. Put a trial off long enough, and anything could happen, with most outcomes favorable to the defense: Witnesses could move away or die, evidence could be lost, memories could fail. Prosecutors could move on to other jobs. Judges could retire. Even in the absence of any of those, with each day that passes the case loses priority. There is so much crime, so many criminals, out there that a case not tried in a timely manner could easily get lost in the judicial system shuffle.

Debbie Berman – the store clerk whose cheekbone and eye socket had been broken by the defendant – deserved better than that. She was there, in the courtroom, losing more time from work, for which she wouldn't be paid, waiting to testify, to bring her attacker to justice. So was the customer who had been in the store at the time. So was the man who had been out front pumping gas at just the right moment to see Soto run out. So was the cop who had analyzed the videotape. So was *everybody* connected to the case, all brought together in the courtroom today as a result of her, Kate's, painstaking work, all relying on her guarantee that showing up and doing the right thing would be worth it, that this time one of the bad guys was going to get what was coming to him. She had organized everything, assembled everyone, dotted every pretrial i and crossed every pretrial t. The prosecution was set up to run like clockwork, with the case going to the jury by the close of the day, probably less than a day for deliberations, late tomorrow or Wednesday at the worst for the verdict to come in. And it would be guilty.

Guilty, guilty, guilty. There was absolutely no doubt in her mind about that. A solid conviction, justice done all around, one less bad guy on the streets, and everybody could go home happy.

Only now Curry was screwing with the plan. She scowled at him before she could stop herself. Luckily, Moran's attention had already swung back to the defense attorney.

'Mr. Curry, you want to give Ms. White and me a quick idea of who this witness is and what he is prepared to testify to before I rule on admissibility?'

Curry glanced at her again. Kate could see the craftiness at the backs of his eyes. He knew his witness was full of crap. He knew that there was no way anyone could testify truthfully that Soto was not at the scene of the crime, because Soto *was* there, *had* committed the crime, and all the evidence proved it. Her gaze shot to the judge, whose expression was solemnly unctuous.

Doesn't he see it? Doesn't he see that Curry knows this is bullshit? Doesn't he get that he's being had?

Apparently not.

'My witness – and I don't want to give his name here in open court, for his protection, but he is a longtime acquaintance of the accused and his family – says Mr. Soto has a cousin who . . .'

The cheerfully funky notes of the Pussycat Dolls

hit 'Don't Cha' blared without warning from some-where in the courtroom. While Judge Moran stiffened and Curry glanced over his shoulder, his expression surprised as he sought the source of the disruption, Kate froze in horror.

She knew the source of the disruption without any possibility of mistake. It was her cell phone. She – and this was another big courtroom no-no – had forgotten to turn it off. The mortifyingly unprofessional ringtone only made things worse. Ben and his friend Samantha had been experimenting with her phone yesterday when she had driven them through the McDonald's drive-thru on the way to returning Samantha home from a playdate. *This* had been their favorite ringtone. *This* was what they had left on her phone. *This* was what she had forgotten all about, and thus hadn't gotten around to changing back to its usual businesslike chime.

She always turned her phone off before walking into court. *Always*. But in all the rush, today of all days, she had simply forgotten.

'Whose cell phone is that?' Judge Moran asked awfully.

A stricken glance at Bryan's face told her that he knew the distracting sound was emanating from somewhere around their table.

Her briefcase, to be precise. Nestled against the far leg of the counsel table, there on the floor beside her chair. Although she couldn't see the black leather rectangle from where she stood, she guessed the thing was practically vibrating with the energy of the song.

Her phone let loose with the bouncy melody again, and she felt about two inches tall.

'I want an answer!' Moran said.

Everyone glanced around, searching for the culprit. The three deputies stationed around the courtroom looked at one another, then at the judge for a cue as to what to do. Knowing Moran, this was going to get nasty fast.

Kate faced the awful truth: There was no way out. She had to confess.

'It's mine, Your Honor,' she said, doing her best to keep her chin up even though she felt like sinking straight down through the floor. Right on cue, the ringtone sounded again.

If only the damned thing would shut up. Please, let it just shut up.

'I'm so sorry, I . . .'

'Turn it off.' Moran's voice was like thunder. His face was taking on color like a quickly ripening tomato. 'Now.'

'Yes, Your Honor.'

Toddling off in the direction of counsel table while doing her best to maintain some semblance of professional cool, she was hideously conscious of being the cynosure of all eyes. Bryan's face was a study in dismay. Beyond him, in the galleries, Kate faced a sea of wide eyes all focused on her. Except for another exuberant burst of melody from her damned phone, the silence in that courtroom was absolute.

Oh my God, I don't believe this. I've made an absolute fool of myself and Bryan and the entire district attorney's office. Moran's going to wipe the floor with me. How could I have let this happen?

Those, and more along the same line, were only some of the happy thoughts that pounded through Kate's head as, teeth clenched, she crouched beside the prosecution's table, flipped the clasps open on her briefcase, and thrust her hand into the side pocket to grab her vibrating phone.

Kate found the button and turned off the ringer with a quick, vicious jab even as recognition dawned: The phone number dancing across the little digital display on the front of the phone was that of Ben's school.

Even so, her uppermost feeling for the next split second was relief that blessed silence now reigned.

Then anxiety of a different sort raised its head, playing havoc with her already frazzled nerves.

Ben.

She had dropped him off at seven-thirty, as she did every morning so she could get to work on time. He was part of the breakfast group, which was maybe a quarter of the school's population of two hundred under-twelves, basically the kids whose parents had to be at work by eight. They had juice and cereal or whatever in the cafeteria until seven-fifty, when they were allowed to go to their classrooms for the official beginning of the school day. This – fourth grade – was Ben's first year at the school, because they'd moved into the district at the beginning of the summer when she'd been hired on at the DA's office. So far, he had told her, it had been 'okay.' Which in Ben-speak meant he didn't want to talk about it. Which worried her. Which was no surprise. Practically everything to do with raising Ben worried her.

She was so afraid she wasn't doing it right.

Now the school was calling, and the knowledge made her stomach tighten with anxiety.

Was Ben sick? Was he hurt? Or was it something else that the school wanted, something administrative maybe? Yes, that was probably it: a form she'd forgotten to fill out, a check she'd forgotten to send, something of that nature. Whatever it was, though, she couldn't possibly return the call now. The best she could do was wait until she could somehow manage to squeeze in a break.

Please don't let Ben be sick or hurt, she prayed as she stuffed the now silenced phone back into her briefcase, slid Bryan an apologetic look, and, cringing inwardly in anticipation of what she knew she was about to face, rose to her feet.

Crack! Crack! Crack!

The sounds, faintly muffled, came out of nowhere.

With her peripheral vision, Kate caught a blur of sudden movement: a door – the tan metal door to the secure corridor where prisoners were kept in a series of holding rooms until their presence was required in court – flew open. As she whirled to face it, someone in the gallery screamed.

Those are gunshots was her instinctive first thought as the courtroom erupted into chaos around her.

To her astonishment, Little Julie Soto sprang to his feet and ran around the far end of the defense table, his wiry, five-feet-six-inch frame conveying a surprising amount of menace despite its diminutive proportions and the ill-fitting gray suit he wore for the benefit of the jury. His long black hair and pale blue tie bounced as he moved, and his narrow face was alight with savage triumph. From somewhere he had acquired a pistol; it was in his hand.

Kate sucked in air. Her heart gave a great leap.

No! But her throat didn't work; her lips didn't move. She screamed it only inside her head.

'You ain't putting me back in jail,' Soto shouted to the accompaniment of an explosion of frantic screams.

Judge Moran was on his feet, she saw as her disbelieving gaze followed Soto's. The judge raised his hands, palms outward, as if to ward off the threat. His eyes were wide and his mouth was opening, as if he was about to speak, or yell, or something. Whatever he meant to do, she never knew, because she was just in time to watch – *bang!* – as his head was blown to pieces.

4

Kate experienced the horror of Judge Moran's murder like a punch to the stomach. She gasped. Her ears rang. A sour taste sprang into her mouth.

This can't be real.

Blood and brains splattered the wall behind the bench. The gruesome cloud of red-tinged mist that was left where the judge's head had been just a split second before was still hanging in the air when his body dropped like a rock, disappearing from view. Kate's knees buckled at the same time. She collapsed into a kneeling position right there at the far side of the counsel table, eyes huge with disbelief, heart pounding. Her clenched fists pressed hard against her mouth. After that, she couldn't move. She couldn't breathe. She felt suddenly disembodied, as if she was viewing what was happening from a great – safe – distance.

Please, oh please, let this be a bad dream.

Men – two of them, at least one a prisoner, judging from the short-sleeved orange jumpsuit he wore – burst from the secure corridor. Pistols were in their hands. Soto glanced over his shoulder at them.

'Vámonos! Let's go!'

Crack! Crack!

More shots rang out, coming from roughly the direction of the jury box. One of the deputies firing back, Kate thought, although she couldn't see who was shooting exactly because she still couldn't move. At the same time, panicked confusion erupted everywhere. In the space of just those first few seconds, the courtroom turned into a terrifying kaleidoscope of color and sound and movement.

Ducking low, Soto and the newcomers ran toward the front of the courtroom as one of them – the one in the orange jumpsuit – shouted at him, 'What the hell did you just do?'

'I killed him, so what?' Soto yelled back.

'You stupid shit!'

'Go to hell!'

With two of the three cursing at each other, they converged, dashing around the side of the bench toward the window, dodging bullets and snapping off shots as they ran. Curry hit the ground in front of the bench, his arms flying to cover his head as a bullet smacked into the smooth mahogany not two feet above where he lay. Hands in the air, the court reporter fled shrieking toward the jury box. The deputy nearest the bench – the one whose sleep-inducing drone Kate had tuned out earlier – screamed and dropped; he'd been shot, she knew, even before she saw the blood rolling out from beneath his head. Screams and curses and pounding feet and gunfire – even after all these years, Kate would recognize those sharp bangs anywhere

– mingled hideously, exploding off the walls and floor and ceiling like rapid-fire thunder, filling the room with deafening, terrifying noise. The smell of cordite and carnage was everywhere.

The blood now pouring from the slain deputy's head continued to roll toward her like a scarlet river across the black-speckled stone floor.

The smell hit her.

Human blood smells like raw meat. Oh, God, I remember that smell . . .

Kate's stomach turned inside out. She wanted to gag, but she couldn't. She seemed to be paralyzed. Shock – it was good that she could at least recognize that cold, dead feeling as shock, wasn't it? – rendered her immobile, rooting her to the smooth, hard terrazzo beneath her bent legs.

Blood – so much blood . . . blood everywhere . . . splashes of scarlet on the walls, splatters of scarlet on the floor, gushers of scarlet pumping from destroyed flesh . . .

Time seemed to slow to an impossible crawl. Her stomach churned sickeningly. Her heart pounded in hard, fast strokes. Icy with horror now, she knew there was nothing she could do to save herself or anyone else as the nightmare unfolded around her.

'Where are they?' the guy in the orange jumpsuit screamed, sharply enough to pierce the explosion of noise, which was so loud she felt her brain might self-destruct from the sheer, unbelievable volume of it.

'The fuck should I know?' Soto screamed back. 'They oughta be here!'

'*Get out, get out, get out!*' This, from the gallery, was some other, innocent, man's yell, rising over the tumult, urging others to flee.

'Mama, where are you?' It was a child's frantic screech, also from the gallery.

'God help me, Jesus help me . . .' a nearby woman wailed.

These and other disembodied voices reached her ears through the hair-raising sounds of dozens of people screaming and fighting to escape what in just a matter of seconds had turned into an abattoir. If she'd been able to move, she would have clapped her hands over her ears, but her muscles, seemingly heavy as lead, obstinately refused to respond to her brain's signals. Her breathing came fast and shallow. Her pulse raced. Cold sweat poured over her in waves. She knew she should move, run, hide, right now on pain of death, but she didn't. She couldn't. For the second time in her life, she was frozen to the spot with fear. Only her eyes moved, glancing desperately around.

Oh, God, how many dead?

Some people in the galleries were hunkered down, she saw as her terrified gaze darted toward them, doing their best to hide from the flying bullets as the remaining deputies and prisoners exchanged fire. Others jumped screaming over the backs of the benches or charged down the center aisle, bent double, pushing and slamming into one another as they tried to escape by way of the double doors she and Bryan had hurried through just moments before. A fleeing man was shot in the back and flung forward out of sight, knocking down two people in front of him as he fell. Those rushing up the aisle behind him leaped over the fallen bodies. In the jury box, some were on their feet, stampeding like crazed cattle toward the door to the jury room. Others dived out of sight behind the box's low wall, impeding their fellows.

Bullets flew everywhere.

Another deputy, retreating along the courtroom's left wall, shot steadily at the murderous trio now sheltering behind the bench before being hit by a barrage of return fire that cut him down. The jack-hammerlike *crack* of the shots blasted Kate's eardrums. She screamed along with the rest – but once again, the sound was only inside her head.

'Kate, for God's sake, get under here!'

The urgent summons came from nearby. Something warm and faintly moist grabbed at her leg. She squeaked, jumping, and sucked in a great gulp of air. Reality hit her like a bucket of ice water to the face.

I could die here – only I can't. What would happen to Ben?

As her son's beloved face rose in her mind's eye, panic clawed at her insides. Her survival instinct kicked in. Even as she recognized Bryan's pudgy fingers sliding away from her ankle she saw him, hunkered down under the dubious protection of the counsel table. He crouched on the balls of his feet, breathing hard, visibly sweating. His eyes were shiny-scared as he met her gaze.

Oh my God, they killed Judge Moran. We – the prosecutors – are probably next on the list.

Time resumed its normal ferocious pace. Twisting around, she speed-crawled toward Bryan. Her heart pounded like a marathon runner's. Her palms were so sweaty that they slipped a little on the terrazzo. Although she knew she really wasn't, she *felt* safer once the thin slab of mahogany was over her head. Crowding next to the sturdy warmth of Bryan's side, she strained to look out beneath the overhang, desperate to find out where the shooters were. What she could see was limited: briefcases and umbrellas and a scattering of papers that had fallen to the floor from the counsel table, part of the wall to the jury box, the lower half of the bench, podium, witness stand, and court reporter's station, the area beneath the defense table and dark paneling all around. The only people visible to her from that angle were the fallen deputy and Curry, who, while still hugging the floor, was moving in a fast, commando-style crawl toward the defense table and, beyond it, the wall that separated the well from the gallery.

'This is bad,' Brian said in her ear, his voice shaky.

'We've got to get out of here.' Terror squeezed her throat, making it difficult to force words out. Their dark little cave might have felt safe, but she absolutely knew it was not. For Ben's sake if for no other reason, she had to survive.

What would he do without her? His dad was dead; she had no family to take him in. He would be all alone. The thought of it imbued her with the worst kind of fear.

'Is that bastard even out there?' Orange Jumpsuit shrieked. 'Pack, you see him?'

'Can't see nothing through the damned rain.'

'We gotta chance it. We gotta *go*.'

At least two of the trio were scarily close, Kate estimated, judging from the clarity with which she heard their shouted exchange. Their guns sounded like they were being fired almost directly overhead. She still couldn't see them, which made the panic flooding her just that much worse. At the thought that at any second now they might remember her and Bryan, Kate shuddered.

Please, God, don't let it be my time to die.

She was breathing so fast that she feared she might hyperventilate. Her pulse raced. Her heart pounded. Loud crashes from the general vicinity of the bench made her cower, but try as she might to see, Kate couldn't tell what caused them. All she was sure of was that she and Bryan were in deadly danger. Knowing that the counsel table offered only an illusion of protection, she desperately looked around for the best way out. The presence of the wall separating the well from the galleries, designed to keep the principals in a trial at a safe distance from the public gallery, worked against them now. It was about three feet behind them, cutting them off from any chance at an easy escape. As she saw it, they had three choices: They could go over the wall and start leaping galleries, they could dash toward the small swinging door that led to the center aisle and bolt with the rest of the crowd for the exit, or they could stay put. The first two exposed them to the bullets that were still flying everywhere, and, if they were spotted by the bad guys as they were almost certain to be, might be the equivalent of painting targets smack in the middle of their backs. The third seemed safer, but in reality it left them vulnerable to being hit by a stray bullet – or discovered at any time by the gunmen.

Who would, she had no doubt at all after what happened to Judge Moran, kill them with glee.

The idea of being trapped and at the prisoners' mercy gave her the willies.

'We need to make a break for it,' she whispered to Bryan, who was looking around just as desperately as she was.

He nodded.

Before they could even think about making a move, the last remaining deputy, the one who earlier had been standing nearest to the jury box, popped into view. He was, she saw, middle-aged, his brown hair going gray around the temples, a little paunchy in his uniform. He shot out from behind the jury-box wall in an awkward, crouching run, yelling, 'Officer down! Officer down!' into a walkie-talkie even as he fired his weapon multiple times to cover himself. Seconds after she spotted him, he took a bullet in the back. The walkie-talkie went sailing as he was flung forward. He landed, hard, just a few feet from where she and Bryan cowered. Kate looked with horror at his blinking eyes – and at the growing circle of crimson that blossomed like a fast-opening rose on the back of his dark blue shirt. The man wasn't dead, though, or at least not yet, because after he hit the floor his hand moved, closing into a loose fist.

Her heart turned over.

He needs help . . .

But there was nothing she could do. She couldn't even go to him without exposing herself to potentially deadly fire.

'Hang on,' she mouthed to the deputy, whose eyes had quit blinking. He was staring at her in a fixed way that she feared meant nothing but bad news. She was nearly positive he wasn't seeing her.

As she looked back at him in horror, two things happened almost simultaneously. First, there was a quick barrage of shots accompanied by the crash of glass shattering. From the sound of it, the window closest to them had been shot out. Shards rained noisily to the floor, breaking again on the stone and sending a cloud of sparkling glass dust flying into view. Second, from the opposite end of the room where the doors to the hall were located came a mighty bellow loud enough to be heard over the chaos.

'Police! Freeze! Get down, get down!'

Thank God, we're saved . . .

'Shit,' one of the bad guys – she was sure it was one of the bad guys, though not Orange Jumpsuit – cried, to the accompaniment of another burst of gunfire and a crescendo of screams that told Kate that the courtroom was still plenty full.

'There's a fucking army of pigs outside!' Orange Jumpsuit shrieked, sounding way too close for Kate's liking.

'I'm going for it.' The voice was high-pitched, hysterical.

'Little Julie, no!'

If there was an answer, Kate didn't hear it, maybe because the words were swallowed up by another bellowed '*I said freeze!*' followed by a deafening burst of gunfire. Bullets whistled through the air, so close she could hear their passing. One smacked into the side of the jury box just a few feet away. Another gouged a chunk from the floor just beyond her briefcase. She and Bryan instinctively covered their heads, getting as low to the ground as they could while staying under the table. They were pressed so closely together now that it was hard to know where his body left off and hers began. From the sound of it, Kate was almost sure that more shots were being fired outside the building. A muffled scream, abruptly cut off, sent a chill racing down her spine.

'I think they've got the building surrounded,' Bryan whispered. 'I think that guy jumped from the window, and they shot him.' They were both shaking all over. Brian's teeth chattered, and the sound of his clattering teeth punctuated his words.

'I wish they'd all jump.'

Another bullet smacked into the table leg just inches

away from Kate, sending splinters flying. Gasping, her gaze flying to the damaged leg, she shied violently, her shoulder butting hard into Bryan's side.

'God save and protect us . . .' The desperate mutter came from Bryan, who, she saw with a despairing glance, was folded into tight thirds now with his eyes closed and his arms wrapped around his head.

Footsteps pounded nearby. Kate's eyes widened and her mouth went dry as her head jerked instinctively in the direction of the sound. She could hear them, but she couldn't see whom they belonged to. Being effectively blind, she discovered, was terrifying.

But not as terrifying as the realization that came to her an instant later: The footsteps had to belong to the gunmen, because there was no one else left standing in the well.

As she scanned what little she could see beyond the table, her heart thumped wildly. Her stomach cramped with fear. Her eyes darted desperately all around, but there was nothing new in view. Crouching as low to the floor as she could get, sucking in ragged gulps of air as she tried to look everywhere at once, she became aware that the quality of what she was breathing had changed: It was cooler and smelled of rain, which confirmed her guess that the window almost directly in front of the prosecution table had been blown out. Apparently, the prisoners had planned to jump but had been dissuaded – all but Soto, anyway – by some sort of police presence outside. She could hear the rush of the downpour, and, cutting through it, sirens. Lots of sirens, as if the entire PPD was now converging on the Justice Center.

If I can just survive a little longer, it'll all be over.

'Drop your weapons *now*!' a police officer yelled from inside the courtroom. Instinctively, she and Bryan huddled closer, bumping shoulders and hips, keeping their heads low, shuddering together as guns cracked and screams filled the air. With the cavalry's arrival and a gunfight going on above their heads, making a break for it suddenly seemed like the stupidest thing they could do.

Please, please, let us be saved . . .

Another quick flurry of running footsteps sent cold chills racing over her body. Anxiously, she scanned as much of the area as she could see. There was still nothing there except the empty lower third of the front of the courtroom and the two dead deputies – she was sure the second one was dead now; his eyes had glazed over and his fist had gone slack. Then, suddenly, the view changed: A pair of feet in black sneakers jumped into view. Kate's heart lurched as Orange Jumpsuit accordioned down on top of the feet, crouching like a malevolent frog directly in front of the counsel table. A big black pistol was in his hand. It had been fired so recently that Kate could smell the scent of hot cordite emanating from it. Like Soto, this guy appeared to be Hispanic, mid-twenties, a street punk. His face was round, clean-shaven, almost babyish, with full cheeks and a dimpled chin. He was sweating, panicky-looking, breathing hard. He was looking over her head, over the table, she thought, probably at the cop or cops at the other end of the room, and his eyes were small and hard and cruel.

Then his gaze lowered, and their eyes locked.

'Throw down your weapon!' a cop roared from the gallery. Kate's pulse was pounding so hard in her ears now that the voice sounded muffled, as if it were coming from miles away.

Orange Jumpsuit gave no indication that he heard. He never even blinked. He just kept holding her gaze. The realization that she was in all likelihood eyeball to eyeball with her own death broke over Kate like an icy wave.

She quit breathing.

Oh, please, oh, please, oh, please, don't let him shoot me.

'Throw down your weapon!' the cop screamed. Only then did Kate notice that he was saying 'weapon,' singular, instead of 'weapons,' plural, as he had earlier. Did that mean that there was only one gun left for the cops to take out? The one Orange Jumpsuit was holding right in front of her?

'Come on.' Orange Jumpsuit grabbed her arm above the elbow, fingers clamping roughly into her flesh. Pointing his gun at her face, he pulled her toward him. She didn't resist; she had no doubt whatsoever that he would shoot her if she did. Her knees bruised on the hard terrazzo. Her sweaty hand kept slipping as she crawled awkwardly out from under the table. She stared at the gun's little round black mouth, and remembered Judge Moran's head exploding: That's what would happen to her if he pulled the trigger.

No, no, no.

But there was nothing she could do to save herself. Bryan didn't try to help her. He shrank away instead, and for that she couldn't blame him: It was abundantly clear that he would have been shot dead in an instant if he had interfered in any way.

'Please, I've got a little boy,' Kate said as her knee bumped Orange Jumpsuit's leg. She tried to hold his gaze, tried to find and appeal to any scrap of human feeling he might possess, but he was looking over the table again, presumably at the cops (she hoped it was plural) at the other end of the room. Her heart pounded like a jackhammer. She was so scared she was nauseated.

'Shut the fuck up.' Orange Jumpsuit shifted his grip, pulling her around so that they were facing the same way, then wrapping an arm around her neck so that he had her in a choke hold, all the while keeping his head below the table. 'Now we're gonna stand up. Together.'

The cold, hard muzzle of his pistol jammed into Kate's cheek. Her heart gave a great terrified leap. She went all light-headed. Her knees trembled and threatened to fold, but Orange Jumpsuit forced her up with him regardless. Plastered against her back, his surprisingly muscular arm locked around her neck so that there was no possibility of escape, he felt hot and sweaty and loathsome. He was just a little taller than she was in the heels, but stockier and far stronger. She could smell him – BO and some bad cologne. She could feel his damp, sticky cheek against her ear. She could hear his labored breathing.

She wanted to puke.

'I'll kill her,' he yelled, holding her tight against him as they slowly straightened together. His arm forced her chin up. The pistol ground into her cheek. 'Back off, or I'll blow her fucking head off.'

'Hold your fire!' A man – she thought it was a cop but her head was tipped up at such an angle that she couldn't see the speaker – at the other end of the room yelled in warning to, presumably, his fellow cops. *'Don't shoot!'*

His grip shifted again, and she was able to lower her chin slightly. Weak-kneed, stretched to her full height and then some, Kate found herself staring at a courtroom in which all the remaining civilian occupants – there were maybe ten – were curled into protective balls, hiding among the galleries, with only a few daring to peep up at her. A wedge of armed deputies and cops was frozen in place in the back of the courtroom, with some fanning out of the open doors and into the hall. The ones inside were hunkered down, with some sheltered behind galleries and others exposed in the center aisle. A couple wore protective gear; the rest didn't. All had weapons, and all were pointing them at her. Nobody was moving. The black-haired, olive-skinned cop in the lead was in plainclothes – a navy jacket, white shirt, and red tie that were soaked with rain. His clothes were plastered to a lean, wide-shouldered body. His wet shirt stuck to his chest in places. Maybe in his mid-thirties, he was good-looking enough to have rated a second glance from her under other, better circumstances. He was down on one knee in the aisle at the head of the wedge, holding his pistol with a two-handed grip. Like the others, it too was aimed straight at Kate.

No, not at me, she told herself, trying to slow her racing heart. Like the others, his gun was pointed at the man using her as a human shield.

She just happened to be in the way.

Her eyes locked with the cop's. He had dark, heavy-lidded eyes that looked almost onyx in the stark overhead light. Their expression was cool, calm, and reassuring. He held her gaze for the briefest of moments before shifting his attention to the man behind her. If he was agitated at all, it didn't show.

'Let her go,' the cop said. Like his eyes, his voice was calm. His pistol never wavered. She knew she was breathing again, because when Orange Jumpsuit tightened his arm around her neck it cut off her air. Gasping for breath, she clutched at his hairy forearm with both hands, not daring to dig in her nails or scratch him for fear he might shoot her if she did. Her heart thundered. Her stomach twisted into a tight knot. Her terrified eyes never left the cop's face.

He didn't look at her again. His attention was all on the man holding her prisoner.

'Yeah, right.' Orange Jumpsuit gave a jeering laugh and began pulling her to the right, toward the doors to chambers and the secure corridor. She stumbled in the impossible shoes, and he jerked her painfully upright. But the action shifted his grip, and she was once again able to breathe. Relieved, she greedily sucked in air. 'What, do you think I'm fucking stupid? You think I don't know I'm looking at the death penalty here?' He hesitated fractionally, and Kate could feel the too-rapid rise and fall of his chest against her back. 'I want a helicopter, see. Out in front of this building. In fifteen minutes. Otherwise, I kill her.'

'You kill her, we kill you,' the cop said. His tone was the verbal equivalent of a shrug. His lean, dark face was expressionless. His eyes never wavered from her captor. His gun tracked them.

'Without that helicopter, I'm dead anyway.'

'Not today.'

'Fuck today. I want that helicopter, you hear me? Or she's dead.'

They reached the door to the secure corridor.

'Open the door,' Orange Jumpsuit said in her ear. When Kate didn't immediately comply, he jabbed the mouth of the gun viciously against her cheek, gouging her skin. The pain was quick and sharp. Wincing, she gave a choked little cry and reached for the knob, which she could just see out of the corner of her eye. It was shiny silver and, she discovered as her hand closed around it, slippery beneath her clammy palm.

Don't turn the knob. Try to delay . . .

'Look,' she said through dry lips, knowing it was futile even as she tried. 'Maybe we could work out a deal . . .'

'Open the goddamned door. *Now*.'

'*Oh*.' The gun jabbed her cheek again, grinding painfully into the hollow below her cheekbone. This time she felt her skin rip. A warm trickle that she knew was blood spilled down her cheek. Breathing hard, the stinging in her cheek a puny thing compared to the terror flooding her veins, she gave up. The tension in his body, the rapid rasp of his breathing, the copious amounts of heat and sweat pouring off him all told her how very desperate he was. If she pushed him, she was as certain as it was possible to be that he would kill her here and now. Moving as slowly as she dared, she did as he said, managing to turn the knob despite her sweaty skin.

Inch by reluctant inch, she started to ease open the heavy, solid metal door.

'Let her go, and you got years to figure out some way to beat the death penalty,' the cop said, still conversational, like he was discussing the weather. Her eyes clung to his face beseechingly. Not by so much as the flicker of an eyelash did he acknowledge her in any way.

She didn't even want to think about what might happen to her if Orange Jumpsuit got her inside that door.

Oh, Ben. Mommy loves you, Ben.

At the idea that she might never see her little boy again, she could feel the tears starting.

'Smart guy like you, that should be a piece of cake,' the cop continued. 'You know how the system works. On the other hand, if you kill her, I guarantee you won't live out the day.'

'You're full of shit,' Orange Jumpsuit said, and to Kate's horror used his foot to shove the door the rest of the way open. Then he backed into the secure corridor, pulling Kate in behind him. 'I ain't ridin' the needle, *amigo*. No fucking way. You got fifteen minutes to get me that helicopter.'

5

The door, which closed automatically, clicked shut in Kate's face. Her heart lurched. Cold chills raced down her spine. She was now alone with Orange Jumpsuit and whoever else might be left in the secure area. It was eerily quiet – so quiet she could hear the hum of the ventilation system ebbing and flowing like a critically ill patient's life support. There was a security camera mounted on the wall just above the door – or, rather, what was left of a security camera. It was clearly useless, having been shot to smithereens. The air smelled stuffy and stale, like the inside of an airplane cabin. Only prisoners and deputies were permitted in this area, and she doubted very much if any deputies were present – at least, none who were still alive.

'Lock it,' Orange Jumpsuit ordered. Glancing down, Kate saw that there was a dead bolt below the knob. He didn't expect or want anyone to join them, and that confirmed her impression that both his buddies were now out of the picture, either dead, wounded, or escaped. Despairing, feeling like she was cutting off her last best hope of rescue, Kate did as he told her. The dead bolt clicked into place. The smooth metal door was bulletproof, she knew. It was also, as far as she could tell, soundproof. If anything was happening in the courtroom – and she prayed that something, namely the urgent organization of a rescue attempt, was – she couldn't hear it.

'That's a good little prosecutor.'

The venom in his voice as he said 'prosecutor' made her even more certain than she already was that her fate was sealed. Whatever happened, he was going to kill her.

Unless she was next in line for a miracle, or she could think of some way to save herself.

Within the next fifteen minutes.

No pressure, though.

'You got a watch?' Without waiting for her to reply, he added, 'What time is it?'

Glancing down at her wrist, she saw that it was nine-sixteen, and told him so.

'You got till nine-thirty-one. Walk.'

Swinging her around so that she faced the opposite end of the hall, he force-marched her forward, shifting his grip so that his hand curled into the neck of her jacket and thrusting his gun hard into her spine just above the small of her back. She grimaced at the sudden jab but didn't dare protest. Her shoes cut into her heels, but the discomfort was so minor now compared to the direness of her situation that she barely even felt it. She was sweating and shivering at the same time, while her heart thundered in her chest and her mind raced.

Stay calm. Think. There has to be a way out of this.

The corridor was part of a labyrinth of connected passages that led from the large, subbasement prisoner holding area throughout the building. They were designed to keep the public separate from the prisoners even when they were of necessity sharing the same general space. Constructed with security in mind, they allowed deputies to move prisoners about inside the Justice Center in virtual invisibility. In an emergency, each section of hallway could be isolated from the others by the bulletproof doors. The safeguards designed to protect the public from the prisoners worked against her now. From what she knew about them, and what she could see, the hallways were all but impregnable.

This particular one was narrow, brightly lit by fluorescent lights glowing out of recessed panels in the ceiling, and painted a depressing shade of gray. The floor was smooth concrete. Two doors, both gray metal, both with small glass-enclosed grills that allowed deputies in the hallway to check on the prisoners inside, opened through its right wall into holding cells. The left wall was a smooth, unbroken expanse of gray paint. A black telephone hung on the narrow wall at the end of the hall. Beneath it, a folding metal chair for deputies to use while waiting to escort a prisoner into court waited beside another solid metal door. That door was the twin of the one that led to the courtroom, and it led into another corridor, world without end. It, too, was closed and, she presumed from his lack of interest in it, locked from this side. The bottom line was, the secure corridors constituted an interior prison hidden inside the soaring, designed-to-impress public areas of the Justice Center. For her to be rescued from this one by force would, she feared, require a Herculean effort on the part of the police – and would give her captor plenty of time to kill her as they tried.

All of a sudden, the possibility that the cell doors were almost certainly bulletproof, too, occurred to her, bringing with it a ray of hope. If she could somehow break away from Orange Jumpsuit, maybe she could dart inside a holding cell and lock herself in . . .

'You better be praying for that helicopter,' he said, nudging her in the spine with his gun.

Oh, yeah. She took a deep, steadying breath. *Say I whirl around, manage to shove him off balance, then run inside the nearest cell and slam the door . . .*

'Maybe a helicopter's not the only option. Maybe we could work something else out – like a plea deal.' She was proud of how steady her voice sounded. Her mind continued to race, turning over the pros and cons of her not-quite-ready-for-prime-time escape plan. It was so quiet in the hallway that the click of her heels on the concrete was clearly audible. Her voice seemed to echo. 'For example, if you let me walk out of here now, I can one hundred percent guarantee you that I can fix it so you won't face the death penalty.'

'Don't give me that. You can't guarantee shit.' His fingers tightened on the neck of her jacket, and his gun jabbed into her spine. Her back curved in a reflexive attempt to escape the pain – without success – as she winced. 'And if you don't shut your fucking mouth so I can think, I'm going to kill you right now.'

O-kay. Deep breath.

So much for trying to talk her way free. She kept walking forward, her heart thundering as the reality of her situation hit home. If this thug didn't get the helicopter he wanted – and he wouldn't, she knew how the whole barter-a-helicopter-for-the-hostage thing worked – or if something else didn't happen that would allow her to escape, she was dead meat.

After the carnage in the courtroom, he clearly knew that he had nothing to lose. He was already looking at the death penalty probably six times over. One more corpse – hers – wouldn't make a particle of difference to what happened to him.

And he clearly wasn't a fan of prosecutors.

Please, God, don't let me die.

Unbidden, Ben's face rose in her mind's eye again. At the thought of how destroyed her son would be if something happened to her, she once more felt the hot sting of welling tears.

Man it up, she told herself fiercely. It was more Ben-speak, and realizing that just twisted the vise that was squeezing her heart a little tighter. Blinking rapidly to dispel the tears before they could overflow, she forced all thoughts of Ben from her mind. To have any hope of surviving, she was going to have to keep her mind clear and focused and in the present.

Make like Winnie-the-Pooh and think, think, think.

They had just reached the first cell when its doorknob rattled. Jumping a little, eyes widening in surprise, Kate saw a face pressed to the grill in the door. It was a man with deeply tanned skin and a shiny bald head, his features faintly distorted by the glass. What was clear, however, was that he was looking at them as he tried without success to open the door.

'Fuck.' Her captor sounded angry. 'Open the door.'

This was addressed to her, and she did as he told her. There were dead-bolt locks on each cell door, but the latches were on the outside. Of course. The prisoners needed to be locked *in*. In all likelihood, there weren't locks on the inside.

Her stomach knotted as she realized just how close she had come to making a fatal mistake.

She was just registering with some confusion that the dead bolt didn't seem to be engaged after all when the door was thrust open and the newcomer pushed through it. He was, she saw, a little taller than her captor, maybe five-eleven or so, with an unnaturally muscular, wide-bodied upper torso that told her he was a fan of steroids and he'd had plenty of time to work out – probably in prison. His orange jumpsuit strained at the shoulders and around the sleeves. His biceps bulged. His neck was as thick as a bull's. He had bushy, dark brown eyebrows above smallish brown eyes; a meaty, triangular nose; and a thin-lipped mouth wrapped in a neatly trimmed dark brown mustache and goatee.

There was a big black pistol in his hand.

'The hell happened to you? And where's Newton?' Her captor growled, pushing her face-first against the wall as he spoke. As the cell door closed right beside her nose, she got a glimpse inside before it clicked shut. Three men sprawled motionless on the floor. She could see only the legs of two: One was wearing an orange jumpsuit. The other was a blue-uniformed deputy. The third man was another deputy. Unnaturally pale, he lay facedown, dead or unconscious, she couldn't be sure which. He had short, thick black hair and was thin and looked young.

'Newton's in there, dead. Damned deputy who brought him over from the jail still had a shot left in him. We were on our way out when Newton bought it. I stopped to finish the deputy off, and the damned door jammed.' In contrast to her captor's obvious agitation, this guy sounded untroubled. Kate stayed where she had been shoved, cheek and palms pressed against the smooth, cool wall, heart thundering like a herd of wild horses. Now she had two armed murderers to contend with, and nothing even resembling a plan. 'Couldn't believe it. Damned door wouldn't open for nothing. I was stuck as a duck.' His tone changed. 'It went to hell, huh?'

'Hell, yeah, it went to hell. You think I'd be back in here if it hadn't gone to hell?'

'Pack and Little Julie?'

'Dead, both of 'em. Meltzer never showed with the truck, damned unreliable shit. Maybe he couldn't get through. There was po-po everywhere, all around the building, already there when we shot out the window, like they'd been tipped off or something. Little Julie jumped anyway, and they tore him up. Pack bought it in the courtroom. I grabbed her' – Kate could feel them looking at her – 'the hot little pro-se-cu-tor' – he drew the word out mockingly – 'and . . .'

He broke off as the phone at the end of the hall began to ring.

The shrill peals made all three of them start and look toward the source.

'Who's that?' There was an anxious edge to the new guy's voice now.

'How the fuck should I know? Wait – maybe it's the cops. Maybe they got the helicopter.'

Up until that point, nobody had made a move to answer the phone, which continued to ring imperiously. Now a hand closed around Kate's arm: Orange Jumpsuit swung her away from the wall and shoved her toward the phone.

'Move your ass,' he said to her as she stumbled in her thrice-damned shoes before finding her footing.

'Helicopter?' the new guy inquired.

'I gave 'em fifteen minutes to get me a helicopter or I pop her.' Orange Jumpsuit sounded proud of himself. 'Hey, Miss Prosecutor, what time is it now?'

Kate didn't want to know, but she looked at her watch anyway.

'Nine-twenty,' she answered.

'They got eleven minutes left, then.'

'You think that'll work?'

'How do I know, shit-for-brains? If they want her alive, it'll work.'

'You sure she's a prosecutor?'

'Hell, yeah, I'm sure.'

The phone was still ringing as they reached it. Kate was first, with Orange Jumpsuit right behind her and the new guy behind him.

Orange Jumpsuit shoved her against the wall beside the phone. It rang again just then, setting her teeth on edge. Doing her best to tune it out, she rested against the cool plaster and tried to concentrate on getting her heart rate and breathing under control. Hyperventilating would do her no good at all. She had to keep her mind clear so she could come up with another plan.

Then, despairingly, she realized that a clear mind wasn't going to help her one bit because the sorry truth was that she was fresh out of ideas.

'Don't you even think about trying nothing,' he said to her, letting go of her arm. The gun moved. Cold and hard and terrifying, its mouth nestled against the vulnerable side of her neck just below her jawline. She closed her eyes as he picked up the receiver, silencing the phone at last.

'Yeah?' he said into it. Then, a moment later, 'Don't give me that crap. You ain't getting more time.'

'Tell 'em you need money,' the new guy said behind them. He was antsy now, jiggling on the balls of his feet. She could sense the movement, hear the rustle of his clothing. 'A hundred thousand dollars, along with the helicopter.'

'I want money, too,' Orange Jumpsuit said into the phone. 'A hundred thousand dollars. In cash, unmarked bills no bigger than twenties, waiting in the helicopter. And you're under ten minutes now.' He listened, then said, 'Sure. Talk to her. Long as you remember the clock's ticking.'

Talk to her. Kate's eyes flew open.

Orange Jumpsuit pressed the receiver to his chest and glared at Kate.

'Says he wants to make sure you're alive,' he said, trailing the mouth of the gun across her skin until it nestled below her ear, where her pulse beat against the bruising metal like a small, trapped bird. Her eyes were wide as they met his. She was breathing too fast, through parted lips. The feel of the gun against her skin was making her dizzy. One slip of his finger, or a single quick, deliberate squeeze, and she was history.

Will it hurt?

'Watch yourself, bitch, 'cause I'm watching you,' he said.

Then he held the receiver to her ear.

Please, God. Please.

'Hello.' Wetting her parched lips, she spoke into the phone.

'Kate White?' a man asked in her ear. It was the cop from the courtroom, the one with the calm, reassuring eyes. His voice was calm and reassuring, too. She latched on to the steady strength he projected at her like a lifeline.

Must stay calm, must stay cool . . . Her knees went weak. *Oh, God, don't let me die.*

'Yes.' She didn't know how long she would be allowed to talk, and she wanted to make sure she got the essentials across first. 'I have a little boy.' Despite her determination to remain cool and calm, her voice was no longer even. It was hoarse and cracked with fear, and her breathing was ragged. 'I'm a single mother. Please give this man what he wants.'

Orange Jumpsuit nodded at her approvingly.

'We're going to do our best to get you out of there in one piece,' the cop said. Orange Jumpsuit watched her intently. She thought that he could hear only her side of the conversation, but she couldn't be sure. 'Are you the only hostage?'

'Yes.' She thought of the bodies lying in the holding cell, and the other holding cell that she hadn't seen the inside of. 'I think so.'

Orange Jumpsuit frowned.

'That's enough.'

He pulled the phone away from her. The gun dug in deeper. She could still feel her pulse beating frantically against the hard little metal circle. Taking a deep, shaken breath, she rested her cheek against the plaster and closed her eyes once more.

Please. Please. Please.

'You heard her: She's a single mother,' he said into the receiver. There was a taunting undertone to his voice. 'You call me back when you get that helicopter. And the money. And remember, tick tick.'

As he hung up, Kate could hear the cop talking on the other end of the phone.

'You ain't going to get that helicopter,' the second guy said.

Her eyes opened.

'What do you mean? Why the hell would you say a stupid-shit thing like that?' Orange Jumpsuit whipped around to face the speaker so fast she felt a breeze from his movement. Either he was so agitated he forgot about her, or he figured she wasn't a threat and was going nowhere because there was nowhere to go, because his gun went with him. Kate let out a silent breath of relief now that it was no longer pressing into her flesh.

'They're just yankin' your chain.' The second guy stood his ground. 'You ain't going to get it.'

'They're not yankin' my chain. The helicopter's coming. They know I'll kill her.'

'And if you kill her, what good does that do, huh? That doesn't get us out of here.'

There was no good answer to that. Orange Jumpsuit knew it as well as Kate did, apparently, because he paused before answering. She could sense the sudden uncertainty in him, the anger, the rising fear. Tension between the two men electrified the atmosphere.

'They want her alive. They'll give me what I want.' But he no longer sounded sure.

'Say you get the helicopter. How you gonna get to it?'

'What?'

'How you gonna get to it? Where's it gonna be?'

'I told 'em the roof.'

'There's a helipad up there.' The second guy seemed to be thinking aloud, weighing the possibilities. 'But how you gonna get to the roof without them offing you?'

'I'm gonna use her like a fucking shield, that's how. And I'm gonna tell 'em if I see a cop, if I even so much as smell a cop, I'll blow her head off.'

The second guy shook his head. 'Not gonna work.'

'What the hell do you mean "Not gonna work"?'

'Too far to go. Gotta get to the elevator, go up to the roof, get out and get across to the helicopter. With her. They'll for sure get you with snipers.'

Orange Jumpsuit practically vibrated with rage and frustration. He bounced up and down on the balls of his feet and flung out his arms in challenge. 'You got a better plan? Huh? You got a better plan? If you do, let's fucking hear it.'

'Yeah, I do,' the second guy said. 'I got a way better plan. For me, that is.'

Kate never even saw his hand move. There was an ear-splitting *crack*, and Orange Jumpsuit smacked into the wall right beside her, hitting so hard the back of his head bounced off the plaster. Her heart leaped. Screaming, she jumped back out of the way. Eyes huge, jaw dropping, her scream still echoing off the walls, she watched with disbelief as his mouth opened soundlessly, like he wanted to scream but couldn't.

Then he slid down the wall as bonelessly as a rag doll until he was sitting on the floor with his legs splayed out straight in front of him. His eyes were still open, and so was his mouth. His head slipped sideways until it rested limply on his shoulder. Even before she saw blood spilling from his mouth and more blood pouring down the front of his jumpsuit, she knew he was dead.

Her stunned gaze flew to the second guy's face. He was looking down at Orange Jumpsuit with a twisted smile, still holding the just-fired gun. The smell of cordite and fresh blood hit her nose at the same time as his eyes rose to lock with hers.

Her blood froze. She stopped breathing.

'Hey, there, Kitty-cat,' he said. 'No need to look so scared. What, don't you remember your old buddy Mario?'

6

Tom's hand was rock-steady as he picked up the receiver. His breathing was under control. His legs never quivered, he didn't blink, and he wasn't sweating. There was nothing about his appearance to give away the sick feeling he was experiencing in the pit of his stomach, the heavy thudding of his heart, the surging adrenaline that pumped through his veins.

They – the small group of cops and sheriff's deputies clustered with him around the bailiff's phone, which the courtroom used for communicating with the deputies guarding the prisoners – had just heard the muffled sound of a gun going off inside the secure corridor. Tom thought of Kate White, slim and lovely with her Scandinavian blond hair, flawless pale skin, and wide blue eyes, helpless as a mouse between the paws of a hungry cat in her current situation, and felt his gut clench.

Was she dead?

What about Charlie, whom he hadn't been able to locate yet? If Charlie was anywhere in the Justice Center where he could get to the heart of the action, he'd be with them already.

Was Charlie dead?

The possibility was making Tom crazy. The dispatcher in the subbasement had thought, but wasn't sure, that after logging his prisoner in, Charlie had escorted him on up to the second floor. Instead of taking the same labyrinthine secure corridors that his brother had used, which he didn't have clearance for anyway, Tom had opted for the easier, civilian route to the second floor in pursuit of Charlie. He had just leaped off the elevator with a pair of deputies alerted by Johnson in tow when he'd heard the first shots being fired in courtroom 207. He'd had to battle his way through the stampede of people exiting the building, exiting the courtroom, running for their lives. In the midst of all the carnage, he still hadn't found Charlie, and his bad feeling about that was growing exponentially.

But at the moment, his first duty was to Kate White.

'If he won't put her on the phone, we got to assume he probably shot her, right?' Mitch Cooney asked. The pudgy, balding, fifty-something deputy was gray-faced. The massacre of so many of his friends and fellow officers had hit him hard. But like the rest of the group around Tom, he was still standing, still serving, still doing his duty, semper fi.

'He'd be stupid to kill her. Then he's got nothing. No bargaining power.' Police Corporal LaRonda Davis, a petite black woman with a bodacious figure that made even her uniform look good, sounded shaken. She was part of the group huddled around the phone because she'd been on her way to an adjoining courtroom to testify when the shooting had broken out.

'Shut up, everybody. I'm calling in now.' Tom pushed the button that rang the secure corridor.

'We got nothing. What are you going to say?' Police Officer Tim Linnig sounded on the verge of panic. The truth was, none of them felt qualified to be the ones responsible for nurturing the complex web of greed, hope, and stupidity that was all that was keeping Kate White alive. But unless and until somebody with better qualifications showed up, the motley crew now gathered around the phone was all she had.

'I'm gonna ask to talk to the lady again,' Tom said grimly. 'If he puts her on the phone, I'm gonna lie like a mother, tell him he's getting everything he wants. If he doesn't – well, we'll cross that bridge when we come to it.'

The call went through. In his ear, he could hear the phone in the secure corridor start to ring. Every nerve in his body was on edge as he listened.

Brriing . . .

He waited. The suspense was making him as jittery as a caffeine addict outside a closed Starbucks. Determined not to let it show, Tom set his teeth.

Brriing . . .

Four minutes were left before the fifteen-minute deadline Nico Rodriguez had given them ran out. The helicopter – they were getting Rodriguez the helicopter he'd demanded, but he wasn't going to be flying away in it; it was basically bait to lure him into the open – was at least ten minutes out. The hundred thousand dollars – which, again, he wasn't going to be going anywhere with – was still being assembled, just in case Rodriguez had the time and smarts to check the money bag. The SWAT team, with its contingent of crack snipers, was on the way: ETA three minutes. So was a hostage negotiator. So was the bulk of Philly's police and sheriff's departments that weren't already on the premises.

All he had to do was keep Kate White alive long enough for the real professionals at this kind of thing to arrive and take over.

If she wasn't already dead.

The thought made him grimace.

Brriing.

'Pick up the damned phone,' Davis said aloud, echoing what all of them were thinking. They were all getting wound tighter than a Roger Clemens fastball, but letting their emotions take control would not help the woman they were trying to save.

His hand gripping the receiver so hard his knuckles showed white, Tom frowned Davis down.

Brriing.

The courtroom was chaotic, teeming with cops and medical personnel and civilians and even reporters who had happened to be in the courthouse when the shooting had started and who had immediately converged on the scene. Blood and gore were everywhere. Victims were being treated where they lay. First-aid carts rattled around the room and emergency triage was being attempted by people with no training for it, and over in a corner a defibrillator let loose with its distinctive *zap*. Women cried hysterically. There were a few shrieks, which Tom deliberately closed his ears to, as loved ones discovered victims. From outside, dozens of sirens, only faintly muffled by the pounding rain and distance, screamed through the broken-out window.

Reinforcements were coming. Soon there would be somebody more qualified than he to take over.

Brriing.

An attempt was being made to cordon off the courtroom; another attempt was being made to clear the room of nonessential personnel. The Criminal Justice Center was being evacuated, except for those who needed to be on the premises, but it wasn't happening fast. Nothing was happening fast. There were too many nooks and corners, too many people, too many prisoners, too many arrangements to coordinate, too much confusion.

So far, the necessary organization to accomplish what needed to be accomplished wasn't happening. Everybody was too shocked, too unprepared for this horror that had so unexpectedly exploded in their lives.

His job, because right now he was the senior cop on the scene, because he knew Rodriguez from having arrested him before, because he wasn't willing to entrust it to anyone else until the trained hostage negotiator who was coming was actually present, was to keep Rodriguez talking, keep him believing he was going to get what he wanted, keep him from killing Kate White.

For as long as he could.

Her eyes, clinging to his as if she actually thought he could save her, haunted him. So did her voice, cracking with fear as she told him she was a single mother.

He refused to let himself think about her kid.

Brri . . .

The sound broke off. Somebody was picking up.

He tensed.

The others must have been able to see that something was going down from his expression or body language, because they all leaned in a little closer, their eyes on his face.

On the other end of the line, nobody said anything. But Tom was sure – almost sure – he could hear somebody breathing.

'Rodriguez?' Tom hazarded a guess. His voice was grim. The sleazeball was a hardcore criminal with a felony record as long as Tom's arm. Killing his hostage wouldn't cause him to bat an eyelash.

'No.' It was Kate White. He recognized her voice instantly. It was low-pitched and shaky, but the good news was she was alive. Only then, when relief loosened the death grip fear had on his senses, did he become aware of the roaring in his ears, and only because it started to subside.

He had been hideously afraid that she was dead.

'You doing all right?' he asked, as the tense group around him, obviously able to either hear her voice or tell that she was alive from his reaction, let out a collective breath.

'Yes.'

Her breathing was ragged, and he sure couldn't blame her for that. All things considered, she was hanging tough, being very calm, very aware, acting as a functioning participant in the attempt to keep her alive, and he admired her for that. Under the circumstances, the majority of people would have been blathering blobs of terror by now. Maybe even himself included.

'We heard—' he began, but she cut him off.

'A shot,' she said. 'I know.' He could hear her taking a deep breath. Then she stunned him. 'I shot him. He's dead.'

For a moment Tom wasn't sure he had heard her right.

'What?' He must have sounded astonished, because the others leaned in again, all ears.

'He's dead. It's all over.' She drew in another long, shaky breath, then let it out slowly. He heard the sigh of it through the line. 'I'm coming out.'

'How did—' Tom began, stupefied, but again she cut him off, this time by hanging up.

Just like that.

Tom listened to the hum of the dial tone in his ear for only a few seconds before hanging up himself and then staring down at the phone in bemusement.

'What?' The question pulled his head up. Roughly a dozen pairs of questioning eyes pinned him.

'She said Rodriguez is dead.' Tom couldn't quite bend his mind around it. 'She said she shot him. And she's coming out.'

'Alone?' Linnig asked.

'I guess. She didn't really say, but if Rodriguez is dead, I'd say that's the logical assumption.'

'You mean that shot we heard was *him* biting the big one?' Davis sounded as gobsmacked as Tom felt. 'And *she* did it?'

Tom shrugged.

'I don't know. This don't sound right.' Cooney, the veteran, shook his head. He was frowning hard at the closed metal door as if he could somehow divine what could have happened behind it if he tried hard enough.

Tom saw the same thought that had already occurred to him hit Cooney and the rest of them at just about the same time: Was it a trick? Was Rodriguez setting them up for something?

That seemed a hell of a lot more likely than the possibility that Rodriguez had been shot dead by Kate White.

With that thought in mind, they scrambled to isolate the door to the secure corridor from the rest of the courtroom, which fortunately, except for the corpses that had been left in place for the coroner's office, and a few people – medics, he hoped – working on the wounded, was nearly empty now. Two of their number – a pair of deputies whose names Tom didn't know –

rushed to clear the courtroom completely except for the casualties and essential medical personnel, in case Rodriguez came out shooting or a gunfight should erupt. The rest of them, weapons drawn, took cover behind galleries and chairs and flattened themselves back against the wall, anything to keep out of sight while still permitting them to take a shot if necessary.

When the knob first started to turn, they were ready. The door was surrounded. Whoever emerged would be instantly covered by a host of guns.

Tom was the only one positioned to be immediately visible. He stood about ten feet back in the well, near the defense table, facing the opening door as if he had taken Kate White at her word and was waiting for her to walk out of there alone. His Glock was in his hand – he didn't have quite that much of a death wish – but his hand rested unthreateningly at his side.

Ready to snap off a shot in just about a second, if need be. Although that should not be apparent at first glance to anybody he needed to shoot.

The knob stopped turning. The door didn't open. Nothing happened.

Jesus H. Christ.

Every muscle in his body had gone taut with tension. His heart pounded. His jaw clenched. A knot of wary anticipation tightened in his chest. His right hand itched to jerk the Glock up into firing position.

Not yet . . .

The waiting was killing him. The thing was, he'd been shot at before, and he hadn't liked it. He figured the chances were at least fifty-fifty that it was getting ready to happen again, and he wasn't going to like it any better this time than the last.

No matter how you sliced it, playing dodge-the-bullet just wasn't any fun. Especially if you lost, like he had.

Finally, the knob turned again.

He held his breath, waiting.

This time, when the knob stopped turning, the door began to open, slowly and soundlessly. Tom held his breath as Kate White came into view. She stood just inside the secure corridor, pale as a ghost and fragile-looking as a porcelain doll in her figure-hugging black suit, her blond hair loose now and spilling in a profusion of waves to her shoulders, her body seemingly unbloodied and in one piece, her face as expressionless as a doll's as she pushed the door open with one arm stiffly extended.

Except for her eyes. They were huge with what he presumed was shock.

As far as Tom could tell, she was, indeed, alone. Her build was too slight to allow Rodriguez or anyone else to hide behind her. Tom's eyes slid beyond her anyway, searching along as much of the secure corridor as he could see: nothing. No one. Only gray walls and doors and empty space.

And Kate White.

Unbelievably, there didn't seem to be any trick to this.

'Kate? Is Rodriguez dead?'

As he said her name, she looked directly at him for the first time since she'd opened the door. Their eyes met. Hers were shadowed now with trouble, and far darker than the robin's-egg hue he remembered from earlier, probably because her pupils had dilated with some combination of fear and trauma. She nodded, then seemed to take a deep breath before she started walking, or rather stumbling, toward him on slim, unsteady legs made to seem even longer than they already were by a pair of surprisingly sexy high heels.

'Hold your fire,' he ordered sharply over his shoulder. 'She's alone.'

As his backup slowly emerged from their concealed positions and the door swung closed behind Kate, he holstered his gun and strode to meet her.

She was so white she looked like she was drained of blood, he saw as he got closer. He deliberately made his voice gentle. 'Are you okay?'

She nodded again, and stopped walking. Her lips parted, but she didn't say anything. As he reached her, Tom saw the ladders in her stockings, the little trickle of dried blood on her cheek, the horror in her eyes.

She was alive, possibly unhurt, but definitely not okay.

Her eyes fell away from his. She took another deep breath, shuddered, then pressed a hand to her chest, to her white T-shirt, right in between her small but shapely breasts, as if her heart had suddenly started doing something it shouldn't and it scared her.

'What happened in there?' he asked, even as his backup moved in cautiously toward the now closed door, ready to search the secure corridor for themselves.

'I shot him,' she said, looking up at him again, the words cold and clear. 'He's dead.'

Then her knees gave way and, with a little cry, she crumpled.

Tom was just close enough to catch her in his arms before she hit the floor.

7

'You sure you don't want to ride on over to the hospital, get checked out, just in case?' the EMT asked. Laura Remke was her name, according to the silver name tag pinned to her pale blue shirt. About five-four and stocky, with boyishly short brown hair and no discernible makeup on her round face, she looked to be in her early forties. She had been kind and efficient, and asked the minimum of questions, which were characteristics Kate greatly appreciated at the moment.

'No thanks.'

Kate was sitting on a high-backed wooden bench nestled against the wall just outside courtroom 207, having been deposited there by the same cop who had scooped her up and yelled for an EMT when Kate's knees betrayed her. Someone had called to him urgently right after he had summoned Remke, and Kate hadn't seen him since he'd practically dropped her on the bench.

She didn't even know his name.

Not that it mattered. What mattered was surviving this nightmare the best way she could. She was alive, anyway, when so many others weren't. That was the most important thing. The rest of the horror she would find a way to deal with, just as she had found a way to deal with everything else life had thrown at her so far. As soon as the panic subsided, as soon as her mind cleared, she would surely be able to think of some way to take care of this latest disaster, too.

'I need to go pick my son up at school. He's sick,' Kate said. Which was true. While the EMT had been checking her vital signs – 'Your blood pressure's way up, honey; 'course, with what you've been through, that's not a surprise' – and applying antibiotic ointment and a Band-Aid to the small cut on her cheek, she had remembered the call from Ben's school, and asked for her briefcase. An obliging deputy fetched it, and she had fished out her phone and returned the call. As she had known they would be, the shootings were a media sensation. The school secretary was agog about the massacre at the Criminal Justice Center – as it was apparently being called all over TV – but more than pleased to hear from her.

Ben was terribly afraid that his mother might be caught up in the tragedy, the secretary told her, despite her repeated assurances that it wasn't very likely. Kate didn't have the heart to tell the woman that Ben was right.

The original call had been made because Ben had thrown up in class, and was even now lying in the little anteroom off the school office, which served as the school's sick bay. Kate had promised to come get him as soon as possible.

'The world could be coming to an end, and we mothers would still be on the job, wouldn't we?' Laura Remke shook her head as she started packing up her supplies. Band-Aids, ointment, blood pressure cuff, thermometer – all disappeared into her bright blue bag with its iconic white cross. 'I got three of my own, so I know.'

Before Kate could reply, the doors to courtroom 207 flew open with a *whoosh* and were held by a pair of grim-faced deputies as a gurney rolled through them. It was moving fast, wheels rattling, with EMTs on either side pushing it and a couple of cops flanking it. Everybody was running, which told Kate that the condition of the person on the gurney was grave.

'Hold that elevator!' one of the EMTs yelled to someone Kate couldn't see. The wide hallway with its soaring, vaulted ceiling was busy and noisy, with cops and deputies and official personnel of all types rushing around, going in and out of various courtrooms calling to one another and talking on cell phones and two-way radios. Heavily armed SWAT officers in their helmets and bulletproof vests moved from room to room en masse. Kate assumed the building, which was still being evacuated, was being thoroughly searched. The staff from the coroner's office was on the scene now, as well, and their bright lights and painstaking procedures added to the general confusion. But the EMT's voice was loud and sharp enough to cut through the din. A path was cleared even as the gurney barreled past.

Kate caught a glimpse of an IV bag swinging crazily on a thin metal pole as it dripped clear liquid down into the arm of the man on the gurney – who, Kate realized with a shiver of recognition as he went past her, was the young, thin, black-haired cop whom she'd last seen lying on the floor of the cell in the secure corridor.

'He's alive,' she said aloud, and realized she was glad. It was a glimmer of hope, a shred of something positive, to hold on to on this hellish day.

'They leave the dead ones lay,' Remke agreed, snapping the latch closed on her medical kit. Kate shuddered. Judge Moran, the slain deputies – all were still in the courtroom. Deliberately, she tried to push from her mind the horrible images the thought conjured up.

The gurney trundled noisily toward the elevators, and Kate's head turned as she watched it go. She recognized one of the two cops loping behind it: the lean, black-haired man in plainclothes – a detective, she guessed, from his clothes – who had been her lifeline throughout the ordeal. From his tense expression and the way he was sticking close to the gurney, she guessed the man on it must be someone of importance to him. A relative, possibly, because they shared the same raven hair.

She hoped he would not lose someone he loved today.

With all eyes still craning after the gurney, which had just disappeared from view, Kate figured this would be a good time to make her exit. She knew the cops would want to talk to her, she knew she should give a statement and stay on the premises until she was told she could leave, but she couldn't.

Her emotions were too raw. The shock was too new, too awful, for her to trust herself to be thinking properly. She could not make a mistake. For Ben's sake as well as her own, she had to be very careful, very calculating, in what she said and did next.

A mistake could cost them everything.

Accordingly, she put down the now half-empty can of Sprite that Remke had procured for her from a nearby vending machine, curled her icy fingers around the handle on her briefcase, and stood up, ignoring the light-headedness that immediately assailed her. Her knees wobbled, but she ignored that, too. Her despised shoes were under the bench where she had kicked them off, but she left them where they lay. Their torment was more than she could deal with at the moment. She would be better off escaping – because that's what she was doing – in her stockinged feet.

'Thanks,' she said to Remke with a quick, grateful smile. It was good to know that even in such extremis she could smile, that she could look and sound normal enough for the EMT to smile back at her.

'You start feeling funny, you give us a call, hear? Sometimes shock keeps people from realizing what bad shape they're in for a couple of hours.'

'I will,' Kate promised, and started walking toward the stairs. The terrazzo felt slick and cool beneath her feet. Taking the elevators would be quicker and much easier, considering the uncertain state of her legs, but they were in heavy use, and she was afraid of who she might run into. The DA's office was almost certainly on the scene in full force by now, although, probably because nobody except law enforcement types and medical personnel were being allowed to enter the building, she hadn't seen anyone she knew. At the very least, witnesses were surely being rounded up and segregated until they could give their statements. And she – by taking the blame, or credit, depending on one's point of view, for the killing of Orange Jumpsuit – had made herself far more than just a witness. Anyone in authority who knew the details of the events in courtroom 207 should by rights prevent her from leaving until her statement was made and all the pertinent questions were asked and answered.

That's what she would have done herself.

She knew what the right thing to do was. And she had no intention of doing it. Not if there was any possible way to avoid it.

What she needed, all she needed, before all the official stuff kicked in was just to buy herself a little time in which to calm down, assess the situation, and think everything through.

Fortunately, she had the perfect excuse: Ben was sick and needed her. Who could blame a mother for rushing to her son? The truth was, though, right now she probably needed him more. Since the moment of his birth, he had been her rock, her anchor, her touchstone in a hard, cruel world. His dependence on her was the engine that had brought her this far, and remembering that she was all he had gave her the strength to gird her loins and face the need to work through one more crisis one more time.

I thought it was all over.

What she was feeling was grief. A profound sense of loss made her chest ache. The happy, hopeful future she had been building for the two of them had just been popped like a soap bubble.

So cry me a river, she told herself grimly.

Hanging on to the banister, being careful because the steps were damp and slick from all the people running in and out and she didn't want to slip and delay her exit and maybe even end up needing another EMT, she reached the bottom of the enormous curved staircase without attracting any undue attention. But even before she took the first step across the lobby toward the contingent of cops now guarding the entrance she saw, through the tall windows and banks of revolving doors, the pandemonium going on in front of the building, and stopped in her tracks.

Her eyes widened.

It looks like the entire city's out there.

Ambulances and fire trucks and police cruisers with their red and blue lights exploding like fireworks on the Fourth of July jammed the narrow street for as far as she could see. Dozens of specialty units, including an armored SWAT vehicle and the bomb-squad truck, filled the lawn. On the sidewalks, crowds of onlookers holding a motley collection of umbrellas and shopping bags and newspapers over their heads to protect them from the rain gaped at the action while jostling the police officers charged with keeping them back. Closer, on the wide concrete walkway that led to the Justice Center's front steps, TV trucks with their antennae and satellite dishes jockeyed for position. A blond reporter – Kate couldn't be sure from the back, but she thought it might be Patti Wilcox from station WKYW – stood beneath an umbrella at the top of the wide front steps, talking excitedly into a microphone as a cameraman under another umbrella a couple of steps below filmed her. More reporters talked into cameras from various spots on the steps. Thick black cables snaked downward, shiny in the rain.

Oh, no.

Frozen no longer, Kate turned and padded quickly across the bustling lobby to the hallway where the public restrooms were located. A small smoking room furnished with a couple of card tables and chairs and a plethora of ashtrays had been elbowed in next to the ladies' room. As she had hoped, it was empty. At the far end of it was a little-used side door. On the stoop outside stood a tall, stocky cop planted four-square with his back to her, almost certainly stationed there to prevent unauthorized persons from entering. The stoop must have been covered by a roof, because the area where he stood was dry, while around him the rain fell like a gently undulating silver curtain.

She stopped, eyeing his uniformed back uncertainly.

He's there to keep people out, not in. Just walk on past.

Easy to say, but her heart thumped wildly as she approached the heavy glass door. From guilt, she knew. Guilt combined with fear to tighten the hard knot in her chest, ramp up the queasiness in her stomach, increase the dryness in her throat.

You're a lawyer, remember. A respectable, upstanding citizen.

A shiver went down her spine at the thought. She felt like – no, she *was* – a fraud. And it seemed to her in that moment as though the truth of what she really was should be so obvious that anyone could see it at a glance, like Hester Prynne's scarlet A.

Keep going, damn it.

The door was unlocked. When she pulled it open, the cop glanced around in surprise, then registered her apparent harmlessness before stepping aside to make room for her. As she stepped out onto the stoop beside him he nodded a greeting, and she nodded back. Shrieking sirens assaulted her eardrums, their impact muted only slightly by the dull roar of the rain. More cop cars crept into view, strobe lights flashing, moving super-slowly as they jolted over sidewalks and curbs in an effort to get around the ever-increasing crowd.

Momentarily, she was glad for the pandemonium. It gave her a legitimate excuse to look anywhere but at the cop.

She could feel his gaze on her face.

A rush of cool air, redolent of damp earth but innocent of the terrible smells of cordite and blood and death that permeated the Justice Center, swirled around the stoop, catching stray strands of her hair and reminding her that it now hung loose. She was also shoeless and disheveled, she realized nervously. Maybe she even had blood on her somewhere. Would he notice? And what would he do if he did? She breathed in greedily, sucking in the smell of the outdoors, trying to purge the other smells from her system, even as her gaze slid warily toward the cop. He was young, younger even than she was, she guessed, a beat cop with a square, earnest face and dark hair shorn high and tight in an unbecoming military-type haircut that made his ears seem to stick out.

'Terrible thing.' With his voice raised to be heard over the commotion, he made small talk with her, shaking his head.

'Terrible,' Kate agreed, heart thumping, and kept walking.

'You're going to get wet,' he warned.

'I don't have far to go.'

Just as easy as that, she moved past him and out into the rain, squinting as the rain came down, her hand sliding along the slick iron handrail as she went down the quartet of narrow metal steps to the sidewalk below. The concrete felt wet and rough beneath her feet. Water rushed by in the gutters. She was almost instantly soaked, and had to push her hair back from her forehead to keep wet strands from straggling onto her face. The downpour was merely chilly rather than cold at first, but as the moisture quickly worked its way through her clothes to her skin, she was suddenly freezing. Ordinarily, she would have gone right, then headed straight down Fulton Street. But then, ordinarily there was not a mob of police and reporters and onlookers blocking the way that she would have to fight her way through. Some of whom would surely recognize her. Some of whom might try to stop her, or ask her questions.

She shivered, from a combination of the cold and the prospect of being stopped and questioned. Turning left away from the front of the building, she stayed on the sidewalk, which put her some six feet in front of the surging throng that was being allowed no closer than the weeping, golden-leaved linden trees lining the curb, and walked steadily in the opposite direction. Two cops in navy rain slickers with PPD emblazoned on their backs strung yellow crime scene tape in front of the crowd; the whole building was being sealed off.

Using her briefcase as a shield, ostensibly from the rain but mostly to keep from being recognized by anybody who might know her, Kate ducked her head and hurried past another stream of newly arriving law enforcement and crime scene types rushing down backstreets toward the Justice Center. The emergency vehicles' flashing bubble lights were reflected in windows and puddles and shiny car bumpers, providing a distraction, making the scene surreal, like it was being lit by a revolving disco ball. The noise was deafening. The tension in the air was palpable. The good thing was, with so much going on she was just one among hundreds, and no one noticed her.

'Kate!' she thought she heard a woman yell, but she didn't look around. She didn't even slow down. There were lots of Kates in the world, anyway. The call probably hadn't even been meant for her. And if it had been – well, she didn't want to know.

Her feet splashed through the freezing, shallow stream the rain had turned the sidewalks into as the street sloped slightly downhill. Her briefcase kept the brunt of the downpour out of her face. She was glad to gradually leave the insanity behind, glad to turn one corner and then another through the narrow colonial lanes with their boxy, modern buildings before finally emerging some five minutes later onto the busy corner near Benington's Department Store.

From there it was easy to hail a cab.

'Wait! What do you think you're doing? You can't get in! You're all wet.' The driver, a young man with dreadlocks and a goatee, turned around to look her over with horror as she slid into the backseat, thankful to get in out of the driving rain at last. 'You gonna get the seat wet. Next customer not gonna want to sit on a wet seat.'

He had a point: She was oozing water like a squeezed sponge.

'Out, out.' He made shooing motions with his hands toward the closed door. Kate stared at him.

I don't believe this.

Considering her other problems, this one was almost ludicrous. Kate thought about informing him that it was illegal to refuse a fare, and never mind whether terminal wetness actually qualified as a legitimate reason under the law, but she didn't have the energy for the argument she was sure would ensue.

'The seat's vinyl,' she pointed out, glancing down at the worn black surface. It was an old yellow cab that had clearly seen years of service. Its interior smelled like moldy pine, and she saw the reason – a tree-shaped air freshener hanging from the rearview mirror. 'A little water won't hurt it. Anyway, I'm already in, which means the seat's already wet, which means it's too late. How about if I tip you five dollars on top of the fare?'

And there goes more of the last of this month's money. But under the circumstances, being broke till payday was the least of her problems.

'Okay,' he agreed, his eyes lighting up, then turned around and pulled out into traffic.

If only all my problems could be solved that easily.

Giving the address of the parking garage next to the DA's office – she'd ridden to the Justice Center with Bryan that morning, leaving her own car at work – Kate slumped in the seat. She was soaked and freezing, and the interior of the cab felt as cold as a refrigerator, so she tried to cope by folding her arms over her chest and squeezing her legs together and curling her wet toes in their shredded nylons in an effort to warm herself up a little.

Her eyes closed. Instantly, images of the carnage in the courtroom began replaying against the screen of her closed lids. Judge Moran, the deputies – they had all gone to work that morning just like she had, and now they were dead. It was unbelievable. Horrible.

It was almost me.

Her shivering intensified. She had to clench her teeth to keep them from chattering. The families of the dead would have been notified by now. Picturing police officers arriving at each victim's door made her stomach turn over. If she had been among the victims, they would have gone to tell Ben at school . . .

Stop that, she told herself fiercely as her heart started to pound. *It didn't happen. And it won't. Whatever it takes.*

Which brought her right back to the nightmare she didn't want to face.

What am I going to do?

Panic clawed at her insides. As the cab progressed in fitful starts through the gridlocked streets, her mind raced, frantically searching for a stratagem, a loophole, any possible means of escape from the new nightmare in which she was trapped. Gritting her teeth, clenching her fists, she finally faced the terrible truth.

Her past had caught up with her.

And now that it had, there was no stuffing the genie back in the bottle. She was just going to have to deal.

Her stomach knotted. She swallowed hard. Her eyes opened but remained blind to the mix of old and new, ornate and plain, mid-rise and high-rise stores and office buildings and condominiums shoehorned into every downtown block. Likewise, she did not register the crawling, honking traffic, the changing traffic lights, the dripping, autumn-bright trees, the sheets of rain.

Instead she saw, through the mist of years, the crowd she'd hung with once upon a very bad time.

8

She had always disliked Mario Castellanos. As a teen, he had been a loudmouthed braggart and a bully. A thug. A lowlife. Bad news in a big way.

As far as she could tell, he hadn't changed a bit. Except now he was bigger. Badder. Way scarier. The street punk had morphed into a hardcore criminal.

Who held her life – and Ben's life – in the palm of his meaty hand.

There had to be some way out, but if there was, she couldn't see it. Right now the best she could come up with was that she was going to have to do exactly what he said, because there just wasn't any other choice.

Which sucked. In fact, recognizing the awful truth and facing it for what it was made her stomach feel like it was being turned inside out.

Claiming that she had shot Orange Jumpsuit was just the first step down a road that, in the worst way, she didn't want to take. Doing it terrified her. She wouldn't face any legal liability over the killing – if ever there was a case that screamed self-defense, shooting the man who had taken her hostage at gunpoint would have been it – but the lie shook her. Her life wasn't about lies anymore. That was all over, all in her past.

Or at least it had been.

'Long time no see,' Mario had said, smiling, after he'd told her who he was immediately after murdering Orange Jumpsuit right in front of her eyes. Orange Jumpsuit was slumped dead at his feet. The shot that had killed him still echoed in the narrow corridor. The smell of cordite and blood and death and fear – hers – had hung heavy in the air.

Her eyes, wide with shock and disbelief, had met Mario's. She could see the swaggering teenage boy she had known thirteen years before in the steroid-pumped man standing in front of her. He would be thirty-one now. The bulk of him, the bald head and deep tan and facial hair, the automatic depersonalization of the orange jumpsuit, the sheer unexpectedness of the encounter – all had combined to keep her from recognizing him until he had called her by her old nickname: Kitty-cat. Then she had known him at once, with a certainty that was as painful and shocking as an unexpected blow to the gut.

I didn't get far enough away. I should have kept running, to Florida maybe, or California.

Looking at him once she knew, she realized that his eyes were the same, a warm spaniel brown that belied the casual cruelty that had disgusted her more than once. His thick nose still bore the crescent-shaped scar from where Roger Friedkin's grandmother's poodle had bitten him. The dog had disappeared not long afterward, a coincidence that Kate had not questioned until months later. Mario's mouth was still thin-lipped and tight, so that even when he smiled he looked mean.

He had been unpredictable and dangerous then. She had no doubt at all that he was even more unpredictable and dangerous now.

'I just saved your life,' Mario had added when she didn't say anything. 'You owe me.'

Her pounding heart beat like a drum in her chest. Her mouth went so dry she had to swallow before she could speak. She tried to breathe normally, tried to stay cool. Tried to ignore the fact that a still-warm corpse was bleeding out at her feet, and one of the monsters that had haunted her nightmares for so long had crawled out from under her bed at last to terrify her by the hard, cold light of day.

'Thank you,' she said.

He laughed, a low, genuinely amused sound that sent a chill racing down her spine. She'd known he was after more than her gratitude, just like she'd known that had it been in his best interests to do so, he would have let Orange Jumpsuit kill her without so much as turning a hair. Mario didn't give a flip about her. The only person she'd ever known Mario to give a flip about was Mario.

'Thank you's not gonna cut it, Kitty-cat.' His tone was playful, and he reached out to tug on a strand of her hair, which had given up the ghost and fallen from its neat bun to spill over her shoulders sometime back.

'I figured.' Putting up her chin, she jerked her head back just enough so that her hair was pulled from his grasp. He let it go. She knew how he worked, knew how all thugs like him worked, because she'd grown up in a world that was chock-full of them. The first rule of survival was don't ever let them see fear. That was also the second, third, and fourth rule. 'So, what do you want?'

'Out of jail. And I want you to get me out.'

He squatted down and began wiping the gun on the hem of Orange Jumpsuit's pants. The dead man's face was gray now. His eyes were still open but glazed over. Blood still trickled sluggishly from his mouth, and the blossoming stain on his chest was still spreading. He sat in an expanding scarlet puddle. Kate looked because she couldn't help it, then deliberately averted her gaze to Mario. He was still wiping down the gun. The fact that he didn't feel the need to hold her at gunpoint, didn't even feel the need to keep his bulk between her and the door, told her that he didn't fear she would make a run for it.

And he was right. Their shared past held her in place like invisible, unbreakable strands of spider silk.

'I can't do that.' Her tone was abrupt. No need to pretend they were friends. They had never been.

'Don't give me that.'

Apparently satisfied with his cleaning efforts, he let the murder weapon slide to the floor beside Orange

Jumpsuit's leg without touching it again. Then he picked up Orange Jumpsuit's dropped gun in its place. He stood, his size menacing in such tight quarters. He held the gun negligently, not pointing it at her, but *still* . . .

She had always been ninety-nine percent certain that it had been Mario who had pulled the trigger.

Kate had to fight the instinctive urge to step back a pace. That was Kate's natural reaction to a thug with a gun, anyway. But Kat – and she had once been Kat – had never backed down from anybody in her life. And it was Kat, who she discovered in that instant was still alive and well and functioning inside her body all these years later, who kept her standing tall, standing her ground.

'So you're a big-time *prosecutor* now. Hey, girl, I'm proud of you!' Mario smiled at her and gave her shoulder a gentle, 'good going, good buddy' kind of punch. When that didn't elicit anything more from her than a narrowing of her eyes, he dropped the good-buddy act and continued in a harder tone: 'That's good for you, and I'm thinking it's even better for me.'

'Are you? How so?'

'I'm looking at some hard time here, twenty-to-life, for nothing. *Nothing*. Violating probation. Possession of a firearm. Persistent felon.' He grimaced. 'Bullshit charges, but looks like they're going to stick. Assholes wouldn't even let me post bail. For nothing, I'm stuck in jail, right, probably till I'm so old my dick shrivels up. When these guys started hatching their little get-out-of-jail-free plan, I told 'em, hell, yeah, count me in. But they were idiots. They blew it. Nobody was supposed to get killed. Guy on the outside was supposed to drive up under the window with a U-Haul. The plan was to blast out a window, leap down onto the truck, get inside, and haul ass. Once Soto shot that judge, far as I was concerned it was all over. I knew they'd hunt us all down to the ends of the earth. I aborted the mission. I was unclipping the keys from that deputy's belt so I could get the hell out of this hallway when Rodriguez here came back in with you.' He smiled. 'I took one look at his little prosecutor friend, and I couldn't believe my . . .'

Brriing.

The phone's shrill summons had sliced the tense atmosphere like a knife. Kate had jumped, looking at the phone with horror. It was almost certainly the cop in the courtroom outside. Her lifeline, but also, now, in a new and terrible way, her enemy.

'Bottom line is, I came up with a better plan,' he continued, ignoring the ringing phone. 'Want to know what it is?'

'What?' It was all she could do to get the word out. She already knew, she already knew . . .

'You. My old friend Kitty-cat. 'Member that security-guard dude we took down that night in Baltimore?'

Oh, yeah. His name was David Brady.

Brriing . . .

As the phone rang again, Kate practically jumped out of her skin. Her nerves were twitching, her heart thumping, her blood pumping so fast that it was all she could do to stand still. This could not be happening . . .

Do not show fear.

'I had nothing to do with that.'

He smirked. 'Baby, you were there just like the rest of us. You know the law better than I do. You know that's all it takes. Somebody lets the cat out of the bag, we're looking at Murder One.'

He's right. Oh, God, he's right.

Brriing . . .

'I was a kid! Fifteen. And I didn't even go inside the store.'

'Doesn't make you any less guilty.'

Youth is a mitigating circumstance.

But as she'd learned later, David Brady had been an off-duty cop. Justice tended to come down hard on people who killed cops.

'Don't worry, I'm not going to tell on you.' Mario must have read the fear in her face, because he smirked at her. ''Less you don't do what I tell you, that is.' His gaze shifted downward. 'Pick up that gun.'

He nodded to the gun he'd used to kill Orange Jumpsuit.

When Kate hesitated, staring down at it without moving while her mind raced a mile a minute, he looked at her again and added in a sharper tone, *'Do it.'*

At the moment, he held all the cards.

Brriing . . .

She did what he said numbly, without another question or protest, not even bothering to make a show of standing up to him. It was useless, anyway. He knew how completely at his mercy she was. And so did she.

As she straightened, she saw that the gun in Mario's hand – Orange Jumpsuit's gun – was now pointed straight at her. Her heart skipped a beat. For a moment she didn't understand. Then she did. She was now holding a loaded weapon. Once upon a time, under similar circumstances, Kat might have thought fast enough and been ruthless enough to have shot him with that gun.

Problem solved.

The intervening years had rendered Kate too civilized.

She took a deep breath. Her pulse thundered in her ears. Her stomach twisted itself into a pretzel. Her knees turned to Jell-O.

'You can't tell on me without telling on yourself,' she said.

Their eyes met. He smiled at her. It was a small, self-satisfied smile.

'But see, that's the beauty of it. Way I see it is, of the two of us I got a whole lot less to lose.'

Brriing.

Oh, God.

'Okay, baby, listen up. Here's how this thing is gonna go down.'

She sucked in air. Her insides shook. Her grip tightened on the gun.

She listened.

And when she was done listening, she picked up the phone.

9

Ben's school, Greathouse Elementary, was a large, boxy, two-story brick rectangle with neat rows of aluminum-clad windows looking out over a grassy playground and sports field in back and a tree-lined circular driveway in front. The building was old and institutional-looking. The trees were redbuds, pretty when they bloomed in the spring, according to some pictures Kate had seen, but shapeless and gray now under the steady onslaught of the rain. The driveway curved to the edge of an overhang that sheltered the front steps and the main entrance. Matching signs on either side of the covered part of the concrete walk that led to the stairs warned *No Parking, Fire Lane.*

Kate ignored the signs, pulling her blue Toyota Camry next to the yellow-painted curb right in front of the overhang. She'd had the heat blasting on high in hopes of drying her wet hair and clothes during the twenty-minute drive between the DA's office at 3 South Penn Square and Ben's school in the Northeast Philadelphia suburb where they lived, but she still felt cold and clammy. A quick glance in the mirror confirmed that except for a few wavy tendrils in front that had been hit by the full blast of the heat, her hair remained a damp mess. Twisting it up in back and stabbing the resultant wet knot through with a pair of bobby pins she fished out of the cup holders between the seats, she grabbed her umbrella from the backseat and got out. The cool air made her shiver; the drumming cascade hitting her umbrella echoed the still-accelerated thudding of her heart. Rain poured onto the umbrella but left her untouched, and she felt like sticking her tongue out at it as she made it to the overhang without getting any wetter than she already was. Closing and shaking the umbrella as she went up the shallow concrete steps, she did a quick mental inventory and decided that except for the gray sneakers from the gym bag she kept in the car, which, having shed her ruined hose, she now wore over bare feet, she looked relatively normal.

Which was important, for Ben's sake.

She had to try three of the four side-by-side front doors before happening upon the one farthest to the right, which was unlocked. Keeping the others locked was one of the security measures, she supposed, that were now being implemented in even the safest schools. A sign printed on red construction paper was taped to the glass part of the chosen door: *PTA meeting, Thursday, 7:30 P.M., Cafeteria.*

Kate felt a constriction in her chest. Since Ben had started kindergarten, she had made it a point to be at every single PTA meeting, no matter what. Having a mother who attended PTA meetings was part and parcel of the life she wanted him to have. A *normal* life. A life so different from her own hardcore childhood that they might have been lived on different planets.

She was still finding it almost impossible to believe that the world she was so carefully constructing for the two of them was in danger of being shattered.

Unless she did what Mario wanted.

Kate felt herself beginning to shake inside, and gritted her teeth.

Not now. Don't think about it now.

'Ms. White?'

The secretary – they were new to the school, and she was rattled, and thus Kate couldn't quite remember the woman's name – greeted her in a low, pleasant voice as soon as she stepped inside the wide front hall, which was painted creamy white with a gray linoleum floor and garlanded with streamers of colorful autumn leaves cut out of construction paper. In her early sixties, a grandmotherly type with short white hair and bifocals and a fluffy blue cardigan with a ring of white benchies embroidered around the neckline, she sat at her desk behind the counter that separated the office area from the main hall that ran the length of the school. She was positioned so that she could see all the comings and goings through the front door: another security measure, Kate had no doubt. When Kate had been looking at the school in conjunction with looking for a place to live after she had been hired as an assistant DA, the parent volunteer who had shown her around had assured her that at Greathouse they were, among other things, very security-conscious.

'Yes. Hi. I'm sorry it took me so long.' Kate dodged a giggling quartet of ponytailed girls as they carried a piece of plywood supporting what was obviously some kind of class project down the hall. She crossed to the counter and glanced over it and into the office area. Like the hall, which was brightly lit and cheerful despite the rain darkening its windows, the office area appeared kid-friendly and welcoming, with a cherry-red back wall adorned with magnetic strips crowded with children's pictures. 'I came as quickly as I could.'

'Oh, listen, I understand. With everything that's been going on downtown – well, I'm just glad you called back when you did. Ben was really getting worried. The TV was on back there, but I had to turn it off. They started showing live pictures of what was happening on every channel, and he was just sure you were in the thick of it.' She stood up as she spoke, and Kate saw that she was comfortably full-bodied in her beige polyester slacks and white blouse, and was also able to read the name tag pinned to the sweater: Mrs. Sherry Jackson. *Right. Got it.* The secretary's voice grew hushed. 'They're saying that ten people were killed, including a judge.'

She looked at Kate as if for confirmation.

Kate felt her stomach tighten. *Don't think about it.* She shook her head. 'I don't know.'

'Well.' Mrs. Jackson smiled at her. 'Ben's lying down

in the back. If you'll just sign him out' – she indicated a clipboard on the counter – 'I'll go and get him.'

While Kate signed Ben out, Mrs. Jackson disappeared through a door at the rear of the office. Loud voices and the sound of running feet coming toward her made Kate start and glance around. The noise was coming from a group of six or so boys who looked to be about Ben's age. They were wearing sneakers and bright blue gym uniforms – Kate recognized them because she had shelled out fifty bucks for two sets for Ben just a little more than a month before – and one was clutching a basketball. Kate didn't know them – she was still too new to the school for her to recognize many of the children – but she smiled at them anyway. One grinned back at her as they ran past, and then they turned a corner into a stairwell and were gone. The thunder of their footsteps echoed through the hall as they headed down to the walk-out basement level.

'Mom?'

Kate's head whipped around at the sound of Ben's voice. He was emerging through a door to the right of the office with Mrs. Jackson right behind him. His backpack, which she knew from experience would be unbelievably heavy for a nine-year-old, hung from one shoulder, giving him a lopsided appearance. Kate's eyes softened as they moved over him. Towheaded and shaggy-haired, a handsome boy with her own light blue eyes, fair complexion, and fine features, he was small for his age, and thin. Today he was wearing jeans, a blue-and-green striped polo, and sneakers. His hair was, as usual, falling in his eyes, and he brushed it aside with one impatient hand.

Considering what had almost happened, what they had almost lost, the sight of him brought tears to her eyes. Her heart swelled with overwhelming love for him even as she forced the tears back so he wouldn't see. She would have hugged him, but he was at the age where being hugged by his mother in public embarrassed him. Instead, she smiled at him.

He didn't smile back.

'Hi, pumpkin.'

Ben grimaced, and immediately Kate knew that she had said the wrong thing. Now that he was in fourth grade, 'pumpkin' sounded babyish to him. In fact, she was forbidden to call him anything except (and these were his instructions) plain old Ben. Because she was a very good mother, she had only succumbed to the urge to call him all three words once or twice.

To his annoyance, of course.

If I don't do what Mario wants, what will happen to Ben? The tinny taste of panic flooded her mouth. She swallowed. *Don't think about it now. Later . . .*

'He says he's feeling better,' Mrs. Jackson reported as Kate stepped forward to relieve Ben of his backpack. As she had suspected, the thing felt like it was loaded with bricks. Another pack of boys in blue gym uniforms burst into view at the end of the hall, but upon seeing Mrs. Jackson slowed to a decorous walk. As they approached, Kate became aware that there were four of them, and that Ben was sidling behind her, clearly trying to get out of sight.

She frowned.

'Hi, Mrs. Jackson,' a couple of the boys chorused.

Kate could feel their curious glances at her, and, she thought, at Ben, who had all but vanished behind her. She could sense his shrinking, feel the shape of him close against her back, and her heart contracted. Leaving their little apartment and the tough South Kensington neighborhood where they had lived while she had attended first Drexel University and then Temple Law School had been hard on him, she knew. But she wanted so much more for him than to grow up in an impoverished area where she was afraid for him to go outside without an adult, or to attend a school where gangs walked the halls, fights were a daily occurrence, and apathy had set in among the staff. She wanted him to have a happy, ordinary childhood in a normal, middle-class suburb where bike rides and neighborhood trick-or-treating and children playing summer games of flashlight tag in front yards was part of the fabric of life. She wanted him to get a good education in a warm, nurturing school, like this one was reputed to be. She wanted a sense of security to be so much a part of his life that he never even thought about it. In short, she wanted him to have everything she had not had.

'You'd better hurry up. Mr. Farris won't like it if you're late for gym,' Mrs. Jackson warned the boys as they passed.

'How can we hurry up? We're not allowed to run in the halls,' one of the boys answered, and the group started snickering.

'And you would never do anything you're not supposed to, would you?' Mrs. Jackson asked in a mock stern tone as she planted her fists on her hips and watched them go by.

This brought forth more not-quite-smothered laughter and a round of answering head shakes, and then they were past and speeding up until they reached the stairwell, where they vanished.

'With this weather, playing basketball for gym class is about all Mr. Farris can have them do.' Mrs. Jackson glanced at Ben, who was once more visible, having sidled back into view as the boys disappeared. 'Some of those boys are in your class, aren't they, Ben?'

'Yeah,' Ben said glumly. He looked up at Kate. 'Mom, could we go? I don't feel so good.'

'Sure.' Kate smiled at Mrs. Jackson, who smiled back. As the secretary headed back toward her office, she called over her shoulder to Ben, who was already trudging for the door, 'Hope you feel better tomorrow.'

'Thanks,' Kate answered when Ben didn't.

He slid into the backseat while she hurried around the front of the car and got in. Shoving the wet umbrella and his backpack into the front passenger-seat footwell, she started the Camry and glanced around at him at the same time.

'So, you want to make a pit stop by the pediatrician's

office?' Putting the car in gear, she pulled away from the curb.

'No.'

The *swish* of the windshield wipers, the hum of the heat, and the heavy patter of rain on metal combined to almost drown out Ben's muttered reply. The smell of burning, which always seeped from the vents in the first few seconds after the heat was turned on, started creeping into the five-year-old car. Knowing that Ben hated the smell, Kate switched the heat to defrost and turned it way down.

'If you're sick . . .'

'I'm not that sick.'

Kate sighed.

'This wouldn't have anything to do with the fact that they're playing basketball in gym today, would it?'

Silence.

Which she translated to mean *Oh, yeah.*

As she turned left onto West Oak Road, the quiet residential street that ran in front of the school, Kate glanced in the rearview mirror at her son. His thin shoulders were hunched, and he was looking gloomily out the rain-drenched window. He looked small and defeated sitting there, and she felt a familiar burst of love and guilt and worry. She was trying so hard – but what if she was doing this mother thing all wrong?

What do I know about raising a kid?

'Ben White, did you even really throw up?'

More silence. Translation: *no.*

'Okay, let's have it. Tell me the whole thing.'

She braked at a stop sign, waited her turn as a red Honda splashed through the intersection in front of her, then turned right onto Maple Avenue. They lived on Beech Court, which was just a little way farther along, within walking distance of the school, in one of the least expensive sections of Foxchase, an upscale neighborhood that she had to really scrape to afford. Of course, she had signed the year's lease on the small house with visions of a smiling Ben and his buddies skipping along the tree-shaded sidewalks to and from school. The reality was that every morning she drove him to school and Suzy Perry, mother of Ben's friend Samantha and two other younger children, picked him up afterward and drove him to her house half a mile away, where he stayed until Kate fetched him after work. The rest of the reality was that Ben didn't seem to have any buddies except Samantha, who was a grade below him and was (as Ben would say despairingly) a *girl*, and Ben rarely smiled anymore.

Which killed her.

'I suck at basketball.'

The small voice from the backseat was truculent and pathetic at the same time. Kate sighed again, inwardly this time. After one of the most horrific events of her life, after the terror and trauma that had struck out of nowhere, this was only a small pain. But it was nonetheless sharp.

'You do not,' she protested loyally, glancing at him in the mirror. He was looking at her in the mirror, too, and their gazes met.

'I do too.' His voice grew even smaller, and with all the other sounds in the car, she had to strain to hear it. Then, after the briefest of pauses, he added, 'Nobody wants me on their team.'

Kate's heart broke. He didn't usually tell her when things went wrong for him – *You've got enough to worry about, Mom,* as he had said on one memorable occasion when she'd asked him why he hadn't told her that some bigger kids at his previous school were stealing the lunch she packed for him every day – so, since he was telling her this, it must be bothering him a lot. She almost said, *Sure they do,* because her instinct was to deny the pain in his face, to buck him up, to do what she could to persuade him that he was mistaken. But the thing about Ben was, he was good at spotting bullshit. Especially hers.

The other thing was, he really wasn't very good at basketball, or any other sport. He took after her in more than looks: Jocks they were not. He was good at school, especially language arts and math. He was a whiz with computers. He watched the Discovery Channel with the same fanatical devotion some people lavished on sports teams. He loved to read, and one of the reasons his backpack was always so heavy was that he always had a couple of books – the one he was reading at the moment and the one he meant to read next, in case he should finish the first one unexpectedly and be caught unprepared – stashed in there along with his schoolwork. When he got the chance – before class started, when he completed an assignment early, even at lunch or recess, unless an adult objected – he would pull out his book and bury his nose in it. This tended to endear him to teachers, but to classmates, not so much. Add that to the fact that he was small for his age, shy around strangers, and just getting started in a new school, and it shouldn't be surprising that he was having trouble making friends.

Which didn't mean that it didn't hurt. A lot.

How do I handle this? Oh, God, I don't have a clue.

'They choose teams?' Kate asked carefully, trying to get a feel for what was actually happening. 'In gym?'

She glanced up in time to see him nod.

'So who chooses?'

'Some of the guys.' He shrugged. It was such a masculine-sounding appellation – 'the guys' – and the shrug was such a masculine gesture that Kate got a quick, poignant vision of the man he was struggling to become.

One day. Right now, he's just a little boy. Desperation squeezed her insides at the thought. *A little boy who thinks his mother can make things all better. Only sometimes I can't.*

Panic tried to rear its ugly head again, but she forced it back. Taking a deep breath, she braked at another intersection, then turned right onto Beech Court.

'Well, who picks the guys who choose?'

'Nobody.'

Of course not. That would be too easy. One quick phone call . . .

'We have to run laps at the beginning of gym. The first four guys to finish – they're the captains, and they get to pick who they want on their teams. We play half-court, with two teams on each end of the court.' He paused. 'I usually finish the laps last. Then I get picked last. Shawn Pascal has a broken arm, and he even gets picked before me.'

Another quick glance in the rearview mirror told her that he was drawing aimless designs in the condensation on the inside of his window.

'That sucks,' Kate said.

'Yeah.'

'What about the girls?'

'They pick their own teams. They play in the little gym.'

'We should practice. You and me, kid.'

'Mom, you suck at basketball. You know you do.'

'That doesn't mean we can't practice. We could both get better.'

Ben snorted. 'Like that would help. Anyway, I hate basketball.'

Kate eyed her son in the mirror.

'I bet you're one of the best readers in your class.'

'Like anybody cares about that.'

'I do. And I bet your teacher does, too.'

Ben snorted again.

'We have a basketball net over the garage. You could practice in the driveway.'

'I don't want to practice. I told you, I hate basketball. Look, just drop it, okay?'

Kate pressed her lips together, swallowing her tendency – which Ben frequently pointed out – to worry subjects to death, as their house came into view on the left. This was, for Philly, one of the newer suburbs, a grid of carefully laid-out streets punctuated by strip malls not too far from I-95 and the Delaware River. It was convenient to her job, with good schools and very little crime. Most of the houses dated from the fifties and sixties. They were either small Cape Cods or modest split-levels, tucked in side by side with postage stamp–sized front yards. Lights were on in a few windows up and down the street – this was a family neighborhood, and several of the mothers stayed home with their kids – but their own house was quiet and dark. It was a pretty little Cape Cod with gray-painted brick and black shutters and two picturesque gables. Right now, rain pelted the tall pin oak by the sidewalk that was just starting to turn red and the smaller, glossily green holly by the front porch and rolled off the black shingle roof to cascade like a waterfall onto the neat line of round bushes that hugged the front of the house.

Kate looked at the overflow in dismay. Clearly the gutters needed to be cleaned. She had never leased a house before; was that a job for her, or for the landlord?

File that under one more problem to worry about later.

As they drove up the driveway, Kate pressed the garage-door opener and the sound of water spilling over the gutters was drowned by the growl of the garage door rolling up. Of all the things she liked about this house, and there were many, the attached garage had to be right up there at the top of the list. For years she'd had to park on the street, and she and Ben, along with whatever packages, groceries, backpacks, or anything else they needed to transport, had had to struggle through everything the weather cared to throw at them to get inside. Driving into a garage, even a small, cluttered, one-car garage without an overhead light, felt like a real luxury.

If I don't do what Mario wants, we'll lose the house. I'll lose my job and my freedom. Maybe even my life. And Ben. I would lose Ben.

Her heart clutched at the thought.

She parked in the garage and pressed the button so that the garage door would go down. As it did, her gaze slid sideways to the lone basketball and kickball in a plastic crate near the trash cans. Maybe she could . . .

'Mom?' Ben's voice sounded a little louder now that she had turned off the car. 'Who would take care of me if something happened to you?'

The garage door met the concrete floor with a metallic *clank*. Kate sat in the gloomy, musty-smelling darkness for a second with her hands still curled around the wheel.

The question struck icy terror into her soul.

Because today it was just too close to home.

She knew why he asked, of course. He had seen parts of what had happened at the Criminal Justice Center on TV. No doubt they had talked about the dead judge, the dead deputies, the dead, period. She only hoped he hadn't seen much of it. She was going to have to talk to him about it, to explore what he knew and thought and feared, to tell him an edited version of how she had been caught up in the horror, sometime within the next few hours, because if she didn't, someone at school almost certainly would. But not yet. She just could not face it yet.

She was still too shattered.

'Nothing's going to happen to me,' she said firmly, and got out. Ben followed suit, and they went into the house. The garage opened into the kitchen, with its cheerful yellow cabinets and white Formica countertops. The appliances were white, too. They had come with the house, so they weren't new, but they worked, and that was all Kate asked of them. On the far side of the refrigerator, a door led out into the small, fenced backyard. The middle of the room was dominated by a round maple table with four chairs. It was, like most of the rest of her furniture, secondhand.

She flipped on the light. There were dishes in the sink from breakfast – she'd been too rushed that morning to load the dishwasher – and a few Cheerios were scattered across the scuffed hardwood floor. Upstairs, the beds weren't made. A couple of loads of laundry waited to be done in the basement.

So Supermom she wasn't. She was trying.

'You hungry?' she asked, as Ben dropped his backpack on the table.

'No.' Then he flashed her a cheeky grin. 'I just threw up, remember?'

'I remember.' Her tone was dry, and she aimed a not-entirely-playful swat at his backside. He dodged, grinned at her, then vanished into the living room. She called after him: 'No more faking sick, understand?'

'Yeah, okay.'

I should probably ground him or something, just so he knows I really mean it.

But she was so relieved to see him looking more cheerful that she dismissed the thought almost as soon as she had it. Then she found herself worrying that a more experienced mom would probably be stricter about discipline, and gave it up.

Like the overflowing gutters, Ben faking sick was the least of her problems at the moment.

Fear twisted inside her.

What am I going to do?

But she was hideously, horribly afraid she already knew the answer. Ben's question about who would take care of him if something happened to her had crystallized the situation for her.

To hell with ethics and morals and personal integrity and criminal liability. Unless she had some kind of brainstorm within the next few hours and saw some way out that hadn't yet occurred to her, she was going to do just exactly what Mario had told her to do. Dance with the devil, just this once, and get him off her back and out of her life.

There simply wasn't any choice.

For Ben's sake.

And never mind that her heart pounded and her pulse raced and she got all light-headed at the thought.

While Ben headed upstairs to his favorite sanctuary, his bedroom, Kate called the office. Her administrative assistant, Mona Morrison, a forty-one-year-old recently divorced mother of a college-aged daughter, answered.

'Oh my God, Kate, where are you? Bryan – the police – a couple of reporters – everybody's been calling, looking for you. Are you all right? What happened?' It was clear from Mona's tone that she was desperate to know all.

'I'm fine. Ben got sick at school, so I had to go pick him up. I'm at home now.'

'What do you mean, you're fine?' Mona screeched. 'There's no way. You were taken hostage. You got hold of a gun and killed the guy to get free. The story's all over TV. How can you be fine?'

I can't handle this now. Then came the corollary thought: *I have to handle it.*

'I really am,' Kate insisted, even as her heart sank at the idea that her lie was already being broadcast all over the city. 'And Ben really is home sick. I just need some time to decompress, so I'm taking the rest of the day off. Tell everybody I'll be in tomorrow.'

'But—'

Kate didn't give Mona time to protest any further. She hung up and walked into the living room. The curtains were open, and through the wide front window she saw that the waterfall thing was still happening.

I'm looking at the back side of water here, she thought with what even she recognized was a sad attempt at mood-lightening humor, and moved to close the draperies, which were a heavy faux silk in a rich tan color (another eBay special, of which she was particularly proud; curtains cost a fortune). A large brown-and-tan plaid couch (courtesy of Goodwill), a gold, plush rocking recliner (consignment store), matching oak coffee and end tables (yard sale), an earth-toned braided rug (another yard sale), and a TV on a cart beside the fireplace made up the furnishings. The walls, like all the walls in the house, were white, except for those in Ben's bedroom, which at his request she had painted a deep blue. For art she had framed some black-and-white sketches of the city, which she had picked up at a street fair early in the summer. The result was attractive, she thought, and not too feminine, which, as the single mother of an only son, she tried to guard against. Along with a separate dining room, which she had turned into an office so she could work at home, a tiny half-bath squeezed in under the stairs, the entry hall, and the kitchen, that was the entire ground floor of the house.

With the draperies closed, the room was dark. Kate switched on one of the brass lamps that graced the tables on either side of the couch, then looked at the TV. For a moment she simply stood there, undecided, then shook her head: Right now she didn't want to know.

Instead, she went upstairs to take a shower.

When she came down again some half an hour later, a little warmer and a whole lot drier but still as sick inside as before, fixing lunch for Ben, who was happily reading in his room, was next on her agenda. Halfway down the stairs she stopped dead. She had finished her shower just in time to watch through the small glass window in her front door as a police cruiser pulled into her driveway.

Followed a scant moment later by a white TV van.

Her stomach did a nosedive for the floor.

10

The Federal Detention Center was just around the corner from Kate's office. She waited after lunch the next day, until after the in-office brouhaha about her and Bryan's survival and her supposed heroism in killing her abductor had died down a little and everybody was once again hard at work, to walk the few blocks to the tall stone building located right in the crowded, tourist-friendly heart of Center City.

Stay calm. It's only your imagination that everyone's looking at you.

Or not. Yesterday, stories on the massacre at the Criminal Justice Center had aired on CNN, MSNBC, Fox News, CourtTV, and all the local channels, and was featured on shows like *Nancy Grace* and *Hannity & Colmes*, just to name a few. This morning *Today, Good Morning America,* and *The Early Show* had kept America in the loop. The story took up the entire front page in all the local dailies, including *The Philadelphia Inquirer* and the *Tribune*. Walking past a sidewalk newspaper stand, she was appalled to see a picture of the post-massacre interior of courtroom 207 splashed across the front page of *USA Today*. She had little doubt that her own picture would be featured in there somewhere. Luckily, her third-year law-school yearbook photo, the one that seemed to be getting the most play, featured her smiling and with her hair loose around her shoulders. Today her hair was pinned in a severe upsweep, and she definitely wasn't smiling.

The way she felt, she might never smile again.

Just thinking about Mario sent cold chills running down her spine. She had put him and all the old gang out of her mind years ago – she had never thought to see any of them again. She had never wanted to see any of them again. But like the proverbial bad penny, Mario had turned up, and if she did not meet with him – today, as he had instructed before hoisting himself up into the ventilation shaft and disappearing – he might start making good on his threat to start talking about their shared past.

The thought made her shiver.

It was a beautiful crisp fall day, sunny, with a cerulean sky dotted with soft white clouds that soared high above the jagged edge of the city's skyscrapers. Yesterday's rain had left behind only a few isolated puddles and some squishy grass. She was walking fast in the black flats she was reduced to because she had abandoned her only black heels in the Justice Center, hugging the charcoal pinstriped blazer she wore with black slacks and a white Hanes T-shirt close because she was freezing, cold to the bone, which was, she knew, more the result of emotional distress than of the weather. The smell of car exhaust and melted asphalt from some construction work up the street and hot dogs from the stand on the corner hung heavy in the air. She breathed deeply anyway, trying to calm her jagged nerves.

It was a waste of bad air.

I feel like a criminal.

A jackhammer's sharp *rat-a-tat* mixed with the *whoosh* of passing cars and the jumble of voices from the people around her on the narrow sidewalk to create a deafening background noise. It was all but drowned out by the too-fast pounding of her own pulse in her ears.

Guess what? You are a criminal.

Kate felt sick at the thought. Catching a glimpse of her own reflection in the window of Ye Olde Candy Shoppe, which was located in one of the dozens of brick-fronted colonial-era row houses that crowded Juniper, she saw that she was way too pale, with dark shadows beneath her eyes and a grim set to her mouth. She looked like someone who had just received a boatload of really bad news.

Wonder why?

Turning the corner onto Arch Street, she glanced up at the plain stone rectangle of the detention center. The narrow slits in the stone that served in place of windows were the only outside indication that some of the most dangerous criminals in the city were housed inside. When the complex had been built, there had been much controversy about locating a prison right in the tourist-hungry heart of the City of Brotherly Love. What visitors didn't seem to realize was that

Philly was one of the most dangerous metropolitan areas in the nation. The police chief, throwing in the towel over the rising crime rate, had recently called for the formation of a vigilante force of ten thousand civilians to patrol the streets, hoping to stem the rising tide of murders, rapes, armed robberies, aggravated assaults, and various other assorted crimes.

Good luck with that.

As she passed beneath it, the U.S. flag snapped sharply in the gust of wind that barreled through the canyon of buildings. It was only as she looked up at the Stars and Stripes, and the blue Commonwealth flag flapping beside it, that she realized both were at half-mast.

Her throat tightened. Her heart gave a sad little hiccup. For Judge Moran, of course, and for the four deputies and two civilians who had lost their lives yesterday. The prisoners who had died weren't included in the official mourning, but as she looked up at those lowered flags she felt sad for them as well.

If things had worked out differently, she might well be dead now, too. The fact that she was alive was something to be profoundly thankful for, she reminded herself grimly.

Even if I am caught like a rat in a trap.

'I saw you on TV this morning,' the black female guard exclaimed as she processed Kate through the entrance. Kate handed over her ID, then walked through the metal detector, watching the steady stream of people entering and exiting the security stations around her. 'Honey, after what you went through, you should be home in bed with the covers over your head. What in the world are you doing working today?'

Kate managed a smile and a shrug. 'Gotta eat.'

The woman made a sympathetic face as she handed Kate's ID back to her. 'Ain't that the truth. Okay, you're good to go.'

By the time she was seated in a cheap plastic chair in one of the banks of grubby, graffiti-scarred cubicles where attorneys met with prisoners, Kate felt like she had run a gauntlet. Nearly everybody she came into contact with had a question or comment about what had happened yesterday. Those who didn't have an opportunity to speak to her directly tracked her with curious stares. Fortunately, for her composure, the detention center was having a busy day, which meant nobody had time to indulge in a prolonged chat. The Criminal Justice Center had been closed to the public as part of the ongoing investigation into the shootings and attempted escape. The detention center itself was on high alert. All trials scheduled for the near future were being moved or postponed, which translated into massive confusion as well as a tsunami of lawyers rushing to visit clients and a ton of extra work for all involved. Kate viewed the chaos as a blessing. It had the double virtue of keeping everybody almost too busy to think as well as scrambling time lines and case files and assignments and court proceedings.

It made doing what Mario wanted just that much easier.

If I don't do what he wants . . .

Her throat went tight. She licked her lips. Her hands curled involuntarily into fists. The consequences would be too much to bear.

Kat the expedient would have had no trouble doing what she had to do to make this whole thing go away. But Kate the conscientious did.

Calling up Mario's file on the computer system had been simple. An ADA from the felony waiver unit had been assigned to the case, but it didn't look like anything much had been done on it. Kate had read through the file, not once but several times. It was mostly low-level stuff, a couple of drug busts, petty theft, check kiting. There were two felony convictions, one for aggravated assault and one for dealing. He'd done time – six months for the aggravated assault and nine months on a five-year sentence, the rest off for good behavior, for dealing. He'd been released on probation eight months ago, picked up again three and a half weeks ago. This time, somebody had decided to get tough with him. The possession-of-a-firearm charge counted as another felony, which meant he fell under the guidelines of the 'three strikes and you're out' law. As he'd said, he was looking at some serious time.

Personally, she felt there were few people more deserving.

The thing was, she was getting ready to put him back on the streets.

Her stomach knotted at the thought. Besides the

crimes that had caused him to be thrown in jail, he was guilty of taking part in yesterday's escape attempt, which had left so many dead. If anyone knew, he would be charged with Murder One. But no one did – except her. And she wasn't in a position to do one thing about it.

If they find out about David Brady, the first thing they'll do is fire you. Then they'll arrest you, and take Ben away . . .

Her chest constricted. For a moment it was hard to breathe.

Maybe you should just confess the whole thing. Get it out in the open and deal with the consequences.

The thought entered her head unbidden. Instantly, she rejected it.

How can I? I can't. What about Ben?

Panic was just starting to curl through her insides again when the door to the cubicle opened. Still wide-eyed and breathing fast from the fresh burst of fear pumping through her veins, Kate looked up through the bulletproof glass wall that rose from the center of the bolted-down table where she was sitting in time to watch Mario swagger in on the other side.

Every muscle in her body tensed. Dread balled into what felt like a rock in her stomach. Her teeth clenched. Her hands flattened on the table's smooth metal surface as her fight-or-flight response kicked in and she battled the urgent need to spring to her feet and flee.

But she stayed seated.

Mario saw her through the barrier. His eyes swept over her. His lips quirked with transparent satisfaction before he looked over his shoulder to say something to someone – she presumed it was the deputy escorting him – behind him.

Still the same cocky asshole.

She took a deep, and she hoped calming, breath. Deliberately, she relaxed her muscles and averted her gaze. Opening her briefcase, which was lying on the table near her left hand, she grabbed a pen and a yellow legal pad from it before closing it again, then scribbled her name at the top for the sheer sake of occupying herself. The worst thing she could do was let Mario see how stressed – get real, how terrified – he was making her.

Never let them see fear.

Clearly Mario had managed to rejoin the general population of prisoners being held in the Justice Center yesterday without anyone's suspecting that he had played a role in the botched escape. Otherwise, he wouldn't be here. He was dressed once again in the ubiquitous orange jumpsuit that all the prisoners wore, and his bald head gleamed in the harsh fluorescent lighting. As a youth, he'd had a head full of frizzy black curls, and their absence, plus the neatly trimmed mustache and goatee and the sheer overdeveloped muscularity of him, made it hard to keep straight in her mind that this 'roided-up thug was the kid she had once known. He looked even broader and more menacing in the close confines of the small space. For the first time, she noticed a tattoo of what looked like a snakelike black dragon curling around his right wrist. Was it some sort of gang symbol? If so, she hadn't come across it before. She was surprised she hadn't spotted it yesterday, but then, her attention had been on other things.

Like staying alive.

She looked up as he approached the table. His gaze found hers, and she thought she saw a flicker of triumph in his eyes.

So much for playing it cool.

He's got me where he wants me and he knows it.

The deputy escorting him glanced at Kate, nodded once, said something to Mario that she couldn't hear because of the glass barrier between them, then withdrew, leaving them alone together. She knew the drill: When she was ready to leave, or if she needed help, all she had to do was press a button on the wall near her elbow. For security purposes, deputies remained stationed outside in the hall at all times.

There was no video or audio surveillance in the booths. By law, attorneys and prisoners were accorded complete privacy.

I can't do this, she thought on another burst of panic as Mario slid into his seat. He propped his elbows on the other half of the table and folded his arms, leaning forward, looking at her confidently through the glass. *I just can't do it.*

Not that actually getting him out would pose any real problem. The ADA assigned to the case would never even miss it. On an average day, each one of them took care of something like forty cases, and most of those didn't even make it onto their radar screens until the night before. The DA's office handled about seventy thousand cases a year; the system was drowning under the sheer volume of proceedings. In the previous year alone, sixty percent of felonies were dismissed at preliminary hearings simply because someone – prosecutor, witness, cop – didn't show up or was unprepared. The justice system was a revolving door that turned crooks lose every single day. Everybody knew it: judges, lawyers, cops, crooks. Only the public remained in blissful ignorance.

Mario's just one more cretin in an ocean of them. Dozens like him go back on the streets every day. By shaking him loose, you're not doing anything that hasn't been done a million times before.

All she had to do was take over his case, and then just fail to do anything. Show up in court unprepared, with no prosecuting witnesses. It would be a slam dunk: case dismissed. Just one more hood back on the streets.

No one would know. She could get on with her life.

I'll know.

Smiling at her, Mario picked up the telephone that allowed them to communicate. After a barely imperceptible pause, she did the same, settling the hard plastic receiver against her ear. Her heart raced; her palms grew damp. But to the best of her ability she kept her face absolutely expressionless as their eyes met and held through the glass.

'Looking good, Kitty-cat,' he said through the phone. 'Real high-class nowadays. And hot.'

Fuck you, Mario.

'If I'm going to do this . . .' Her voice was cold, abrupt. She couldn't just roll over and play dead for him. She was one of the good guys now; she had worked too hard to turn her life around to go back. There had to be some way out of this, some way to save herself and Ben without giving in to his blackmail. But what? She didn't know. Not yet. She needed to get over her panic, take some time to think. Thus her immediate strategy became obvious: delay, delay, delay.

'Oh, you are,' he said. And his smile widened.

Kate fixed him with a steely stare.

Pretend you're in charge here, even if maybe you aren't. Don't let him think he has the upper hand, even if – no maybe about this – he does.

'*If* I'm going to do this,' she repeated icily, 'you're going to have to give me something in return: the name of your supplier, maybe. Or the details of some crime you know about, and who committed it.'

His eyes narrowed and he lost the smile. 'What? Hell, no.'

'I don't have any get-out-of-jail-free cards stashed in my pocket, you know. If you want me to spring you, you're going to have to work with me here. Give me something to use as a reason. Something that I can take to a judge.'

'You can forget that. I ain't no snitch.'

'And I'm not a miracle worker.'

His eyes narrowed. 'I saved your life yesterday, bitch. Rodriguez would have wasted you for sure. Don't you go forgetting that.'

'You call me bitch again, and I guarantee that what I'll forget is that we ever knew each other.'

'I'll call you whatever the hell I want.' His expression turned ugly. 'I own you, baby. You better get me the hell out of here.'

'You don't own squat.' Through the glass, she matched him threatening glare for threatening glare. 'You start shooting off your big mouth, the person who's going down is you. *You* were the one who was carrying the gun that night. You think twenty years sucks? Try looking at the death penalty.'

'Believe me, if I'm looking at it, you'll be looking at it right along with me. And anyway, it wasn't me who pulled the trigger. Keep pushing me, and I'll swear on my sweet dead mother's life it was you.'

Impasse.

'Get real. I'm a lawyer. You're a felon. If I deny everything, who you think they're gonna believe?'

Unnervingly, he smiled at that. Crinkles appeared around the corners of his mean little pit-bull eyes. His teeth showed white through his beard.

Kate's heart skipped a beat. Hopefully, there was no way he could tell.

'Names and places, Kitty-cat. I know names and places.'

He did, and they both knew it. She also knew that

she would crumble like a stale cracker at the bottom of the pack before she let it come to that.

It was time to dial the confrontational tone down a couple of degrees.

'Look, Mario, I want to help you, for old time's sake and all that, but I've been on the job only a couple of months. It's not like I can just tell them to let you go and they'll do it. I still need my boss to sign off on everything I do, and if I'm going to go to him and tell him I want to bargain the charges against you down, I'm going to have to give him a reason. You're going to have to give me something I can use.'

His lips compressed. For the first time, he looked uncertain.

'I'm not giving you shit.'

She shrugged as if to say, 'Your call,' then pressed the round gray button on the wall that summoned the deputy. Mario's eyes widened in surprise.

'What the hell are you doing?'

'Leaving. I've got to get back to work.'

'What about getting me out of here?'

'Like I said, I need your help to do that.'

'Kat . . .' Alarm and anger mixed in his tone.

'And by the way, just so you're aware, calling me that, or anything except Ms. White, is a mistake. Let on that you know me in any way, shape, form, or fashion other than as a lawyer, and you're screwed, because if any whiff of the fact that we have a previous acquaintance gets out, I'll be yanked from your case. And that won't work for what you've got in mind.'

The door opened. As the deputy stepped into the room, Kate smiled at Mario through the glass.

'I'll be in touch,' she said, and hung up the phone.

There was no way he could possibly know her knees were shaking.

His mouth moved, and she was pretty sure the words coming out of it were mostly curses. His eyes shot bullets at her through the glass. But then the deputy was beside him, sliding a hand around his arm, glancing at her, saying something to Mario, and Mario had to hang up.

She didn't look at him again, but instead busied herself with restoring her legal pad and pen to her briefcase as he stood up and was led from the room.

Left alone, she stood up herself. It was no surprise at all to discover that her legs were as wobbly as rubber bands. Her heart pounded; her stomach churned.

She felt like a worm on a hook, wriggling madly as it fought to avoid a hungry trout.

But she'd bought herself some time. Exactly what good that would do she didn't know. But it was something.

By the time she was back inside the ornate stone building at the corner of Juniper and Penn that was home to the DA's office, she was almost calm again. Her nerves were still jittery, but her breathing was normal, her heart had calmed down, and her legs once again felt like they could support her weight. It was a little after two-thirty, late to be returning from lunch, so there was no one she knew in the crowd waiting for the elevator. Instead, a motley collection of people – a raggedy old man who looked (and smelled) like he'd spent the morning with a bottle, a college-age girl in blue jeans, two fiftyish guys in suits, a well-dressed older couple discussing something in whispers – crowded in around her. Punching the button for the ninth floor, she stared into the shiny brass panel facing her and concentrated on relaxing her face.

The only word that came to mind to describe her expression was grim.

The Major Trials Unit occupied all of the ninth floor, and it was bustling, Kate saw as the elevator door opened. A chattering group of what looked like high school students was being given the grand tour by John Frost of the Public Relations Office. A loudly wailing old woman – Kate assumed she was either a victim or a witness – in red polyester slacks and a brown poncho was being hustled into the nearby ladies' room by another, much younger woman in a suit whom Kate knew to be an ADA, although she could not immediately recall her name. An administrative assistant, Nancy somebody, emerged from the break room beside the restroom with a steaming cup of coffee in her hand and hurried down the hall, blond and lithe in a long-sleeved blue T-shirt and flowy skirt, sloshing coffee into a saucer as she went. The smell of it wafted through the air. Kate waved at Cindy Hartnett, the twenty-five-year-old receptionist whose semicircular desk faced the elevators, as she stepped off and the elevator doors rumbled closed behind her.

The voluptuous brunette waved back as she reached to answer her ringing phone. Ron Ott, a fellow ADA in the Major Trials Unit, was leaning against Cindy's desk, probably trying to get her to go out with him as nearly all the single males in the building did. He glanced over his shoulder as Cindy waved, saw Kate, and waved, too. Behind Cindy, a large room full of cubicles was home to the paralegals, who did much of the grunt work on the cases. Several were on their feet, standing and chatting, looking over the shoulders of seated individuals whom Kate could not see, or walking around with files or cell phones in their hands. The walls separating their desks were only six feet high, so the row of windows overlooking the street bathed the room, and the reception area Kate was walking through, in shafts of sunlight thick with dancing dust motes. A long, pale green hall with dark wood doors opening off it ran to the left and right of Cindy's desk. Kate headed right, toward her own office, waving to a few of her colleagues whose doors were open. Bryan's door was closed, she saw as she passed it. She had talked to him on the phone last night when he'd called to check on her, but she hadn't seen him all day. Which suited her just fine. As far as she was concerned, the fewer people who wanted to discuss yesterday's events, the better.

I have to get my act together about this.

'Oh my God.' Mona shot to her feet as Kate hurried past her administrative assistant's office, which was right next door to hers. 'Where have you been?'

Kate had hoped to reach her own office and safety without eagle-eyed Mona spotting her. With that hope shot to hell, and with Mona hurtling toward her like a heat-seeking missile, Kate stopped and turned to face her. Aware that her grip on her briefcase was tightening into viselike territory, she forced a smile.

'What's up?' she asked, guiltily aware that it wasn't an answer. Nervous flutters in her stomach made her tone more abrupt than the smile might suggest, but she couldn't help it. Clearly something was afoot, though, for Mona to spring up after her like that.

Mona didn't appear to notice anything amiss. With her short, flaming-red hair framing an animated face dominated by big brown eyes and wide, scarlet-painted lips, and her pin-thin body clad in a burnt-orange turtleneck and gold plaid skirt, brown opaque hose, and heels, she resembled nothing so much as a living finger of flame.

'You're not going to believe this.' Mona stopped, steepling her hands with their long, scarlet-painted nails beneath her chin. Several rings glinted on her fingers. '*The View* called.'

'*What?*'

Mona nodded eagerly. 'They want you to be a guest on the show. They're calling you the heroine of courtroom 207! They want to fly you out there and everything.'

For a moment Kate was rendered speechless. She stood rooted to the spot with growing horror. For her part, Mona practically vibrated with excitement.

Appalled blue eyes connected with thrilled brown ones for a pregnant instant. Then Kate broke eye contact, shaking her head.

'No.'

Trying to ignore the fact that her pulse had just made like a race car when the driver stomps the gas and jumps from zero to sixty in a couple of seconds, Kate turned and continued walking toward her office.

'What do you mean "no"?' Mona screeched. Mona definitely wasn't the shy, retiring type. She was vocal and opinionated, and one of the firmest of her opinions was that Kate needed to be taken under her wing. 'Do you realize what a chance this is for you? You'll be famous.'

'I don't want to be famous.' Kate was getting almost used to the feeling of her heart pumping furiously in her chest. But that didn't mean she had to like it.

'But-but . . .' Mona sputtered. 'Think what it could mean for your career. You'd get noticed! Maybe you could even use it to get a TV gig, like Greta Van Susteren or somebody.'

'I don't want a TV gig.' Just the thought of appearing on national television under the circumstances gave her the willies. The whole 'heroine of courtroom 207' thing was a terrible lie that she just wanted to move as far away from as fast as she could. It was already all over the news. The thought of compounding that lie by appearing live and in person on national TV to repeat it filled her with fear. To say nothing of the fact that such exposure would give Mario even more ammunition, and might even flush out additional rats from her past.

'But, Kate . . .' Mona was right behind her as Kate turned on her heel and resumed the march toward her office. Kate was looking straight ahead at the gilt-framed portrait of the governor that adorned the far end of the hall, but she didn't have to see Mona to know that she was wringing her hands.

'No buts,' Kate said, reaching her door and turning the knob. She looked back at Mona as she pushed the door open. 'I don't want to be on *The View*, or any other television show, thank you very much.'

'You can't just . . .' Mona protested. Whatever else she said after that was lost as Kate stepped inside her office to find a man already in there, standing in front of her desk, turning to look at her as she entered.

The black-haired cop who'd been her lifeline in courtroom 207, to be precise.

11

'What are you doing in here?'

Kate was so shocked that her tone was a whole lot sharper than it would have been if she'd had even a few seconds' warning to prepare. A cop – even this cop, especially this cop, with whom she discovered she felt a weird kind of connection, like the courtroom thing had linked them in some mysterious way – waiting in her office right on the heels of where she had just been and what she had just been doing was as unnerving as a skeleton popping out unexpectedly from behind her desk. No, make that *more* unnerving. Mona practically bumped into her before stopping dead behind her. Even as Kate breathed in the faint but unmistakable scent of cigarette smoke that always hung around Mona, she could feel her administrative assistant peering over her shoulder.

'Umm, that's the other thing I meant to tell you,' Mona said in her ear, sounding sheepish. 'There's a couple of cops waiting in your office.'

'Thanks for the heads up.' Kate's voice was dry.

A couple of cops . . .

She spotted the second one as he stepped out from

behind the first. Stylishly dressed in a dark blue pinstriped suit with a pale blue shirt and a yellow tie, he was about five-ten, stocky, with close-cropped sandy hair, a ruddy complexion, and a blunt-featured, good-humored face. Stubby-lashed eyes the color of his suit moved over her appraisingly. The cop from the courtroom smiled at her – he really was as good-looking as she remembered, tall, dark, and lean, with a hard, angular face, heavy-lidded coffee-brown eyes, and a slow smile – and held out his hand.

'Thought I'd stop by to see how you're doing,' he said as she took his hand and gave it the brisk, businesslike pump that lawyers give people. Gratitude for his efforts to save her life yesterday was swamped by an uprush of extreme wariness: What did he want? His hand was big and warm and firm, and she dropped it like it was hot while vivid images of him scooping her up in his arms after her knees gave way and carrying her out of the courtroom yelling for an EMT danced in her head. He was broad-shouldered but didn't look overly muscular in his loose-fitting tan jacket, limp-looking white shirt, red tie, and nondescript navy slacks. Still, she knew from personal experience that he was strong. Slim as she was, she was no feather, and he had lifted her with ease. 'I'm Tom Braga, by the way. Detective, Homicide Division.' His eyes touched the small Band-Aid on her cheek, then slid quickly over her. 'I'm glad to see you've recovered so fast.'

Gulp.

Her heart was beating a mile a minute, and not because he was cute. Probably because he was a cop – a homicide detective, yet – and she felt like a criminal. Like he *knew* she was a criminal. Like he could somehow tell that what he believed had happened in the secure corridor yesterday was a lie.

Which he couldn't. No possible way.

Could he?

Get a grip, Kate. As far as he knows, you're the victim here, remember?

Forcing a smile to her lips, she sucked in air through her nose so he wouldn't notice, hoping the deep breath would prove calming.

It didn't.

'This is Detective Howard Fischback, also from Homicide,' Braga added, gesturing at the other man. The second cop stepped forward with his hand out. His was fleshier, with stubbier fingers. He smiled at her, and she noted the white gleam of his teeth and the deep dimples on either side of his mouth. His suit was immaculate, and his shirt and tie looked new. This guy might not be as classically handsome as his partner, but clearly he worked it.

'Kate White.' She pumped his hand and let it drop.

'Pleased to meet ya.' His smile was broad and genial. His eyes were warm on her face.

Okay, he was definitely trying to charm her. *Fat chance.* She glanced at her watch – time, two-fifty-five – desperately searching for an excuse to shoo them away. She was due in court? No, the courts were closed. An urgent appointment? Mona would know it was a lie.

'And I'm her administrative assistant, Mona Morrison.' Obviously operating under the assumption that Kate had forgotten all about her – which she had – Mona stepped forward with her hand out. Both men shook it briskly, and Fischback flashed her that dimpled smile, but it was Braga who she made big eyes at. *Of course.* Mona made no bones about being perpetually on the hunt, and Braga was nothing if not sexy.

'I've seen you around the building for years, so it's nice to finally meet you,' Mona gushed, her gaze targeting Braga like a laser.

'You've worked here for years?' Braga's eyes slid toward Kate. He had thick, straight black brows, and they lifted slightly in surprise.

She shook her head.

'Oh, I've only been with Kate since she came to work here in June. Before that I was in the RO unit.'

'Ah,' Braga said.

'Thanks, Mona,' Kate said. Her nerves were raw, and watching Mona flirt was the last thing she wanted to do. What she desperately needed was to be alone, to have a small window of time to get her thoughts in order and her emotions under control.

Fat chance at that, too.

Her administrative assistant flashed her a reproachful look, but took the hint. 'Well, I'll be in my office if you need anything.'

Kate nodded. Fischback's gaze followed Mona as

she left the room. Braga, on the other hand, was watching her, Kate discovered when she looked back at him and their eyes met. He smiled at her. The office suddenly felt way too small. She and Braga were maybe a yard apart, so close that she could see that his jacket was worn around the edges of the lapels and his morning shave was starting to grow out.

'After yesterday, I'm surprised you're at work,' Braga said.

'You're working today,' Kate pointed out.

'I already used up my sick days for the year.'

From the hint of humor in his tone, Kate knew not to take that seriously. She was walking as he spoke, putting some much-needed distance between them by moving around the two men to set her briefcase down on her desk. That gave her a moment with her back to them in which she tried to relax the muscles of her face. They were so rigid with tension that the smile she had given them had felt like it had been dragged out of hardening cement.

Stay cool. They have no clue.

When she faced them again, they were glancing around her office. Like all the ADA's in her division, she had a ten-by-twelve rectangle with pale green walls (it was officially called celadon, but as Ben said, the shade was more akin to squished caterpillar), a standard-issue, L-shaped black metal desk with a faux-wood top that claimed the center of the room, a matching black metal bookcase and a pair of file cabinets shoved against the wall behind the desk, a big black leather desk chair that she used, and two small black-leather-and-steel chairs positioned in front of her desk for visitors. On the wall behind her desk were her framed diplomas. On her desk was last year's school photo of Ben. An empty coatrack stood in one corner. In another, a spindly fake ficus tree – Kate had given up on real plants long since, because she always forgot to water them – stood forlornly beside a double-hung window. The window was outfitted with narrow gray blinds that were almost always open, providing Kate with a thrilling view of the plain stone front of the office building across the street. Occasionally, her day was enlivened by watching pigeons perch on her windowsill or, for variety, the sills across the street.

If she went to the window and looked straight up, she could see a river of sky snaking above the high-rise canyon in which she worked.

'I saw you leaving the Justice Center behind a sheriff's deputy on a stretcher yesterday. I hope he's doing okay?' The best defense was always a good offense, and taking the lead in the conversation was a classic diversion strategy. A warm, interested tone was what she was shooting for. She wasn't sure she succeeded. Like her face, her voice felt stiff and unnatural.

Braga shrugged, and a shadow passed over his face. 'He's alive, and the doctors say he's going to make it. He's still in ICU, though.' His eyes flickered. 'He's my brother.'

That pierced her wariness a little bit. Clearly, he cared about his brother. She nodded with genuine sympathy. 'I thought I saw a resemblance. The black hair.'

A small smile touched his lips, lightening his expression, as he gave an acknowledging nod.

'Which brings me to the *other* reason why we're here. Do you mind answering a few questions?'

Caught off guard, Kate felt her face freeze. Her heart lurched. Her stomach clenched. Hoping against hope that it wasn't already too late, she tried her best to keep her instant, instinctive rejection from becoming apparent.

'I gave my statement yesterday. Some officers came by my house.'

God, she'd been so rattled then – could she even remember what she'd said? The TV truck had been only the first of a wave of media that had descended on her house. They had knocked on her door and rung her doorbell incessantly until one of the pair of uniforms who had arrived to take her statement had gone to the door and told them to knock it off. By the time she'd finished giving her statement and walked the cops to the door, her front yard had become a sea of reporters and cameras and umbrellas and satellite trucks and dozens of flashing lights that popped at her like balled lightning through the falling rain as she stepped out onto the porch.

'Kate, is it true you shot your captor with his own gun?' 'Kate, did you think you were going to die?'

'Kate, can you tell us about your ordeal?' 'Ms. White, how are you feeling?' 'Ms. White, what did Rodriguez say to you?' 'Kate, look this way!'

She had looked at the throng, horrified, and said, 'I have nothing to say' when a reporter stuck a microphone in her face, stepped back inside the house, and slammed the door on them, carefully locking it behind her. Through the door she'd heard the cops yelling at them to leave the area. Even as they grudgingly obeyed, her phones had started to ring, both landline and cell. Her insides twisted into one big Gordian knot. Gritting her teeth, she turned the ringers off on both phones, then walked through the house, methodically closing all the drapes, checking the doors and windows to make sure they were locked. She ended up in Ben's room, where he was propped up in bed reading. Automatically, she turned on the lamp beside his bed – he was always reading in what she considered the dark – and he took his nose out of his book for long enough to look up at her.

'Mom, what were all those people doing outside? Did you really shoot somebody today?' He was wide-eyed with interest and – no mistake about it – awe at the thought that his mother might have actually done such a thing.

Clearly, all the commotion had pulled him from his book and he had looked out his window. No doubt he'd heard some of the questions shouted at her.

Her heart sank.

'No,' she said, because she couldn't lie to him about

something as enormous as that, because she didn't want him to think of his mother and violence in the same breath, because that wasn't part of the life experience she wanted for him. Then, because she had to, because if anybody asked him questions she couldn't have him saying, 'My mom said she didn't shoot anybody,' she then changed her answer to 'yes.'

And then his eyes got even wider and he scooted up taller against the pillows to stare at her, and she sat down beside him and told him the whole story. Sort of. With a lot of editing and a few crucial lies.

Just like she was getting ready to do again with these guys. Just like she'd done in her official statement.

The truth – most of her story had been the absolute truth. Because in almost every way that mattered, she *was* the victim here. She had nothing to hide. Except for the end . . . and the beginning.

Her heart beat faster at the thought.

'It won't take very long.' Braga correctly interpreted her hesitation as reluctance, although he was wrong about the reason for it.

She fought the urge to swallow. Her hands – damned telltale things! – had clasped at her waist without her even being aware of it. Now that she *was* aware, it was all she could do not to not to jerk them apart. But that would be a giveaway, too.

Fortunately, Braga was looking at her face, not her hands. Casually, she let them drop so that her fingertips just rested on the surface of her desk.

'Everything's in my statement,' she tried again.

'I read through it this morning. But there's still a few things – while they're fresh in your mind.'

'This won't hurt a bit, scout's honor,' Fischback assured her with a flashing smile. He pulled the guest chair closest to him out a bit. Its sturdy metal legs made a scraping sound against the hardwood floor. 'Mind if we sit down?'

He was already suiting the action to the words.

'Of course not. Go ahead,' Kate said, like she had any choice. Braga sat, too, and pulled a small, flip-top notebook and a pen from his jacket pocket. She sank into her own chair, facing them across her desk, acutely aware that he was reading through scribbled notes. Notes, she had no doubt at all, pertaining to her statement.

'After Rodriguez pulled you back into the hall, did you see anyone?'

It took everything Kate had to keep her eyes from widening. *They know about Mario.* That was her first, instantaneous thought. She went cold all over. Her pulse raced. Her stomach cramped. Then she remembered Braga's brother, the other fallen deputy, and the other downed prisoner in the holding cell. Of course, Braga meant them.

She picked up a pen and fiddled with it to hide her relief.

'Besides Rodriguez, do you mean?' Her voice was amazingly steady despite the fact that her mouth had gone as dry as the Sahara in the split second before reason had regained its grip on her. She prided herself that her expression was just right – a little painful remembrance, a little curiosity, nothing more.

'Besides Rodriguez,' Braga agreed.

'There were three men lying on the floor of one of the holding cells. I just got a glimpse. Two of them were deputies – your brother was one although I didn't know that at the time – and the third was wearing an orange jumpsuit, so I assumed he was a prisoner. I . . . I thought at the time that they were all dead.' A quick vision of them lying there made the little catch in her voice all too real.

He nodded and wrote something in his notebook. Fischback, Kate saw, was looking over her desk. A quick, searching flicker of her eyes confirmed that there was nothing incriminating – such as Mario's file, which earlier she had called up on her computer – to be seen. Her laptop was open but in sleep mode, and she didn't think he could see anything on it anyway, positioned as he was in front of her desk. The phone, stacks of files, piles of paperwork, a trayful of mail, a couple of plastic boxes crammed with computer discs, a few assorted books, a construction paper-covered tin can (Ben had made it; it was supposed to be a dog) full of pencils and pens – her desk was clean. She dared not look behind her, but she knew what he would see back there: big brown accordion files lined on top of the bookshelf, shelves crammed with books and manila folders and papers, a big seashell she and Ben had found during a visit to the shore. Both file cabinets were closed, with only a few yellow Post-its adorning their fronts. A fax machine was on top of one of them. Her calendar, which was stuck to the side of the other file cabinet by a pair of black Scottie dog magnets that had been a gift from Ben last Mother's Day, had nothing about today's appointment at the detention center on it. She was too much the lawyer now to ever write down anything that could possibly be used against her at a later date.

There was, she was sure, no trace of Mario to be seen anywhere on the premises.

She was just heaving a silent sigh of relief when her gaze fell on Braga again. He was watching her hands.

She was still fiddling with the pen, turning it over and over, end over end.

It took every bit of self-control she possessed not to clench her hands into fists and let the pen fall.

Instead, she set it down carefully, then folded her hands primly in front of her, fingers laced, so that they could give nothing away.

There was no way he could know that her palms were damp.

'So how did you come to "just get a glimpse" inside the cell?' Braga asked.

Kate frowned. Here was one of the places where she had lied about what had happened, where she had to lie, because of course the reason she had seen inside that cell was because Mario had come out of it.

'Rodriguez pulled the door open for just a moment, I don't know why. He shoved me against the wall first, and I was in a position to look inside the door when it opened.'

'And what did you see?'

'I told you. The three men – the deputies and the prisoner – lying on the floor. Like I said, it was just a glimpse.'

'Did you see any weapons? A gun?'

'No. Except for the one Rodriguez was holding, of course.'

'Okay.' Braga consulted his notebook again. Kate tried not to sweat.

'Any idea where Rodriguez got that gun, Ms. White?' Fischback asked.

Kate was on solid ground here. 'None. Not at all.' She thought back. One minute Rodriguez had been sitting at the defense table, the next he'd sprung to his feet, gun in hand. 'When he jumped to his feet in the courtroom, the gun was just there in his hand.'

'And that's the first time you saw it?' Fischback's expression was unreadable.

Again, she didn't care, because on this point she was on solid ground. 'Yes.'

'So where'd you get the gun you shot Rodriguez with?' Braga asked, his pen poised over the notebook. There was only mild inquiry in his eyes, Kate discovered as she met them. Absolutely no suspicion at all.

Regardless, Kate felt sweat prickling to life under her clothes.

'It was just there – on the floor.'

'It was lying on the floor in the hall?'

'Yes.'

'You didn't see it earlier?'

'No.' She had to fight the urge to look away, or to lick her lips. 'He pushed me down, and I landed, and there the gun was just lying on the floor up against the wall, right next to the wall. I hadn't noticed it earlier.'

Silence filled the room as he seemed to be waiting for her to continue. She met his gaze straight on, while her heart pounded and her nerve endings crawled and she had to fight the physical urge to jump to her feet and walk away. Her fight-or-flight response screamed *flight,* but she couldn't, she had to sit there and look calm and lie through her teeth and wait. As a lawyer, the one thing she had seen suspects do over and over again that got them into trouble was talk too much. She wasn't going to fall into that trap if she could help it.

'So you saw a gun on the floor against the wall,' Braga said finally. 'To your right or left?'

Kate tried to visualize the scenario she was creating in her mind.

'To my right.'

'Okay.' He paused to scribble something in his notebook while her nerves stretched taut as piano wire. 'You said he pushed you down. How did you land?' Kate must have frowned because he elaborated almost immediately. 'Stomach, back, side . . .'

Oh, God, get this over with. Please.

'On my butt. I landed on my butt and saw the gun. I knew Rodriguez was getting ready to shoot me, so I grabbed it and just pointed it and pulled the trigger.' She took a deep breath, both for effect and because she really, really needed the oxygen. 'And I shot him.'

'Where was he? Rodriguez?'

Kate could feel sweat trickling down her spine. Her antiperspirant had already given up the ghost. Luckily, her jacket would hide any telltale rings under her arms.

'Near the wall, the back wall where the phone is. He was facing me.' Kate tried to picture the scenario she was creating again. Could she have grabbed a gun, aimed, and fired it while Rodriguez was just standing there with his own weapon? In a word, no. 'He . . . he dropped his gun, and bent to pick it up. I didn't think I'd ever get a better chance. So I . . . went for it. The gun on the floor.'

Braga wrote something down. Then he looked up at her again.

'So Rodriguez dropped his gun, and while he was picking it up again you grabbed the gun you saw on the floor. Had he recovered his gun when you shot him? What position was he in?'

Forensics. Mustn't forget about forensics. They'll be able to tell what position Rodriguez − and I − was in when the fatal shot was fired from the trajectory of the bullet.

If they cared to go to that much trouble. But she had to assume they would.

'He was holding the gun, lifting it. He was standing again. I think . . . I'm pretty sure he was getting ready to shoot me.' She took another deep breath, because she needed it and because she was pretty sure at this juncture one would be considered an appropriate response to remembered stress. A picture of Mario shooting Rodriguez came crystal clear into her mind's eye. She tried to put herself in Mario's place. 'I was on my feet by that time. We were both on our feet when I shot him.'

'So let me see if I have this straight: He was standing facing you, his back to the wall, and you were standing facing him when you pulled the trigger.'

Kate nodded.

'Was the safety on?'

That caught her by surprise, but she hoped she didn't show it. Her eyes didn't widen. Her mouth didn't tighten. Her body didn't stiffen. She stayed perfectly composed, perfectly relaxed – but it cost her big-time. As a prosecutor, she had been trained to read body language as one part of an arsenal of tools to judge if someone was lying. She was absolutely certain that homicide detectives looked for the same things.

Accordingly, she frowned slightly, as if trying to remember. Her stomach felt like butterflies were doing somersaults inside there. She could hear her pulse beating against her eardrums. She had to fight the impulse to swallow hard.

But a slight, thoughtful grimace was what appeared on her face, while, she hoped invisibly, her mind raced.

The thing was, she hadn't actually worked out in

her mental recreation of events the exact physical details of how firing a gun under such circumstances would have gone down. She'd fired one before, both in her misspent youth and later, at a practice range, with a fifty-dollar special she'd bought for protection, but the thing was, she didn't know that much about pistols in general. Thinking fast, she tried to see the possible pitfalls attached to each answer – for example, Braga could say, *Show me how you did it,* and hand her a gun identical to the one she'd supposedly used, and she would have to locate the safety – and came up with what she considered the safest response.

Her frown cleared. 'No.' Her voice was confident, her face serene.

Bravo.

He nodded, and wrote that down, too. So simple. So easy. So why was she sweating fricking bullets?

Her phone rang, and she jumped a mile.

12

Kate didn't know why that startled her so. Just the sheer unexpectedness of the noise when she was so tense, she supposed. It was her cell, and it was a normal, *brriing* type of ring. After yesterday, she'd had enough of custom ringtones to last a lifetime.

But for whatever reason, her heart had picked up the pace until it was now threatening to beat its way out of her chest. Braga and Fischback were watching her, both of them curious, expectant.

Never let them see you sweat. Even if beneath her clothes she was wringing with it.

'Excuse me, I have to take this.'

They nodded.

It was Ben. She knew it as soon as she came back to earth after that first alarming ring, even before she retrieved the phone from her briefcase and saw the number crawling across the screen and answered it. To begin with, the phone in her office had been routed through Mona for the day, because it had been ringing off the hook from the moment she arrived at work that morning. And only a few people – Ben and the people connected with him in some way – had her cell number. Anyway, Ben always called her as soon as he was in Suzy's car, so she would know he had been safely picked up from school.

So she wouldn't worry.

Get real. You always worry.

'Hi, pump – Ben,' she said, remembering in the nick of time that 'pumpkin' was a no-no.

'Hey, Mom. I'm on my way to the Perrys'.'

'Did you have a good day?'

'It was okay.'

She imagined him sitting there in the backseat of Suzy's Blazer. The music would be blaring – Samantha liked loud music – and the three Perry kids, plus Suzy, would be grooving to it. But not Ben. He'd be hunched against his door to get as far away from the noise as he could, probably with a finger in his ear while he talked on the phone.

She sighed. In a perfect world, she would get to pick up her own kid. Unfortunately, there was no such thing.

'I'll be there to get you as soon as I can. Probably a little early today. Grab a snack. Have fun. Do your homework.'

'Yeah, right.'

Kate had to smile. That last had been thrown in there as a kind of parental Hail Mary pass. Homework almost never got done at Suzy's, which was a place for hanging out with Samantha. Homework was for home – and for Mom to help with.

Which made for some grueling evenings when both

parent and child were tired, cross, and mutually stumped by fourth-grade math. Still, when it came right down to it, Kate wouldn't have it any other way.

Braga and Fischback were still watching her. Braga's eyes were dark and unreadable. Fischback's were bright with curiosity. Kate became aware of the smile that still lingered around her lips, of the lessening of the tension in her neck and shoulder muscles.

Hearing Ben's voice, picturing him on the other end of the phone, had both calmed her and given her a renewed sense of purpose.

She was going to get them through this with their lives intact, whatever it took.

For Ben.

'Got to go, sweetie,' she said into the phone.

'*Mom,*' he protested the endearment. Then, 'Okay, bye.'

'Bye,' she echoed, even as the sound of him disconnecting reached her ear. Closing the phone, she placed it on her desk.

'That your son?' Braga nodded at the photo of Ben on her desk. It was a standard-issue school photo, taken the previous year. Ben was looking solemnly at the camera – he'd been missing a front tooth, and thus had refused to smile – and had a big chunk of hair missing from the front of his shaggy blond bangs where he'd taken a pair of scissors to them in a do-it-yourself effort to remove a splash of red paint he'd gotten in his hair in art class. At the time she'd been horrified. Now it made her smile.

Kate nodded. 'Yes.'

'Cute kid.'

'Thanks.' Talking to Ben, realizing all over again what was at stake, had done the trick. She had her nerve back and her guard up. Placing her hands flat on her desk as if she was getting ready to stand up, she looked at the two detectives with cool inquiry. 'If there's nothing else?'

'No.' Braga flipped his notebook closed and slid it and his pen into his pocket, then stood up. Fischback was a second or so behind him, and Kate rose with Fischback. 'I think that's all.'

'You've been a big help,' Fischback said, and smiled at her. 'We have a whole lot of new areas to explore.'

Kate refused to allow herself to read anything into that.

'If you think of anything else, you know where I am.' Her tone was brisk. She held out her hand, first to Braga and then to Fischback, then walked around her desk to escort them to the door (with much more eagerness than she hoped was apparent).

'We do,' Braga agreed, pausing to glance over his shoulder at her as his partner went ahead of him into the hall. He was just inside her open door when he stopped, and, having been mentally pushing him along, she was right behind him when she had to stop, too. In her flat shoes, her head just topped his shoulders, and she revised her estimate of his height upward by an inch or two, to, say, six-two-ish. From her fresh vantage point behind him, his shoulders really were impressively broad. His black hair was short, but not so short that it couldn't curl at the back of his collar. Seen in profile, his forehead was high, his nose was long, with a faint curve to the bridge, his lips were a little on the thin side but well-shaped, his jaw was square, and his chin was determined. He looked tired, and a little older than she'd first thought. The good looks were still abundantly apparent, but there was a cynicism to his eyes, a hardness to his mouth, a grimness to the set of his jaw, that reminded her that this was a veteran detective with years of experience in digging through bullshit. As their eyes met, the thick black slashes of his eyebrows slanted toward his nose, and she saw that he was frowning at her.

She frowned herself, nervous all over again and hoping it didn't show.

'Was there something else?' she asked.

'I just want you to know, I wasn't sure you were going to make it out of there yesterday. I'd had dealings with Rodriguez before: You took out a real bad dude.'

Kate swallowed before she could catch herself, then realized her reaction was perfectly appropriate given all the bad memories that would naturally attach to what he thought had gone down.

'That makes it a little easier,' she said, because it was clear that he was trying to ease some of the guilt he thought she might be feeling over having taken a human life. 'And by the way, in case I didn't say it, thanks for trying to save my life yesterday.'

He smiled a little, his eyes crinkling at the corners. 'All in a day's work.'

Then he walked on out of her office.

Fischback was waiting in the hall, and the two of them headed toward the elevators together, moving with easy synchroneity without ever once looking back. As far as Kate could tell, they didn't talk. Mona's door was open, but she was either on the phone or in some other way preoccupied, because she didn't pop out for one more attempt to hit on Braga, which Kate knew she would have done had she been able.

When they were far enough along the hall so that she was pretty sure they were really, truly gone, Kate closed the door at last and pressed her back to it, leaning limply against the cool paneled wood, her hand still on the knob. The contact, which flattened her T-shirt against her skin, made her unpleasantly aware of how clammy she was. Her heart was still beating way too fast. Her knees threatened to give out at any second. She had to fight the urge to slide down until she was sitting spraddle-legged on the floor. Closing her eyes, regulating her breathing, she fought off the mini-breakdown she could feel coming on.

Stay strong.

'Pretty lady.' Fish's voice was reflective. They were riding the elevator down, just the two of them in the car.

'Yeah.' Tom was leaning back against the wall, his arms folded across his chest, his eyes on the numbers over the door as they blinked successively lower. Kate White *was* pretty, exceptionally pretty, even if she was a little on the skinny side for his tastes. Ordinarily, he didn't like overly thin women. Probably something to do with the Italian blood in him.

'You catch an off vibe there?'

'Just a little one.'

'So, what do you think?'

There was a *ping* as they reached the ground floor and the doors started to slide open. Both of them moved forward to exit the elevator at the same time, with Tom, because he was at the back of the car, bringing up the rear.

'Good question,' he said.

There were maybe a dozen people milling around the lobby, plus a quartet of security guards whose job of the day was to keep the press at bay, so the conversation was suspended until they were through the double doors and out on the sidewalk. The narrow strip of concrete fronting this busy commercial block was crowded, with a tight little knot of people huddled around a TV reporter conducting an interview with some poor fool just to the left of the building's entrance and pedestrians curving around them in both directions. Without a word, they cut straight through the flow toward Tom's car. The Taurus was parked at the curb to the right, illegal as hell because the only open space had been in front of a *No Parking Anytime* sign, but something, either good timing or the police tag Tom had hung from his rearview mirror in hopes that a passing meter maid might see it and take pity, had kept them from getting a ticket. In Philly, parking was a problem. The city was laid out like a municipal designer's wet dream, in neat grids: Broad Street runs north and south, Market Street runs east and west, everything else runs parallel to those two. The only problem was, back when it was Billy Penn's city, cars hadn't been invented. Now that they were, there was no room for them. Most of the city's residents had accepted the truth of that long since, and rode the trains with grim resignation.

'Looks like this is your lucky day,' Fish observed as he opened the passenger door. Tom followed his gaze to see the familiar three-wheeled meter maid truck, its white, bullet-shaped hood gleaming in the bright sunlight, a blue-uniformed woman aboard, rolling slowly along the row of parked vehicles toward them.

Tom moved a little faster, acting under the principle that it was better to avoid a ticket altogether than to try to talk his way out of one. As he rounded the front of the car with the rush of traffic in his ears, a gust of wind spiraling down the street caught him, its cool freshness at odds with the usual city scent of exhaust fumes and melting rubber and asphalt. The sudden blast of it ruffled his hair and set his jacket flapping. Automatically, he started to button the jacket in self-defense, only to have the damned top button pop off. It sailed through the air, hit the pavement with a barely audible *click,* and rolled.

Shit.

With a quick glance over his shoulder – the meter maid was still about a dozen cars away; the TV reporter was still busy – he risked life and limb to retrieve the button from beside the left-front wheel, got into the car, inserted the key into the ignition, and dropped the button into the cup holder between the seats.

'What's that?' Fish asked as the engine turned over, following the movement with a frown.

'Damned button popped off.' Tom put the car into gear and pulled out into traffic. Typical of Center City, it was heavy but slow, which made pulling out more a matter of muscling your way in between vehicles than waiting for an opening.

'Your jacket?' As both of them ignored the indignant honk behind them, Fish looked down at the straggling threads that marked where the button had been and shook his head. 'Hallelujah. Maybe now you'll buy a new one.'

The corners of Tom's mouth curved upward as, safe now in the flow of traffic, he passed the meter maid.

'That's crazy talk. I think I can manage to sew a button back on.'

Fish groaned. Then he rolled down the window. Before Tom realized what he meant to do, he scooped the button out of the cup holder and flicked it out into the street.

'What'd you do that for?' Tom caught the arc of it out of the corner of his eye.

'To save you from yourself. Jeez, Tom, you need to go shopping. If that jacket was human, it'd have its driver's license by now.'

Tom braked for a light. A crush of tourists complete with cameras and city guides, businesspeople, students from one of Philly's four major universities, suburban shoppers in town for the afternoon, and street types hurried through the crosswalk two stopped cars ahead. He registered details about them without even being aware that he was doing so, courtesy of years on the job. 'So?'

'So it deserves to be retired. Get a new one. Hell, get a couple of new ones. Get a whole new wardrobe. Live a little.'

'Hey, Fish? Fuck you.' It was said without heat. They both knew where Fish was coming from. They'd been friends since they'd played football together at St. Aloysius High School in South Philly. Fish had joined the PPD the year after Tom had, and had been his partner for the last four years. Fish knew his history, knew it all, about the divorce and everything else, knew that since then he had done his best to allow nothing permanent in his life that wasn't already there, renting an apartment rather than buying a house, seeing a perpetually changing string of women rather than having an exclusive girlfriend, not keeping any pets, using a department-issue car that was replaced every few years. Hell, when he was home he even ate off paper plates. Tom kept a low profile, did his job to the best of his ability, and saved his money rather than spent it. Why everyone, from his family to Fish was starting to have a problem with that he couldn't begin to fathom.

Nor did he much care.

'Fine.' Fish was clearly exasperated. 'Be that way, asshole. Wear your crummy old clothes. Work all the time. Don't have any fun. See who gets all the women.'

Tom grinned. So did Fish, reluctantly. They both knew who was number one when it came to women, and who tried harder. Though Fish, having worked for it, usually did all right.

'You don't think she planted the gun, do you?' Fish asked after a moment, referring back to their earlier subject.

'Kate White?' Tom had been there in that courtroom. He had seen first-hand her terror when Rodriguez grabbed her. If she'd been faking any of that, he would turn in his badge. 'No.'

Where Soto got the gun he killed Judge Moran with was, in the detectives' judgment, the key to unraveling the conspiracy that had culminated in the homicides. They were only one of several teams working on different angles of the crime, to which they had been assigned largely because of Charlie, which made it personal, and because Tom had been there in the courtroom at the beginning and thus had a perspective the others didn't have. The thing was, though, all the known perps were dead, which was blunting the fury of the investigation to a certain degree. Rodriguez, Soto, Lonnie Pack, and Chili Newton – they were the ones who had physically committed the murders, and each of them had already paid the ultimate price. No arrest, no prosecution, no death penalties were possible, although the law-enforcement community was foaming at the mouth to exact retribution. But under the circumstances, retribution was going to require painstaking and therefore relatively slow detective work.

The bottom line was, the killers had to have had help, and that was where their investigation was presently focused. Tom was almost sure that the weapons had been planted either in courtroom 207 itself or in the holding cells or the secure corridor associated with that particular courtroom, or, as seemed most likely from the available evidence, both, because if the prisoners had gotten hold of weapons anyplace else, there would have been more areas of attempted egress. And there hadn't been. The only escape attempt had happened in courtroom 207.

All of which meant that the weapons had to have been planted by someone with access to that area. Which pointed to an inside job.

The light changed, and Tom hung a left. He was, as they both knew, headed toward the police administration building at Eighth and Race, aka the Roundhouse, because of its distinctive shape.

'Something was off about her. She was nervous,' Fish said thoughtfully.

Tom was aware. She had tried hard to hide it, but there had been too many subtle signals to ignore. But something, perhaps the memory of terrified blue eyes clinging to his like he was the only hope she had in the world when Rodriguez took her captive, or maybe the shaken urgency of her voice over the phone when she had told him that she was a single mother, or maybe even the very feminine feel of her in his arms when he had carried her to the EMT, made him feel unexpectedly protective toward her. Whatever was making her nervous, he didn't think she had planted any weapons, or helped with the escape attempt in any way. Although he was prepared to investigate the possibility, and even to be proved wrong if that was how it worked out.

'Maybe it was seeing me. Maybe I brought up bad memories from yesterday or something for her.'

'Possible,' Fish said.

'Maybe she fudged her résumé or something to get her job, and she's afraid it's all going to come out in the investigation.'

'Also possible,' Fish agreed.

Tom hung a right on Market, and the Roundhouse came into view. It was a large, multistory, oval-shaped building with a stubby rectangular tail. In Tom's opinion, which he'd shared freely over the years, it looked like a giant stone sperm. Right now there were TV trucks out front, and the entrances and parking lot were being manned by uniforms controlling access. The flags over the central dome were at half-mast, flapping sadly against the soft, blue sky, reminding him of yesterday's horror, of the men who had died.

He counted himself lucky that his brother wasn't one of them.

'Hell, maybe she's just a high-strung type and gets all tense and jumpy whenever anything goes wrong,' Tom said.

Fish made a noncommittal sound. 'You buying what she's selling about finding Charlie's gun just lying there on the hallway floor? Right smack-dab in the spot when she needed it?'

Forensics had already determined that Rodriguez had been shot with Charlie's service revolver. Determining how it had gotten into Kate White's hands had been one of the primary reasons for their visit to her office.

'I don't see any reason *not* to believe it, for now.' Tom paused to pull into the parking lot, where a uniform, recognizing him and Fish, waved him on in. 'The safety was off, she said, which means somebody was getting ready to fire it before she got her hands on it. Maybe there was a struggle, and Charlie dropped his weapon out there in that hallway. Maybe somebody took it off Charlie and dropped it.'

'And maybe she's lying through her straight little white teeth.'

Tom's lips tightened. So did his gut. Truth to tell, that was the suspicion that was worming through his thought processes, too. 'Why would she?'

'Because she has something to hide?'

Tom didn't reply.

Fish shifted in his seat, folded his arms over his

chest, and gave him a long, appraising look as Tom slowly circled the lot, searching for an open spot.

'Turns you on, does she?'

'*What?*' It took Tom a second, but then the truth of it hit him like a crowbar to the head, and he wondered why he hadn't realized it before. Because he hadn't wanted to, of course. It complicated things, and one thing he didn't go in for anymore was complications. But truth was truth, and the truth here was that the instant he'd seen her, willowy, blond, and more than pretty, wide-eyed with fear and yet fiercely brave in Rodriguez's murderous grip, he'd felt an intense reaction that went far beyond anything in the typical cop/victim-in-need-of-saving relationship. Why? Because as Fish had so tactfully pointed out, she turned him on. *Shit.* Not that he meant to admit it, ever. And not that it made any difference. 'You're nuts.'

Ah, there was a black-and-white pulling out of a spot. Tom gunned toward it and was just in time, barely beating out a dilapidated blue van that he had no trouble identifying as belonging to the narc squad. Officer Phil Wablonski, undercover and barely recognizable in a heavy beard and sunglasses, rolled down the van's tinted window to shoot Tom the bird as the Taurus cut him off. Tom returned the favor.

'Stay objective, that's all I'm saying.' Fish released his seat belt as Tom parked and cut the engine. 'Just because she looks like an angel doesn't mean she is one.'

Tom popped his seat belt, too.

'You're projecting, is what you're doing,' he said to Fish's back as his partner got out of the car. 'She turns *you* on.'

'Yeah, but the difference is, I freely admit it,' Fish replied when they were both heading toward the building. Reporters were camped out front, so they moved by unspoken agreement toward a side entrance. Neither one of them wanted to take the slightest chance of being the unfortunate cop captured on live TV in connection with the ongoing investigation. The commissioner had put a gag order on the entire PPD: no talking, no exceptions. Fish reached the unobtrusive metal door first and held it open. 'You, on the other hand, are in denial, which is dangerous. Anyway, I may be looking, too, but I guarantee you it's not me she's looking back at with those big blue bedroom eyes.'

'Fuck you, Fish,' Tom said for the second time that day, and walked by him into the Roundhouse.

The Duty Room of the PPD homicide unit was located on the first floor. It was a big, untidy rectangle that provided work space for the unit's sixty-four deputies, plus supervisors and support staff. Tom pushed through the glass doors first, with Fish behind him. There was always plenty going on in the Duty Room – Philly was third in the nation when it came to homicides, which had numerous bad points but at least provided an appreciable degree of job security for the harried detectives who worked them – no shortage of dead bodies here. Today, though, the chaos and activity level and noise were cranked up to a whole new level. Multiple murders were nothing new to Philly, but multiple murders by prisoners, of deputies and a judge in their own backyard – which the Criminal Justice Center was – well, that was new. It was also embarrassing. A black eye for the whole Philly law-enforcement community.

This case, in other words, was both extremely high-profile and personal. *Way* personal. The PPD was pulling out all the stops.

A chorus of voices greeted them as they entered and separated, each heading to his own desk. Tom waved by way of reply, and was just dropping into his own creaky desk chair when Sergeant Ike Stella, a twenty-eight-year veteran of the PPD and the shift supervisor, stopped by his desk. Stella was a big man, six-foot-three and a good three hundred pounds, most of which he carried in his gut. He was fifty-five years old, with walnut-colored skin, a strip of black hair stretching around the back of his head from ear to ear that left him bald on top, rugged features, and a gruff, no-nonsense demeanor. The thing about Stella was, he might not be universally loved, but he was universally respected. He might bawl you out to your face, but if you found trouble, he had your back.

'You got anything?' Stella asked, turning his habitual scowl on Tom.

'Nothing worth anything – yet.'

'Any inkling where they got the weapons?'

'Working on it.'

'Work faster,' Stella said, his lips thinning. 'Inquiring minds want to know.'

He moved away, and Tom got to work, spending the next hour or so at his desk, writing up the interview with Kate White, answering phone calls, going through witness statements, trying to get a handle on all the paperwork that was piling up in connection with this case. The problem wasn't that they didn't have enough information. It was that they had too much, reams of it. And they were just getting started. He had little doubt that the truth was in there somewhere, buried in the mountains of paper that would just keep piling higher until the case was resolved. The problem was, finding it was going to be akin to finding a specific grain of sand on the beach.

Quitting time, five o'clock, found Tom on the phone with the medical examiner, Dr. Mary Hardy, who confirmed that the shots that had wounded Charlie and killed Deputy Dino Russo had come from Russo's department-issue weapon, which had been found near Chili Newton's body. Newton's fingerprints were on it, along with Russo's.

Hanging up, Tom went back over his notes, pondering. It was fairly obvious that the weapon had been taken from Russo either pre- or postmortem, and thus the origin of one of the murder weapons was accounted for. The Sig that Soto had used, however, that had killed the judge and a deputy, was not department-issue, nor was it immediately traceable, as all identifying features had been filed off. The other two pistols – each had killed a deputy and a civilian – were a PSM and a non-department-issue Glock, likewise minus identifying features, almost certainly smuggled in from the street. The mystery was how, and by whom.

He meant to find out.

'You planning on pulling an all-nighter?' Fish asked. Tom looked up from the notes he was cross-checking to find his partner standing beside his desk. Fish's suit coat was on, which meant he was getting ready to leave. A glance at the digital clock on his desk told Tom that it was a couple minutes after six. He was, he realized, dead tired. The previous night he had stayed all night at the hospital with Charlie, alternating between spending fifteen minutes every couple of hours with his unconscious brother (all that the ICU would allow) and the rest of the time hanging out in the waiting room with various combinations of his mother, sisters, sister-in-law, and the flocks of other assorted relatives, friends, and fellow officers who had descended to comfort the afflicted family.

'Nah.' He put down his pencil, rolled his shoulders and neck in a mostly futile attempt to relieve some of the stiffness there, and stood up. His jacket hung on the back of his chair. He pulled it free and shrugged into it. 'I'm out of here.'

'I checked with forensics. The distance checks out,' Fish said in a grudging tone as they headed out of the building together. 'And her prints are all over the murder weapon. It's looking like your smokin' little ADA could have shot Rodriguez the way she says she did.'

By calling Kate White *his* smokin' little ADA, Fish was deliberately needling him. Tom knew it, and so ignored the effort.

'Good to know,' he said mildly.

They pushed out of the door, pausing on the sidewalk. Fish's car was in the lot behind the building, so that was the point where their paths diverged. Dusk was deepening into full night, and a few aggressive stars had already breached the deep purple-gray of the sky. The soft, white glow of halogen security lights illuminated the outside of the building and the surrounding parking lots. A slight breeze carried the smell of car exhaust.

'You wanna get dinner?' Fish asked.

Tom shook his head. 'I'm going on over to the hospital.'

'Want company?' Fish had come by the hospital last night, too, but the demands of the investigation had pulled him away. Just like the demands of the investigation had brought Tom to work today, leaving the rest of the family to hold down the fort with Charlie.

'Hell, my whole family's there. Last night there were cousins I've never seen in my life. At the hospital, I *got* company.'

'Still, I'll probably stop by later.'

Tom nodded, then lifted a hand in farewell as they both started walking toward their respective vehicles.

'Word of advice,' Fish called back over his shoulder, and Tom looked his way inquiringly. 'Before you get there, lose the jacket.'

Tom looked down at himself, at the clump of threads where the button had been, and grimaced. Okay, so maybe – thanks to Fish – the jacket was a lost cause. He would have yelled, 'Go to hell,' after Fish, but he was afraid the TV types in front of the building might hear, and the next thing he knew a story about discord in the homicide unit would be on the air.

That wouldn't be good.

Half an hour later, still wearing the jacket because he needed it to cover his shoulder holster and he wasn't about to go home to get another one just to please Fish's GQ sensibilities, Tom walked into the crowded, brightly lit waiting room outside the ICU, and found himself, as he had known he would be, engulfed in relatives.

'Tommy.' His mother stood up from the red vinyl couch where she'd been sitting with her sister Miriam and his middle sister, thirty-year-old Vicky, to embrace him. He hugged her back affectionately, breathing in the faint smell of the Shalimar perfume that she had worn for as long as he could remember. Christmases, his dad used to buy her a big bottle of the stuff, and after his death she had continued to wear it faithfully. Anna Braga was sixty now, short and pleasantly rounded, unlike her children, all of whom had taken after their father in build, with black hair (she dyed the gray) that she kept fashionably styled, and a soft, still-pretty face with very few lines. Today her hazel eyes were red-rimmed and less bright than usual from yesterday's tears, but her lipstick was a deep, defiant red and her cheeks were dusted pink. Just because she was a widow didn't mean she was dead, as she was always telling her children. She dressed well – today in a pale pink blouse and gray slacks – worked as a hostess at Rocco's in the Italian Market, and even occasionally dated. Her children, as she was also always telling them, were her life. 'Charlie's better, praise God.' She made the sign of the cross. 'Have you eaten?'

'I grabbed a burger on the way over,' he lied as his mother stepped back to look him over critically. His answer was pure self-defense. If he said no, his mother would dispatch somebody – probably his youngest sister, Natalia – to fetch him something to eat, and then watch him until it was consumed to the last crumb. Then she would tell him he needed to eat more, because he could stand to gain a few pounds.

'You've lost a button on your coat.' Her disapproving gaze focused on the telltale dangling threads. She frowned, then looked up at him, shaking her head. 'You need somebody to take care of things like that for you. A wife. A man doesn't think of such things.'

It was all Tom could do not to roll his eyes. The only thing that stopped him was the certain knowledge that his mother would bop him upside the head if he dared. She'd been on this Tom-needs-a-wife kick for almost the last year, and it was starting to drive him insane. His gaze found twenty-nine-year-old Natalia, who was slim and attractive in jeans and an orange sweater, with her thick black hair cut boyishly short and the minimum of makeup – at least, that Tom could see – on her angular face. Seven years married, a stay-at-home mother of two, she was standing near the couch engaged in conversation with a woman Tom didn't know. As their eyes met she grinned at him, having clearly overheard their mother's harassment, and waggled her fingers at him in saucy greeting.

'So what's going on with Charlie?' He figured the best way to get their mother's attention off himself was to focus it on his brother.

'They've taken him off the ventilator. Terry's with him.'

ICU rules allowed only one person in the room with a patient at a time.

'That's good.'

'Hey, Tom.' Vicky stood up and gave him a hug, too. The oldest of his sisters, thirty-two-year-old mother-of-three Tina, was not in the room, Tom saw as he hugged his middle sister back. Vicky was tall and thin, with long, black hair worn in a braid that hung down her back. She'd been married for ten years – the Bragas all tended to marry young and reproduce like rabbits – and had two girls and a boy. A kindergarten teacher and part-time artist, she wore a loose, ankle-length pale blue dress that was covered with tiny white flowers. She pulled out of his arms, looked at his face, and frowned.

'You poor thing, you've got bags. Have you gotten any sleep at all?'

'For God's sake, don't get Mom started on that,' Tom said to her in a low voice, casting an alarmed glance at their mother, who fortunately had her head turned as she said something to Aunt Miriam. 'She'll have me napping on the couch here.'

That made Vicky grin. And the reason it made Vicky grin was because she knew, just like Tom did, that it was absolutely true. Anna Braga worried about all her children, but Tom, because he was male and the oldest and had no family of his own, most of all.

'I think I'll just go look in on Charlie.' Tom spoke a little louder as he sought to escape before his mother could discover for herself that he was looking tired. 'Maybe Terry wants to take a break.'

His sister-in-law, Terry, a short, athletically built, freckle-faced, redheaded, fiercely independent accountant whom Tom was convinced Charlie had been attracted to because she was the antithesis of the women he'd grown up being (s)mothered by, looked around when Tom opened the door of the ICU ward. Seeing him, she smiled, then rose from the chair she'd been sitting in and came over to him.

'I'm glad you're here,' she said quietly, after they had exchanged hugs. 'Go to him.'

She came out, and he walked on inside the ICU, wrinkling his nose at the strong smell of antiseptics and who knew what else that reached his nostrils. The nurse on duty gave him a careful look as he moved toward where Charlie lay at the far end of the four-bed ward, but must have been satisfied that he was harmless because she disappeared behind a white curtain drawn around another patient's bed.

It was cold in the ICU, Tom thought as he stopped at the foot of his brother's bed, and eerily quiet. Except for the sounds of various life-saving machines, there was nothing: no voices, no telephones or TVs, no footsteps. It was like the patients were in limbo, caught in a white world somewhere between life and death.

His hands closed over the foot of Charlie's bed. A curtain separated his brother from whoever was in the bed next door, but it didn't extend all the way to the foot of the bed. Tom registered the machines blinking and beeping around the bed, the IV pole and myriad tubes attached to his brother's body, the white swath of bandages wrapped around his chest, and felt his gut tighten.

It could so easily have gone the other way.

Then he looked at his brother's face – something he'd been putting off, because seeing Charlie so unnaturally pale and still bothered him more than he liked to admit, even to himself – to find that Charlie was looking back at him.

13

'I must've got your genes,' Ben said glumly as he watched Kate's shot smack into the brick above the garage a yard to the left of the goal, then go bouncing away. The bugs swooping around the rusty light fixture that illuminated a fuzzy circle at the top of the driveway scattered, then came looping back in. Their low drone never faltered.

'You say that like it's a bad thing,' Kate panted, running into the dark front yard for what felt like the thousandth time to retrieve the ball. Trying to maintain her outward good humor at a little after eight-thirty P.M. on the day after she'd seen roughly half a dozen people murdered before her eyes and her life had gone to hell, when she was so scared she was sick with it and so frazzled she jumped at every unfamiliar sound, wasn't easy under the circumstances. Which were, to wit, she was out in her driveway after supper and homework were over, trying to help her unenthusiastic son practice for the basketball tournament that was scheduled for the following week in gym.

That was the thing about having a kid, Kate thought as she jogged across the yard in pursuit of the thrice-damned basketball: No matter what disasters were happening in your own life, your kid's regimen of school and homework and extracurriculars kept on keeping on, and your kid's problems did, too.

The yellowish glow Ben stood in only made the night beyond it seem darker. Overhead, a pale fingernail moon and a few shy stars played peek-a-boo with scooting clouds. Trees swayed and leaves rustled, stirred by the breeze that carried an autumn-ish hint of smoke on it. Black chiffon shadows undulated across patchy charcoal grass. The lingering moisture from the previous day's rain made the ground slightly squishy underfoot, and the leaves that had already fallen were treacherously slippery. As she spotted the ball in the line of scraggly bushes that marked the delineation between the yards and bent to scoop it up, the scent of damp earth filled her nostrils. Straightening, she stretched her back, in no huge hurry to return to the fray. She was wearing jeans, a ratty gray Phillies sweatshirt that she'd pushed up to her elbows, and sneakers, and her hair was caught up in a haphazard ponytail. Despite the fact that the temperature had dropped into the low sixties, she was hot, sweaty, and so tired she was drooping.

And as of now she officially really, really hated basketball.

'Was my dad any good at sports?' Ben asked wistfully, as Kate, carrying the ball, walked back into the light. They'd been out there for maybe fifteen minutes, shooting hoops and missing a good ninety percent of the shots between them, and she was getting a stitch in her side from chasing the ball. But Ben was so afraid that he was going to be the worst player in the class, that he was going to make a fool of himself and the other kids were going to laugh, that she was prepared to do whatever it took to try to make sure it didn't happen. Not that he had expressed his fears in so many words. He wouldn't. But she knew. When he had told her about the upcoming basketball week in gym as she had driven him home from Suzy's, she'd been able to read between the lines without any trouble. He'd been thinking of missing school for a week. She'd been thinking, *Not possible*. And so here they were.

And now he was breaking her heart anew with questions about his father.

'Yes, he was,' she lied. As far as she knew, Ben's father, Chaz White, whom she had married at eighteen and who had deserted her at nineteen, two months after Ben's birth, had never played any kind of organized sport in his life. She'd met him in Atlantic City, where she'd fled after David Brady's death. He'd been a handsome street tough who'd worked as a bouncer in the casino where she'd been a cocktail waitress (complete with her own fake ID to match the underage customers). In the year that she'd known him, she'd learned that along with the abundant charm that had attracted her in the first place, he had a violent temper and a nose for trouble. Less than a month after their split, he had died in a drive-by shooting. And she had read the handwriting on the wall, grabbed

Ben, and run again, this time to Philly, where she had been working her ass off ever since to give her precious son a better life. Not that she meant to tell Ben any of that, at least not for many, many years. And some of it she would never tell him.

'He was good at lots of things, including sports. Hey, you know what? I think he was even pretty good at basketball. But I remember he told me that he wasn't very athletic until he got to high school. He had to grow into it.'

She bounced the ball to Ben as a way of distracting him from asking more questions about his father.

'Are you telling the truth?' Holding the ball in both hands, he looked at her hard, his voice laced with suspicion.

Kate planted her fists on her hips. 'Would I lie to you?'

'Yeah,' Ben answered without hesitation.

Okay, he knew her too well. She occasionally did lie to him when she thought it was necessary. And over the years she had fudged the facts to create a kinder, gentler father who had loved Ben devotedly but had died in a car accident shortly after his birth. At some point, she might tell him more, but she was never, ever going to tell him that Chaz had freaked when their screaming, colicky baby had come home from the hospital and then left them flat.

That Ben never needed to know.

'Well, I'm not,' she said, resisting the urge to bend over and place her hands on her knees while she caught her breath. She couldn't believe how winded she was. It must have something to do with either emotional distress or plain old exhaustion. 'Just shoot the thing, would you please?'

'This is lame.' Ben groaned but obediently turned around and heaved the ball at the goal. This time it actually hit the rim before bouncing off.

'Good job. That was close,' Kate encouraged as she looked after the damned ball, which was rolling across the lawn toward the big oak by the sidewalk. 'Your shot, your rebound.'

'Can't we just go in?'

Ben trudged off after the ball, which had disappeared in the inky shadows at the base of the tree. She followed his small figure with her eyes. His hands were jammed into the front pockets of his jeans. His shoulders slumped, and his movements were dispirited. Like her, he was wearing a sweatshirt, although his was a forest-green hoodie and not ratty. A few porch lights were on up and down the street, and here and there uncurtained windows glowed yellow. But still, the night was so dark that the sidewalk was only visible as a pale ribbon snaking over the ground between the street and the tree. She was able to track Ben mostly because of his blond hair.

A car drove slowly past, its headlights catching Ben for an instant and throwing his shadow against the big oak's rough gray bark. He had almost reached the basketball, which was nestled in the roots. Kate watched the car's red taillights receding down the street, relieved that it kept going. There had been a knot of reporters waiting in front of her house when she'd pulled in from picking up Ben, and once more she'd had reason to be grateful for the attached garage and automatic opener. Driving right inside and closing the door, she'd managed to avoid them. She had stayed inside with the curtains drawn, refusing to come out or answer the phone, and as dark had fallen, they had finally given up and gone away. She was still wary, however. But the car kept going, and as she exhaled she shifted her gaze back to Ben, who was moving so slowly and reluctantly that he could have been a mobility-impaired turtle.

She was seriously considering the pros and cons of just sending a note to school on Monday saying that Ben had twisted his ankle and couldn't play basketball next week when she saw a figure slide around the oak and approach Ben, who was finally bending over to pick up the ball.

Her eyes widened. Her breath caught.

Although she was too far away to hear it, the person must have said something to Ben, because, holding the ball in both hands now, he straightened way too quickly to look at whoever it was.

The hair stood up on the back of Kate's neck. All she could tell through the darkness was that whoever was standing there in the dark talking so quietly to her little boy was an adult. A large adult.

It was probably a neighbor. Or a reporter. But she didn't like the feel of it. Something just felt wrong.

'Ben!' She shot like a homing missile across the few yards separating them. The dark swallowed her up just as it had Ben, and for a few seconds, until her eyes adjusted, it was difficult to see much more than shapes.

'Mom.'

Holding the basketball against his chest, Ben was backing toward her even as she reached him. Of course, she'd spent his entire life warning him about strangers, and here was one – a big, menacing one – in the flesh. Her hands closed protectively over his thin shoulders. She could feel the tension in the rigidity of his shoulders and the rapid rise and fall of his chest. As he pressed back against her, his small body warm and faintly sweaty from basketball, his tousled head not yet reaching her shoulders, she looked over his head at the man – it was definitely a man, she saw, now that she was closer – standing only a few feet away. He was watching them both with a kind of still purpose that brought her heart into her throat.

She didn't recognize him, but, of course, it was dark. But her sixth sense screamed danger.

'Kate . . . White,' he said before she could speak, pronouncing her name like a judgment. It wasn't a question. His voice was low and deep with a rough West Philly accent, and she absolutely, positively didn't recognize it. Her eyes were growing more accustomed to the dark now. A knit watch cap was pulled down low over his eyes, and some kind of dark jacket or shirt was zipped up to his throat. It was impossible to tell his ethnicity with any certainty, but his skin was pale enough so that she could see the square-jawed shape of his face in the moonlight. He was about six feet tall, with a stocky, muscular build. But the night obscured the details of his features. All she could see of them with any clarity was the gleam of his eyes. She couldn't see his hands, she thought with some confusion as he folded his arms over his chest, then an instant later realized it was because he was wearing dark gloves.

It wasn't that cold.

'Go in the house,' she said fiercely to Ben, and thrust him behind her.

'Mom . . .' There was fear in his voice. She glanced at him over her shoulder. He hesitated, looking back at her.

'Do what I tell you!'

She never spoke to him in that tone, and he clearly recognized that she meant business. Still clutching the basketball, he headed at a trot toward the closed garage door and the opener that waited in the grass by the pavement. The front door was locked. They had come out through the garage, and it was the only way back in. She thought about going with him, tried to gauge the possibility of both her and Ben making it safely inside the house if they ran for it, and concluded that if this guy wanted to grab them, it wouldn't be likely. No matter how fast they were, he was almost certain to be faster. And the garage door took a long time to rise, and then an equally long time to close again. Likewise, a scream might not be heard or responded to.

She planted herself foursquare and solid in front of the man.

'Who are you?' she asked sharply. Her heart was beating way too fast. Her hands had closed into fists of their own volition.

'I got a message for you,' he said, without answering her question. He didn't move, didn't come any closer, did nothing overt, but Kate felt the threat emanating from him like a wall of heat. 'Mario says you owe him.'

'*What?*'

Horrified as the message registered, Kate sucked in air. The groan of the garage door lifting up rumbled in the background, and she was conscious of Ben joggling anxiously from foot to foot as he waited and watched her through the dark. As she stood rooted to the spot, more headlights cut through the pitch blackness at the top of the street, coming toward them steadily. Just when the beams would have illuminated the stranger's face, he stepped back out of their path. She strained to see him.

The voice turned ugly. 'He says you better not screw him over.'

Kate felt a wave of dizziness. It had not occurred to her that Mario would have confederates, or that he constituted a physical threat. Terror blossomed in her anew, and her heart pounded. Her throat went dry. The headlights caught Kate in their glare, and she turned instinctively to glance at the oncoming car. To her surprise, instead of sweeping past, the headlights arced across her yard, and she realized that this car was pulling into her driveway. The *swish* of tires on pavement reached her ears even as she looked toward the stranger again. But she could no longer see him. As far as she could tell he was gone, faded away into the shadows.

Oh my God.

Her eyes cut to the car now parking in her driveway. Its headlights illuminated Ben, who had turned to look at the car as it pulled in, and the slowly rising garage door behind him. Ben was wide-eyed and pale in the bright beams, obviously scared, a small blond boy in jeans and a dark green hoodie who was clutching the garage door opener like it could somehow save him from whatever threatened.

'I'm coming, sweetie,' she called, and his eyes, huge with uncertainty, turned in her direction.

Sick at the fear in Ben's face, she jogged across the yard toward him. Whoever this was, friend, neighbor, reporter, anyone, she could only be thankful that they'd come when they had. Though no violence had been threatened to her or Ben, the taste of fear was tinny in her mouth, and her pulse raced out of control.

We could have been hurt. Or worse.

The car stopped just outside the circle of light. Swathed in shadows, it was impossible to identify.

When the headlights went dead, it occurred to her that this, too, might be someone connected with Mario. Her eyes widened. Her pulse leaped. Her jog turned into a mad dash toward her son.

'Mom!' Ben's eyes searched for her in the dark. Behind him, the garage was opening into a black, cavelike maw as the door passed the midway mark. He could duck inside – but the door wouldn't close in time to keep whoever this was out. He would have to keep on running, into the house with its flimsy lock on the door that led in from the garage, then, with luck, if he remembered, to the phone to dial 911 . . .

'I'm right here.' She just reached the circle of light when the driver's door opened. Looking fearfully in the direction of the sound, she reached Ben just as a man got out and straightened to his full height. He was tall . . .

Heart in throat, she grabbed Ben by the arm and prepared to dart with him through the garage and into the house. Then the man turned his head, and a shaft of moonlight struck hair as shiny black as a crow's wing.

In an instant, his height and build and that black hair all came together for her: Detective Braga.

As she recognized him, he said, 'Ms. White?'

'Who is he, Mom?' Ben's voice was urgent. He clutched the door opener, clearly frightened and ready to run into the garage.

'It's all right,' Kate told him as relief washed over her, leaving her feeling weak all over in its wake. Earlier today, the sight of the detective had nearly given her a nervous breakdown. Now she was ready to fall at his feet. 'I know him. He's a police officer. He's safe.'

'Is something wrong?' The sound of the car door

slamming was followed by a tiny beep as Braga locked it. Then he came toward them, frowning as he walked out of the darkness into the circle of fuzzy yellow light where they still stood. Kate realized that Ben was pressed against her side and she was clutching his forearm and, if her expression was anything like his, they both looked like they had just escaped a near-death encounter.

Trying to pretend that nothing had happened would be stupid. It was obvious from his expression that Braga could tell something bad had just gone down. Unable to help herself, Kate compulsively glanced toward the oak, visually searching the shadows around the tree and beyond. Was Mario's emissary still there? Was he watching?

The thought made her dizzy.

'Kate?' Braga's frown deepened as he reached them. His head turned, his gaze following hers to probe the encroaching darkness.

Get a grip. Downplay this.

'It's nothing. Just . . . oh, come inside, would you, please?'

He was looking at her now, the frown still in place. Her voice sounded croaky, because she was still shaken to the core. Her heart pounded, her pulse raced, and adrenaline rushed through her veins. Their eyes met, and Braga's frown deepened. But he didn't argue.

'Thanks.'

Kate didn't wait for more. Instead, she turned away and headed inside.

'Are you sure he's okay, Mom?' Ben whispered urgently as she pulled him with her through the dark garage.

'I'm sure,' Kate whispered back.

Braga was right behind them, and she thought he probably heard what they said, but she didn't care. Reassuring Ben had to be her first priority. The thought that her son didn't feel safe was almost unbearable.

Not that she felt safe, either, even with a presumably armed homicide detective who she knew would protect them with his life just a step behind them. She felt hideously, unexpectedly vulnerable. Even her own familiar belongings seemed ominous at the moment. The garbage cans and bicycles and even her good old reliable Camry took on a shadowy life of their own when viewed through a prism of newly awakened fear. Anyone could hide in those shadows. Anyone could appear when she least expected it, just like that thug had popped out from behind the oak in her front yard.

Kate realized that gradually, over the past eight and a half years, ever since she'd run from Atlantic City with Ben, she had forgotten what it was like to be afraid.

Now she remembered.

'Close the garage door, please,' she said to Ben in as calm a tone as she could muster as they reached the door that led into the house. He obediently pushed the button on the remote, and the grinding sound of the garage door going down followed them into the kitchen.

Warmth and bright light and the lingering smell of the hamburger patties with beef gravy and canned green beans they'd had for dinner greeted them. The supper dishes piled in the sink and the notebook paper and calculator and pencils strewn haphazardly on the table – detritus from Ben's homework – greeted them, too. As did the half-empty brown grocery bag on the counter – she'd put away the perishables, but peanut butter and bananas and bread were still inside. A big yellow box of Cheerios perennially lived on the counter beside the refrigerator, because they both ate a bowl for breakfast every morning and she never quite got around to putting it back in the cabinet. Her purse and cell phone and Ben's backpack were on the counter, too, crowded together near the door. The kitchen was messy, no doubt about it, and it bothered her because she was suddenly seeing it as she imagined Braga, who had stepped past her and was now glancing around, would.

Which was stupid. Keeping an immaculate house was not and had never been one of her priorities. At least the place was clean (well, reasonably), if not entirely tidy.

'Who was that man, Mom?' Ben asked as she closed and locked the kitchen door, then turned back into the kitchen. She folded her arms over her chest, rubbing her upper arms with her hands to ward off the sudden chill that beset her despite the supposed warmth-giving properties of the oversized sweatshirt. Braga was watching her. Hoping to hide as much of her agitation as she could from his too-keen gaze, she dropped her arms to her sides as she forced a smile for Ben. Her little boy's eyes were big on her face; his small mouth was tight with anxiety. His expression killed her, but with Braga watching, she tried not to let it show.

'I don't know.' Shaking her head, she took the garage door opener from him and put it in their catchall place on the counter by the door along with all the other things they would need before they dashed out in the morning.

'So, you want to tell me what's going on?'

Braga's eyes were on her face. They were almost black in the unforgiving light, and narrowed with speculation. He looked even more tired than he had earlier, she thought, and on edge. His lean jaw was dark with stubble, and the set of his mouth verged on grim. The lines bracketing his nose and mouth had deepened, and there were fine lines around his eyes and shadows beneath them that she hadn't noticed before. The top button of his white shirt was undone, and the knot of his dark red tie had been loosened. He wore the same worn tan blazer – minus its top button now – and navy slacks as before.

'There was a man outside,' Ben said, before Kate could reply. Of course Ben was going to tell what he knew; she wouldn't expect, or want, him to do anything else. Unlike her, her son had no reason to lie. 'He was scary.'

'Just now?' Braga stiffened and glanced past Kate toward the door, as if he was prepared to head back outside. 'When I pulled up?'

'He left,' Kate said. 'It really wasn't anything.'

'What did he do?'

'He came out from behind the tree and said, "Are you Ben?"' Ben told him. 'And then my mom came.'

The idea that the stranger had known she had a son named Ben took Kate's breath away. She felt dizzy all over again. But she couldn't let it show, not now, not with Braga there. He was too perceptive, and she had too much to hide.

'He just said my name,' Kate said. 'Like this: "*Kate – White*."'

She imitated the ominous tone. Then, for Braga's benefit, she shivered ostentatiously. As if that alone had been enough to terrify her silly.

Braga frowned. 'That's all?'

'Mom told me to run into the house. That's what I was doing when you came.'

Braga's gaze shifted back to Kate. She nodded agreement.

'Who was it? Did you know him?'

Kate shook her head. 'No.'

'Can you give me a description?'

Kate complied.

'I thought he was going to kill us.' Unzipping his hoodie as he spoke, Ben looked earnestly up at Braga. 'So did my mom.' He glanced at her for confirmation, and when she didn't say anything, he added, 'You know you did. I could tell.'

Braga's gaze fixed once again on her face.

'It was . . . a little unnerving,' she admitted. That

had to be one of the great understatements of her life. 'I think it scared us so much because it was dark and . . . he just appeared out of the blue.' She followed up with a small smile and a shrug, diminishing the importance of the event. 'It was kind of bizarre.'

Braga evidently did not read body language very well, because he was moving purposefully toward her – and the door – even before she finished. His jacket parted to give her a glimpse of a businesslike black shoulder holster and gun lying flat against the left side of his chest.

'Where are you going?' She still stood in his path. But unless she meant to physically block his exit, there wasn't anything she could do to keep him in the kitchen. Bowing to the inevitable as he kept coming, she stepped aside to let him pass.

'Outside to look around.' Reaching for the knob, he glanced back at her as he spoke. 'In case this joker's still close by. You can fill me in on any details I missed when I come back in.'

'He's long gone.' Kate was certain of that. Besides, if he wasn't, she certainly didn't want Braga to find him. She didn't want this veteran detective grilling any acquaintance of Mario's about anything. The thought was almost as scary as the stranger's sudden appearance had been.

Almost.

'I'll just check.' He picked up the garage door opener and left the kitchen, closing the door behind him.

Pressing her lips together, trying to slow the still-frantic racing of her pulse, Kate was left staring at the white-painted panels of the closed kitchen door. While she listened to the muffled growl of the garage door rising, she said a little prayer that the thug was indeed long gone.

'Are you okay, mom?' Ben asked from behind her.

Kate jumped, caught herself, then turned to smile at him. The last thing she wanted was to frighten her child any more.

'Of course I'm okay. I'm fine.'

'You don't look fine.' He regarded her critically. 'You look really upset.'

'I am upset,' she admitted, because there wasn't any point in denying something he already knew. 'But I'm getting over it. Just having somebody pop up like that would upset anybody. But he didn't really *do* anything.'

'It was like something out of a horror movie,' Ben said. 'I thought he was going to start slashing us up or something. Like in *Halloween*.'

Kate was starting to feel a little more normal, normal enough at least to put up a front of normalcy for Ben. She narrowed her eyes at him. He wasn't allowed to watch R-rated movies, and he knew it.

'Which you saw when?'

He looked guilty. 'Uh . . . Samantha was watching it one time.'

'Uh-huh.' But Ben seeing a forbidden movie was near the bottom of her list of worries at the moment. She shook her head reprovingly at him, then moved toward him and wrapped her arms around his thin body, hugging him tight. What would her life be like without Ben in it? She didn't want to find out. 'You were so brave out there. You did exactly what I told you to do, too. Good job.'

Instead of protesting or trying to wriggle away, which ordinarily he would do, Ben hugged her back, quick and hard. Kate knew from that that he was still shaken by the encounter.

They heard the rattle of the garage door closing a split second before the kitchen door opened. Ben was already pulling out of her arms as Braga walked in.

'Nobody,' he said in response to Kate's questioning look. 'I have a black-and-white looking around the neighborhood, though, just in case.' He glanced at Ben, who stood by Kate's side regarding him with some caution, then smiled and held out his hand. 'I'm Tom Braga, by the way.'

'Ben White.' Ben shook hands, looking and sounding so grown up suddenly that Kate felt a tightness in her throat. There was such a man-to-man air about the exchange, and again she felt she was being given a glimpse of the man her son would someday become.

If she could just keep the monsters at bay long enough.

That thought was enough to make her tense all over again.

'What are you doing here, anyway?' Moving toward the table, she started to gather the remains of their homework session as she frowned at Braga over her shoulder. As an aside, she added, 'Ben, would you put these away?'

She passed the two pencils they had used to Ben, who took them without comment and put them in the cup by the microwave where they kept writing implements of various descriptions. It was a measure of how rattled she had been that it was just now occurring to her that Braga's opportune arrival couldn't simply be chalked up to good fortune.

'I wanted to talk to you.' His tone was easy. But there was something, some expression, in his eyes as he watched her move around the table that made her apprehensive in a whole new way.

She tried to keep her tone and her expression casual. 'About what?'

'Nothing that important. Just a few details about what you told my partner and me earlier.'

Kate's heart lurched. She wondered if he was acting like it was no big deal for Ben's benefit, and decided he was.

'If it wasn't important, I'm surprised it couldn't wait until tomorrow.'

He shrugged, and she turned away, crouching down to put the notebook paper and calculator away in the cabinet where she kept school supplies, glad for a chance to hide her face until she could school her expression. The whole time, she could feel his gaze on her back.

'So, are you a friend of my mom's or what?' Ben's question came out of nowhere, bristling with sudden protectiveness.

Kate took a quick – and she hoped unseen – breath, stood up, and turned around. There had been just the two of them for so long that they naturally took care of each other, but she didn't want Ben thinking he had to fight her battles for her. Her son had paused in the act of stripping off his hoodie to look at Braga with clear challenge, she saw. Obviously, he had sensed something in the atmosphere that worried him.

Braga answered before she could say anything.

'I'm a friend,' he said. With a quick glance at Kate, who nodded confirmation, Ben relaxed. Braga's gaze shifted to Kate. His lips stretched into a smile that didn't reach his eyes. 'You wouldn't happen to have any coffee available, by any chance, would you?'

Actually, she did. The last two days had been long and exhausting, and she couldn't have gotten through them without massive infusions of caffeine.

Her eyes narrowed at him. She appreciated the fact that he had scared away Mario's henchman, and reassured Ben just now, but she completely recognized his present show of relaxed affability for what it was – a show. Clearly, he had a question about something she had told him, and just trying to imagine what it might be made her stomach knot. Not that she meant to let him know it.

'Detective, would you like a cup of coffee?' A healthy dose of irony underlaid the question.

'Thank you. That would be great.' He responded with aplomb. 'And please call me Tom.' There was the tiniest of pauses. 'Kate.'

So we're Tom and Kate now, are we? Just so you know, that doesn't fool me into thinking we're friends.

'Milk or sugar, Tom?' There might well have been bite in her tone if Ben hadn't been standing there listening.

'Black,' Braga answered, then turned to Ben. 'Maybe you and I could go sit down somewhere, and you could tell me exactly what happened outside again. Just to make sure I've got it straight.'

'Okay.' Ben finished taking off his hoodie and dropped it on the table. 'You want to come in the living room?' Suddenly uncertain, he glanced at Kate, probably picking up on something she was subconsciously projecting in her face or stance. 'It's all right, isn't it?'

Kate just barely managed not to purse her lips. She suspected that Braga thought that without her presence he could get more information out of Ben. Which was probably true, except for the fact that, minus a few unimportant details, Ben had already told Braga everything he knew.

Thank God he didn't hear the last part of that man's message.

'Sure.' She glanced at the big, round clock that hung on the wall above the refrigerator. It was eight-fifty. 'You'd better talk fast, though. You've got till nine o'clock. Tomorrow's a school day.'

Ben groaned.

'I hate school,' he said glumly, and headed toward the living room with Braga following.

As Kate turned to get the coffee out of the cabinet – there were only dregs left in the four-cup pot she had made when she got home from work, she discovered when she checked – she was suddenly conscious of her heart knocking against her ribs.

14

In the living room, which was just off the kitchen, close enough so Tom could hear Kate clattering around as she made coffee, Ben clambered into a gold plush chair – a rocker/recliner, Tom saw as it moved beneath the kid's weight. Ben settled in with a serious expression on his face and both arms on the armrests. His feet didn't touch the floor. Tom sank down near him on the couch, which was big and comfortable, and glanced around the room, which was small and comfortable and decorated in earth tones. A pair of brass lamps on either end of the couch were already switched on, giving the room a cozy glow. There was a good-size TV on a stand by the fireplace at the far end of the room, and a multipaned glass-and-wood door that appeared to lead into another room. Both the TV and the other room were dark. To his left were the front door and stairs leading up to the second floor.

The smell of coffee wafted beneath his nostrils, drawing his attention back toward the open doorway to the kitchen.

Probably not going home and crashing before

tackling Kate White had been a mistake, but what Charlie had told him had disturbed him to the point where he knew he wasn't going to be able to sleep until he had at least made a stab at clearing it up. According to Charlie, who admittedly had been lapsing in and out of consciousness as he lay on the floor of the holding cell after being shot, when everybody else was gone and just before he'd been rescued, there had been two men and a woman alive and on their feet in the secure corridor. *Two* men, not one, both wearing prisoners' orange jumpsuits. The woman, whom he'd only glimpsed from mid-calf down through an opening door, had great calves and ankles and had been wearing sexy black high heels.

Bingo. Tom remembered those calves and ankles, and the shoes, too: Kate White.

But there shouldn't have been two men.

'So, what do you want to know?' Ben's question penetrated his reverie.

Tom looked at the kid. Like his mother, he was thin and fine-boned, with a shock of white-blond hair and big, vividly blue eyes. He guessed him to be about seven or, at most, eight years old. Just about the age of two of his nephews and one of his nieces.

'Okay, let's start at the beginning: What were you doing outside in the first place?'

Ben grimaced. 'Practicing basketball.'

'You don't like basketball?' That much was clear from the kid's tone.

Ben shook his head.

'So why were you outside practicing it? After dark?' He remembered what Kate had said. 'On a school night?'

'Because I suck. And we're having this dorky basketball tournament in gym next week.'

Tom nodded. 'So you were outside practicing basketball. Then what?'

'The ball rolled away and I went to get it and that man just came out from behind the tree and asked me if I was Ben.'

'What did you say?'

'I didn't say anything. I was too scared.'

'Where was your mom?'

'Over by the goal. I think she saw the man talking to me, because she came running.'

'When did she come outside?'

'She was out there the whole time. She was helping me practice.' He made a face, and his voice lowered and his expression turned confidential as his eyes sought Tom's. 'Don't tell her I said this, but she really isn't much help. She sucks at basketball, too.'

'Your dad's not around?'

Ben shook his head. 'He died in a car crash when I was a baby. There's just me and my mom now.'

'I'm sorry to hear that.' Tom felt bad for bringing it up. If he weren't so tired, maybe he would have picked up on the fact that there was no evidence of Ben's father being present earlier. On Kate's desk, for example, there had been one photo: her son. No family shot, no husband. 'Just for the record, my dad died when I was a kid, too. I wasn't a baby, though. I was nine.'

'That's how old I am.'

'Oh, yeah?' His estimate had been off by a year or so. The kid was small for his age.

Ben nodded.

'Do you guys usually go out and practice basketball – or just go outside – about that same time? When it's dark?'

Ben shook his head. 'This is the first time. 'Cause Mom thinks if I practice, I'll get better.' He pulled his knees up to his chin and wrapped his arms around them. 'I won't. I don't know why people even like stupid old basketball anyway.'

'Sometimes it can be fun. Once you get the hang of it.' Tom looked at Ben's huddled form, and felt a twinge of sympathy. He remembered what it was like growing up without a dad: in a word, hard. 'Your mom's right: Practice helps. You throw the ball at the basket enough times, you start to make a few, and one day something clicks.'

'Did you ever play basketball?'

'I was pretty good in high school. I made the team, but I had to quit after freshman year.'

'Why?'

Tom shrugged. 'I had to get a job after school to help out my family. There were five of us kids, so it took a lot to keep us going.' He turned the subject back to the topic at hand. 'Look, Ben, have you noticed anybody hanging around your house or yard lately?'

Ben shook his head.

'Your mom have any old boyfriends who might be mad at her?'

Ben shook his head again. 'She doesn't have boyfriends. She's pretty busy all the time.'

Tom let that pass without comment, although he figured that it was nearly impossible that a looker like Kate White didn't have a boyfriend or two in the wings. Apparently, she kept her love life separate from her kid.

'Did you see which way the guy went when he left?'

Once more with the head shake. 'I was over by the garage by then. Mom told me to go inside, and pushed me away.'

Tom frowned. 'She stayed?'

Ben nodded.

'Did you hear what the guy said to her?'

'No. I was trying to get in the house to call the police. Then you came.' Then, before Tom could ask anything else, he added in a small voice, 'Is somebody trying to hurt my mom?'

'What?' Tom's attention was caught. He processed that, then leaned a little toward Ben, his forearm pressing into the thick rolled arm of the couch, his gaze suddenly intent. 'Why do you ask that?'

Ben's brow wrinkled as if he was thinking hard. 'There was that thing yesterday at where she works. Somebody at school said she was almost killed. Then that man came to our house tonight. And you're a cop, and you're here, too. And . . . and . . .' his voice trailed off, then picked up again. His eyes held Tom's. 'I think she's scared.'

Smart kid. Tom almost said it aloud, because there it was: That was the vibe he was picking up from Kate. She was afraid. Not just tonight but earlier today as well, when he and Fish had visited her in her office. But then he heard rattling sounds approaching, accompanied by soft footsteps. The lady of the house must be heading their way with the coffee. Time to redirect the conversation until he could think this whole thing through.

'So you were chasing your ball and the man just appeared from behind the tree,' Tom said to Ben. 'Did you say anything to him?'

Ben shook his head. His gaze shifted to his mom, who walked into Tom's line of vision with two thick white mugs, a couple of napkins, and a saucer in her hands.

'Nine o'clock,' she said crisply to Ben as she handed Tom one of the mugs and set the saucer and napkins down on the coffee table. The saucer, he saw at a glance, held a few chocolate-chip cookies. The packaged kind. Chips Ahoy, unless he was mistaken.

It was only as he looked at them that he realized he was hungry. He'd forgotten all about dinner.

'Thanks,' he said, meaning it, and reached for a cookie.

'You're welcome.' Her gaze shifted to Ben. 'Bath and bed.'

Ben groaned, but apparently this was a

nonnegotiable issue, because he slid to his feet without argument. Tom was impressed. His nephews and nieces did argue about bedtime. Loudly and vehemently, every time Tom was around them and they were sent to bed.

'Say good night to Detective Braga,' Kate directed as Ben trudged past them on his way to the stairs.

Ben flicked a sideways look at him. There was meaning in it, and after a second Tom could tell that Ben was silently charging him not to repeat what he had been told.

'Good night.'

''Night, Ben,' Tom replied.

'Call me when you're ready,' Kate said to her son. Ben nodded. Then Tom lost track of him as Kate, steaming mug in hand, sat down in the gold chair the kid had just vacated, and of its own volition, his attention focused completely on her.

With her hair pulled back in a ponytail that allowed just a few wavy blond tendrils to frame her face, she looked more like a teenager than a prosecutor. The small Band-Aid under her cheekbone reminded him of how close she had come to being killed yesterday, and he sent an automatic little prayer of thanks winging skyward that she had survived. Her bone structure might or might not be classically beautiful – hell, what did he know about classic bone structure, anyway? – but it appealed to him. Her rounded forehead, high cheekbones, and square jawline made him wonder if maybe she had Vikings in her family tree somewhere. Her mouth – wide and soft-looking and deeply pink

– was both feminine and determined. Her nose was long and elegant, her chin obstinate. Her collarbone was just visible above the loose neckline of the too-big gray sweatshirt she wore with faded jeans and sneakers, and the sweatshirt itself swallowed her up so that her curves – and slight as she was, she did have curves, as he was more than well aware – weren't readily apparent. Okay, she was on the skinny side, no doubt about it, but it was a lithe, fine-boned kind of skinny that he was actually starting to find sexier than the voluptuousness he usually preferred.

Her eyes – Tom tried not to remember Fish describing them as big, blue bedroom eyes – were unmistakably wary as they focused on him.

She's hiding something.

He was almost certain.

'Thank you for coming to my rescue again.' Kate took another sip of coffee, watching him over the rim of her mug.

Tom helped himself to another cookie to give himself time to consider how best to play this.

'Not a problem.' He smiled at her. 'That's what us police officers do.'

'Was Ben able to add anything to what he already told you?'

Was she fishing? Oh, yeah.

'Not really.' He polished off the cookie and gulped some coffee to wash it down. 'By the way, you got a great kid there.'

He smiled at her again.

'Thank you.' This time she smiled back, a crocodile smile if he had ever seen one that didn't touch the wariness in her eyes. It was becoming almost crystal clear: Something was up with her. The question was, what? He thought of Ben, and found himself suddenly hoping that it wasn't what he was beginning to fear: that she was, in some way, part of yesterday's murderous plot.

'Must have been hard for you, raising him on your own.'

'We've managed.' She must have heard the sudden frostiness in her own voice, because barely a beat later she added in a softer tone, 'But, yes, it was hard.'

'You have family around to help you out?'

'No.' This time she didn't even attempt to mitigate the coldness. Instead, she took another sip of coffee, then set the cup down on the lamp table between them before looking directly at him. 'So, Detective, what can I do for you?'

'Tom,' he corrected.

'Tom.' If there was impatience in her tone, only someone as attuned to the nuances of her voice as he was beginning to be would have noticed it.

'You can tell me what you're afraid of, to begin with.' It was a shot in the dark, but it definitely hit home. Her eyes widened, flickered. Her lips parted, and she sucked in air. He knew then, without a doubt, that he was on the right track. But as quickly as her expression changed, it changed back, closing down, hiding the truth from him. Her eyes went big and blue and innocent. Her brows went up in questioning surprise.

'What in the world are you talking about?'

She was good, he had to give her that. But it was too late: He had already seen everything he needed to see.

'What really happened yesterday, Kate?' His eyes never left her face. His voice was almost tender.

There it was again – that telltale flicker of her eyes. A quick downward sweep of her lashes that she was probably not even aware of. Then the lids snapped up and she met his gaze head-on.

'You know exactly what happened – I told you. I gave a sworn statement and I answered your questions. All of them.' She sat taller in the chair. Her nails – oval, well cared for, shiny with clear polish – dug into the ends of the armrests. Her nostrils flared. Her eyes blazed at him like twin blue headlights. 'What exactly are you accusing me of?'

Her attempt to take the war into the enemy camp was pitch-perfect. Her voice was steady. Her spine was straight. Her chin was up. Her eyes shot indignant sparks into his.

Too bad it all happened just a split second too late.

'I'm not accusing you of anything. But I think there's something you're not telling me.'

For a moment she simply held his gaze. Then she gave a short, derisive laugh.

'Like what? My shoe size? What I had for lunch?

My mother's maiden name? Tell me what you're asking for, and I'll tell you if I know anything about it.'

'Who was the other man in the corridor with you and Rodriguez?'

She didn't move, didn't flinch. There was no flicker, nothing.

'We've been over this. Your brother and another deputy and a prisoner were lying on the floor of one of the holding cells. Other than that, there was no one.'

'I believe there was.'

Her brows twitched together. 'Ben believes in Santa Claus, but that doesn't mean he exists.'

Touché.

If she was lying, she'd just gotten exponentially better at it. Maybe Charlie was wrong. Maybe there hadn't been another prisoner besides Rodriguez in the corridor. Hell, maybe Charlie had been hallucinating. Or seeing double. Even if he hadn't been, even if he was one hundred percent correct, given the condition he'd been in at the time, his uncorroborated testimony would never hold up in court.

'Who else do you think was back there, Detective?'

Forget calling him Tom. She was hostile now. Her eyes held a militant gleam, her lips had thinned, her jaw was tight. All hallmarks of an innocent woman wrongly accused.

Or a very good actress.

Anyway, she had him there. He had no idea – yet.

Not that he meant to tell her so.

Let her stew.

'Look, Kate. We have a whole lot of people, including a judge and a number of deputies, dead. Murdered. Shot in broad daylight in and around a high-security area of the Criminal Justice Center by prisoners attempting an escape. It's my job to get to the bottom of what happened. I'm attempting to do that.'

'And you think I had something to do with it?'

The incredulity in her voice struck him as sincere. Tom narrowed his eyes. It almost – *almost* – made him believe in her innocence.

But if she was innocent, what was she afraid of?

'Mom!' The yell from upstairs caught them both by surprise. It was only then, as Ben's voice sliced through it, that Tom realized how thick the tension in the air had become. 'I'm ready!'

Kate's eyes bored into Tom's for a moment longer, and then she glanced toward the stairs as she rose.

'I'm coming,' she called back. Her gaze shifted back to him. Her expression was stony.

'I always go up and tuck Ben in and read to him before he falls asleep. So . . .'

Her voice trailed off, but it was obvious from her expression that she was asking him to leave.

Tom smiled.

'Would you mind if I wait here until you're finished? If you could come back down, that would be great. I still have a few more questions to ask.'

Her eyes turned to ice.

'I've told you everything I know. I have nothing to add.'

'I understand. But I still have to ask the questions. Of course, if you'd rather, we could do it tomorrow. At the Roundhouse.'

It was clear from her expression that she understood the implied threat. If she didn't cooperate, he could always show up at her office the next day and take her down to police headquarters for additional questioning. Of course, given the fact that she was an ADA, the whole thing got a little trickier. When they found out about it, as they certainly would, the DA's office would be outraged. The powers that be at the PPD probably wouldn't react much better. In any case, he had little doubt that she could make some phone calls, file a motion, slap a harassment charge on him, or in some manner find a way to prevent it from happening, at least for a day or two, until he could get all his ducks in a row, explain things to the DA's office, to the brass at the PPD. But he was betting on the fact that she wouldn't want that to happen. Any word that she was being asked to come in for questioning at police headquarters, with its implication that she was under suspicion of something in this most high-profile of cases, would raise a lot of eyebrows. Something like that wasn't good for careers, especially the career of a young, newly hired prosecutor.

On the other hand, if she had nothing to hide, she might just tell him to go to hell.

Instead, she glared at him. 'Are you trying to intimidate me?'

'Absolutely not.'

'Mom!'

'I'm coming!' she called. Then she looked back at Tom. Her hands curled into fists at her sides. Her face was tight with displeasure. 'Fine. I'll be upstairs for about half an hour. Please, make yourself at home until I come back.'

Sarcasm practically dripped from that last sentence.

'Thank you,' Tom said gently. Then he watched as she stalked toward the stairs, rounded the newel post, started to climb, and disappeared from sight, all with her back rigid and her head held high.

She was a beautiful woman, no doubt about it. Those eyes of hers alone were big, blue pools deep enough for a man to drown in if he wasn't careful. Her mouth was soft and alluring, even when it was telling what he was almost sure was a pack of lies. Her silken blond hair and delicate features and smooth, white skin would have been right at home on a Christmas tree angel. Her body – well, no need to go there. Suffice it to say that if he let himself, he could have the hots for her big-time.

Plus, she had a kid she obviously doted on, who just as obviously loved her a whole lot in return.

None of which, under the circumstances, added up to anything good.

Tom found himself wishing she had told him to go to hell.

15

Panic tasted sour and vinegary in the mouth, as Kate had already discovered. Some forty minutes after she had left Braga waiting downstairs for her like a fat spider crouched in the middle of its sticky old web, she was in the small, utilitarian bathroom off her small, utilitarian bedroom, brushing her teeth vigorously to rid herself of the taste. A glance in the mirror told her that she was pale and big-eyed, with her hair – she'd pulled out the coated elastic that had held her ponytail while she'd read to Ben, in the vain hope that her headache could be blamed on a too-tight ponytail – tangled around her face and her lips gone dry and devoid of color.

She looked like she was scared to death, and for a very good reason: She was.

How had Braga known there was a second man in the secure corridor?

Even considering the possibilities made her heart pound. The security camera had been shot to hell. She remembered it clearly, dangling above the door over her head. Could there have been another one that she had missed? Thinking back, she wasn't one hundred percent certain either way. But as she considered it, she grew increasingly sure that Mario and company wouldn't have been so careless as to have missed a security camera – unless, of course, it was hidden and they hadn't seen it.

She had never heard of anything like that in the Justice Center, which didn't mean it wasn't possible.

At the thought of the cops possessing a tape of everything that had happened in that corridor, she started to sweat.

If Mario had been caught on tape, you wouldn't have been visiting him in the detention center because he would have been taken into federal custody so fast smoke would have been coming out of the windows.

Okay. Deep breath.

Which left another possibility: She wasn't the only person who had made it out of that corridor alive. Charlie Braga had survived, too. Maybe he had seen something. Maybe he had seen Mario.

Kate's stomach knotted as she thought about it. In the glimpse she'd gotten of him, Charlie Braga had looked dead. But maybe he'd been conscious the whole time, and just playing possum. Maybe he'd seen Mario before he'd been shot. Maybe – maybe . . .

You can drive yourself crazy with maybes.

Anyway, he couldn't have seen her with Mario. He couldn't have seen Mario shoot Rodriguez and then force her to take the gun. He couldn't have overheard anything she and Mario had said. Given Charlie

Braga's position on the floor of the holding cell, it was impossible.

Almost impossible. *Wasn't it?*

Yes, she thought it was.

Therefore, Tom Braga couldn't *know* anything, she tried to reassure herself as she rinsed her mouth clean. Not for sure. If he did, he'd already have put her under arrest. He might be scarily on target with his accusations, but he could only be bluffing, trying to see if he could rattle her into making some kind of damaging admission. She had seen cops do it time after time after time.

But she'd never been on the receiving end of it before. She'd never known how truly frightening the technique could be.

Especially if you're hiding something.

But Braga didn't know that, either. If he did, she would be sitting in one of the interrogation rooms at the Roundhouse at that very moment, with more cops buzzing around her than bees around a trash can. She would already have been read her rights. Her life would already have been destroyed.

As it was, right now everything that mattered to her, everything that she'd worked so hard to build, was still intact.

But it was a very specific guess.

Specific enough that something or someone had to have put him on the right track. Though trying to figure out who or what would take longer than she had to spare right now, if she could even do it with any certainty.

The bottom line was, Braga clearly didn't *know* anything, and unless and until he did, she could still hold everything together if she just kept her cool.

That conclusion should have made her feel better, Kate thought bitterly as she ran a quick brush through her hair and slicked a little pink gloss on her lips to give them some color before heading back downstairs to face the enemy. But it didn't. She still felt sick to her stomach, cold to the bone, and absolutely wretched.

She felt guilty.

Turning off lights was second nature to her, to save on the electricity bill. She clicked off her bathroom light, then her bedroom light, and stepped out into the small landing at the top of the stairs that, with the shade pulled down on its single window, was now so dark she could barely see into the cavelike gloom that was Ben's room on the other side. She paused to quietly close his door before heading downstairs, because if he should wake up – he never did, he slept like a rock, but just in case – she didn't want him to overhear any part of her conversation with Braga. He'd fallen asleep to a chapter of *A Wrinkle in Time,* which they were currently reading, and as she'd pulled the covers up around his shoulders and kissed his cheek – proof positive that he was asleep, because he would have protested otherwise – she'd felt an overwhelming surge of love for him, and with it a strengthening of her resolve, a rush of renewed courage.

She was all Ben had in the world, and she would do what she had to do to keep him safe.

Including lying to Braga as often and as convincingly as necessary.

Despite the cold, hard knot that felt like a rock in her stomach.

Standing outside Ben's door, she looked down the stairs toward where she knew Braga was waiting for her, and took a deep – and she hoped heartening – breath. She tried to summon that fresh upsurge of resolve and courage again, but despite her best efforts, it wasn't happening.

All I feel is scared. And alone. And even if I do manage to get Braga off my back, there's still Mario to contend with.

With that happy thought, she gave up.

One crisis at a time.

Braga was first.

Conscious of her heart knocking against her ribs with every step, she headed down the shadowy stairs toward the pool of soft lamplight below. Halfway down, part of the coffee table and the couch came into view.

Kate found herself looking at a pair of long, unmistakably masculine legs in navy pants that ended in boat-sized feet in black wingtips, with sturdy ankles in black socks bridging the gap between the two. The ankles were crossed, the feet were propped up on her coffee table, and the legs bridged the gap between the table and the couch.

She frowned. Braga had his feet up on her coffee table, and she didn't like that. Except that actually, under the circumstances, she did like it, because it gave her something to yell at him about, and thus she could begin their forced tête-à-tête by putting him on the defensive.

Taking heart a little at that, tightening her mouth and narrowing her eyes with what she hoped was clear disapproval, she proceeded on down the stairs.

Only to discover as she reached the bottom that Braga had fallen asleep on her couch.

The discovery took her aback. What was she supposed to do now?

She moved toward him, meaning to wake him, then stopped when she was near. For a moment she stood on the other side of the coffee table, eyeing him across it, thinking the situation through. He was definitely soundly asleep. He was sitting up, his broad shoulders stretching across fully a third of the couch, his feet propped on her coffee table, his long body, still completely dressed, even to his jacket, relaxed. His head was tipped back against the rolled top of the couch. His exposed throat looked very brown against the open collar of his white shirt. Black stubble roughened his throat and the chiseled line of his jaw. His eyes were closed; his lashes formed stubby black crescents against his cheeks. His lips were slightly parted, revealing a hint of even, white teeth. Lamplight bathed his olive complexion in a warm, golden glow, smoothing away some of the lines she had noticed in his face earlier, picking up blue highlights in his black hair.

Unwillingly, she registered it: Even asleep, he looked sexy.

A slight snore issued from between his lips.

Still.

Kate thought about waking him up. But if she did, she would have to answer his questions. Her gaze slid to the cable box on top of the TV. According to the digital numbers there, the time was 10:06. If she left him alone for an hour, or an hour and a half, and then woke him, she could immediately send him on his way, pleading the late hour and her own need for sleep.

Sounds like a plan.

Leaving Sleeping Beauty where he was, she quietly picked up the coffee mugs and empty saucer, carried them into the kitchen, and loaded them and the other dishes into the dishwasher. She put the remaining groceries away, tidied the kitchen, and made sure everything was set out for the morning. Then she turned out the light and returned to check on her unwelcome guest.

He was still sleeping like a baby. As far as she could tell, he hadn't so much as twitched since she had last looked at him. A sideways glance told her that it was not quite ten-thirty. For optimum results, she needed to let him sleep at least half an hour longer. An hour longer would be even better.

Okay, she had work to do anyway. With one last careful look at the man snoring away on her couch, she quietly turned off the lamp farthest from him – she was afraid that turning off the one at his elbow might waken him – then went into her office, which, since it was the former dining room, was connected to the living room by a glass-paned door that was located on the other side of the fireplace from the TV. The other door in the room was an open archway that led into the kitchen. Her office was a small room that she hadn't bothered to try to decorate, with plain white walls, cheap white tab-top curtains covering the single double-hung window, and Ben's artwork from school stuck up everywhere with poster tape. Her desk and chair, along with a wastebasket and unopened boxes of books and mountains of files, were the only furnishings. Her cluttered desk was a Goodwill special, a scarred oak monstrosity that she thought probably had once been a teacher's desk. It sat in the middle of the floor facing the living room so that she could, when seated behind it, see Ben in the living room as he watched TV. Her briefcase waited unopened on the desk.

So get to work.

A sudden, vivid memory of Mario's friend appearing in her dark yard earlier popped without warning into her mind, and she glanced quickly toward the window, relieved when the plain white fall of the curtains blocked her view of the night beyond. Then she looked closer. Was there a sliver of space between the thin panels where someone might be able to see in?

Yes.

Her heart started to pound as her eyes fixed on the gap. Crossing quickly to the window, she tugged the panels together, making certain they overlapped. Still, she felt exposed. It was almost as if she could sense a presence beyond the curtains, beyond the glass. *Was* someone out there? She could not bring herself to part the curtains again, to look. Even if she did, as dark as it was outside, all she would be able to see would be the night crowding close around the house, she told herself.

All you're doing by dwelling on what happened earlier is freaking yourself out.

Turning away from the window required a real effort of will, but she did it. The open doorway to the kitchen was dark; beyond it, the kitchen itself was thick with shadows. The only illumination came from the single lamp that still burned in the living room. Except for the low hum of various appliances, the house was silent. Spookily so. Kate shivered in spite of herself, and was conscious of a kind of sneaky gladness that she and Ben were not alone in the house.

Even if Braga was almost as dangerous to them in his own way as Mario and company.

Don't think about it. Any of it. Put it out of your mind.

Sitting down in the blue-upholstered office chair that was also courtesy of Goodwill, Kate deliberately ignored the fact that once she scooted the chair up to her desk she could see Braga sprawled out on the couch anytime she cared to look through the glass door. She *didn't* care to look. She didn't care to think, either, about anything except work. Instead, she got busy, clicking on the small lamp on her desk, opening her briefcase, and plunging deliberately into the minutiae of her upcoming cases. Details of beatings, robberies, aggravated assaults, and attempted homicides were spelled out in the most graphic terms in the files in front of her. Many of the worst cases were 'twofers,' where the victim had as long a rap sheet as the alleged perpetrator. Those were the most difficult to try, because it was an uphill battle working up sympathy for the victim among the jurors. Genuinely innocent victims, on the other hand, were what a prosecutor lived for, and there were a few of those in the mix, too. Usually, the hardest thing for Kate was to remember not to let certain cases and victims invade her heart. Tonight, though, with her own life threatening to come apart around her, the hardest thing was just to concentrate.

These people are counting on you to get them justice.

Even with all the chaos the attack at the Justice Center had thrown into the system, legal life had to go on. Motions still had to be heard, charges filed, pleas negotiated, cases tried. Though this week was clearly going to be a lost cause for everybody, she had to assume that by next week things would be up and running again. Accordingly, she had to prepare. She owed it to the people she was being paid to represent.

But with the best will in the world, finally she had to admit it just wasn't happening. After reading the same witness statement three times before she realized that it was the same, she acknowledged defeat. She was doing no one any good by sitting there staring at pieces of paper that weren't registering while her mind wrestled fearfully with her own situation. She would be better off heading up to bed and starting fresh in the morning.

Closing the file she was working on, she slid it and the others she would need for tomorrow back into her briefcase, then looked through the glass door at last.

Braga was still asleep. In the same position. If he had moved at all, she couldn't tell it.

Frowning, she glanced at the small clock on her desk and registered the time with surprise: eleven fifty-seven. Even though she didn't think she had retained a single word she'd read, the time had passed swiftly.

Standing up, stretching, she turned off the lamp on her desk, picked up her briefcase, and padded in her white athletic socks – her sneakers were under her desk, where she'd kicked them off – into the kitchen, wanting to put off waking Braga for as long as possible. Number one, she didn't want to deal with him, and number two, she really wasn't looking forward to being left with just herself and Ben all alone in the house. There was something reassuring about being under the same roof as a cop with a gun, even if said cop was not exactly her best friend.

Get over it. You've got to deal with this on your own. Which was, of course, the story of her life.

She didn't turn on the kitchen light. Moonlight filtering through the window in the top half of the back door, plus the diffused glow of the living-room lamp, provided plenty of illumination when all she was doing was dropping off her briefcase on the counter by the garage door and grabbing a couple of Tylenol. Her headache was back, her mouth was dry, and her eyes felt grainy. And she was tired. Exhausted, really, with the kind of fatigue that probably had as much to do with overwhelming anxiety as lack of sleep. Without work to distract her, she was once again aware of the tension in her shoulders and the heaviness in her stomach.

As much as she needed it, sleep, she feared, might be a long time coming.

One foot in front of the other.

Shaking a couple of Extra Strength Tylenol into her palm from the bottle she kept in the cabinet beside the stove, she turned to the refrigerator for a glass of milk – she hoped its sleep-inducing properties weren't just a myth – to wash it down. The dim white glow of the appliance's interior light made the rest of the kitchen seem very dark. It was almost a relief to finish pouring the milk and shut the door again.

Swallowing the Tylenol and chugging the milk, she moved over to the sink and turned on the water, rinsing the glass. Turning off the water, she left the glass in the sink to be loaded in the dishwasher tomorrow and faced the fact that time was up. It was midnight, and she had run out of excuses not to wake Braga.

I'll tell him he was sleeping so soundly I couldn't bear to . . .

That was the thought running through her mind

when it was interrupted by a sound. A small, metallic sound. A sound that in the normal scheme of things probably wouldn't have caught her attention at all. But it did catch her attention, because it shouldn't have been there, in her dark, quiet kitchen at midnight.

It was the *scritch* of the doorknob turning.

Kate recognized it with a thrill of horror even as her head slewed in its direction. It was coming from the door to the backyard, and as she was still standing at the sink it was perhaps five feet to her left. For a moment her gaze was riveted on the brass knob, which was just barely visible through the gloom. She wouldn't have been able to see it at all if it had not been for a thin little sliver of moonlight slanting through the window above it.

But she did see it, and her breath caught as she watched: It was turning back and forth impatiently.

Someone's trying to break into the house.

She registered it incredulously.

Her heart leaped into her throat. Her blood ran cold. Her stomach dropped.

Then she realized that she could no longer see the night sky through the window. And the reason she couldn't see it was that a huge black shape – a man; she could make out the outline of his head, his shoulders, his arms – was standing on the other side of the door blocking out the stars, trying to get into her kitchen, trying to get to *her*.

16

Kate screamed like a banshee.

Screaming, she leaped away from the sink, bolting for the living room.

'Kate!' Braga met her in the doorway. She ran into him, colliding full-tilt with his solid body, which didn't give an inch despite the considerable force of the impact, and would have bounced off if he hadn't grabbed her upper arms to prevent it from happening.

'What the *hell* . . .'

'A man . . . at the door.' She was panting with fear and exertion. 'Just now . . . *there*.'

Pulling an arm free, she pointed at the back door. 'Stay here.'

Braga let her go and leaped toward the door, pulling his gun from his shoulder holster as he moved. Just before he reached the door the refrigerator blocked her view of him, but she could hear the *whoosh* of the door being jerked open, followed by Braga's quick footsteps on the small wooden deck and a rush of cool night air.

It has to be Mario. He's sending people to break into my house now. To deliver another message? Maybe to get physical so I know he means business?

Her knees gave way without warning at the thought of what might have happened had she and Ben been alone, and she sank down abruptly to sit cross-legged on the hardwood floor.

This can't go on.

Residual adrenaline sent her heart to fluttering. Her pulse raced. She tried to consider the possibility that maybe this had nothing to do with Mario, maybe it was just a garden-variety burglar or psycho intent on committing a random crime, without success. But the timing was too pat. She wrapped her arms around herself to ward off the cold, then realized her teeth were chattering and clenched them to stop it.

I've got to find a way to make this go away.

Braga came back inside, closing the door behind him. Kate heard the *click* of the lock being thrown. Then he came into view around the refrigerator, a tall, dark silhouette with a gun in his hand. As she watched, he holstered the weapon, sliding it beneath his jacket and out of sight, then came walking toward her through the shadows.

Now that it was over, her racing pulse started to slow a little.

Thank God he was here.

He stopped just a couple of feet away and stood with his hands at his waist, looking down at her. 'Nobody there.'

She shook her hair back from her face and met his gaze. 'Somehow I knew that.'

Unclenching her jaw and keeping her voice steady

had required some effort, but she thought the results sounded laudably normal.

'Are you sure . . . ?' His voice trailed off.

She nodded. Then, because she wasn't certain he could see the gesture in the dark, she clarified. 'That there was a man trying to get in the back door? Oh, yeah.'

'Did you recognize him? Was it the same guy who was out in the yard earlier?'

'No, I didn't recognize him. And since I never got a good look at the other guy, I don't know. It could have been.' She thought about it. The general size and shape matched well enough, as far as she could tell. 'Maybe. Or maybe not. I just don't know.'

'I fell asleep on your couch,' he said. 'Why didn't you wake me up when you came back down?'

She shrugged. 'You seemed tired.'

'I was.'

Reaching into his jacket pocket, Braga pulled out something that fit in the palm of his hand. With it being dark and all, she wasn't quite sure what it was until he flipped it open and it responded with a soft blue glow. Then she knew: his cell phone.

'What are you doing?'

'Calling it in.' He was already pushing buttons. 'Somebody will . . .'

'Please don't.' Her voice was sharp.

'What?' He stopped pushing buttons and looked at her. 'Why?'

She took a deep breath and decided that the

soothing effects of a couple of lungs' worth of oxygen had been overrated as a calming device, because she still felt as shaky afterward as a drunk doing a field sobriety test.

'Because it won't do any good. They won't find anybody. And I've been at the center of so much' – she groped for the word – 'turmoil these last couple of days that I just can't face any more right now. So please. Let it go. As a favor.'

Braga looked at her a moment longer without saying anything, then closed his phone with a snap and returned it to his pocket.

'We need to talk.' His voice was grim.

'You keep saying that. I still haven't figured out why, exactly.'

He grunted by way of a reply, then reached a hand down to her with the obvious intent of helping her to her feet.

'Come on. Upsy-daisy.'

Kate looked at that hand for a moment, and made a monumental effort. She gripped it and felt its warm strength close around her own clammy palm. Then he was hauling her up and she was going with the flow until she was upright again. Almost upright, that is. Her knees sagged, and she sagged, too, stumbling forward a little in an effort to regain her balance.

'Hey.'

His arms came around her as she lurched into him, and for a moment, just a moment, her hands flattened against his shoulders and she rested against him, using him as a support. He was tall and solid and felt unmistakably masculine. His arms were hard and strong around her waist. Her cheek lay against the soft cotton of his shirt, and beneath it she could feel the firmness of his muscles, the warmth of his skin. The faint smell of Downy fabric softener reached her nostrils. She recognized it because it was the brand she used herself.

She was conscious of a sudden strong urge to stay where she was for a very long time. To burrow her face against his shoulder and wrap her arms around his neck and just cling. To let somebody else carry the burden of taking care of things for a while. The thing that had struck her first about Braga, above and beyond his good looks, of course, was his aura of being the calm, competent center in the midst of a storm. From the moment she had first laid eyes on him in courtroom 207 when Rodriguez had had a gun to her head, she had never doubted that Braga would do everything he could to get her out of there alive. He was suspicious of her now, and she was rightfully wary of him, but still she had absolute confidence that as long as he was with them he would keep her and Ben physically safe.

Sometimes – just every now and then – it would be good to have somebody else to lean on.

The thought appeared out of nowhere and resonated with surprising force through her entire being. Since Ben's birth, she'd had to be strong and smart and resourceful for the both of them. How wonderful would it be to just lay down the burden for a while? To know that there was someone else around to be strong and smart and resourceful for them, too?

As in 'Someday my prince will come'? Yeah, right.

As she had learned the hard way, she was the only person she could count on to take care of her and Ben.

And she was four kinds of a fool to even begin to let herself daydream about anything else.

'You okay?' His voice broke the spell.

'Fine.' Reluctantly, she pushed away.

'You always fall into someone's arms when you're fine?'

'It's been a rough couple of days.'

'Tell me about it.' His voice was dry. His hands rode the sides of her waist, light but protective, as if he wasn't entirely sure she wasn't going to collapse on the floor again.

Which, frankly, neither was she.

'How's your brother?'

She was still standing much closer than she should, with her head tilted up so that she was looking into his face. The soft incandescence from the living room just touched him, while she had her back to it. Her inquiry elicited the slightest of sudden frowns, but there was a touch, too, of what she thought was ruefulness about his eyes and mouth as he looked down at her.

'Recovering.'

'I'm glad.'

'Me, too.' His grip on her waist tightened fractionally. She could feel the size and strength of his hands through the layers of her sweatshirt and T-shirt all the way to her skin. His eyes, black in the gloom, moved over her face. There was something in them . . .

Kate's eyes widened in surprised response, and her heart picked up the pace again, but for an entirely different reason. There was suddenly – what? A flicker of heat, a kind of chemistry? – sizzling in the air between them.

It hit her – she was attracted to him. And he was attracted back.

Oh, no. No, no, no.

'So, you want to tell me what's going on here?'

He spoke before she could even begin to process all the reasons why developing a thing for Braga was such a bad idea. Whatever might or might not have been struggling to life between them, his question, asked in a hard, impersonal, cop kind of voice, killed it stone-cold dead.

And thank goodness, too.

She stiffened. 'We've been over this.' Her voice had hardened to match his.

His face was now as hard as his voice. His hands dropped away from her waist.

'How about we go over it again?'

She turned away from him, wrapping her arms tighter across her chest to ward off the chill that she couldn't seem to shake.

'How about we don't?' She tossed the question over her shoulder as she padded toward the living room. 'It's late. I want to go to bed. Do you mind?'

He was behind her. 'You're not worried about your visitor – oh, sorry, *one* of your visitors – coming back?'

Okay, he had her there. Yes, she was.

'I have a gun.' Unloaded, in a gun safe in a drawer in her room. With the bullets stored separately. As a mother, she considered such precautions an absolute necessity. But in practical terms, it made actually snatching up the gun and using it in an emergency problematic. 'And I know how to use it.'

'Believe me, I'm well aware.' There was a dry note to his voice. It took Kate a second before she remembered she was supposed to have shot and killed Rodriguez. Like it or not, that lie was now part of what everyone – colleagues, friends and acquaintances, police, the general public, Braga – now thought they knew about her.

So be it.

'I've been taking care of myself and Ben for a long time.'

She was striding across the middle of the living room now, heading for the front door, meaning to show him out and be done with this. As soon as he was gone, she had already decided she would go straight upstairs, check on Ben, go to her room, retrieve and load her gun, and sit up in a chair for the rest of the night with it, just in case. Probably the man who'd tried to break into the house wouldn't be back.

Probably even if he'd gotten in he'd meant only to frighten, not harm, her as a way of underlining the message Mario had sent earlier.

But with Ben's safety on the line, too, that wasn't a chance she was prepared to take.

'Mom.' Ben's sleepy voice calling from the top of the stairs stopped her in her tracks. Braga stopped, too, right behind her. She could feel him just inches behind her back. 'Is everything all right?'

'Everything's fine, sweetie.' Regaining her composure, she walked to the foot of the stairs and looked up at him. He was standing at the top, just outside his open bedroom door, wearing his favorite blue pajamas with rockets on them, his face flushed with sleep. Even as he looked down at her, he was rubbing his eyes with one fist. This was her baby, her little boy, and her heart swelled with fierce love for him. Whatever it took to keep him safe, she would do. 'What are you doing up?'

'I thought I heard you scream. But I was so tired it took me a long time to get up.'

Kate's blood ran cold at the thought that if Braga hadn't been there, Ben might have gotten up to find her at the mercy of whoever had been trying to break into the house. If he had the brains to realize Ben was her most vulnerable point, the thug might well then have turned his attention to her son.

'It must have been a bad dream,' Kate said firmly. 'Go on back to bed. I'll be up in just a minute.'

Ben yawned. 'Okay.'

And he turned and went back into his room. A beat passed in which Kate remained standing at the foot of the stairs looking up, and then she heard the distinctive creak that meant he had climbed into bed.

She looked at Braga.

He was standing where she had left him, about eight feet away, almost in the middle of the small room. His hands were thrust partway into the front pockets of his pants. His hair was ruffled, his chiseled jaw was dark with stubble, and his eyes were tired. And he looked totally fed up with the situation in which he found himself.

Their eyes met. She was waiting to open the door for him until she was pretty sure Ben was once again asleep – the way the child had looked, she estimated that would take just a couple of minutes, max.

Then he jerked his head at her as if to say 'come here.'

She frowned. But she moved away from the stairs and toward him. There was, she saw, a grim twist to his mouth. When she stopped in front of him, their eyes met again. He rocked back on his heels a little.

'What?' she asked. It was an impatient near whisper.

'How about I stay the night?'

Her eyebrows went up. He had shocked her. *'What?'*

He didn't look any too thrilled about what he was suggesting. By now – a moment after the thought hit her brain – she was guessing – assuming – it wouldn't be for sex.

'It's already after midnight. By the time I get home

and get to sleep, it'll be closer to one A.M. I could sack out on your couch, go home in time to shave and change for work.'

A beat passed in which they stared measuringly at each other.

'Why would you want to do that?' she asked at last.

'I don't like the idea of leaving you and the kid alone.' His lips tightened. 'That's twice in one night somebody's tried to get at you. What is it they say? Third time's the charm?'

Kate didn't say anything for a moment. Much as she hated to admit it, she didn't like that idea, either.

'It's nice of you to offer,' she said at last, grudgingly. By not turning him down, she was, in effect, accepting, and they both knew it.

'You're welcome.' His tone was dry. His eyes slid over her. 'You look beat. If you'll toss me down a blanket and a pillow after you get upstairs, we can both get some sleep.'

Kate hesitated. Letting him sleep on her couch just felt like a really bad idea. But she was so tired, and so scared, and having him in the house would make all the difference to how the remainder of her night went.

And then maybe, if she got some decent sleep, tomorrow her head would be clear enough to allow her to figure some way out of this.

Still, she hesitated.

'There were reporters out in front of the house this morning from about seven on, waiting for me to come out and head for work. If they show up tomorrow, having you spend the night might cause more problems than it solves.'

At the thought of the kinds of stories that would go around in that case, Kate practically shuddered. Even if 'the heroine of courtroom 207 sleeps with the detective who tried to save her' angle didn't make the newspapers or airwaves – and surely it wouldn't – local reporters knew the Philly legal and law-enforcement communities well. Gossip about her and Braga would spread like wildfire. She didn't know how he felt about that, but as one of the low prosecutors on the totem pole at the DA's office, she definitely didn't need it.

He grimaced. 'I'll be out of here long before seven, don't worry.'

'I usually get up at six. I could wake you.'

'I imagine I'll already be up. Look, go on to bed, would you? I got everything at this end covered. Quit worrying.'

Worrying was one of those things she was really good at, even when life was normal, but he couldn't know that. Pursing her lips, looking at him consideringly, Kate knew there just wasn't much else to say. The truth was, the idea of having him under the same roof was so tempting it was impossible to turn down. She wasn't going to argue anymore. She was going to go upstairs and go to sleep, secure in the knowledge that at least she and Ben were safe for the rest of the night.

'All right, then. I'll just go get some things for the couch.'

With that she turned and headed for the stairs. When she came back, loaded down with a pillow and a couple of mismatched blankets and a set of Ninja Turtle sheets – the only twin-sized sheets she had that were clean – he had taken off his jacket. With just a couple of steps to go before she reached the bottom, she faltered, looking across the room at him. He had his back turned to her, and his shoulders looked very broad in his white dress shirt. The black straps of his shoulder holster stood out sharply against it, and she was reminded – as if she needed reminding – that he was a cop. He had an athlete's narrow hips and a great butt – had she really expected anything else? – that was small and tight-looking in the navy slacks. His head was tilted slightly forward, and she could just see the clean angle of his forehead and cheek and jaw. His hands were at chest height in front of him, moving in such a way that she thought he might be unbuttoning his shirt. Her breath caught at the thought, and she stood there on the second step from the bottom without being able to move or say a word while, with no warning at all, a rush of awareness of him as a totally hot guy engulfed her. Once again, to her total dismay, she felt the unwanted pull of sexual attraction.

It caught her by surprise, set her heart to beating just a little faster, quickened her breathing, warmed her like nothing else had been able to do all night.

Whoa. Chill. Hold it right there. Not happening. Put it out of your mind.

'I've got blankets,' she said in a firm voice before the temptation to just remain mute and watch while he stripped off his shirt could get the better of her, and walked down the remaining stairs.

'Thanks.'

He glanced over his shoulder at her, sliding his shoulder holster off at the same time. Even as he folded the thing and placed it – and his gun – on the lamp table at the far end of the couch, she realized that that was what he had been doing all along: unfastening his shoulder holster.

Her breath escaped in a small sigh of relief and disappointment that to her ears sounded like a deflating balloon. He didn't appear to notice, but she did, and it annoyed her.

'You know, you might want to think about getting a security system put in here,' he said, as she reached the coffee table, where she dropped the pillow and blankets before moving on to the couch with the sheets.

'I am thinking about it.' She focused on shaking out the bottom sheet over the couch cushions, determined not to notice that at the same time he was pulling off his tie and tossing it onto the gold chair, where his jacket already waited. 'But a security system is expensive, and I'm just leasing this house.'

'If your life keeps on being this exciting, it still might be better than the alternative.'

He had moved to help her. They were at opposite ends of the couch, and he tucked his part of the sheet around the cushions with aplomb.

'Yeah, well, I hope my life doesn't go on being this exciting. Really, boredom's more my thing.'

He smiled at that. Kate smiled wryly back. They were standing there not doing anything except smiling at each other, and the atmosphere in the room had gone all cozy, and she was suddenly starting to feel way too comfortable with him. Her brows snapped together, and she dropped her gaze, looking around for the top sheet. It was on the coffee table. When she picked it up and started to shake it out, he took it from her.

'I can do this. Go to bed.'

His tone was abrupt. Kate flicked a quick look up at his face. There was nothing in his expression at all now: His face was wiped clean. Every bit of warmth and humor – and, yes, even his earlier aggravation with her – had disappeared.

The thing she had to keep in mind was that he might be spending the night, but they weren't even friends. At best, he was a cop with an oversized sense of responsibility doing his job. And she was a scared potential victim grateful for the protection.

At worst, he was a homicide detective and she was one of the objects of his investigation.

'Okay.' She stepped away from the couch, moved around the coffee table, and headed toward the stairs. No protest at all. Keeping it impersonal.

'Good night,' he said.

With one hand on the newel post, she looked over her shoulder at him.

'Good night,' she answered, and headed on up the stairs.

17

Despite everything, Kate slept like the dead. If she had dreams, she couldn't remember them. When her alarm went off at six, she felt like she was swimming through fathoms of deep water before she finally surfaced, heard the shrill beeping, and silenced it. It was only then, as she lay there blinking in the first few moments of 'I really want to go back to sleep, but I know I can't' stupor, that she remembered Braga.

Then she was out of bed like a shot.

It took her less than five minutes to do everything she needed to do and, barefoot and wrapped in her ratty blue terry robe, head downstairs. Her mission: make sure he was up and on his way out before anyone knew he'd been there. It was still dark outside, but now that her mind was clear and a new day was at hand she felt embarrassed that she had allowed him to stay the night.

No need to compound the error by getting the fact in the news.

The smell of coffee greeted her as she neared the bottom of the stairs. Clearly, Braga was up. A quick glance around showed her that the couch was empty;

the sheets were stripped off the cushions and folded along with the blankets at one end. The pillow was stacked on top. And while the rest of the house was dark, a light was on in the kitchen.

She headed toward it.

The coffeemaker was on, she saw as she reached the kitchen doorway and cast a single sweeping glance around, along with the overhead light. One of her thick, white mugs waited, empty and apparently unused, beside the coffeemaker. But there was no sign of Braga.

Kate turned back toward the dark living room just as the door to the powder room under the stairs opened and Braga walked out. He was wearing his pants, for which she was thankful, and was rubbing his face with a towel. Despite a narrow black belt, the pants rode low on his hip bones. His chest was bare.

She looked. Of course she did.

It was a very masculine chest, a classic V shape, wide and broad-shouldered on top, then tapering down to a narrow waist and hips. His leanness when dressed was deceptive. Shirtless, he was surprisingly muscular and tanned, with well-developed pecs, impressive biceps, and brawny forearms. A wedge of curling black hair adorned the center of his chest, then tapered down before disappearing beneath his pants. His nipples were flat and dark, barely visible beneath his chest hair. It was difficult to see his abs in the gloom, and if he possessed a six-pack, its definition was lost in the shadows. But his stomach was definitely flat.

Also, sexy didn't begin to cover it.

Her eyes jerked up and away at just about the time he emerged from beneath the towel.

'Morning,' he said, sounding surprised to see her.

She looked at him again, all innocent greeting, just as if – she hoped – she hadn't been looking at him in a whole other way seconds before. He crumpled in one hand the small maroon guest towel she kept in that bathroom, and continued walking away from her, toward where, she saw now, his shirt waited with his tie and jacket on the gold chair.

'Good morning,' she managed, a little feebly. His back was almost as impressive as his chest. The same wide shoulders. Strong shoulder blades. A straight spine. Smooth skin over sleek, powerful muscles.

'Sleep well?' He dropped the towel on the coffee table and picked up his shirt, glancing at her over his shoulder. He was casual, like having her see him without his shirt on was no big deal.

It probably wasn't – for him.

'Pretty well.' If he could do casual, so could she. She tightened the belt on her wraparound robe, which covered her from neck to knees, and adjusted the neckline. Beneath it she wore a pink mid-thigh-length T-shirt that said *Kiss Me* above a picture of a frog. Luckily, there was no way he could know that. 'How about you?'

'Good.' He shrugged his shirt on and proceeded to button it. Kate tried not to watch. 'That's a comfortable couch.'

'Thanks.' The conversation felt ridiculous and stilted. The awkwardness inherent in having the cop who suspected you of God knew what sleeping over at your house was something that only became truly apparent the morning after, she was discovering. See said cop half-naked and have him be dishy as hell, and the awkwardness could not be overstated.

She wondered if he felt the awkwardness, too. If he did, it didn't show.

'I'm just going to grab a cup of coffee,' she said, as it occurred to her that standing there watching him get dressed was probably a really stupid thing to do.

'I already put a pot on.'

'I smelled it coming downstairs.'

Padding into the kitchen, she filled his cup, remembering that he took it black. Then she poured herself one as well, added generous amounts of sugar, stirred, and sipped the hot brew, savoring the smell, the taste, and the promise of a caffeine kick. Her gaze was drawn inexorably to the window in the door. This morning there was nothing to see except the soft gray dawn as it crept over the backyard. She shuddered, remembering. It seemed clear that the intruder had known she was in the kitchen, had perhaps tracked her movements from the time she went into her office. The crack in the curtains – had he been watching her through them? The thought made her sick.

Who's going to protect Ben and me tonight?

When Braga walked in, she was leaning against the counter in front of the sink, cradling the thick mug in both hands. A quick glance told her that he was now fully dressed, down to the shoes. His tie was slung around his neck. He looked only marginally less tired than he had the night before. His eyes were bloodshot. His hair was unruly. He badly needed a shave.

He looked scruffy, disreputable, and way more like a bad guy than a cop.

Considering everything, it was actually surprising how safe he made her feel.

'Did I miss anything during the night?' she asked, thrusting the cup she'd filled at him as he came toward her.

'Nope.' He accepted it and took a healthy swallow. His eyes met hers. 'Except maybe me snoring.'

She smiled involuntarily. 'Um, too much information?'

A glimmer of an answering smile appeared in his eyes. Then it vanished as he took another quick chug of coffee, set his mug down on the counter, and started walking away.

'I'm out of here,' he said over his shoulder. 'Come lock the door behind me.'

Setting her own mug down, she followed him through the kitchen and across the shadowy living room. He paused with a hand on the knob to look warily out the small window in the door. Apparently, he saw nothing to give him pause, because he opened it. A rush of crisp air, fragrant with the scent of fall, hit her, blowing the hair back from her face, swirling around her bare legs and feet and raising goose bumps in its wake. Moving to the door to close it behind him as he stepped out onto the small front porch, she looked past him to see that his car was still in the dark driveway and pink fingers of dawn were just beginning to climb the sky above the houses across the street. Nothing stirred. No one was in view.

He looked around at her. 'Try to stay out of trouble, will you?'

Kate blinked. *Like I asked for any of this?*

Before indignation could well and truly take hold, she thought of how soundly she had slept, and how differently the night might have turned out if he had left her and Ben on their own.

'Hey,' she said to him. Stepping off the porch, he glanced back at her inquiringly. 'Thanks for staying.'

'You're welcome.' His eyes slid down her body and he grinned suddenly. 'Nice frog.'

Taken aback, Kate frowned in incomprehension before suddenly stopping to look down at herself. Sure enough, the lapels of her robe had parted. A good-size section of her pink nightshirt, including a big green head topped by googly eyes and the words *Kiss Me,* was clearly visible.

She felt her face growing warm with embarrassment. The sound of a car door closing caused her to look up. Braga was already in his car, she saw. Seconds later, the headlights came on and his car started backing out.

She stepped inside, quickly shutting and locking

the door. As the shadowy stillness of her now quiet house enveloped her, she was conscious of fear closing like a fist around her stomach.

Braga suspected there had been a second man in the security corridor. And Mario was sending goons to threaten her.

As the new realities of her life came crashing down, her heart started to pound. Her pulse began to race. Her throat went dry.

And the sad thing was the day was only beginning.

Tom knew he had trouble even before he got the call back from Wade Bowling in forensics.

Located in the lab in the Roundhouse's basement, forensics was conducting tests on the various guns used in the shootings, trying to ascertain which victim had been shot by which weapon and which perp had been responsible for firing said weapon. Tom had called Bowling for an update as soon as he'd gotten to work that morning. He hadn't considered it all that important, because he was pretty sure he knew the answers anyway, although forensics' confirmation would provide needed verification. After that, he'd been so busy with other facets of the investigation that the unreturned call to forensics had almost slipped his mind.

Which, when it wasn't wrestling with trying to determine how the original guns – he was almost certain there were only two that hadn't been taken from deputies – had gotten into the inmates' hands, was continually being infiltrated by stealth thoughts of Kate White. By staying the night at her house, he had overstepped the boundaries of professional distance, and he knew it. Still, playing overnight protector to a scared woman and her kid was not actually against any rules, nor did it violate any departmental ethics codes. She was not – officially – suspected of anything. And he had slept on the couch.

The problem was, he was attracted to her.

Okay, get real. You've got the hots for her big-time.

Last night, after someone had terrorized her for the second time in about four hours – which, in his experience, was something of a record – she had stumbled into his arms. What he had felt as he'd held her could not be characterized by any stretch of the imagination as professional disinterest.

He had wanted her. Bad.

Which wasn't exactly surprising. His smokin' little ADA, as Fish had called her, was a desirable woman. Any man worth his testosterone would want her. He could deal with wanting her. He might not appreciate the ramifications, but he could deal.

What was complicating the situation was that he also liked her much more than he should.

When she wasn't scared to death – her typical state since he'd made her acquaintance – it turned out that she was funny, smart, and assertive, and from everything he'd been able to observe, a hell of a good mom.

And her boy seemed like a nice little kid.

Under different circumstances, he would turn tail and run like hell from the pair of them.

Which had been his firm intention when he'd left her house that morning.

Unfortunately, that didn't look like it was going to be possible.

Like any careful investigator would, he had spent a portion of the morning doing a quick background check on a person of interest in the case whose story wasn't quite adding up. That person was Kate.

First things first: She had no criminal record in the state of Pennsylvania, which, while not a surprise, was definitely a relief. Then, starting from the present, he'd worked his way back through her life. What he had found had both increased his admiration of her tenfold and raised a number of red flags. Hired at the DA's office at age twenty-eight with stellar recommendations, she had spent the three previous years funded by student loans and scholarships at Temple Law School, where she had excelled despite what one source referred to as 'the pressures of being a single mother.' Before that, she had taken five years and change to earn a degree in psychology from Drexel University. Both were urban schools, with a large percentage of dropouts because of the nature of the student body. Getting through college had taken her five years because, in addition to receiving financial aid, she had supported herself and her son by working nights as a waitress.

Before that, the picture started to get a little murky,

but he traced her back to Atlantic City, New Jersey, with minimal trouble. There, public records indicated, her son had been born – she'd been nineteen at the time; one Chaz White was listed on the birth certificate as the father – and she – Katrina Dawn Kominski – had married Charles Edward White, age twenty-four, seven months before. On the marriage license application, she had listed her occupation as waitress; White had put CEO, White Security Company. Tom assumed that Charles Edward White was the Chaz White on the birth certificate and, thus, Ben's father, and that either he had a quirky sense of humor or was given to elevating his own importance, because other records – notably, his obituary – listed his occupation as a bouncer at Harrah's Casino. He was twenty-five at the time of his death, which was called 'sudden,' though no cause was given.

Tom remembered Ben saying that his father had perished in a car accident not long after his birth.

The marriage license also named Kate's parents – Lois Smolski Johansen and Walter Sykes Kominski – and place of birth: Baltimore, Maryland. Both parents had criminal records, the mother for drugs and a variety of other nonviolent crimes, the father for drugs and a list of offenses, some violent, some not, as long as Tom's arm. Both were now deceased.

It was in Maryland that the trail got really interesting. Kate had a juvenile record, which he couldn't access; from the age of nine she'd bounced around the foster-care system, with her longest placement being one year, and at age fifteen she had apparently disappeared without a trace, not to resurface until she'd filed for a marriage license three years later in Atlantic City.

He was still pondering what that meant for the investigation when Bowling in forensics finally called him back.

'So, what'd he say?' Fish asked, referring to Bowling, after Tom hung up.

Tom was seated behind his cluttered desk, a cup of coffee at his elbow – his sixth or seventh of the day; the truth was, he hadn't slept worth a damn on Kate's couch – his notebook in front of him, a pen in his hand. They were in the Duty Room at the Roundhouse, it was past lunchtime, and Fish was kicked back in the chair across from Tom's desk, waiting for them to head out on their usual midday run to Margee's for cheesesteaks. Fish was resplendent as always in one of his snazzy suits – today's was solid navy blue, with a striped shirt and a patterned tie. Tom was showered and shaved and dressed in an old favorite gray corduroy jacket – hey, it had all its buttons – black slacks, white shirt, and red tie. (Red ties, he had discovered by trial and error over the years, pretty much went with anything.) The day had been going well, or at least as well as a day could in which the murders of four fellow law-enforcement officers and a judge were his top priority, while from points all across the city more murders just kept rolling in, and he was tired as hell and slightly distracted by an inconvenient attraction to a woman lawyer with a juvie record and a murky past who might or might not be a player in the crime he was investigating.

Then Bowling called and, in the course of an ordinary cross-check of facts Tom already knew, threw a wrench in the works that threatened to send a perfectly good day straight down the toilet.

That was when Tom knew he had it bad. Because right after he hung up the phone and Fish asked what Bowling had said, his first impulse had been to lie to his partner, his longtime friend, his fellow detective, and say, 'Nothing new.'

Instead, he hesitated, tapping the notebook in which he kept track of things with the end of his pen, frowning at Fish across the desk.

'What?' Fish knew him well enough to sit up a little straighter in anticipation.

Tom was conscious of a sense of extreme reluctance to part with the information he had just received. He forced himself past it.

'The usual. What we knew. Except, whoever shot Rodriguez was probably left-handed.'

There, he'd said it.

It took Fish a second, and then his eyes widened. 'Is the pretty prosecutor left-handed?'

'I don't know.' His memories on that point were admittedly a little hazy, but he didn't think so. 'But I mean to find out.'

'So . . .' Fish began, but was cut off by Ike's looming presence behind him.

'Glad you two are still here.' Ike looked about as

cheerful as Tom felt. 'A call just came in. Two bodies found in a burnt-out U-Haul in Montgomery County. Looks like they might be our guys.'

'The ones who were supposed to drive the getaway vehicle?' Fish's voice quickened with interest. He surged to his feet. 'Yippie-i-ay, we're really cooking now.'

Ignoring the bad joke that had Fish (and Fish alone) grinning at his own wit, Tom rose, too. He might feel grim as hell, but as a cop he played no favorites. 'We'll check it out.'

'You do that.' With a nod, and a quelling stare for Fish, Ike went on his way.

Feeling tension tightening his nerves until they were stretched as taut as piano wire, Tom headed out with Fish, and tried not to think about how this whole thing was going to play out if Kate White, as he suspected, was right-handed.

'What do you mean the charges were dropped?' Kate yelled into her cell phone. One hand covered her free ear in an effort to block some of the street noise. 'The charges couldn't have been dropped.'

'Let me check again,' the woman on the other end of the phone said, and there was a *click* followed by canned music. Grinding her teeth at the delay, Kate had to face the facts: She had been put on hold.

These were the first moments Kate had had to herself during a very hectic day. She had been working flat out since she stepped onto the ninth floor at five minutes before eight that morning, eating lunch at her desk, taking bathroom breaks on the run. Rescheduling everything was a backbreaker that had the entire criminal justice system scrambling. The first funerals were scheduled for the next day, and reworking timetables around them was creating even more of a snarl. Anything that couldn't be postponed had been moved to today in the Federal Building, and getting witnesses, defendants, lawyers, judges, and assorted support personnel all together at the right place at the right time was a logistical nightmare. She had been running around like a chicken with its head off all day going back and forth. Most everybody in the DA's office was doing the same. Finally, telling Mona she needed a breath of fresh air to clear her head, she had at last managed to get away.

Now, at just a few minutes shy of five P.M., she was striding purposefully toward the detention center on a glorious late-fall afternoon that was bright and beautiful enough to bring the tourists out in droves. Golden sunlight sparkled off the top windows of the skyscrapers. The sidewalks were thick with pedestrians. The streets were crowded with vehicles, even more than usual, as people were starting to get off work. The purple Philly Phlash tourist bus that looped around to local attractions rumbled past, and she saw that it was standing room only on board. Hot-dog vendors, pretzel stands, soft-drink carts, and street peddlers hawking freshly printed T-shirts with sayings like *I Love Philly* above Monday's date and *Survivor:*

Criminal Justice Center had sprung up like mushrooms after a rain. Their combined smells, along with car exhaust, perfumed the air. It was as if the sensational nature of the killings was acting as a magnet, drawing even more people and activity than usual into Center City.

On the bright side, there had been only a few reporters outside her house when she had left that morning, and none at all outside the DA's office at any time during the day that she had seen, so it seemed that the message that no one on their side was going to talk to the media was getting out.

'I'm sorry.' The woman on the phone was back. Kate had to strain to hear her over the street noise. 'But our records show that all charges against Mr. Castellanos have been dropped and he was released from custody about an hour ago.'

Dumbfounded, Kate stopped dead, oblivious to the people streaming around her. 'That can't be.'

'That's what our records show.'

Kate sucked in air. She was attracting curious looks as passersby brushed past her, but she barely even noticed.

'Who signed the release order?' she demanded.

It was too late. The woman had hung up. A dial tone buzzing like an angry wasp in Kate's ear was the only reply. For a moment, a long moment, she kept the phone where it was while she stared blindly at the busy intersection in front of her and the news slowly sank in.

Mario's out on the street.

The morning's chill had mellowed, and although she was wearing a black blazer and slacks with a long-sleeved blue oxford-cloth blouse and had been walking very fast in her flats before she stopped, she was suddenly freezing cold. Her stomach knotted and her heart began to pound as she gripped her cell phone – which she was using out of utter paranoia because she didn't want the calls to come up on the office log, just in case anyone ever checked them, which she was pretty sure no one ever did – to call the detention center to arrange for another meeting with Mario. In which she had meant to threaten to trump up enough charges to see to it that he was put away for life if any of his goon pals ever came within spitting distance of her or Ben again. And never mind that he would almost certainly threaten her back if she didn't get him out.

She had even been prepared to promise that she *would* get him out and forget about the whole confidential-informant thing. Whatever it took to keep him and his associates away from Ben.

But she had still meant to make him sweat for it as much as she could. The one thing she had known from the beginning she could not do was just roll over and play dead. If Mario knew he had succeeded in frightening her last night, she was toast. Once a bully, always a bully.

Oh my God, maybe Mario thinks I already did what he asked. Maybe he thinks I got him out. Or maybe he'll be satisfied with just being out however it happened and leave me alone.

Kate savored that thought for a calming second or two before reality hit.

Yeah, and maybe there's a tooth fairy, too.

'Are you okay, miss?' a man's voice penetrated the fog she was lost in. Blinking, she saw that a nice-looking, mid-thirtyish man in a business suit had stopped walking and was looking at her in concern.

Kate met his gaze, saw the inquisitive glances she was attracting from her fellow pedestrians, and forced herself back into the moment.

If a breakdown was on the agenda, she was just going to have to have it later.

'I'm fine, thanks.'

She even managed a quick smile for the Good Samaritan as she lowered her phone, snapping it shut, stowing it away in her pocket. Aware finally of the attention she was attracting, she started walking again. The Good Samaritan nodded and moved on. She now had no reason to go to the detention center, she reversed course, heading back toward the office. She actually felt proud of how well she was coping until she caught a glimpse of her reflection in a store window. Her shoulders were hunched. Her movements were jerky. With her hair scraped back in its lawyerly bun, she had a really good view of her face: Strain was apparent in every feature.

She looked shocked. Blindsided. Scared.

Big surprise. That's exactly how she felt.

Mario's free.

Little curls of panic spiraled to life inside her at the thought.

What do I do now?

She was just realizing that she didn't have an answer for that when, out of nowhere, someone grabbed her arm.

18

Kate jumped like she had been shot. Her head snapped around so fast to see who had grabbed her that she almost gave herself whiplash.

'Did I startle you? Sorry 'bout that.' Bryan grinned at her. It was his hand curled around her upper arm. Her heart slid out of her throat to settle back into something like its normal position in her chest. Its galloping slowed to the point where she no longer feared dropping dead on the spot. She was able to move again, to breathe, to resume walking down the crowded street. 'You heading anywhere interesting?'

'Depends on what you call interesting. I'm on my way back to work.' Kate dredged up a smile. She had seen Bryan only in passing since Rodriguez had dragged her out from under the counsel table in courtroom 207. He looked unchanged by the ordeal. His round face was cheerful. His brown eyes twinkled at her. His stocky body in its business-friendly gray suit, white shirt, and blue tie seemed to radiate energy. He was carrying his briefcase, which, as usual and like most of the other briefcases associated with the DA's office, was bulging with way too much work. 'How about you?'

'Actually, I'm just on my way back from a meeting with the mayor.' Bryan dropped her arm and fell into step beside her. His tone was nonchalant, but Kate could tell from the pinkening of his cheeks how proud he was of that. 'Or should I say, *we're* just on our way back from a meeting with the mayor.'

That was the first indication Kate had that Bryan wasn't alone. She followed his sideways glance to the tall, portly, white-haired figure just a step off the pace on Bryan's other side. As he saw her looking at him, he gave her a nod and a smile.

Sylvester Buchanan, the district attorney himself, Kate's boss of bosses. As she recognized him, her eyes widened.

She had met him only once before, for a few brief moments at a reception for the retiring head of the Major Trials Unit. That had been in July, when she'd been on the job for just more than a month. They had been introduced, exchanged a brief handshake. She doubted he remembered, or had a clue who she was.

'We were just talking about you,' Bryan said happily, dodging a stream of oncoming pedestrian traffic.

'Really?' Kate's eyebrows shot up. If they were talking about her, maybe Buchanan knew who she was after all. A career plus – if she even had a career left after this thing with Mario shook out. Still, her eyes slid in Buchanan's direction again. He sidestepped closer to Bryan as a couple of young women armed with baby strollers plowed past.

'Yes, indeed,' he confirmed, beaming at her. 'And I'm happy to be the one to give you some good news. The mayor wants to honor you with a Shining Star award. And he wants to present it to you personally next Friday night at the fund-raiser he's cohosting for Jim Wolff.'

From his tone, it was clear that he expected her to be overwhelmed. Which she was, but not with the excitement he obviously anticipated. Jim Wolff was James Arvin Wolff IV, the front-running Republican candidate for President in 2008. *Not* the candidate she was anticipating voting for, although admittedly anything could happen between now and next November. And a Shining Star award was part of the mayor's new crime-fighting initiative: It recognized citizens who had played a significant role in the citywide effort to combat violent crime. The last one she remembered hearing anything about had been presented, sometime this past summer, to the widow of a small supermarket owner who had vowed not to give in to the robbers who continually targeted his store. If she recalled, the award had been posthumous: The supermarket owner had been killed in a shoot-out with the last thugs who had tried to rob him.

And she had supposedly shot the man who had taken her hostage.

Considering the fact that it was an award honoring the effort to combat violent crime, there was irony in there somewhere.

'It's a very exclusive event, you know,' Buchanan

confided, looking slightly anxious, as if he feared she didn't quite realize how significantly she was being honored. Kate suspected she might be looking as appalled as she felt, and tried to adjust both her expression and her body language to something more closely resembling pleased surprise. 'Black-tie. All the local movers and shakers. Good for you. Good for all of us at the DA's office. Lots of publicity. Might even make the national news.'

Oh my God. Can this get any worse?

Kate fumbled for a response that would get her off the hook without offending Buchanan. 'I . . . I really don't think I deserve an award.'

What she truly wanted to say was *No way, José. Not happening. Unh-uh. Forget about it.*

'I told you she's modest,' Bryan said to Buchanan as they reached the imposing stone edifice that housed the DA's offices and took up the entire corner. Getting to the door nearest them first, Bryan pulled it open for her. 'But the way she handled herself – she's deserving. Believe me, I was there.'

Kate groaned inwardly as she walked past Bryan into the spacious lobby. Buchanan followed. Glancing over her shoulder to say something, anything, to try to convince them that this was a hideous mistake, Kate was disconcerted to hear a stampede of footsteps on the marble floor and a way-too-familiar symphony of whirring sounds before she could get so much as a word out.

Her head snapped forward again. Just as she had

suspected, the sounds came from half a dozen reporters converging on them, complete with a phalanx of cameras. Hoping she didn't look as much like a deer in the headlights as she felt, Kate veered toward the elevator banks with Bryan and Buchanan moving fast right behind her.

'Mrs. White, how does it feel to know you've been selected to receive a Shining Star award?' 'Mrs. White, are you a supporter of Jim Wolff?' 'Kate, why won't you talk about what happened in courtroom 207?' 'Mr. Buchanan, did you suggest Mrs. White's name for this award when you met with the mayor today?'

'No comment,' Kate said, feeling like an animal at bay as they backed her against the wall between two elevator shafts. She jabbed furiously at the button as the handful of others who had been waiting for the elevators moved away like the newcomers were radioactive. A harried glance up showed her that the closest elevator was on the left. It was on the third floor, coming down.

She edged toward it.

'Ms. White is both honored to be chosen and deeply deserving of a Shining Star award,' Buchanan said in the kind of deep, authoritative voice she had heard him use before in public forums. It was quite different from the soft, kindly tones he used in private conversation, or at least the private conversation he had so recently directed at her. 'And no' – he broke off briefly as a *ping* announced the arrival of the elevator – 'I did not suggest her name to the mayor.'

A few people got off the elevator, looking surprised to find themselves in the midst of a media frenzy. Kate slid inside. Bryan and Buchanan followed with alacrity as Kate pressed the button for the ninth floor.

'Kate, will you be at Judge Moran's funeral tomorrow?' 'Mr. Buchanan, do you have any idea about the timetable for appointing a replacement judge?' 'Kate, do you think you—'

The doors slid shut. Kate slumped against the side wall in relief.

'How did they get in here?' Buchanan shook his head in annoyance as Bryan shrugged. 'I'll have to have a word with security. Kate . . . may I call you Kate?' – she nodded assent – 'would you press four, please?'

Kate wordlessly pressed the button for the fourth floor.

'And where the *devil* do they get their information? The mayor hasn't made any kind of public announcement about that award yet. Damned leaks.'

The elevator rocked to a stop.

'Well. I guess I'll let the mayor sort this one out.' Buchanan patted her arm. 'Congratulations, by the way. See you next Friday.'

She did her best not to look appalled as he exited the elevator.

'You don't seem too thrilled about getting a Shining Star award,' Bryan observed as they got under way again. Glimpsing her reflection in the brass plate around the floor buttons, Kate saw what he meant. She was pale and big-eyed, and if she had to describe her expression in a word it would be *hunted*. 'The award's a good thing. To begin with, it could really raise your profile around here. Get you on the fast track to the top.'

Once upon a time, that would have been music to her ears.

'I don't have anything to wear,' she said faintly, coming up with the only halfway logical objection she could think of on the spur of the moment.

Bryan chuckled. 'Now *that* sounds familiar. My wife says the exact same thing every time we get ready to go anywhere. I'm sure you can find something.'

'Yes, but . . .' The elevator *ping*ed on nine, and as she followed Bryan through the opening doors onto their floor, Kate decided to give it up for the moment. She had more than a week to come up with a good reason why she would not be attending the fundraiser. If worst came to worst, she could always plead illness. Anyway, at the moment she had more pressing concerns. Like Mario being in the wind. He could show up anywhere, at any time, and the thought made her sick with dread. How much of a threat was he really, in a physical sense? That was the question.

Unfortunately, she didn't really have an answer.

Waving absentmindedly back at Cindy the receptionist, who was talking on the phone as she wiggled her manicured fingers at them in greeting, Kate fell into step beside Bryan as he headed down the hall toward their offices. The ninth floor was, as usual, a beehive of activity. Phones rang with discordant insistence, copy machines whirred, a rolling coffee cart making its way among the paralegals' cubicles clattered over the hardwood floor, and a hodgepodge of simultaneous conversations raised the background noise level to a near roar. Employees flitted from desk to desk and office to office with an unusual sense of urgency. The late afternoon sun was too low in the sky now to provide much in the way of natural light, so if it hadn't been for the whitish fluorescents overhead, the hall would have been positively dark. The smells of coffee and microwaved pastries followed them. Ordinarily, the smell would have made her hungry, but today she was too tense for such a mundane bodily reaction. In fact, she was too tense to eat: Lunch had consisted of half an apple and a nibble of a peanut-butter cracker.

'How are you doing?' They had almost reached his office when Bryan glanced at her. His tone made it clear that he felt slightly awkward about asking. 'I mean, are you holding up all right? Lord knows what happened Monday was traumatic as hell, and as far as I can tell you haven't missed a beat.'

If only you knew.

'Working helps,' Kate said. 'I try not to dwell on it, you know?'

'That's probably good.' Brian paused, and cut his eyes at her again. 'There are counselors available. If you should need one, I mean. Just to talk. It would be totally confidential, with no record that you ever even visited one. There should be a memo about it in your e-mail, along with a number to call to make an appointment. Plus, there's a notice on the bulletin board in the break room.'

'I'll keep it in mind,' she promised. Monday had been traumatic – *way* traumatic – and she could probably use all the counseling she could get to deal with it. The problem was that since she couldn't tell the truth about her experience, she didn't think counseling would be of much use. 'How are *you* doing? You were traumatized, too.'

'I was scared shitless, you mean.' Bryan gave her a quick sheepish grin. 'I've already seen a counselor. Yesterday. And it helped. But keep that on the down-low, would you?'

'You got it.' Since they were talking about Monday, there was something she realized she badly needed to know.

'Let me ask you a question,' she said. 'Is there a gang or some kind of group that you know of that uses a dragon as a symbol, or a dragon tattoo as a way to mark its members?'

Bryan frowned.

'Why do you want to know?' They had reached his office. Opening the door, he gestured at her to precede him inside.

As she walked past him she shrugged, elaborately casual as to her reason.

'I've heard some things,' she said vaguely, and

plopped down in one of the two chrome-and-leather chairs in front of his desk. His office was almost identical to hers, except the furnishings were a little nicer and it was bigger and had two windows.

'There's the Black Dragons.' Setting his briefcase down, he settled in his chair behind the desk, leaning back, his arms resting comfortably on the armrests. 'They came in here about four years ago from Baltimore and D.C., mostly. At first they just mixed it up with the other gangs and we didn't really pay all that much attention, but then they started turning up in relation to some pretty heinous crimes. Remember that tenement fire last year that killed sixteen people? That was the Dragons, in retaliation for a drug deal gone bad. There was a family – parents, two kids, grandma – killed in a home invasion a few months back because the dad didn't want to be a Dragon anymore. Lots of things like that. They're a gang like the Crips and the Bloods, only even more vicious and with ties to organized crime. We're trying to uproot them before they get too strong, run them out of Philly. Every time one gets picked up, we make it a point to throw the book at 'em.'

Not reassuring. And if that's so, how the hell did Mario get out of jail?

She felt her panic level start to climb.

'You prosecuting a case involving a Dragon?' Bryan frowned at her. 'Probably not something you want to take on alone just yet.'

Kate shook her head. 'I was curious, is all. I saw a

dragon tattoo on an inmate at the detention center the other day and I thought it looked like something that might be gang-related.'

'You were right.' Bryan started to say something more, but then his phone rang. After a glance at the caller ID and a quick 'Sorry' to her, he picked it up. As he said 'Chen here' into the phone, she stood up to leave. He waved good-bye to her. Closing his door softly behind her, she headed toward her office.

Only to have her steps falter as she spotted Mona. Her administrative assistant was partly visible as she stood half in the hall and half inside Kate's open door, one hand on the knob, clearly talking to someone inside Kate's office.

Mona's ensemble of the day involved a neon-green long-sleeved T-shirt with a peacock-blue skirt that ended in ruffle around her ankles. She was wearing green tights and green, wooden-soled shoes with four-inch heels. A neon-green-and-peacock scarf looped around her neck tied the look together.

Sort of. Or maybe not.

Mona glanced her way just then, and her face lit up as she saw Kate. Kate distinctly heard her say 'Here she comes now' to the person waiting in her office. Accompanied by a huge smile, that bright observation filled Kate with misgivings. Then Mona stepped into the hall, and moved quickly toward her, her gaze focused on Kate, her lithe body radiating excitement, her expression ripe with news.

Defeated, Kate resumed walking her way.

'Who is it?' Kate whispered when Mona was close enough.

Widening her eyes theatrically, Mona mimed fanning herself as if she were dying of heat stroke.

'The hot cop,' she mouthed. Then, as Kate walked by her, she added in a voice meant for public consumption, 'Detective Braga is here to see you.'

Kate shot her a speaking look over her shoulder. Walking backward now, Mona grinned and gave her two thumbs up.

Then Kate reached her office.

Braga stood in front of the window, facing the door. His head was bent as if he were studying something on the floor in front of him; his hands seemed to be clasped behind his back. He looked up quickly as she entered, and she saw instantly how small her office was, because he seemed to take up so much of its available space. His left elbow brushed the ficus; his broad shoulders blocked most of the window. A quick, comprehensive glance told her that he had showered and shaved since she had seen him last – she tried not to remember that it had been that morning, leaving her house after spending the night on her couch, and that he'd glimpsed part of her ridiculous pink nightshirt on the way out – but a significant degree of stubble had reappeared, darkening his lean cheeks. His black hair was rumpled, as if he'd recently run his hands through it. His face was unreadable, although he still looked tired.

The thing was, she felt a little pang of what she

hated to recognize as gladness upon seeing him. As if he were a friend or something.

Which, as she had to keep firmly fixed in her mind, he definitely was not. Last night's sleepover notwithstanding.

19

'Hey,' Braga said in greeting. His gaze tracked Kate as she walked around behind her desk. 'Busy day?'

Her eyes narrowed at him. There was something in his demeanor . . .

'Is this a social call?' she asked, as she set her briefcase down on the floor, almost sure it wasn't. Straightening, squaring her shoulders, she looked directly at him. Standing behind her desk, her hands curling around the smooth leather back of her chair, she braced herself for whatever he was about to throw at her. 'Because if it is, I don't have the time. I have a few more things I have to do before I can leave, and I don't like to be late picking up Ben.'

'This'll only take a minute.' His hands came out from behind his back. He was holding a thin white plastic grocery bag that bulged with whatever was in it. 'I brought you something.'

'You brought me something?' *Not* what she had been expecting. Kate reached out to take the bag, mystified, glancing from it to his face just in time to catch an almost imperceptible spasm of harshness that appeared briefly around his eyes and mouth as its possession transferred from his hand to hers. *What's that about?* She frowned as she tried to make sense of the fleeting expression.

'Actually, it's for Ben.' There was absolutely no intonation whatsoever to his voice now. 'A basketball. I happened to run across one that has hands printed on it to show him the correct shooting position. I thought it might help.'

Kate peeked in the bag. There was a basketball in there, all right. Orange leather, with small magenta hands tooled into it. A training ball for beginners? Because that's what it looked like to her.

Her eyes met his.

'Thank you,' she said, and meant it. Because it was for Ben, because he'd thought of Ben and the problem her son must have told him he was having in gym, the gift touched her. She smiled at him, a slow, sweet, and charming smile of the sort that she almost never directed at anybody these days.

He nodded brusquely in response. His feet were braced slightly apart, his expression was inscrutable as he met her gaze. No trace of an answering smile. In fact, if she had to characterize the vibe she was getting, he almost seemed angry.

Okay, so much for being nice. She set the bag down beside her briefcase and looked at him again, this time minus the smile.

'Is there anything else?'

'Yeah, there is.'

Then he moved, crossing the room in two quick strides and closing the door while she watched with growing surprise. With the door closed, he came to stand in front of her desk, looking at her across it with that unreadable poker face that she was beginning to learn meant he was in full cop mode.

Uh-oh.

'What?' She glanced at him, trying not to seem nervous, although nervous was starting to feel like her middle name.

'I need you to clarify something for me. About how you shot Rodriguez. Go over that one more time for me, would you please?'

Her heart started thudding like a kettledrum. A hard knot formed in her chest. Her mouth went dry. All instant, spontaneous physical reactions that she couldn't control.

Oh, God. Could he tell? Could he see?

Get a grip, she told herself. *He's a cop, not a psychic.*

'I don't want to talk about it anymore. Talking about it upsets me.'

His lips tightened. Placing his hands flat on her desk, he leaned toward her. That put their eyes almost on a level. Sexy eyes – or at least they would have been if they hadn't been boring like lasers into hers.

'You're going to have to talk about it with somebody sooner or later. If I were you, I'd choose me. And now.'

She gripped the back of the chair hard and lifted her chin at him. As a lawyer, if there was one thing she knew, it was her rights.

'I don't have to say a word. It's my legal right not to answer your questions, or anybody else's.'

'That's right, it is. Are you exercising it?'

They both knew that an ADA such as herself refusing to answer the legitimate questions of a homicide detective investigating a case she was involved in would raise all kinds of red flags throughout the Philly legal and law-enforcement communities, including with her bosses. In short, they wouldn't like it. In shorter, it would seem suspicious, as if, perhaps, she were trying to hide something.

Go figure.

'No.' It was all she could do not to sound sulky. What good were all those constitutional protections if you couldn't use them when you needed to? 'What do you want to know?'

Like she didn't remember. Like he hadn't zeroed in on the one thing she most feared being questioned about. Like the lie she had told wasn't burned into her soul.

'How you shot Rodriguez. And I'm sorry if the question calls up painful memories.'

Kate curled her lip at him. He didn't sound sorry. He didn't look sorry. He looked tense.

Like he was waiting for her to mess up.

What, exactly, did he know? Was this about the second man in the security corridor again? Or something different?

Don't panic.

Instead, she tried to concentrate on recalling the

story she had told exactly the way she had told it. Consistency, that was the key. As an ADA, what she always looked for was somebody telling three different versions of the same event. Because sure as she found it, that somebody was telling a lie.

Deep breath. No, wait, that's too revealing. Just stay cool.

'So?' he asked.

Kate's fingers tightened on the back of the chair until her nails were digging into the leather.

'He pushed me down. I saw a gun on the floor. He dropped his gun. I grabbed the gun on the floor and jumped up and shot him. The bullet hit him right in the middle of the chest.'

Kate gave a very real shudder at the very real memory of Rodriguez being shot. She was almost positive she had the sequence of supposed events right. She even remembered claiming that the safety had been off. Was that what this was about? Had they somehow determined that the safety had really been on? If so, she could . . .

'Which hand were you holding the gun in when you fired it?'

For Kate, for a split second, everything stopped. This was an 'aha' moment if she had ever had one. It was almost as if in that instant of realization, her life passed before her eyes. *This* was what he was after. *This* was the discrepancy. Because as vividly as she had ever recalled anything in her life, she suddenly recalled that Mario had been holding the gun in his left hand when he shot Rodriguez. That Mario was left-handed. That was why she hadn't noticed the dragon curling around his right wrist in the security corridor. Because he had been using his left hand.

'My left.' She only hoped her expression hadn't changed as the awful truth had unspooled through her mind. She didn't think it had; the whole process had been too quick. But even if she was wrong, a changing expression was a hard thing to base an indictment or anything else on.

'You're right-handed, aren't you?'

Something about the surety with which he said it made her frown. Then it hit her. *Of course.* The basketball – he had handed her the bag containing the basketball. And she had taken it from him. With her right hand. Easily and automatically, because she was indeed right-handed.

He had done it deliberately, as a test.

The knowledge burst on her like fireworks exploding in the night sky.

She glared at him, pointed at the door. 'That's it. Get out.'

He straightened, clearly surprised. 'You haven't answered the question.'

'And I'm not going to. This conversation is over. And I want you to leave. Right now.'

Because she'd been touched at his gift, because she'd thought for a moment that maybe they were friends, because she had allowed herself to imagine that he cared in some small way for Ben and for her, because she'd been wrong and tricked, and it hurt worse than she had ever guessed it could. Stepping out from behind her desk, she stalked toward the door, meaning to open it for him and stand there beside it until he left. But he caught her arm as she went past, swinging her around to face him.

'You're right-handed, Kate.'

She jerked her arm free. He was very close, so close she had to look up to meet his eyes. They were dark and angry. His mouth was set in a thin, hard line. His whole expression was grim – which was fine with her.

Grim was a puny thing compared to how savage she felt.

'Keep your hands off me. Get out of my office.'

'If there's an explanation for why a right-handed woman would shoot a man with her left hand, I'd like to hear it.'

Fuming, she resumed her march toward the door, flinging her response over her shoulder. 'Then I guess I'd have to say you're shit out of luck, Detective, because I'm not answering any more of your questions.'

'Kate . . .'

Reaching the door, she flung it open and turned to face him. 'Get out!'

His face was hard. 'I'm not the only one who's going to be asking.'

'I said, *get out!*'

Mona popped out of her office, her eyes wide, her expression startled as she stared down the hall. Behind her, a couple of paralegals who'd been crossing the hall just then turned to look, too. It was only then that Kate heard she was yelling.

Don't cause a scene.

'Is something wrong?' Mona said. Braga was already moving toward the door.

'Detective Braga was just leaving.' Ice dripped from Kate's voice. Mona arrived, panting at her elbow, her wide-eyed gaze shifting to the man now practically looming over Kate.

He was so close that Kate could see the fine-grained texture of his skin. His eyes swept her face. She returned his gaze stonily.

Leaning into her, his mouth almost brushing her ear, he whispered, 'Just for the record, you're a lousy liar. Your face gives you away every time.'

Then, as she sucked in an infuriated breath, he left.

'I have to say it: That man is *fine.*' Mona was still wide-eyed as she and Kate both watched him walk away down the hall. 'I wish he was whispering in *my* ear.'

Kate quit watching Braga to glare at Mona, who flung up both hands.

'Sorry.' Mona grimaced apologetically. She cast one more regretful glance after Braga before focusing once again on Kate. 'So, what was that all about?'

'Nothing.' Mona's expression told Kate that more was definitely required. Unfortunately for Mona, that was just about all she was going to get. 'He just overstayed his welcome, is all.'

'Uh-*huh*.'

'Listen, I have work to do.' Kate retreated into her office, closing the door in Mona's curious face. Then she leaned against it and closed her eyes.

In the end, she was too shaken up to get anything done. She'd meant to call the detention center back and have someone check to see who had signed the release order on Mario. She'd meant to call a couple of key witnesses who'd been slated to appear in court at her behest tomorrow before the whole schedule got hopelessly mangled and make sure they knew the trials had been postponed. She'd meant to check over the details of a suppression hearing still on the docket for early tomorrow morning, before everything in the judicial system stopped for Judge Moran's, and, later the same day, two of the deputies' funerals. She'd meant to . . .

To hell with it. She was going home. A glance at her watch confirmed it: She wouldn't even be leaving early. It was just a few minutes before six o'clock.

For once she picked up her briefcase without bothering to check the contents – something she always did, adding and deleting files so that she had what she needed to work at home after Ben was in bed. The bag containing the basketball was on the floor behind her desk, too. She glanced at it, hesitating. Hating the fact that the reason it had been given to her still bothered her so, she picked that up, too, because if she didn't it would just be sitting there with its bad juju in the morning. Then she headed out.

Mona's door was closed, and the light in her office was off, Kate saw as she passed it, and from that she surmised that Mona had left for the day. Bryan's door was closed, but his light was still on, which meant he was still working.

As she neared the end of the hall, Kate got an unpleasant surprise.

Cindy was still seated at her desk, laughing and making big fluttering eyes at the man standing on the other side of it, who didn't see Kate approaching because he had his back to her. Lean-hipped, broad-shouldered, black-haired, tall – there was no mistaking him for anyone else.

Braga.

As she recognized him, Kate felt a swift infusion of mixed hostility and unease.

What's he still doing here?

She didn't like to think. In fact, she wasn't going to think. Whether he was flirting with Cindy or trying to pry information out of her, she just didn't care.

She was physically and emotionally exhausted. And once again scared to death.

Because Mario could be anywhere. And tonight it would be just herself and Ben, on their own.

She shouldn't have let Braga stay last night. Whatever his motives had been – and she was too tired to even try to sort out the possibilities – allowing herself to depend on somebody, even briefly, just made it that much worse when that somebody was no longer available.

You knew that. How could you have forgotten?

It was just that she had gotten used to not being scared.

With a quick, silent wave for Cindy – she was too mature to glare at Braga's back – Kate hung a sharp left toward the elevator banks, where about a dozen assorted employees waited. She joined them, responding as needed to greetings and comments without ever really registering what was being said. With luck, she calculated, Braga would never even look around.

Unfortunately, luck didn't seem to be on her side.

'Feel like talking yet?' A moment later, Braga had sidled up behind her, asking the question in a quiet voice that she was pretty sure only she could hear. With her back firmly turned to Cindy and her desk, Kate had been tracking the elevators' positions by watching the numbers over the doors, and never even saw him coming.

Conscious of the potentially listening ears of her sporadically chattering coworkers, Kate didn't respond. Instead, she stared fixedly at the closed elevator doors in front of her. Which, unfortunately, were brass. And reflective. So that she could see him, a little to her left and behind her. Looking at her.

Their eyes met through the brass.

She glared at him.

'Nope,' he concluded.

An elevator arrived just then. Kate and everybody else crowded on. Once again, Braga was behind her. And once again, she could see him in the brass.

Damned brass.

When the elevator reached the ground floor, Kate filed out with everyone else. Heading toward the door closest to the underground parking garage beneath the retail space next door where she had left her car, she was annoyed to find Braga right behind her.

'Go away,' she said over her shoulder as she pushed through the door, took a dozen steps across the alley between the buildings, and shoved through another door, all with Braga still following.

His reply was mild. 'My car's parked in here, too.'

Without replying, Kate walked briskly down a short stairwell into the cavernous parking garage. It was six levels deep, a vast, echoing concrete vault that smelled of gas fumes and rubber and was lit by small white lights recessed in the ceiling. The walls were solid, the corners shadowy and dark. Only people with permits were allowed to park here. *She* had a permit. She was almost sure Braga did not, but then cops seemed to be able to park just about wherever they wanted. A few people were in sight, heading along the uppermost level toward their parked cars. It looked to be about half-full, although during business hours there was usually not a spot to be had. Of course, a number of people would already have retrieved their vehicles and headed home. The sound of cars being driven up and down the spiraling ramps echoed throughout the structure. An occasional horn blared. As darkness had fallen – and it was almost full night now – the temperature had dropped. It was even colder in the garage than it was outside, and Kate shivered a little as she headed toward the nearby elevator.

'You want to talk to me, Kate.' Braga was right behind her. Of course, he would claim he was heading toward the elevator, too. 'Believe it or not, I'm on your side.'

'Oh, right.' Furiously, she jabbed the elevator button. These doors, thank God, were painted a very unreflective yellow. He might be standing beside her, but she didn't have to look at him. 'Does that work on many people? Because I have to tell you, it didn't convince me.'

The elevator arrived. It was a small, dingy metal box that smelled of things Kate preferred not to think about. As the doors cranked slowly open, she stepped inside. Braga did, too.

'Maybe you're ambidextrous,' Braga said. 'You know, I never thought of that.'

At his baiting, Kate saw red.

'Go to hell.' She turned on him, her voice fierce. 'And take your damned ball with you.'

She thrust the bag containing the ball at him. Surprised, he took it. Then she turned and stepped back through the narrow fissure in the closing doors. The opening was now way too small for him to follow – she hoped. He lunged for the elevator button. The doors closed.

Hah.

Her last glimpse of him found him jabbing at the button and looking after her in frustration.

Just to make sure he didn't catch up with her again, she turned and ran down two flights of fire stairs to the third level, where she had left her car. The place was so silent now, her footsteps echoed in her ears; the chilly gloom of all that empty concrete made her shiver. As she power-walked to her car, it occurred to her that Braga might come looking for her, but since – presumably – he had no idea where she had parked, he was unlikely to find her before she could get in her car and drive away. And if he had the gall to show up at her house later, she would order him to leave.

If she had anything to say about it, she would never speak to him again.

Still fuming, she clicked the unlock button, opened the door, chucked her briefcase into the passenger seat as she got in, then started the engine and backed out of the space. Changing direction, heading toward the ramp that led up and out, she was just noticing how very eerie and deserted the third level really was when she sensed – not saw but sensed – movement in the backseat.

Glancing compulsively over her shoulder, she almost jumped out of her skin when she saw Mario levering himself up off the floorboard.

20

Kate squeaked. It would have been a scream, but she caught herself before the full force of the shriek that instinctively burst from her lungs could get out.

'Holy shit, watch where you're going!' Mario yelped, planting his butt in the center of the backseat and bracing himself against the front passenger seat with one arm. In the tight confines of the small car, that was way too close for Kate.

Eyes flashing forward again, Kate saw that she was headed straight toward one of the fat concrete pillars that supported the structure, and corrected course just in time. The Camry swerved sharply but didn't hit anything.

Heart thudding, she took a deep, much needed breath, which she hoped he would ascribe to the close call, and hit the brakes. The car rocked to a halt inches from a line of small cars parked against the opposite wall.

'Don't stop,' he said. 'Just keep on driving and we'll get along fine.'

For a moment fear all but paralyzed her. Her breath caught. Cold sweat popped out along her hairline.

Oh my God, what should I do?

Kate did a lightning-fast mental assessment of the chances of getting away if she jumped from the car then and there and ran for it. She had not yet put on her seat belt. Still seething at Braga, she'd forgotten all about it, although she probably would have remembered before she'd reached the street. So getting out of the vehicle fast was doable. The problem was, this level of the parking garage was nearly deserted. And it was a long way to the nearest door. If Mario gave chase, he could probably catch her. The knowledge that Braga was almost certainly still somewhere in the garage provided a spurt of hope, but she didn't know that for sure, or have any idea where exactly he was. She did know that he wasn't on the third level. If she jumped from the car and ran away screaming, he might not hear her. She might not be heard, or heeded, by anyone, or help might not arrive in time. Then, if he caught her, Mario would be mad at her. And that would not be good.

Better to hang tough for now, and see how things went.

But she bitterly regretted ditching Braga in that elevator. And she kept her seat belt off.

'What the hell do you think you're doing hiding in my car?' Her voice was tough, angry, as she gently hit the accelerator again and steered away from the parked cars, heading toward the exit ramp. She gave no indication that inside she had turned into a quivering mass of Jell-O, shaking and quaking and completely spineless in reaction to his presence. She had no doubt at all that this was not a friendly visit.

Never let them see fear.

O-kay.

'Waiting for you, baby.' Mario's voice was silky-smooth. Something about it sent a cold finger of dread trailing down her spine.

Asking him how he'd gotten into her locked car was pointless. The Marios of the world never had any trouble doing things like that. Come to think of it, once upon a time she wouldn't have had any trouble doing it, either.

'What do you want?' Reaching the ramp, she turned onto it and started heading up toward the street level. Whatever happened, she figured she would have a better chance of responding to it once she was out of the garage. The white lights were brighter and more garish on the ramp. She had the sense, fueled by moving shadows and whooshing sounds above and below them, of other cars also using the ramp, but she couldn't see them. For all intents and purposes, they were alone.

'You didn't come through for me. I'm pissed.'

Okay, so he knew she'd had nothing to do with getting him out. She could feel herself starting to sweat. The Mario of old never let a wrong go without exacting some kind of payback. She doubted he'd changed much over the years.

'You're out, aren't you?'

'No thanks to you.'

'I was working on it. I told you it wasn't going to be easy.'

'Know what? You're full of shit.'

'So why are you here?'

'I got some friends I want you to meet.'

Kate remembered Mario's 'friend' who'd showed up at her house, and shuddered inwardly. Were they Black Dragons? She figured the chances were good the answer was yes. Her hands were clamped so tightly around the wheel now her knuckles showed white. Her back was so rigid it was starting to ache. The Camry's headlights flashed along the graffiti-covered concrete wall that rose straight and smooth to her right, while the car climbed the spiraling ramp at a steady pace.

What to do?

'Sorry. Bad timing. I'm busy tonight.'

'I wasn't asking.'

Mario scooted forward so that he was pressed up close to the space between the front bucket seats. He was wearing black sweatpants and a black hoodie with the Eagles logo on it, she saw with a quick glance through the rearview mirror, and had a diamond stud in his left ear. Standard punk attire for Philly. His thick legs were bent at the knees and spread wide to fit into the tight space. His arms were draped over the front bucket seats. She caught a faint odor of onions and something else – sweat, perhaps? He was big, way big for the small rear area, and his posture was intimidating. Deliberately so, Kate knew, and she tried to will herself not to let it get to her. Then she felt something tap her left shoulder and glanced toward it.

A gun. Mario was holding a big black pistol. With him being left-handed and his arm draped over the seat, the weapon was between her and the driver's-side door.

Her heart gave a great leap in her chest. The bottom dropped out of her stomach. Her mouth went dry. So much for making a quick exit from the car.

From somewhere she managed to summon the necessary bravado to keep him from guessing how much he was beginning to scare her.

She gave a faux-disbelieving little laugh. 'What, are you going to shoot me now?'

'Nah.' He rubbed the side of her neck with the barrel of the gun. Under other circumstances, with something other than a gun, it might almost have been mistaken for an affectionate gesture. As it was, it was a terrifying parody. The cold metal made her skin crawl. She tried not to let it show. 'Not unless you make me. I always did like you, Kitty-cat.'

Lucky me.

'Then get the damned gun away from me. I don't like it.'

'Yeah. No can do.' The gun stayed where it was.

So much for the direct approach.

By now the Camry had nosed its way to the surface. The parking garage attendant's hut was empty, as was usual at this time of night, curse the luck. All she had to do was pull up to the turnstile, and the automatic arm would sense the presence of a vehicle and lift.

'Head for the Vine Street Expressway,' Mario directed, as the Camry reached the turnstile.

The arm lifted, and they were through. The parking garage exited into one of the narrow, dark alleys for which Philly was infamous. Along with rats and stray cats, drunks and predators loved them. The rest of the city, not so much. As she turned, the headlights arced over windowless brick walls and a big, green industrial dumpster and clusters of battered garbage cans. The alley ran parallel to Arch Street, ending at Thirteenth. She could turn right there, drive two blocks, and then hit the on-ramp for the expressway. If she were to miss the ramp 'accidentally,' she calculated, as the Camry bumped along the alley, Thirteenth led straight through one of the seediest sections of downtown. Populated by pimps, hos, druggies, and people in search of the same, it was crowded with adult bookstores, strip clubs, and run-down bars. The out-of-town convention traffic kept the area hopping. If she were to drive that way and somehow manage to bolt from the car without getting shot, at least she'd be running down a highly populated street. Whether or not anyone would help her if Mario gave chase was debatable, though, especially if he was flashing the gun. People tended to mind their own business around Thirteenth.

Still, it was probably the best chance she was going to get. Once on the expressway, she would have no chance to jump. And she had absolutely no wish at all to find herself in some deserted area with him, or to meet his 'friends.'

'The way things are going in your life, you ought to thank your lucky stars that you have a friend like me in the prosecutor's office,' Kate tried, operating on the hope that letting him think she was prepared to help him next time he got into trouble was the best way to keep him in line.

Mario snorted. 'Thing is, you were going to screw me over. I don't trust you no more.'

'I was not going to screw you over.'

'Don't matter anymore, does it? I'm out.'

'You got a place to stay? A family, maybe?' She was trying to pretend to be his friend, because at the moment the 'old friend' card was the only one she had to play. The gun on her shoulder wasn't pointed at her, but still its presence was making her sweat.

'I got people who take care of me, just like I take care of them.'

The Black Dragons? The question was on the tip of her tongue, but she swallowed it. Best not to let on that she knew anything about that.

She thought about telling him about Ben, that she was already late to pick up her son, that he was only nine, with no other family in the world, but she didn't. She knew Mario wouldn't care. And although he was aware of Ben's existence, she didn't want to bring any unnecessary attention to her son's presence in her life.

'You in touch with any of the old group? Jason, or Leah, or anybody?'

He laughed. 'Don't you know, baby? They're dead. All of 'em. Car crash, about three months after you left us. I probably would've been with them, except I was in jail at the time.' He leaned closer. 'And just for the record, it was your boyfriend who shot that security guard, not me.'

Liar. It was never Jason; it was you. Kate screamed the words at him in her mind as she reeled inwardly at the news. All of them – her friends, Jason with the blue eyes – dead.

What kind of terrible world was it when she and Mario were the only ones left?

'Turn right up here at Thirteenth. And don't miss the expressway turnoff. I won't like that.'

He tapped her cheek admonishingly with the gun barrel.

Kate's gut clenched. She hadn't realized how tense her facial muscles were until she tried to speak.

'I don't like *that*,' she snapped. 'Keep your damned gun out of my face.'

He chuckled.

They reached the end of the alley and she stopped to look both ways before merging onto Thirteenth. Brightly lit and busy, with heavy traffic moving steadily in both directions and a fair number of pedestrians on the sidewalks, this next block and a half or so before the freeway entrance was probably her best chance of escape. The gun on her shoulder was the biggest obstacle.

Would he shoot her if she tried to open the door and run? She wasn't sure, but she didn't really want to find out. Dead was dead, no do-overs allowed. Besides, if he was quick enough when she reached for the door handle, he might just be able to grab her and keep her in the car that way. He was close enough, so close that she could feel the heat of his arm behind her head and smell the oniony odor of his breath.

'You got any money?' Mario asked. 'I bet prosecutors make a lot of money.'

'Not much.'

She had exactly six dollars tucked away in her briefcase, which, as a result of her sudden stop after discovering Mario in the car, now rested on its side in the passenger-seat footwell. Since she got paid Monday, that six dollars had to carry them through. It was just enough for the fresh milk and bread they needed, and Ben's lunch money.

Headlights shining in the alley behind them caught her attention as she turned right onto Thirteenth, carefully wedging in between a white pickup in front and a small red car behind. Glancing back, she saw a black Taurus waiting in the mouth of the alley for its chance to join the stream of traffic, and her heart skipped a beat.

She was almost positive that was Braga's car.

'How much?' Mario growled.

Kate did a lightning calculation. If that was indeed Braga, and she thought it was, jumping from the car and running toward him was her best hope of escape. But getting the gun out of the way would greatly increase her chance of escaping uninjured.

Go for it.

At the thought, her heart began to pound so hard it felt like it was trying to beat its way out of her chest. Cold sweat poured over her. She flicked a quick look at Mario through the rearview mirror, praying he wouldn't notice. He squatted there on the edge of her backseat like a malevolent Buddha, looking pleased with himself and the situation, observing the scene out the windshield with transparent interest. The gun rested negligently on her shoulder.

He thinks he's got me trapped.

'A hundred bucks,' she lied. 'Give or take a couple of dollars.' Then she glanced down at her briefcase as she braked gently, one of a dozen or so cars braking for the red light at the intersection before the one leading to the expressway ramp. Now, while the light was red and the car was stopped, was the best chance she was going to get, she knew. 'It's in my briefcase. Why?'

''Cause I want it.' Mario looked down at her briefcase, then shifted himself, reaching between the seats, reaching for the briefcase.

The gun moved when he did. Suddenly, it was no longer there.

Kate's heart lurched. Her breath caught.

This is it.

Grabbing the door handle, she shoved the door open, throwing herself from the car with such force that she landed hard on her hands and knees on the pavement. It hurt, but she didn't have time to think about it.

'Shit,' Mario yelled as the car lurched forward.

Adrenaline shot through her system as she caught a terrifying glimpse of him snapping upright and turning toward her, but she didn't stick around to watch. She was already scrambling to her feet, already running screaming down the center line between the stopped rows of traffic. Her heart pounded like a jackhammer. Her shoulder blades tensed in horrible anticipation of a bullet smacking into her flesh at any second. Her stomach cramped as she glanced fearfully back over her shoulder. The driver's door was still open, but the Camry wasn't moving. No sign of Mario – or the gun. Around her, the street pulsed with life, with brightly colored neon signs flashing slogans like *Girls! Girls! Girls!* and *Fully Nude*. Adult bookstores with their big front windows blocked by newspapers glowed from within like jack-o'-lanterns. Seedy locals and business-men in suits and tourists – even women – in casual clothes mingled on the sidewalks and hurried through the crosswalk in front of the stopped cars while hookers, obvious in leather miniskirts and thigh-high boots or bra tops and hot pants or tiny, shiny dresses, claimed the corners and curbs. Music blared from the bars through the open doors as patrons continually went in and out. The air smelled of car exhaust and booze. A few heads turned in her direction. One or two car doors opened, and the men driving popped their heads up, yelling something to her, presumably asking questions or offering help, but Kate was barely aware of them. Her entire focus was on the black Taurus that was maybe six cars back.

Even as she reached its front bumper, the driver's door opened and Tom jumped out, drawing his gun as he moved.

'Kate!'

'Tom! Tom, help!'

He yelled something else, a question, she thought, at her as he raced for her and she bolted toward him, but her pulse was thundering so she couldn't understand what he was saying. She reached him at last, running straight into his arms. Gun and all, they closed around her, catching her up against him, holding her tightly.

Oh, God, I'm safe.

Clinging, burrowing her face into the velvety smoothness of his coat, breathing in the warm, Downy-tinged scent of him as she gasped for air, she was aware that he was cursing and asking her what had happened all in the same breath, but she was too shaken to hear properly or reply. Then the light must have changed, because suddenly all around them everyone was back in their vehicles and traffic began to move and the cars behind the Taurus began to honk their horns impatiently as they started trying to cut around the stopped car.

With a quick glance over her shoulder, Kate could see that her Camry was gone with the rest of the traffic ahead of them.

Mario stole my car. That was her first, instinctive reaction. Then, *I made it. I got out.*

Thinking of what might have been, she shuddered convulsively from head to toe.

'Damn it to hell and back anyway.' Holstering his gun, wrapping his arm tightly around her, Tom hustled her around to the passenger seat of the Taurus and bundled her inside. Then he loped around the front of the car again and slid back behind the wheel, flashing his badge at an irate motorist who made an obscene gesture out the window at him as he drove past. The motorist yanked his arm back inside and sped off.

Heart racing, still breathing way too fast, Kate lay back against the plush leather seat in a boneless bundle of nerves as Tom put the Taurus into gear and drove off. Her face was turned toward him. He glanced her way, his eyes narrowed and dark in the uncertain light.

'What just happened here?' His voice was sharp. His face was tense as his gaze slid over her. 'Holy mother of God, were you just carjacked?'

She was going to have to lie to him again. The thought made her sick to her stomach. The temptation to tell him the truth and let the chips fall where they may was almost overwhelming. But if she did, she would lose everything. For Ben's sake, she had to be strong, had to think fast, had to come up with one more halfway plausible lie. She couldn't tell him about Mario. But if she left out the identity of the man in the car . . .

If you're going to lie, stick as close to the truth as possible.

'There was a man in the backseat when I got in my car.' Her voice was unsteady. 'He had a gun.'

She couldn't help it. She shivered at the memory.

The curses that fell from Tom's mouth then turned the air blue. Kate watched the clean lines of his face tighten, watched his lips thin and the set of his jaw grow grim.

'Did he hurt you?' he asked as he pulled the Taurus over to the curb and shoved its transmission into park. His eyes raked her, as if he were searching for some visible sign of injury. The entrance to the Vine Street Expressway was yards away, and traffic was rushing onto it. She wondered if her Camry was on that expressway, speeding away.

She hoped it was speeding away.

'No.' She shook her head.

'Anybody you know? The guy from last night, maybe?'

She saw that he had his cell phone in his hand and was punching numbers into it. Clearly, the reason he had pulled over was to report her car stolen, along with the circumstances surrounding the theft. She couldn't ask him not to; he would immediately become suspicious. She was just going to have to deal.

And lie, lie, lie.

He was already talking to somebody on the phone. When he asked, she gave him the license plate number and a (slightly wrong, although she had to be careful not to be too wrong in case they actually caught Mario) description of the perpetrator, while claiming she hadn't really gotten all that good a look at him, thanks to the dark, shock, etc. All the while, she prayed that Mario wouldn't be caught, because if he was caught, he might talk. Although if he told the police about Baltimore, at least she would no longer have to lie and the hold he had on her would be broken forever.

If it wasn't for Ben, she thought, she would almost be glad of it.

'They're putting out an APB on your car. Somebody'll come by your house later to take your statement,' Tom said when he was finished. They were still parked beside the curb on Thirteenth Street, with traffic, both vehicular and pedestrian, flowing past in a steady stream. A pink-and-green neon palm tree advertising the Oasis Bar flashed changing rectangles of color over the black dashboard. The headlights of oncoming traffic plus the streetlights that stood on every corner made it easy to see him. He was staring out through the windshield, frowning thoughtfully. Then his eyes cut toward her.

Kate braced herself.

'Put on your seat belt' was all he said. As she complied, he restarted the car and pulled out into traffic. 'Where to?'

'I have to pick up Ben.' She gave him the address.

He nodded. She borrowed his phone to call Suzy and explain about being late, without telling her precisely what had happened, because she didn't want Ben finding out and worrying before she could tell him herself. When she disconnected, they drove in silence for a while. After they crossed the bridge over the Delaware, Philly's glittering skyline gradually receded into the distance. Traffic thinned out and speeded up, and except for the occasional slash of oncoming headlights cutting through the Taurus's interior and the *swoosh* of wheels on pavement, the ride was quiet and dark. Having almost recovered her composure, Kate looked out to see a bone-white moon rising over the jagged line of rooftops to the east. Its roundness was reflected in the black waters of the river that ran alongside the expressway. The scene was beautiful, she thought – and cold.

Almost as cold as she felt. Wrapping her arms over her chest, she glanced at Tom.

Big mistake.

'So, you still hell-bent on stonewalling me?' he asked. They weren't too far from the West Oak exit, the one she took to get Ben. His tone made it almost a throwaway question, no tension behind it at all. But as Kate looked closer, she saw that his jaw was tight and his mouth was thin.

'I don't know what you mea—' she began, but he cut her off with an impatient sound.

'Let's see: A right-handed woman uses her left hand to shoot and kill a vicious punk with a rap sheet as long as my arm. Then she's harassed at home by another punk who just happens to know her and her kid's names. Later that same night, a man – Same punk? Different punk? Who the hell knows? Because it seems to be open season on this woman – tries to break into her house. The following night, an armed man is hiding in her car when she gets into it, and she barely manages to escape.' He slanted a hard-eyed look at her. 'So, what do you think, counselor, in your professional opinion? Is our girl having a run of really shitty luck, or is she involved up to her pretty neck in something she's not coming clean about?'

By the time he finished, Kate was glaring at him.

'You know what? I don't appreciate your attitude.'

'Well, gee, isn't that just the biggest coincidence? Because I don't appreciate being jerked around.'

'You know what else I don't appreciate? You trying to trick me. Why didn't you just ask me outright whether or not I'm right-handed? Instead of pretending that you had a gift for Ben so I would reach for it?' That still stung.

A beat passed. 'I did have a gift for Ben. The basketball is a gift.'

Kate snorted. 'Which you got for him so you could give it to me so I would reach for it.'

'I got it for him so he'd have a decent shot at learning the game of basketball. Handing it to you – okay, maybe I had an ulterior motive in the way I handed it to you.'

'Maybe?' Scorn dripped from the word. But at the idea that the gift itself possibly wasn't part of the trick, she felt a little better. *If* she believed that part of it, which, thinking about it, she guessed she kind of did. After all, he could have handed her anything.

'Get off here,' she added, because West Oak was the next exit.

He pulled into the right lane. The exit was just ahead.

'You want to talk about ulterior motives, seems to me like you might have an ulterior motive in the way you just changed the subject,' he said, as he guided the Taurus off the expressway and around the dark, curving ramp. 'Like dodging giving me any kind of explanation for the run of bad luck I mentioned.'

'Okay.' Her voice was tart. 'You want an explanation? I'll give you the best one I have: Did it ever occur to you that maybe, just maybe, all the publicity I've gotten since I managed to survive being taken hostage has brought these creeps out of the woodwork? That they're homing in on me right now because I'm on TV all the time? And that maybe the reason a right-handed woman – and yes, I admit it, I am right-handed, you've got me there – shot a man with her left hand was because I grabbed the gun with my left hand as I was scrambling to my feet and didn't have time to switch it to my right hand before I fired it to save my life?'

Her words hung in the air between them as they reached the bottom of the ramp and he stopped, looked both ways, and then pulled out onto West Oak. She got the feeling that he was weighing them, testing them, going over them again in his mind.

'That's your story?'

She bristled. 'No, that's not my story. That's what happened.' She glanced out at the passing streets, which were lit only by the moon and the illuminated windows of houses in this residential area. 'You want to turn right up here at Pine.'

They reached Pine, and he complied. 'So you think this guy who was hiding in your car targeted you because you've been on TV?'

The skepticism in his voice was too much. She was lying, he suspected she was lying, and she knew it, and the thing was, she didn't want to lie anymore. She hated telling lie upon lie, especially – and she hated facing this, too – to him. But she could not tell the truth.

'I don't know.' Her voice wobbled with the helplessness she was feeling, and ironically, that made it more convincing. Lying was the only option she had, but she didn't have to like it. 'I don't know, okay? All I know is he was in my car, and he had a gun, and I think he would have hurt me – or worse – if I hadn't gotten away.'

Something, either her obvious emotion or the thought of what might have happened to her had she not managed to escape, shut him up.

Kate took a deep breath, trying to get herself under control, and glanced around. They were just about half a block from their destination. The yards were bigger here where the Perrys lived, and the houses were farther apart. Consequently, it was much darker. Shiny black bags full of leaves were piled beside the road, waiting for city services to come and pick them up, and a few stray leaves blew across the pavement in front of the car like small golden magic carpets caught in the headlights. The Perrys' rambling ranch house was set far back on its lot, and she could see it as they approached. Big trees dotted the yard, most of them nearly leafless now, although a couple of sturdy evergreens did a good job of providing privacy from the street. Kate caught just a glimpse of light spilling from the windows.

Her heart ached at the thought of Ben innocently waiting for her inside. He had no idea of the jeopardy they were both in.

Whatever it took, she had to handle this, for Ben's sake.

'Next driveway,' she said.

'You know, there's just one problem.' He pulled into the long, unpaved driveway that led back to the Perrys' house. Gravel crunched beneath the wheels as he drove toward the house. 'None of what you said explains why you've been scared to death ever since I first walked into your office. The hostage situation had been resolved by then. You were safe. But you were still scared. You *are* still scared.'

She wanted to tell him the truth then. She really did. But she couldn't, and because she couldn't, she had to play the game as if her lies were the truth.

'If I said you were wrong, you wouldn't believe me, so what's the point?'

The car was even with the walkway that led into the house now, although a fat pine tree kept the front door and most of the front of the house except for the garage, which was directly ahead of them, hidden from view. He braked, and the car stopped.

'I'm not wrong.'

'See?' She gave a brittle little laugh. 'Listen, I appreciate all your help, but I wish you'd leave now. I'll get one of the Perrys to give Ben and me a lift home.'

Putting the transmission in park, he turned off the ignition. The headlights shut off automatically. The interior of the car went as dark as the night outside, but she could see the hard outline of his forehead and cheek and chin, and the gleam of his eyes as he turned to look at her.

'You don't want me to leave.' There was cool certainty in his voice. 'I think you're forgetting something. The guy who took your car has your keys. I assume your house key was on the same key ring?'

Kate sucked in air. She hadn't thought of that. Now Mario and company wouldn't even have to break in.

'I'll drive you two home, and I'll sleep on the couch again. Tomorrow, you can have the locks changed, and get a damned security system put in.' His voice hardened. 'After that, you're on your own.'

Kate wanted to refuse, wanted to send him away, wanted to say something like *No way in hell,* but she couldn't. The idea that Mario could now walk in on them at will was absolutely terrifying.

'Fine,' she snapped, and opened her door and got out of the car. It was cold and dark there in the lee of the big evergreen, and the air smelled of pine and wood smoke. Walking quickly around the hood, she was surprised when he got out, too. Before his door shut all the way and the interior light went out again, she saw that he was coming toward her. She could hear the quick crunch of his footsteps on the gravel, see the dark outline of him against the background of light-limned trees.

'You don't have to come in with me,' she said when they converged in front of the Taurus's bumper. He stopped, and she kept on going, meaning to walk past him. 'In fact, I'd rather you didn't. I don't want to have to explain you to Suzy.'

'I just want you to answer one question for me, and you notice I'm asking it outright.' He caught her upper arm when she would have dodged around him. His hold wasn't tight, and it would be easy to break free if she wanted to. But she didn't. She stopped. He was close, standing right in front of her, a solid barrier between her and the sidewalk, and she had to look up to see his face.

'What?'

'Did you have anything to do with planning or helping in that escape attempt?'

Her eyes widened. 'No! I knew you were thinking something like that. I didn't. I swear it.'

'That's what I needed to hear,' he said.

Then his free hand slid around the back of her neck and he bent his head and kissed her.

21

His lips were warm and firm and dry, and as soon as he touched them to hers, she went weak at the knees. When his tongue slid between her lips she felt dizzy. It had nothing to do with him, personally, she assured herself even as her lips parted beneath his and she pressed herself up against his hard body and wrapped her arms around his neck and kissed him back. It was simply that it had been years – since before Ben's birth, actually – since she'd been kissed, years since she'd been with a man, and her body was overreacting.

The pounding of her heart, the racing of her pulse, the quickening of her breathing were simply instinctive reactions. The woman in her responding to the man in him. Nothing personal at all.

At least, that's what she told herself as his mouth slanted over hers and his arms came around her, hard and strong, and his hands splayed over her back, pressing her even closer against him.

She closed her eyes. The inside of his mouth was wet and hot and tasted faintly of coffee, and he was kissing her so expertly and so thoroughly now that she caught fire with the thrill of it.

And she kissed him back some more, with all the pent-up longing of a dieter confronted with a chocolate buffet.

Loving the taste of him. Loving the heat of him. Loving the feel of him.

Her fingers threaded through the crisp curls at his nape, savoring their texture. She rose on tiptoe, or he pulled her up on tiptoe, she couldn't be sure which, and she strained against him, dazzled by the hot prickle of her nipples as they tightened against the firm muscles of his chest, enthralled by the hard bulge that was proof positive that he was as turned on as she was, intoxicated by the urgent quickening of her body, by the fierce demand of his.

'Jesus,' he whispered, as his mouth left hers to trace a fiery trail across her cheek to the hollow beneath her ear. He was breathing hard. She could feel the rapid rise and fall of his chest against her breasts. His arms were so tight around her that she couldn't have broken away if she'd wanted to.

Which she didn't. Not in a million years.

'Tom.' Kate shivered as her head fell back against his shoulder, allowing him access to the tender column of her throat. His mouth crawled toward her collarbone in a chain of tiny, seductive kisses. His lips burned her skin; she could feel the rasp of stubble against the underside of her jaw, and she felt soft and shivery inside.

I love this, she thought hazily, and then his lips were on hers again and she quit thinking altogether. Totally swept away, she tightened her arms around his neck and pressed herself against him until she could feel every hard plane and long bone and flexing muscle, and kissed him back.

Hungrily. Fervently. Feverishly.

'Kate, is that you?'

The voice, calling from some little distance away, blasted them apart like a bomb. Kate jumped a foot in the air, and when she came down, Tom's arms were no longer wrapped around her. Suzy – it had been her voice, Kate recognized now that some of the heat was leaving her brain – stood on her small front porch, peering around the fat evergreen at them.

Kate hadn't even heard Suzy opening the front door.

'Yes, it's me,' she called back, aware that her heart was still thudding and her toes were curling in her shoes. 'I'm just on my way in.'

A quick glance around confirmed that where they stood was deep in shadow. She didn't think Suzy could have seen a thing. But still she couldn't keep her face from heating as she glanced self-consciously at Tom.

He turned his head to look at her. It was too dark to read his expression, but she could just see the hot gleam of his eyes. There was tension in his stance. They were no longer touching, but electricity still hung in the air between them. Its presence was an almost palpable thing.

Suzy be damned. Kate wanted to walk right back into his arms.

'I'll wait in the car for you,' he said, and turned away.

She took a deep breath and tried her best to push the last mind-blowing couple of minutes out of her mind. Suzy still waited on the porch. Now was not the time.

I'll think this through later, she promised herself, and started walking toward the house.

She wasn't gone five minutes. But that was long enough for Tom to get himself back under control. By the time Ben came trudging down the sidewalk toward him, dragging a backpack behind him like a dog on a leash, Tom had finished kicking himself and had his game face on. It was the adrenaline rush he was operating on that had caused him to go off the rails like that, he concluded. Frustration at the runaround she was giving him and fear for her safety had combined with lack of sleep and an overdose of caffeine and everything else that was going on to juice him up until he'd exploded in that debacle of a kiss. Even before he'd gone by her office, he'd already had a hell of an afternoon. Those two charred corpses in the burned-out U-Haul both had criminal records, were known associates of Rodriguez and Soto, and were almost certainly the guys they'd been seeking. Now they were dead, killed with one neat bullet hole between the eyes each before the U-Haul was set on fire. Which meant someone had killed them. Someone who was still on the streets. Someone else involved in the escape? Maybe. It was always a mistake to assume, though. The guy who had stolen Kate's car? Another maybe, but the connection seemed thin. Still, those blackened corpses had been the first thing he'd thought of when she had told him what had happened to her. Seeing her running toward him between those parked cars looking as terrified as if the devil himself were after her, and then hearing what she had narrowly escaped from, had shaved years off his life. It had awoken his protective instincts. He wouldn't like it if she was to get hurt. He would, in fact, take it personally.

And that was bad.

It meant his emotions were involved. He never let himself get emotionally involved with women anymore. Physically, yes. He was always up for a good time, and he made sure his partners had fun, too. But he also made it clear that a relationship wasn't going to happen. When fun time was over, he was going to walk away.

For the first time in forever, walking away wasn't going to be so easy.

Was she in danger? Or was she dangerous? Or both? That's what he was trying to decide. Any way it worked out, as a cop he had good reason to keep close tabs on her. But keeping close tabs on her wasn't really what he was doing. At least, it wasn't all he was doing.

This thing – it wasn't a relationship – with Kate had snuck up on him and bitten him in the ass. He'd thought some about getting her in the sack, yes; but, given the circumstances, he had firmly rejected making any moves in that direction. She might turn him on, but he wasn't stupid. Or at least he'd thought he wasn't. Now it seemed like maybe he was after all.

As someone 'under the umbrella of suspicion,' as the media types in the department would no doubt put it, she should have been strictly off-limits. So she'd said no when he'd asked her if she'd been involved in the escape attempt. What had he expected her to do, confess?

And yet, he believed her – about that.

Which was still no excuse for kissing her. Kissing her was just about the stupidest thing he could have done.

He'd done it on impulse, a quick compulsion he hadn't been disciplined enough to control. The instant his mouth had touched hers he'd gone up in flames. The thing was, she'd been hot for him, too. In fact, she had kissed him back like she was dying to take him to bed. He had it tamped way down now, but he could still feel the hungry heat she'd ignited pulsing through his body. It wouldn't take much to set it off again.

What he should do is give up, give in, and get it over with. Woo the woman. Sleep with her and get her out of his system. It could be just as simple as that.

Or maybe not. Maybe she was playing him. Maybe she could tell how hot he was for her, and was hoping to use the power it gave her to get him on her side.

Despite her denials, he didn't trust her, but that didn't stop him from thinking about her much more than he should. Her evasiveness aggravated the hell out of him, but she still managed to rock his world with her smile. Lately he had pretty much wanted to shake her and kiss her at the same time. One thing was for sure: What was happening between them was a surprise. Never in this life would he have expected to feel this way about her.

Like they were involved somehow. Like there was a connection between them. Like she had become his responsibility.

Hell, he even liked her damned little kid.

Who was opening the rear door and sliding into the car behind him even as he had the thought.

'Hi,' Ben said as the interior light came on. 'Are you here because my mom's car got stolen?'

Tom glanced at him through the rearview mirror. 'Yeah.'

Ben shoved his backpack over and closed the door. 'So, what really happened with that?'

It was such an adult question, uttered in such an adult tone, that Tom slewed around in the seat to look at him. Blue eyes regarded him unblinkingly from beneath fans of thick, dark lashes. Jeez, the kid looked like Kate.

'You need to ask your mom that.'

Ben grimaced. 'She won't tell me. She always tries to protect me from stuff she thinks I'm too young to know.'

Tom was at a loss. 'Well, that's what moms do.'

The passenger-side door opened just then and the interior light, which had just started to fade, brightened as Kate slid in. Her cheeks were rosy, he saw, and her lips were rosy, too, and fuller than usual. The swift little glance she sent him as she settled in was almost furtive, almost shy, and it ignited all that tamped-down heat inside him so that just as quick as that he burned for her again.

Only this time it didn't feel good.

As the interior light faded again and Kate said something to Ben, Tom gritted his teeth against his own impulses and started the car.

She didn't want to like him.

That was the thought that popped into her mind as she watched him with her son.

After Kate walked to the front door with the officers who had come to take the report on her stolen car, after the police yelled good-bye to Tom and got into their car and drove away, she continued to stand in the open doorway, her attention caught by the tableau at the top of her driveway. Ben and Tom were playing basketball in the fuzzy glow cast by the light over the garage, and the sight of the tall, dark, athletic man, still in his work clothes, grinning at her small, blond son as he passed the ball to him disturbed her in a way she couldn't quite put her finger on. The sound of the bouncing ball was muted only slightly by the rustle of wind in the leaves and the creaking of the branches of the big oak. It was full night now, gusty, and starting to get cold. The moon was hidden behind a blowing bank of clouds, which made anything beyond that yellow circle of light difficult to see. The darkness made her jittery, because she knew Mario was out there in it somewhere, and he wasn't done with her. She would have worried about Mario or his friends showing up tonight, but Tom was there, and she had not a doubt in the world that as a consequence she and Ben were perfectly safe. Tired and worried as she was, she was caught by the sight of her son's easy interaction with this man who seemed to be assuming outsize importance in both their lives, and so she continued to stand there in the open doorway with her gaze on the pair of them. As she did, Ben took a shot, missed, and Tom caught the rebound. Then he demonstrated for Ben the correct stance, showing him how to hold the ball – they were using the beginner ball, Kate saw – and stepping back out of the way. Ben shot – and made it. As Ben ran to retrieve the ball, Tom applauded. And Kate saw Ben grin, and watched his face flush with pride.

Unnoticed by either of them, Kate smiled.

The little glow from seeing Ben's pleasure radiated throughout her body like warmth from the sun. It was the most relaxed and at peace she had felt in days.

Because Ben was happy, she was happy.

And she knew: The way to her heart was through her son.

It was a sneaky wormhole in the defenses she'd

established over the years. Until now, because she'd taken care not to become involved with anyone, because she hadn't let a man get close enough to even begin to break into the small circle that was her and Ben, she hadn't realized it was there.

Letting herself fall for Tom Braga would be just about the stupidest thing she could possibly do. Even if she wasn't doing a high-wire act with the truth, even if her past wasn't a ticking time bomb that threatened to blow her life apart at any moment, even if he wasn't a cop sniffing around all the lies she was telling like a bloodhound on a scent, her plate was full. She had Ben to raise. A career to ace. And no room in her life for anything – or anyone – else.

She didn't want a man.

Even if she was still shaky inside from the after-effects of that toe-curling kiss.

Which, if she could help it, she wasn't going to think about ever again.

And just supposing she was softheaded enough to want this particular man, one of the reasons she didn't date hadn't changed a bit: She didn't want Ben getting attached to someone who was just going to disappear from his life.

Men left. She knew that.

But Ben didn't. And one lesson she'd rather he didn't learn was how much it hurt to be left by somebody you'd learned to love.

Ben was shooting again while Tom made a (less-than-all-out, she was sure) try at stopping him.

Kate didn't even watch to see if the ball went in.

Squaring her shoulders, no longer smiling, she turned back into the house.

'Ben,' she called over her shoulder in her best no-nonsense voice. 'Homework.'

The bouncing sound of the ball followed her inside. 'Mo-*om*.'

'Now,' she said, unmoved by the protest, and headed for the kitchen.

Ben came in a few minutes later, flushed and perspiring, the new ball clutched in his hands. Having shed her blazer earlier, Kate sat at the table in her blue shirt and black slacks, going through his backpack, pulling out notebooks and textbooks and crumpled bits of paper, trying to make sense of it all. She was tired and upset, unnerved by the certainty that Mario wouldn't just forget about her, shaken by her reaction to the man she could hear walking around her living room, but school and homework were nonnegotiable facts of life with Ben. She had pulled down the cheap roll-up shades that had come with the house – which, since the kitchen opened only onto the backyard, she had never bothered to use before – so that no hint of the night outside was visible. The room was a bright, cozy, slightly untidy cocoon, with the lingering scent of the carryout pizza Tom had insisted on grabbing on the way home for dinner still hanging in the air.

'You forgot your planner,' she said, looking up at her son. The teacher required them to keep a planner in which they recorded all their assignments. In theory, it was a good idea. In practice, Ben tended to either forget it or forget to write anything down in it.

'I know what I have to do.' His tone was more resigned than sulky. 'Trust me.' Then his voice brightened. 'Look what Tom gave me.'

He held up the ball for her inspection. He looked bright-eyed and pink-cheeked and, yes, happy. Despite her numerous and varied misgivings – Ben sounded frighteningly comfortable calling this near stranger 'Tom' – she found she couldn't bring herself to rain on her child's parade.

'Wow,' she said, and smiled at him. Out of force of habit and because she couldn't help herself, she added, 'Did you say "Thank you"?'

'Yeah.' From his tone, he might as well have added *duh*. 'I think it's really helping.'

'That's good.' Okay, despite any possible ulterior motives on Tom's part, she found that she was really, really glad he had given Ben the ball. 'Think you could put it down now so we could get this homework out of the way?'

'I hate homework.' But Ben obediently put the ball down on the counter and came and sat at the table, pulling his math notebook toward him. Sighing, he opened the notebook, picked up a pencil, and looked up at her with a frown. 'What are we going to do without a car?'

She had told him only that her car had been stolen, without mentioning that she had been in it at the time, so he found the whole thing more exciting than anything else. It was possible that he was really concerned about how they were going to get around, but Kate liked to think she recognized a delaying tactic when she came eyeball to eyeball with one.

'The insurance company is getting me a loaner tomorrow. Do your math.'

'I hate math.'

'I know. Do it anyway.'

The whole time they were doing homework – and it took almost an hour, right up until Ben's scheduled nine P.M. bedtime – Kate was conscious that the two of them were not alone. The house felt smaller with Tom in it, even though he stayed in the living room, out of their way. But she could hear him moving around, hear him flipping through channels before settling on some sports program that neither she nor Ben would ever watch, hear him making calls on his cell phone. They weren't particularly intrusive sounds – even the volume on the TV was turned low – but they unsettled her in some vague way.

When Ben finally finished, he hopped up and started for the living room.

Eagerly.

'Bedtime.' Kate rose, too, and followed him, her chest tightening at the idea of seeing Tom. Since that kiss, she felt wary of him in an all new kind of way.

'Can't I stay up just a little bit later? Since Tom's here?'

'Nope.'

They reached the entrance to the living room with

Ben a couple of steps in the lead. Tom sat sprawled on the couch, his head resting back against the upholstery, his stockinged feet on her coffee table, the remote in one hand, looking totally at home. He'd shed his jacket, shoulder holster, and tie, which left him in his white shirt and black pants. The shirt was unbuttoned at the throat, and he'd rolled up the sleeves.

He looked scruffy, tired, and so handsome anyway that, had Kate been in the mood to be at all romantically receptive, she would have caught her breath.

But she wasn't. Because when she and Ben walked into the room, Tom turned his head, looked up at them, and smiled, a lazy, engaging smile that warmed his eyes and caused her stomach to tighten.

'All done?' he asked.

And it was then that it struck her: She knew why having him in the house unsettled her so.

It felt like they were a family.

And that was somewhere she just wasn't going to go.

22

'Yep,' Ben answered, and made a beeline for the gold chair.

'Oh, no, you don't.' Kate caught Ben's shoulder and turned him from his chosen course, propelling him instead toward the stairs. 'Say good night.'

Kate couldn't see the expression on Ben's face, but she could see Tom: He shot her son a commiserating look. In response, Ben shrugged. She was willing to bet Monday's check that her son was also rolling his eyes.

It felt like they were ganging up on her. Like the two of them, as males, had some kind of special bond.

She frowned.

''Night, Tom,' Ben said. 'Thanks for helping me out with the basketball.'

'Not a problem. Good night.'

By that time, she and Ben were at the bottom of the stairs. She went up with him, because it beat the alternative, which was staying down with Tom. She knew she was going to have to deal sooner or later with him and the whole grab bag of problems he represented, but at the moment later seemed better.

She needed to get her head together first.

'Tom's nice,' Ben told her, as they reached the top of the stairs. He looked over his shoulder at her as she followed him down the hall toward the bathroom.

'Yeah.' Kate's chest tightened. 'But you know, he's just helping us out temporarily here. Once all this mess gets straightened out, we probably won't be seeing him anymore.'

At the bathroom door, Ben stopped and turned to look at her. The happy glow of a few minutes before was gone. He looked worried, and suddenly far older than his nine years, as he met her gaze. 'Is somebody trying to hurt you, Mom?'

'No! Of course not.' Ben knew her really, really well, so she didn't know why she was so surprised he had picked up on her anxiety. But her job was to protect him, not the other way around, and there was no way she was laying even so much as a hint of this on him. 'Why would you even ask that?'

'Because a lot of bad stuff's been happening to you lately. And Tom's a cop, and this is the second night in a row he's spending the night at our house.'

Okay, she should have remembered that nothing escaped Ben.

'That's because . . . because . . .' She was groping, and coming up empty. *Think.* 'It's just a precaution. Because I got so much publicity after that stuff happened at the Justice Center. Tom's kind of just hanging around until it all dies down, which it will soon.'

Ben continued to study her face. 'I was hoping maybe he was going to be your boyfriend.'

Kate tried not to look as surprised and dismayed as she felt. She had never, since Ben had been alive, had a boyfriend. How had such a thought even entered his head?

She wasn't about to ask. One thing she'd learned in law school was to never ask a question unless you're certain you want to hear the answer.

Words to live by.

'No.' Her voice was firm. 'He's not going to be my boyfriend. He's just a nice man who's doing his job. That's all. Go take your bath.'

When he went into the bathroom and shut the door, she leaned against the wall and closed her eyes.

Until Ben just now planted the idea of Tom as her boyfriend in her head, she hadn't realized quite how alone she felt. For nine years now, her every thought and action had been centered on making a good life for Ben. Had making a good life for herself, too, gotten lost in the shuffle?

Maybe. But I did what I had to do.

By the time she had finished reading to Ben and he had fallen asleep, Kate was dead on her feet. With the loss of her briefcase and its contents, which included her laptop and phone, and, because she used it like a purse, her identification, credit cards (and good luck with those, Mario – they were totally maxed out), and various other personal items, tomorrow promised to be a very taxing day. The one positive to it was that with the best will in the world, she couldn't do any work tonight. All her files, etc., were gone with the briefcase.

So with Ben asleep and Tom on guard, she was free to do what she was dying to do: go to bed.

Only she couldn't.

Because she had to go back downstairs first and deal with the problem that was Tom.

He wasn't in the living room, although the TV and lamps were on. As Kate glanced around, she heard faint sounds from the kitchen. Holding fast to her resolution, she headed that way.

The kitchen light was off. With the shades drawn over the windows, except for the illumination spilling over from the living room, the room was as dark as a cave. For a moment she was conscious of a little niggle of fear as she glanced around and didn't see him anywhere. Could something have happened? Could he have gone outside for some reason, or could Mario and company possibly have broken in and overpowered him? Freezing at the thought, she was just about to retreat when he said *damn* very distinctly from somewhere near at hand. There was no doubt that it was Tom's voice, and, relieved of one worry at least, she advanced cautiously to discover him behind the refrigerator, wedging one of her kitchen chairs beneath the knob on the back door.

'What are you doing?' she asked, totally sidetracked by the unexpected sight.

He was still working the chair into place as he

glanced around at her. It was hard to tell in the gloom, but she could have sworn he looked a little embarrassed at being discovered.

'Taking precautions.'

She had to smile. All her illusions about her big, bad cop protector were in danger of crashing and burning on the spot.

'If you weren't here, that's just exactly what I would have done. Only I would have figured it was pretty useless.' She leaned a hip against the table and settled in to watch.

'And you would have been right.' With the chair apparently adjusted to his satisfaction, he left it and moved toward her. 'The thing is, somebody's got your house key, so a minute ago they could've walked right in. Now they have to break something first, and theoretically I'll hear it.'

'Smart.' Glancing around, she spied another chair beneath the knob of the door to the garage, and her smile widened into a full-fledged grin. 'Is there one against the front door, too?'

If so, she'd totally missed it, but given how tired and frazzled she was, anything was possible.

'Not yet, but there will be.'

She looked back at him to discover that he had stopped not two feet in front of her.

'Nice.' She was grinning at him like an idiot, and he was smiling back wryly. The scene was cozy and warm and, yes, damn it, happy, despite the fact that what they were talking about was barricading her house so that some really bad guys who were threatening her and possibly wanted to put some serious hurt on her couldn't get in. He was looking tall and dark and dangerous (and never mind those ridiculous chairs), and sexy as hell, and as she grinned at him her heart was beating a little faster and her blood was heating and she could feel electricity pulsing through the air between them. Then she couldn't help it: She caught herself remembering that blistering kiss.

And the whole thing scared her so badly that her stomach cramped.

No. No. No.

Her grin died like somebody had shot it. Straightening away from the table, then taking a couple of steps sideways and back because the movement had brought her closer still to him and she couldn't deal with that, she fixed him with a level look.

'What?' His eyebrows lifted at her.

'We need to talk.' Turning on her heel, she headed for the (relatively brightly lit) living room.

'Now you're starting to sound like me.'

He followed her, and when she reached the coffee table she turned around to face him again. He stood a few feet away, just over the living-room threshold, and stopped when she did. Kate met his gaze head-on. And forget about how the sizzle was still there in the air between them, and that her heart was still beating way too fast.

'First, I want to thank you for giving Ben that basketball and playing with him out there tonight.'

He shrugged. His hands were hooked in his front pockets, and his face was unreadable now. 'Not a problem. I like Ben.'

'I'm glad you said that. Because Ben likes you, too. And that's part of the problem.'

'There's a problem?'

She'd paused only for a moment to gather her thoughts, and her courage, and his response elicited no more than a brusque nod before she went on.

'Look, about what happened tonight' – okay, as soon as she said it she realized she was going to have to be more specific, because a lot of things had happened tonight – 'when we k-kissed . . .' Jesus, she was stuttering now. How pathetic was that? 'The thing is, I don't do that. I don't kiss people. I don't get involved. I don't date. I'm too busy, and . . . and it's not good for Ben.'

There. She'd gotten it out. Most of it.

'Meaning?'

'Meaning I'm really grateful you're staying here tonight, and I'm grateful you stayed here last night, and I appreciate everything else you've done, but . . . but after tonight, I don't think we should see each other anymore.'

'I didn't realize we *were* seeing each other.'

She made an impatient sound. 'You know what I mean. I don't think you should come by the house anymore. I don't want you seeing Ben. I know you have to do your job, and I'm willing to answer questions from you if and when they come up, but from here on out, I want things between us to be strictly professional. No more . . .'

Her voice broke off as she searched for the best way to put it.

'Kissing?' he suggested.

Her chin came up. 'Yes. Exactly.'

'Okay,' he said. 'You got it.'

His easy acquiescence left her without anything else to say. It also, if she was honest, rankled her just the tiniest bit. Because she had kind of liked the kissing.

No – and again with the being honest here – she had loved it.

'Okay. Good.' Feeling ridiculously uncomfortable with him now, she cast a quick glance at the couch. 'Um . . . the sheets and things you used last night are in the dryer. I'll just get them and—'

'I'll get them,' he interrupted. 'I know where the dryer is, and I can find anything else I need. Go on up to bed. Get some sleep.'

Going up to bed was exactly what she needed to do, she knew, because it would get her away from him. Especially since part of her wanted to take it all back.

'Yes, I'm going,' she said, and headed toward the stairs. She could feel his gaze on her. With one hand on the newel post, she glanced at him.

'Good night,' she said.

He simply nodded in reply.

Climbing the stairs, knowing she had done the right thing, the only thing possible under the circumstances,

Kate nevertheless was conscious of a sickening sense of loss.

Then she got angry at herself: *Idiot! How can you lose something you never even had?*

For the next two days, Philadelphia was a sea of blue. Thousands of police officers from across the Northeast lined up along the streets to pay their respects during the funeral processions for Judge Moran and the slain deputies. In addition, the citizens of Philadelphia turned out en masse. During those hours of mourning, the city came to a virtual standstill. Flags few at half-mast. Bells tolled almost continually. At the huge cathedral basilica of Saints Peter and Paul, where Judge Moran's and Deputy Russo's funeral masses were celebrated within hours of each other, televisions throughout the sanctuary showed scenes from the men's lives, while across the street in the park enormous screens were set up so that overflow crowds could watch the services. Kate attended all the funerals, usually sitting between Mona and Bryan, with both of them holding her hands tightly, although whether for their own comfort or hers Kate couldn't tell. The services were emotionally wrenching; witnessing the grief of the bereaved families was terrible, especially when Kate couldn't shake the thought that she could so easily have been among the dead, with Ben left to cry useless tears for her.

The local and national news media were also out in force. She, Bryan, Public Defender Ed Curry, and

Sally Toner, the court reporter, as the only survivors among the official personnel who had been in court that day, were besieged by cameras and microphones and shouted questions wherever they went. One enterprising CNN crew managed to capture the four of them huddled together near a service elevator as they sought to escape the relentless media scrutiny via an underground garage. The resulting images and the brief, shouted question-and-answer session that accompanied them – Curry, as a public defender, wasn't bound by the same order that had gagged the DA's office, and it was he who responded to the questions – was broadcast, presumably worldwide, much to Kate's dismay.

But there was nothing she could do about it. About any of it. Except get through it the best way she could.

She glimpsed Tom at a distance several times, always in the company of the army of police officers attending the funerals. His mouth tight, his expression somber, he looked so starkly handsome that Mona was poking her in the ribs and pointing him out (like Kate might have missed him) while she sighed over his good looks. But Mona pined alone, because Kate wasn't in the mood to sigh over them herself.

Despite the little speech she'd given him, the one he'd agreed to so readily, he ended up spending Thursday night on her couch. Why? Because, after they had delivered Ben to school Thursday morning and he had driven her on into work where, later in the day, the insurance company had arranged to drop off a rental car for her use, he had dropped a bombshell on her.

'You want to be extra-careful today.' As they had driven over the bridge into the city, Tom had glanced at her, breaking the uneasy silence that had filled the car since Ben had gotten out. 'Yesterday afternoon we found two adult male bodies in a torched U-Haul. Looks like they were supposed to be the getaway drivers Rodriguez and his pals were waiting for. Only those guys were dead long before these two were killed. Which means there's somebody else out there – *still* out there – who killed them. And given the run of bad luck you've been having lately' – here a touch of sarcasm colored his voice – 'I'd say it's not impossible that you might encounter this somebody. So take some precautions, okay? Like not walking through dark garages alone. Like not being alone, period.'

As she processed the ramifications of that, Kate's blood ran cold.

Mario.

Motive, method, and opportunity: Those were the three cornerstones of prosecuting a successful murder case. As she knew only too well, Mario had been back on the streets as of yesterday afternoon, which meant that, depending on the exact time of death, he could have had the opportunity. He'd certainly had motive, if the dead men knew he'd been party to the escape attempt. As for method, she didn't even have to think about that. When it came to violence, she was willing to believe that Mario was infinitely versatile.

But she couldn't tell Tom about Mario. Not a word, not a syllable. The risk to herself was too great.

It was then that she had a stunning epiphany: With the deaths of the others who'd been present that night, just like Mario was the only one who knew she'd been there when David Brady had been killed, she was the only one who knew the same about him. And he had been eighteen, a legal adult at the time, and despite his denial, very likely the trigger man to boot. And she also knew that he had shot Rodriguez. And had been party to the escape attempt that had left Judge Moran and the others dead.

She was even more of a danger to him than he was to her.

And he knew it. He was many things but not stupid.

If Mario was killing witnesses to his crimes, she had to be number one on his hit list.

At this, she went all light-headed.

'Why didn't you tell me this last night?' she asked when she could trust herself to speak.

'I didn't see any point in worrying you. I was there, and I knew you were safe. Today's a different story.'

Oh, yeah. Definitely. She tried to keep her physical reactions invisible, tried not to let him see the sudden need she had to breathe deeply, or the acceleration of her pulse, or the pounding of her heart.

When she didn't respond, he gave her a quick, hard look and continued.

'Look, I called in some favors with some first-rate people I know. By the time you get home tonight, your locks will be changed and you'll have a security system installed. But you know, nothing's foolproof. If there's something going on with you that's putting you in danger, you need to tell me before you – and maybe Ben with you – wind up dead.'

Oh, God. It was her worst fear, and now that he'd put it into words, she reeled inwardly at the terror it invoked. If Mario came for her, and if Ben was around, would he leave Ben alone? She didn't even have to think about it: not likely.

Should she tell Tom everything, and thereby at least make sure Ben would be physically safe?

Physically safe but with his mother in custody and his life destroyed?

Or should she try to come up with another, alternative, solution? Like abandoning her job and grabbing Ben and running for it, maybe? But she had six dollars to last till Monday – no, wait, that was gone with her briefcase; except for what was in the change jar in the house, she was broke. So wait until she got paid, and then run? That small amount of money wouldn't last long. It wouldn't be enough to find a place to live and keep them until she could get another job.

Anyway, Mario might come after her or have someone come after her. In fact, given the magnitude of what she knew about him, the odds were good that he would. He wouldn't feel safe while she lived. She would be forever scared, forever looking over her shoulder.

Forever at risk.

How about making sure Ben was kept safe while she tried to deal with Mario on her own?

Tom glanced at her again, waiting for her reply.

'I keep telling you,' Kate said. 'There's nothing.'

'You keep telling me,' Tom agreed. Like he didn't believe her. Well, she didn't have the heart to try to convince him otherwise. She was getting sick of telling lies.

They were across the bridge now, cutting through the densely populated, kitschy-for-the-tourists area that was Chinatown. Looking out at the crowded streets without really seeing anything, Kate came to a decision.

If this was a game she and Mario were playing, the rules had changed: It had just turned into winner-take-all.

And for Ben's sake, she meant to win.

The first thing she had to do was make sure nothing happened to Ben while she made further plans. Although Tom posed his own particular brand of danger to them, keeping him as their protector until she could get Ben out of harm's way was only smart.

'You know, you're scaring me to death here.' She slewed around a little in her seat to look at him. 'Do you really think Ben and I are in danger?'

He turned left onto Juniper. They were almost there. The skyscrapers formed a canyon closing them in on two sides. The iconic statue of Billy Penn that sat high atop City Hall was just visible through an opening between the buildings.

'My guess is that you know the answer to that better than I do.'

'Just for the record, your suspicious mind is getting old. But I don't want to argue with you. I . . . I have a favor to ask.'

'What?'

'Do you think you could spend the night with us again tonight?'

His lips compressed. The glance he sent her way was unreadable.

'Yeah.'

'But no . . . no . . .' Stupid as it was, she still couldn't put it into words.

'Kissing?' His mouth twisted. 'You don't have to worry, I won't touch you again. That was a mistake, anyway, which I think we both agree on. But I'll spend the night just to make sure you and Ben stay safe until we catch these guys.'

She was surprised to discover that it stung to hear him describe kissing her as a mistake. Even though it had been.

'Thanks. I appreciate it. And I appreciate you understanding that it isn't you. I just can't get involved with anyone right now.'

'Not a problem.' His voice was dry.

By the time Tom let her out in front of her office, a plan was already taking shape inside her head. The first thing to do was to make arrangements for Ben to spend Friday night at the Perrys'. The second was to tell Tom they were going out of town. Then, with her son safely out of the way and Tom no longer hovering protectively, she was going to confront Mario. It had occurred to her that Mario had her cell phone, which gave her a way to get in touch with him. She would set up a meeting at her house to supposedly talk things over, and if Mario showed up – and she felt there was a strong possibility he would, because clearly he still wanted something from her – she would shoot him and claim he was a burglar. Given the way the law was written, if he was inside her house when she pulled the trigger, she wouldn't even be charged with a crime.

Problem solved.

It was a terrible solution, and one that the respectable mother and lawyer she had become shuddered at. But now that she realized she was truly fighting for her and Ben's lives, she could feel the tough inner core of her that had helped her survive her hellacious childhood reemerging.

In this time of extremis, she was prepared to do whatever she had to do.

Which was why on Friday she was alone in the rented Civic as she pulled into her driveway. Tom thought she was picking up Ben at the Perrys' and then going on to a hotel for the night near Longwood Gardens, the former du Pont estate in the Brandywine Valley that was a huge tourist attraction this time of year. What she planned to tell him, if Mario showed up and everything went as planned, was that she had changed her mind about going, deciding instead that she just wanted to be alone for the night to decompress. Tom might have his suspicions – that was nothing new – but with Mario dead, there would be no way for him, or anyone else, to uncover anything that could hurt her or Ben.

They would be safe forever more. They could go on with their lives as if this whole nightmare had never happened.

All she had to do was kill a man first.

Despite her grim determination to see the task through, the thought made her queasy.

Yesterday, she had called her cell phone and left a message: Call me. If ever her phone fell into the hands of the police, she had devised a simple explanation for the call. She was hoping to persuade whoever answered to return her things. But when, as she had hoped, Mario had called back, she told him she wanted to talk and asked him to meet her at her house at midnight Friday. He had agreed.

Even as she had disconnected, the knowledge that she was trying to set Mario up so she could kill him made her want to vomit. But at that point, as she saw it, it was pretty much his life – or hers and Ben's.

Ben tipped the balance.

Since she had no reason to rush home after work Friday, it was almost seven by the time she stopped in her driveway. The remote to the garage had been lost along with everything else in her car, but, courtesy of Tom's connections, she had a new one, along with a whole new garage-door operating system complete with an automatic light. So far she hadn't seen the bill, and it was something that she preferred not to think about until she had to. Anyway, paying for the stuff that had been done to her house was the least of her problems at the moment.

It was full night as she pressed the button to open the garage door, but the silvery moon hanging low on the horizon kept it from being totally dark. A brisk wind blew in from the east, and the trees cast dancing shadows over the house and yard. A lamp was on in the living room – she'd deliberately left it on that morning – and the soft glow visible through the curtains should have been comforting.

It wasn't. She was too nervous.

I'm going to kill a man tonight.

Her stomach churned.

Maybe Mario won't show. It was a sneaking, hopeful thought, followed by the depressing corollary, *If he doesn't, then I'll just be living in fear until he does.*

Which was worse?

That was a question for which she had no answer. What she did have was her gun, safe on the passenger seat beside her. In case there were any surprises, like Mario jumping her unexpectedly, she meant to be ready.

But there had been no sign of him for nearly two days.

Still, her heart was thudding as the garage door finally opened all the way. Given the new locks and the new security system, it was unlikely that Mario could already be inside the house waiting. But she had felt hideously vulnerable sitting in her driveway, and she felt hideously vulnerable now as she drove inside the garage and sat waiting in her locked car for the door to close again before she got out. Once it did, she figured she was relatively safe. She should have plenty of time to get inside and get ready. Get her courage up.

If Mario even came.

She was so busy watching anxiously out the rearview mirror in case anyone – read: Mario – should duck under the door as she waited for the thing to close that she almost missed it.

Or, rather, *him*.

Mario. He was already there, in her garage.

23

Kate gasped as her gaze found him and stopped, riveted. Her eyes went wide with shock. Her hands tightened on the wheel. Her heart threatened to leap out of her chest. Mario was in the front left corner of the garage, partially hidden by some boxes of dishes and things she hadn't yet unpacked. She could see him only from the mid-chest up and from the knees down, but from what she could tell he sat on the concrete floor with his legs splayed out in front of him and his head slumped toward his shoulder.

And unless her eyes were playing tricks on her, there was a bullet hole in the middle of his forehead.

Whatever, she was almost one hundred percent certain he was dead.

Murdered.

Oh, God. Oh, God. Oh, God.

Terror sluiced like ice water through her veins as, all at the same time, it occurred to her that if Mario had been murdered, someone had to have done it, and they had to have been in her garage, and they might very well still be somewhere nearby. Gasping with fear, heart galloping, pulse racing, she looked wildly around, making sure the car doors were still locked and that no one was hidden in the shadows. At the same time, she jabbed at the garage door opener so that the damned door would open back up and she could get the hell out of there, and cringed in hideous anticipation of a bullet finding her at any second.

Mario's eyes were open. His mouth was, too. His face was slack. The hole was dime-sized and black and oozing just a trickle of blood. All this she saw in a series of horrified glances as, with glacial slowness and enough noise to wake the dead, the garage door ponderously rose.

Call 911. Call Tom.

She had just replaced her cell phone the day before, and she thanked God for it as she grabbed it. Tom's number – what was it? She didn't know, but thank God it was programmed into her phone.

Punching the button, she listened to the call connecting and at the same time shifted into reverse with one hand while she waited for the garage door to reach a height sufficient for the Civic to scoot beneath it. But as the door continued to rise and the phone finally began to ring at the other end, and she listened to both and glanced in horror at Mario and kept looking desperately around, she could see how vulnerable she was. Stuck in the garage, she was as exposed as an animal with its leg caught in a trap. Until the opening was wide enough, she couldn't get out. Anyone could get in.

Her skin crawled at the thought.

'Tom Braga.'

Tom's voice in her ear was the most welcome sound she had ever heard.

'Tom. You need to come.' Even as she gasped the words out, she was reminding herself that she didn't know who this man in her garage was. To her, supposedly, he was a dead stranger. Not Mario.

'Kate? What's wrong?'

'There's a dead man in my garage. Please hurry.'

'*What?* Jesus fucking Christ. Is anyone else there? Are you in danger?' His tone was sharp, urgent.

'I . . . don't think so.' The garage door was finally high enough so that the Civic would fit. Taking her foot off the brake, she hit the gas and zoomed backward, flying out beneath the door and down the driveway toward the street. Darkness swallowed the Civic like a giant mouth. 'I don't know. Okay, I'm out of the garage.'

He was swearing a blue streak. He said something in reply to something that was said to him by whomever he was with, but she was breathing so hard and her pulse was pounding so loudly in her ears that she didn't really catch what it was he said. The Civic careened into the street just as another car went past that she nearly hit, but it swerved and honked and went on its way, so she shifted into forward and took off, heading back the way she had come.

She was shaking from head to toe, she discovered. The one thought in her head was to get as far away as she could from the scene.

'Kate!' From the sound of his voice, Tom had called her name more than once without getting an answer.

'I'm here.'

'There's a patrol car close by. It'll be at your house in a few minutes. I'm on my way.'

'Okay.' Kate was at the top of the street, braking for the stop sign, when she heard a siren approaching. She could see the flashing lights coming toward her fast. 'I see it.'

'That's good.' He said something indistinguishable, presumably to whoever was with him, and then the patrol car was in full view, speeding toward her, and the shaking was going away and her heart was slowing down and her pulse was quieting a little because it was starting to seem like she was safe now.

If Mario was dead . . .

The thought remained unfinished as Tom spoke again. 'I can hear the siren over the phone. Are you okay?'

She was still at the stop sign, waiting, watching the patrol car racing toward her. It bore down on her street, and she knew that when it passed an innocent person would follow it back to her house, open the garage door for the officers, let them see Mario, answer their questions . . .

Then it hit her. She *was* an innocent person. At least about this. She hadn't killed Mario.

'Kate?' Tom's voice was more urgent. 'Are you okay? What about Ben?'

'Yes. Yes, I'm fine. And Ben's not with me. I just

got home and . . . there this guy was. I think somebody shot him in the head. Oh, my God.'

The patrol car turned in front of her, heading down her street, heading toward her house. In the distance she saw more flashing lights coming her way.

'I'll be there in about fifteen minutes,' Tom said to her, and then there was a pause. She could hear someone talking in the background. 'We got a call coming through dispatch from the officers who are pulling up in front of your house. Are you there?'

'I'm at the end of the street.' She was actually pulling into a neighbor's driveway and backing out so that she could head home again. Small rectangles of light that she knew were front doors opening were appearing up and down the street as neighbors stepped outside to see what was going on. 'I can see them. Tell them I'm coming.'

She could hear him talking to somebody else again. The patrol car was stopped in her driveway now, and officers were getting out. Kate pulled in behind it, narrowing her eyes against the stroboscopic light as another patrol car turned in at the top of the street and raced toward them.

'That's you in the driveway behind them, right?' Tom said. 'They told dispatch a woman in a red car just pulled in.'

'Yes, it's me,' Kate said, taking a deep breath as she watched the uniformed officers walking toward her. Her mind was already moving at about a million miles a second as she explored the ins and outs of what she was going to say. 'I'm going to hang up now and talk to them. Hurry, please.'

Then she disconnected, turned off the engine, and got out of the car to talk to the waiting officers.

The investigation hadn't been assigned to him and Fish, which suited Tom perfectly. He knew Kate way too well now to be satisfied with her responses if it had been, although he was keeping his opinions to himself and letting the detectives on the case, Jeff Kirchoff and Tim Stone, both relative newcomers to the Homicide Division, take the lead. He propped a shoulder against the wall in her living room and stayed out of the way, watching and listening as Kirchoff, who was young and easily dazzled, gently led Kate through her discovery of the body one more time.

Still wearing the conservative navy blue skirt suit she'd worn to work – he knew because he'd been there when she'd left, and had followed her to the office – she sat on the couch with her slender knees and calves pressed tightly together, her feet in a pair of nude high heels that made her legs look a mile long, her hands clasped tightly in her lap as she leaned toward Kirchoff. With her hair pulled back into a loose bun so that her beautiful bone structure was on full display and her big, blue eyes wide on Kirchoff's face, she looked sexy and fragile and the very picture of innocence. Kirchoff didn't stand a chance. Nodding sympathetically, he was drinking in every word that fell from her soft, pink lips. His notebook lay in his lap, forgotten. He was so convinced that he was dealing with an innocent victim of circumstances that he wasn't even bothering to write things down, or to check her story against things she'd already said.

Tom, on the other hand, was drawing an entirely different conclusion.

Those flickering lashes, the quick downward glances, the tight clasping of her hands – he'd seen them all before.

His smokin' little prosecutor was lying through her pretty white teeth again.

And the thing that was really getting to him about it was the knowledge that he had no intention in the world of calling her on it. At least, not where anyone else could hear.

Finally, he couldn't take it any longer.

Straightening away from the wall, he walked toward her.

'Is she free to go?' he asked Kirchoff. Kate broke off what she'd been saying, interrupted in mid-spiel, but he didn't care. Kirchoff, perched in the gold chair, looked up at him with surprise that quickly changed to respect when he saw the veteran homicide detective who was addressing him.

'Yeah,' he said, and looked at Kate. 'I'm sorry to keep you so long.'

'That's all right.' She smiled at him, a brave little smile that had Kirchoff practically melting in the chair, and stood up. 'If I can answer any more questions . . .'

'I'll let you know,' Kirchoff promised, standing, too, and smiling back.

It was all Tom could do not to roll his eyes.

Kate's gaze just touched his as she moved toward him. The medical examiner's office was still busy in the garage, and, behind him, flashes were popping as investigators finished photographing the premises. They'd already searched the house from top to bottom, dusted for fingerprints, used Luminol for blood, etc. It was after ten now, and things were winding up.

'Go pack a bag,' he said, low-voiced. 'I'm taking you home with me.'

She stopped, looking up at him in mute surprise.

'Would you rather stay here?'

She shook her head.

'You got any better offers?'

She shook her head again.

Kirchoff skirted around them, casting them a curious glance that he quickly averted when Tom met it with a level look. By then, Kate was moving again, heading for the stairs, presumably to pack a bag.

Tom cursed himself for three kinds of a fool as he watched her go. At least Fish, in whose car they had arrived, was already gone. Otherwise, he'd be getting an earful. An earful of hard truths and common sense that he was too far gone to hear.

He was standing in the door between the kitchen and the garage, talking to Lally Cohen of the medical examiner's office when Kate came up behind him and touched his arm through his black wool jacket. With gray slacks, white shirt, and a black tie (he owned just one that wasn't red), he'd been good to go to work, two funerals, and back to work again.

'Ready?' he asked her over his shoulder.

'Yes.'

He nodded good-bye to Lally and turned to Kate. A small black suitcase sat on its end on the ground beside her. Picking it up – it wasn't heavy – he headed toward the front door, with her trailing behind him. When he reached it, he opened it and stood back for her to precede him through it, jeering at himself inwardly all the while.

Clearly, he was a sucker for pretty blondes, too.

'We'll have to take your car,' he said when they were outside. 'Fish drove.'

She nodded, pausing for a moment on the porch to look around. Yellow crime scene tape cordoned off the front of the house just beyond the sidewalk, although it had not yet been extended to the driveway, which was still full of vehicles. A patrol car, dark and still, was in front. The white coroner's van was parked behind Kate's Civic, waiting for the body to be released by the PPD. Two more black-and-whites, dark like the first one, Kirchoff and Stone's Taurus, and a few other assorted official vehicles lined both sides of the street directly in front of the house. Earlier there had been an ambulance, but it was long gone, its services not needed.

The man in the garage was definitely dead.

'How long do you think they'll be here?' Kate asked over her shoulder as she stepped off the porch and onto the walkway.

'Few more hours. You can probably come back tomorrow night, if you want.'

He followed her down the walk, opened the door for her, tossed her suitcase in the back. Then he walked around the trunk of the car to get to the driver's seat. The night was clear. The moon looked like a Ping-Pong ball sailing high overhead. The wind blew in his face, surprisingly cold.

What he was getting ready to do – take Kate home with him – was probably one of the stupider things he'd ever done in his life. And the sad thing was, he knew it and was going to do it anyway.

He got in. 'Keys?'

She passed them over without comment, and he started the car. Because the van had them blocked in, he drove through the grass to get to the street. As he negotiated the streets of her neighborhood, neither of them spoke.

'So,' Tom said as they pulled onto the expressway. 'That was the guy who carjacked you?'

He'd heard her tell Kirchoff so.

'I think so.'

'Who do you think shot him?'

'I have no idea.'

'Must have given you a turn to see him like that in your garage.'

'It did.'

'Thought you were going out of town. To Longwood Gardens, wasn't it?'

'I changed my mind.'

'So you parked Ben with his babysitter so you could spend the night in your house alone.'

He glanced her way in time to see her narrow her eyes at him.

'That's right.'

'Correct me if I'm wrong, but wasn't it just last night that I slept on your couch, at your request, because you were scared to death?' In a (clearly useless) attempt to keep himself from getting dragged any deeper into the ongoing debacle that was his relationship with her, he had not arrived until after eleven, when she'd already been in bed. Hank Knox, a grandfatherly patrol officer who owed him a favor, had filled in for him until then.

'I was worried about Ben.' Her tone was getting snappish. The big overhead streetlights made the interior of the car nearly as bright as day. She was looking pale – maybe it was the lights – and kind of hollow-eyed. But there was no mistaking the thinning of her lips, or the annoyed glint in her eyes.

'Not about yourself.'

'That's right.'

He digested that, sent her a look. 'Remember what I told you that day in your office?'

'What day?'

'The day you got mad at me because I gave Ben a ball.'

'You mean the day you tricked me into reaching

for the ball so that you could see if I was right- or left-handed?'

'That's the one. I said, you're a lousy liar, because your face gives you away every time. Just for the record, that still applies.'

She sat bolt upright in the seat. Her chin quivered. Her eyes spat fire at him.

'*That's it*. I've had it. I'm sick of being questioned, questioned, questioned every minute I'm with you. You turn this car around right now and—'

'Forget it.' He interrupted her in full tirade. 'It's not happening, Katrina Dawn Kominski.'

That shut her up. She sat there gaping at him like he'd slapped her face.

It was a full minute before she said anything else.

'You've been investigating me.'

'I'm an investigator. That's what we do.'

'Was it fun? Snooping into my life?'

'Not fun. Necessary.' The Fitzwater exit – his exit – was coming up on the left. He switched lanes in preparation.

'So you know all about me, huh?'

The brittleness of her voice told him how deep the scars of her past went: so deep that she was doing her best to cover up any hint of hurt or shame about it. He almost kicked himself for bringing it up.

Almost. But if he was going to fall head over heels for a woman who seemed to lie almost as easily as she breathed, the first thing they needed to establish was some small beachhead of truth.

'I know a lot. I know you had a tough childhood, that your husband died, that you've done a truly admirable job of pulling yourself and Ben up by your bootstraps ever since.' They were on the ramp now, whizzing down toward Fitzwater in Italian-centric South Philly. His place was just blocks away. He glanced at her, his voice gentling. 'Why don't you tell me the rest?'

She glared at him. 'What are you, the good cop without the bad cop?'

He turned right on Fitzwater. 'I'm not being a cop now, Kate. I'm just asking.'

'Oh, *right*. You've been trying to catch me in a lie ever since you and your partner first showed up in my office. You were there in the courtroom that day. You saw how it all went down. How can you possibly imagine that I had anything to do with that?'

'I don't think you did have anything to do with that.' He turned onto Seventh. His place – the end segment of a triple row house known locally as a Trinity (as in Father, Son, and Holy Ghost) – was just up the block. So close to the Italian Market, the Italian-food mecca that stretched out over three blocks along Ninth, the street was busy, like most in the area on weekend nights. Cars rattled across cobblestones that had once been paved over but were now missing most of their covering. Tourists walked the uneven sidewalks in pairs and small groups until long past midnight. There were streetlights on the corners, but most of the bulbs were out. Parking could be a problem. Crime could be a problem. The architecture was less than inspiring: old three-story brick buildings, each exactly the same as the last; concrete steps leading up to aluminum-framed screen doors; rusting metal awnings arching over tiny front stoops.

In other words, home sweet home.

'Then what's the point of this?'

'I think something else is up with you. You're lying about something, you're scared of something, and way too many evildoers seem to be popping up in your life for it to be a coincidence. A case in point being this dead guy tonight.' He shot her a quick, assessing glance as his parking space, protected by a sawhorse with a sign that said *Reserved for Police,* which he'd made in self-defense against the tourists, came up on the right. Double-parking beside the car next to it, he got out, picked up the sawhorse, set it on the sidewalk, and then got back into the car. She was sitting there with her arms crossed over her chest, looking royally pissed. Which was fine with him. He was feeling kind of pissed himself, and every bit of it could be traced back to her. Or more accurately, his reaction to her.

'Go to hell,' she said through her teeth as he eased the Civic into the space. 'And leave the keys in the ignition. As soon as you get out, I'm leaving.'

'Oh, yeah?' He put the transmission in park, turned off the car, pulled the keys out of the ignition, and handed them over to her, which just made her look pissier than ever. 'Where are you going to go that comes complete with police protection? Because, not that I mean to worry you or anything, but you probably want to keep in mind that *somebody* killed that dude in your garage.'

Then he got out of the car. She still hadn't moved when he made it around to her door, so he opened it for her. She got out without a word. He retrieved her suitcase and tucked his sawhorse under one arm, she clicked the button to lock the car doors, and they proceeded across the sidewalk and up the quartet of narrow concrete steps that led to his front door.

Then he stepped back to let her precede him inside. By the time he had the door locked again and the sawhorse stowed away in its usual spot, she was in his living room, which – because she was in it – he saw through fresh eyes.

With an inner wince.

Unlike her, he hadn't tried to make a home. This shotgun-style town house was where he slept, watched the occasional ball game on TV, did laundry, and cooked when he got tired of eating out. Otherwise, he was never in it. The room was good-sized, rectangular, with one wall given over to an ornate mahogany fireplace with a mirror built in over it. The couch was old, cracking black vinyl, big and comfy but nothing to look at. The chairs didn't match. The tables (okay, one was a box) didn't match. There was a floor lamp and a table lamp (perched precariously on the box), and a rug on the floor. A plasma TV took pride of place in a corner. The few pictures were on the mantel; they were framed ones of family, placed there by his mom, who clucked over his lack of decorating skills and frequently offered to do the job herself, which he just as frequently declined.

Kate was standing near the fireplace, looking around. He walked past her into the dining room – the rooms opened into each other, three to a floor, and the stairs went up from the dining room – set her suitcase at the base of the stairs, and went into the kitchen, where he opened the refrigerator and snagged a beer.

'You hungry?' he bellowed in her direction, popping the top. 'You want something to drink?'

'No,' she called back.

Taking a chug, he headed back toward the living room.

Having her in his house was making him uncomfortable, he discovered. Like he was heading somewhere he didn't want to go.

Accordingly, when he stopped in the living-room doorway and discovered that she was picking up pictures from the mantel and looking at them, he scowled at her.

'Want to fill me in on your juvenile record?' He took another swallow of beer as her big, blue eyes turned from the picture she held in one hand to focus on him. 'It's sealed. I can get a court order to open it if I need to, but it'd be easier if you just told me about it.'

He watched her shoulders square. 'I shoplifted, okay? And I got caught. And I stole twenty dollars from a foster family I was living with. I got caught then, too. And I hit a boy in the head with a soda bottle. That one I spent three months in juvenile hall for.'

She was looking at him defiantly. He took another swig of beer.

'That was in Baltimore,' he said. It wasn't a question, because he knew he was right. 'So how'd you end up in Atlantic City?'

Her face tightened. Her eyes darkened. Her lips compressed.

And he knew he was onto something.

'You know what?' she said. 'I'm not answering any more questions. It's your turn. The only thing I know about you is that you're a homicide detective with a damned suspicious nature and a brother. Do you have other family?'

Finishing his beer, he lobbed the empty can into a nearly full wastebasket in the corner. Then he leaned a shoulder against the doorjamb and eyed her contemplatively. She was maybe ten feet away, standing in front of the fireplace, looking absolutely gorgeous, a few long blond strands having escaped from her bun to curl around her face, the severe business suit she wore ironically emphasizing the slender femininity of the body inside it.

Changing the subject when the topic under discussion didn't suit was practically an art form with her.

He was willing to go with the flow – for now.

'I have a mother, three married sisters, my brother, who's also married, and so many nieces and nephews

I've lost count. They all live in Philly, so we see each other fairly often. Actually, my mom has a standing Sunday dinner that she tries to shame us all into attending, but I've missed the last few.'

Her face had softened as if the idea of his family appealed to her. 'Why?'

He shrugged. Going into the real reason would, he felt, be stepping onto dangerous ground. 'Too busy.'

'Are your brothers and sisters older? Or younger?'

'I'm the oldest.'

Her lips curved into the slightest of smiles. 'I should have guessed.'

'Why's that?'

'Bossy. Controlling.'

'Oh, yeah?'

She was looking at the pictures on the mantel and didn't reply. He tried to think of which ones were up there – he couldn't really remember.

'Are these your family?' She gestured at the lineup on the mantel.

'Most of them, yeah.'

'Is this a nephew?' She held up the silver-framed picture she was clutching so that he could see it. It was a three-by-five of a plump baby boy in blue corduroy overalls. He was seated on one of those blanket-covered boxes where baby photographers plop babies to take pictures of them. He held a blue-striped rattle in one hand. His eyes were big and brown, he had a mop of black hair, and he was grinning a huge grin that showed two emerging teeth.

Tom's heart began to slam in his chest.

'No.' It was an effort to get the words out. Stupid how, all these years later, it was still so hard to talk about. 'That's my son.'

Her eyes went wide. 'Your *son*?'

'He was killed in a boating accident with his mother – my ex-wife – shortly after that picture was taken. Josh – his name was Joshua – was ten months old.'

'Oh my God.' Kate stared at him, then put the picture back on the mantel and came toward him. 'I'm so sorry. I had no idea.'

He straightened away from the door as she touched his arm – stroked it, really – through his jacket. Despite his best efforts, he could feel a familiar tightening at the back of his throat.

The pain was better. Far better. But it wasn't gone, and he wasn't sure now that it would ever completely go away.

'It happened eleven years ago, so it's not like it's some fresh tragedy.' Her eyes were full of sympathy. He tried to make light of his feelings, tried to keep his voice even, because as he'd learned the hard way over the years, having people pity him totally sucked. 'Michelle and I had just officially gotten divorced about two weeks before, and she and Josh were out on the Delaware River with her new boyfriend in his boat when another boat crashed into them. Everybody had been drinking. Nobody was wearing life jackets. Not that it would have mattered for Josh. He was killed on impact.'

The stark recitation gave no clue about the agonies of grief he had endured, about the horror of the funeral with the tiny coffin, about the nightmares he'd suffered for years afterward about his small son lying buried in the cold ground. It did nothing to describe the hell of darkness he'd been lost in until finally, day by painful day, he'd managed to claw his way out.

'That is so . . . sad.' The catch in her voice made his gut tighten. She was holding on to his arm now, her slender fingers pale as they curled into his jacket. Her lips were parted, and her eyes were huge blue pools of sympathy for him. She was standing close, so close he could smell the soft perfume of her shampoo. 'That must have totally broken your heart.'

Yes. That was exactly what it had done: broken his heart. And it had hurt so much that he wasn't about to ever put the damned vulnerable thing at risk again.

'I survived.'

'I'm so very, very sorry, Tom.'

He wasn't mistaken: Tears were puddling in her eyes as she looked up at him. His gut clenched at the sight. As he watched, they spilled over to slide silently down her cheeks.

'Damn it, are you crying?' His voice was unexpectedly harsh. 'For me?'

Her chin lifted defiantly. 'Yes. Yes, I am. Is there some reason why I shouldn't?'

That was it. He couldn't stand it. The pain for him he saw in her face was absolutely tearing him apart.

His hands slid around her upper arms, and he pulled her up against him, hard.

She didn't resist. Instead, she melted against him. He could feel the soft warmth of her with every nerve ending he possessed.

Their eyes met. Hers were still overflowing with tears.

It was a mistake, he knew it was a mistake, and he did it anyway.

He covered her mouth with his.

24

His mouth was hot and hungry and urgent and tasted of beer, and she caught fire from it. Wrapping her arms around his neck, closing her tear-filled eyes, she kissed him with feverish intensity, taking his mouth as thoroughly as he took hers. He pressed her back against the wall, trapping her there with his weight, and his hand found her breast through the white Hanes T-shirt she wore with her suit. It was big and hard and sure of itself, and as it flattened over her, she made a tiny mewling sound in her throat and arched up against it and felt her bones melt.

He pulled her T-shirt out of her waistband, slid his hand inside, over her waist, up her rib cage. It was warm and faintly abrasive and unmistakably masculine, and the feel of it made her heart pound so hard that its drumming was all she could hear. She was wearing a simple white cotton bra, nothing fancy, but when his hand moved over it the cloth felt as sheer as the finest silk. His thumb found her nipple, rubbed it, and she went dizzy. Then he pushed the bra up and out of his way. His hand was on her bare skin, on her breast, on both breasts, caressing her until her nipples were tight and her breasts were swelling into his hands, until she burned and moaned and pressed up against him with an urgency that turned her blood to pure steam. Even as she recognized that this was crazy, that she was doing something she had sworn she wasn't going to do, he kissed her with a fierceness that robbed her of even the tiniest bit of caution that remained.

What he was doing to her simply felt so good that it was impossible to resist.

She could feel the hardness of him against her, pressing between her legs, the strength of his desire obvious even through the layers of their clothes. He rocked into her, then tore his mouth from hers to press hot, wet kisses to each of her exposed breasts, drawing the nipples into his mouth, sucking them until her head fell back against the wall and she whimpered, mindless with need.

He kissed her mouth again, deeper, harder, with a fierce, hot urgency that made her tremble and quake and feel as if all her muscles were dissolving with the heat of it even as she kissed him back with a flaming hunger of her own. She felt his hands at the small of her back, unbuttoning her skirt. He got the button free, and the zipper made a tiny sound as he pulled it down. Then he pushed her skirt down over her hips and it fell to the floor with a silken whisper.

She still had her arms around his neck when he pulled his mouth away from hers again and then broke free of her grip entirely to pull her pantyhose and her panties with them down her legs. Leaning back, eyes still closed, panting, heart pounding, she pressed her hands flat against the cool plaster as he painted a hot, wet trail with his mouth down her right thigh, and then her left, on the way. One at a time, he guided her out of her shoes, pressing tiny, wet kisses to her knees as he did, and then he tugged her pantyhose and panties off each foot so that she was naked except for her blazer and the T-shirt and bra twisted up above her breasts.

He stood up and pushed her blazer off her shoulders and pulled her T-shirt and bra over her head.

Then she was totally naked, her back pressed up against the cool plaster wall in his living room, her hands flattened against it, breathing hard, weak with passion, and she could feel him looking at her, feel his eyes moving over her breasts and waist and the soft triangle of curls between her thighs. She was trembling, knowing that he could see how aroused she was, that she was totally exposed to him in every way, but she was absolutely too turned on to move, or try to cover herself in any way. For a moment nothing happened. Then she heard him catch his breath, and his lips brushed her nipples, softly, searingly, one at a time. His hand slid between her legs, rubbing her, claiming her, and she sucked in air and went weak at the knees.

She never opened her eyes. She never looked at him. If it was a form of denial – and she guessed it was – she was too far gone to care. Her heart was pounding and she was breathing hard and the quickening inside her was coming fast and close. She shivered and burned and arched her back and moved against his mouth and his hand.

I want you, she thought dizzily, but she didn't say it aloud.

Then his lips molded themselves to hers again, and she wrapped her arms around his neck and kissed him back with abandon. He picked her up, his big hands curving beneath her cheeks, and she wrapped her legs around his waist. He was naked, too, and with the small part of her mind that was still functional, she supposed he must have stripped himself at the same time that he had stripped her.

Seconds later he tipped them both onto the big leather couch and came into her hard. He was big and hot and filled her to capacity. She gave a short, sharp cry at the suddenness of it, the sheer unexpected pleasure of it.

The cry was swallowed up by his mouth. He kissed her fiercely at the same time as he thrust into her again and again, deep and fast, driving her wild, so that she could do nothing but gasp and moan and surge against him, consumed with desire, dizzy with it, burning and writhing and quaking with it. She clung to his broad shoulders and kissed him back with fiery abandon as he made her shudder, made her clench and convulse inside, made her arch and scream and come in long, undulating waves that finally burst into a mind-blowing, earth-shattering intensity that rocked her world.

She was still soaring when he drove inside her one last time and, with a low, guttural sound, found his own release.

She floated back to earth to discover that being naked and sweaty on a leather couch was not such a good thing. In fact, she could hardly move, and not only because approximately two hundred pounds of naked, sweaty male was sprawled on top of her. Her skin felt like it was fused to the couch.

Opening her eyes, she discovered that she was looking at a broad, bronzed, muscular shoulder with a fine sheen of sweat. And a big, masculine hand that still cupped her breast. His head was out of sight, buried in the curve between her shoulders and neck. His beard felt prickly against her skin. She could feel his breath stirring her hair, and could hear the soft sound of his breathing.

He lifted his head and looked at her. With no warning at all. His eyes were still darker than usual, still hot in the aftermath of what they had done. His hair was tousled. A faint flush rode high on his cheekbones. His mouth had a slight, sensuous curve to it.

She was a twenty-eight-year-old lawyer, for God's sake – and yet she still felt herself blush.

'That was unexpected,' she said, because she was rattled, because she had to say something, because he was looking at her. Her tone was way too bright.

His hands rose to cup her face; his thumbs moved

across her cheeks beneath her lashes, wiping away, any residual dampness that remained from her tears.

'Yeah,' he said. 'It was.'

Then he kissed her, a soft, sweet kiss that quickly changed into something entirely different. And he rolled with her, so that she was on top – she was sure she'd lost a layer of skin in the process – but then things got so heated so fast that she didn't even care. It was slower, different, but no less intense. In the end, she was astride him, his hands on her hips, her head thrown back while he thrust up inside her with barely controlled savagery. And finally she came again – and again.

It was about three o'clock in the morning before she stirred a second time. She knew, because somewhere deep in the house she heard the clock strike the hour. She was, she discovered, still as naked as the last time she had checked, sprawled half across his chest and half in the tiny space between his body – he was flat on his back – and the stick-to-your-skin leather on the back of the couch.

He was snoring.

Despite everything, the homely noises he was making made her smile.

Her heart picked up the pace. Her hand, which was resting in the nest of hair on his chest, stroked the firm muscle beneath, strictly of its own volition.

Bad idea. Snatching her hand away, she glanced at his face with alarm. He didn't so much as flicker an eyelash.

Okay, playtime's over.

She levered herself off him, taking as much care as she could not to wake him. The situation was . . . awkward. She needed time to think it through. It would certainly be easier to deal with if, the next time she came eyeball to eyeball with him, she wasn't naked and flushed with sex and wrapped in his arms.

Waking him didn't seem like it was something she had to worry about, she concluded, as, after a series of ungainly maneuvers, she managed to get to her feet at last. It was a surprise to discover that her legs were still a little unsteady, although it probably shouldn't have been. The sex had been wild, unbelievable, far above and beyond anything she had ever experienced. Of course, the last time she'd had sex she'd been nineteen years old. Apparently, her arousal system had fine-tuned itself in the meantime. Or maybe it was because now she was a grown woman, with a grown woman's responses. Or maybe it was just that she hadn't had sex in nine years.

Whatever, just remembering made her go all shivery inside.

So she quit. With determination. Until she decided how she wanted to handle this – handle him – she needed to put how he could make her feel out of her head. Because it complicated things.

Tom complicated things.

Of its own accord, her gaze slid over him.

Lying there stark naked, with one arm tucked behind his head and the other trailing down into the valley she'd just wriggled out of, he looked big and dark and utterly masculine. There wasn't an inch of him that wasn't, to quote Mona, 'fine.' His hair was tousled, his eyes were closed so that his lashes lay in sooty crescents against his cheeks, he was sporting a considerable amount of dark stubble, and his lips were slightly parted to let the snores escape. If she'd ever thought he wasn't particularly muscular, she saw now that she'd been wrong. His muscles were of the lean, ripped variety: honed forearms and brawny biceps, broad shoulders and wide chest, narrow hips, definitely six-pack abs that were bisected by a maybe six-inch-long white and puckered scar below and to the left of his navel. His legs were long and powerful-looking, an athlete's muscular legs, and what lay between them was impressive despite its current, uh, sleepy state.

Her body tightened at the thought of how impressive it was when it was awake. Then he stirred, shifting position slightly, and she hastily turned away. The last thing she wanted was to be caught staring at him.

In fact, the last thing she wanted was to be caught naked in his living room and to have to face this thing that had happened between them before she had herself together again, before she was ready. Before she'd thought it through.

She hastily gathered up her clothes (while trying with indifferent success not to remember how each and every piece had come off) and, following the path she'd seen him take with her suitcase, walked into the next room, which was the dining room, she discovered at a glance. It was furnished with a perfectly serviceable table and six chairs, but as far as she was concerned at the moment the best thing about it was the narrow staircase with her suitcase sitting at the foot of it. Casting a wary glance back – he was still snoring away on the couch – she picked up the suitcase and lugged it upstairs.

Five minutes later she was stepping into the shower.

The bathroom she'd found opened off the hall; it was old and narrow, with avocado tile and black accents and fixtures. The shower was actually a tub/shower combination, with a frosted sliding glass door to keep the water in. But the pressure was good, the water was hot, and there was soap, and that was what was important.

With her hair twisted into a high knot on top of her head to keep it dry, she proceeded to shower – and think.

Mario was dead. That was the good news. In fact, so far it didn't seem to have sunk in, because she should be feeling way more euphoric than she was. But she did feel a slight lessening of tension – or maybe that was due to the mellowing effects of the hot water – as she reminded herself that the hold he'd had on her was broken forever. It was over. There was now no longer anyone else left alive who knew that she had been there at the murder of David Brady.

In other words, all of a sudden her life had been handed back to her.

That was the good news.

The bad news was, someone had shot Mario in her garage. It probably had nothing to do with her personally. Probably Mario's enemies had happened to kill him at her house because that was where he just happened to be, courtesy of his desire to surprise her with an early appearance.

Whoever killed him would probably just fade into the woodwork now, posing no threat to her at all.

Probably.

Although for her money, if she were hunting the killer, the first thing she would do would be check out whoever had gotten Mario out of jail.

But that was a problem for Tom and his fellow cops, not her. And for obvious reasons, that was information that she had no intention of sharing with Tom.

Let the past be gone with Mario.

On that cheering thought, she rinsed the soap from her body, turned off the taps, and stepped out of the shower. The towel she'd found wasn't thick, it wasn't new, and it wasn't particularly large. But it smelled clean, and it was large enough to dry with and then wrap around herself and tuck in while she brushed her teeth. She was in the midst of doing that when her gaze just happened to travel sideways. And that was how she discovered that the bathroom door was open a few inches, and Tom, clad in a dark toweling robe and leaning against the wall opposite the bathroom, was watching her through the opening.

Kate almost choked on her toothpaste.

By the time she had rinsed and thus rendered herself able to speak, he had pushed the door the rest of the way open and was standing in the aperture, grinning at her.

'The latch is broken,' he said by way of an explanation when she narrowed her eyes at him. He propped a shoulder against the doorjamb. His arms were crossed over his chest. 'The damned door never stays shut. You notice I didn't come in, though.'

Okay, she guessed she had to give him that. He could have if he had wanted to, but at least he had that much respect for her privacy.

'Good call,' she said.

'When I woke up and you – and all your things – were nowhere in sight, I thought you'd gotten cold feet and run out on me. But then I heard the shower, and when I came up, steam was pouring out of the door here, so I knew where you went.'

He'd clearly had a shower, too, a much faster one than hers. His hair was glistening wet and brushed back from his face, and there were stray water droplets here and there in the vee of hairy chest she could see and on his bare calves and feet.

Water droplets or not, he looked so handsome he stole her breath.

She was suddenly way, way too aware that all she was wearing was a thin and skimpy white towel that was tucked in between her breasts and didn't even reach to mid-thigh. He wasn't ogling her – he was way too smart a man for that – but she knew he was taking in the view just the same.

She put up her chin, figuratively speaking. 'I was actually meaning to put my PJ's on and go find a bed to sleep in for the rest of the night.'

'You got three to choose from. Two spare beds – or mine.'

Her throat dried up. Her heart began to pound. Their eyes met. He was still leaning against the doorjamb, no longer grinning but with the hint of a smile still lingering at the corners of his mouth. He still looked totally relaxed, but she got the impression that he was watching her carefully.

For one of the few times in her life, she was absolutely devoid of speech.

When she didn't say anything, his eyes darkened and the smile went away. She stood beside the bathroom sink, one hand on the counter, looking at him mutely. Behind him, the hall was dim. The bathroom was steamy but relatively bright. Only a few feet of space separated them.

Heat – and not from the shower – seemed to shimmer in the air.

She knew what he was asking. For the life of her, she couldn't come up with an answer.

He gave her a level look. 'Okay, I know you didn't want this to happen. I'm not exactly overjoyed that it did, either. But the thing is, it did happen. I guess we could just walk away and pretend it didn't, but how stupid would that be? There's something – a connection

– between us that's been there from day one. How about we give it a shot?'

Kate realized that the thumping she was hearing in her ears was her suddenly pounding heart.

There were so many reasons to just walk away from him, from what had happened between them tonight. Ben, for one. Did she want to let a man – this man – into his life, for however long their 'connection' might last? And there was her career. Getting where she was determined to go was going to take every ounce of drive and time and focus she could muster. And there were the lies she had told him, and the things about her and her past that he would never know.

And then – and she had to admit it, this was the biggie – there was her.

People you loved left. And that hurt. Did she really want to prove that to herself one more time?

Then she looked at him standing there, so sexy and strong and absolutely rock-solid in every way, and she felt her heart thudding and her stomach going all fluttery and, yes, her toes curling against the warm, slick tile, and she remembered wondering the other day if, in all this new life-building she was doing, she was maybe forgetting about herself.

'The suspense is killing me here,' he warned with a slight smile.

She had to smile, too, and it was then that she knew she was going to go for it, whatever the future cost might be.

'I guess we could give it a chance,' she agreed.

Then he smiled, and straightened away from the doorjamb and opened his arms to her. And she walked into them.

25

Of course, they ended up not getting much sleep at all, even though they did spend the night together in his big, rumpled bed. They made love, and talked, and dozed off, only to awaken and do it all again. She told him some things about her early life, about how she had met Ben's father when they had both worked at the same casino, about falling crazily in love with him and marrying him in a quickie, impulsive Atlantic City wedding chapel ceremony and then getting pregnant with Ben, only to discover that the last thing Chaz White wanted was a family cramping his style. She told him the truth about Chaz, and why he left, and how he died. And she told him about finding herself broke and alone with baby Ben; about Chaz's associates coming around looking for money he'd lost gambling and still owed them, and demanding she pay it back; about taking a good, hard look at the life she'd led up until that point and deciding that it wasn't the life she wanted for her precious son. She told him about packing up her old car and driving away with baby Ben and their few possessions, about ending up in Philly, where she'd gone on welfare at first to survive, where she'd started college, where she'd started calling herself Kate. Where she'd become Kate. For Ben.

What she didn't tell him was how she'd come to leave Baltimore, or about David Brady.

He told her about his father, who'd been a cop. About his death from a sudden heart attack, how he went to work one day and *boom*, he just keeled over. About trying his best to be the man in the family after that. About getting married young, to his high school sweetheart. About becoming a cop even though Michelle objected. About her getting pregnant and him getting shot on the job – of which the scar on his abdomen was a permanent souvenir. By the time he was fully recovered, Josh had been born and the marriage, torpedoed by Michelle's insistence that he quit the force, was kaput. Josh was only six weeks old when Michelle left Tom for good, taking the baby with her.

What he didn't talk about, not another word, was his son's death. And that Kate completely understood.

Whenever possible, the worst, most painful memories were best left to lie undisturbed.

They must have fallen asleep again at last, because when Kate finally opened her eyes, the room was gray instead of black and she realized that it was from light streaming in around the drawn curtains. There was a weird buzzing sound that she couldn't place, so she lifted her head to look for the source, pushing her hair, which had come out of its knot almost as soon as she'd walked into Tom's arms the previous night, out of her eyes as she did so. The bed, complete with black comforter, mismatched sheets and pillowcases, and a pine headboard, stood in the center of the room. An oak chest with a small TV on top of it was directly opposite. A worn brown armchair sat in a corner. A round table of the sort that was supposed to have a tablecloth thrown over it, but without the cloth, served as a bedside table, with a clear glass lamp on it. The buzzing sound seemed to come from the table.

At about the same time that Kate figured out that the buzzing sound was coming from his phone, which was vibrating away on the table, Tom opened an eye, cocked it toward the table, then stretched a long arm out to pick it up.

'Tom Braga,' Tom said into the phone a moment later, as Kate blinked at the digital numbers on the clock beside the lamp – 7:42 A.M.

With an inner groan, she dropped her head back down in its previous spot on Tom's chest. His arm tightened around her shoulders.

'You need a ride to work or what?' Kate could hear the other man's voice coming over the phone perfectly, although she didn't recognize it.

'I'm taking a personal day,' Tom said.

'A personal day?' The voice sounded astounded. 'You haven't missed a day of work in ten years.'

''Bout time then, wouldn't you say?'

'This wouldn't have anything to do with the red Civic that's parked in your parking space, would it?'

Tilting her head so that she could see Tom's face, Kate watched him frown.

'Where are you?' he asked.

'Circling the block. Your car's at the Roundhouse, remember? I was going to give you a ride in?'

'Oh, yeah. Sorry, I forgot. Thanks for coming by.'

'She got you, didn't she? The smokin' little prosecutor got you.'

Tom slanted a glance down at her. 'Her name's Kate, Fish.'

'Goddamn it, Tom—'

But whatever else Fish had been going to say was lost, because Tom disconnected. Then he punched a number, and told the woman who answered that he was taking a personal day. By the time he finished that call, Kate was making twisty little curls out of the hair on his chest.

' "Smokin' little prosecutor," hmm?' Lifting her head, she gave him a severe look.

He grinned at her. 'I wondered if you could hear that. And I would say, definitely smokin'.'

They were tangled together in the middle of the bed with their legs entwined and only a sheet for covering because they'd gotten hot in the small hours of the night. She was sure they looked very intimate. Very involved. Like a couple, which she guessed they now kind of were. Falling asleep for the last time before the ringing phone woke her, Kate had wondered if she would panic in the morning, if she would regret the night before in the worst way, if it would all seem just horribly wrong by the bright light of day. She hadn't gotten much sleep. Her left shoulder ached from having been wedged beneath his for most of the night. Other parts of her body were making themselves felt in interesting ways. As for her prince, he was bleary-eyed and tousle-haired and in dire need of a shave.

But he was grinning at her, with one arm tucked behind his head now and the other wrapped around her shoulders. He was naked, and the lean, muscular warmth of him felt intoxicating against her smooth skin. And he was right, there was a connection between them, something special happening here, and besides, he'd turned her on to sex for what was really the first time in her life, and she wasn't about to say no to more of that.

The bottom line was, she didn't regret a thing.

'By the way, you look beautiful first thing in the morning,' he said, and rolled with her so that she was on her back and he was looming above her on his elbows.

Kate traced a teasing finger down the middle of the wide, hair-roughened expanse of his chest.

'So do you,' she informed him, because it was the truth, and then, because it was obvious where this was going, she added, 'I need to pick Ben up at noon.'

'Not a problem,' he said, and kissed her.

So maybe he was stupid, Tom thought later that day as he found himself at Southland Lanes Bowling

Emporium, a new, mega–bowling alley not too far from Kate's house, where Ben had been invited to a birthday party by another kid in his class, along with, apparently, the entire fourth grade. Kate had offered to let him off the hook, to let him go do whatever it was he wanted to do while she took care of the party scenario with Ben, then meet up later. But Tom was having none of it, both because he was afraid that, with her penchant for finding trouble, things might go south fast if he wasn't there to keep an eye out and because he wanted to see how he handled the family thing. The last-minute invitation involved rushing around for a present, waiting in the Civic as Kate walked Ben in, and then, two hours later, going in with her to pick Ben up. Only the kids weren't finished bowling yet. And some of the adults had been bowling with their kids. And Ben, excited, had asked Kate and him to bowl with him and his friend Samantha, just one more game. Kate had looked alarmed – once he'd seen her bowl, Tom understood, because she was lousy at it, gutter ball after gutter ball – but she did it, grace under pressure personified in her snug-fitting jeans and black pullover sweater with the sleeves pushed up past her elbows; he, on the other hand, was good, earning Ben's admiration, racking up strike after strike (okay, a couple of spares, too) surrounded by a gang of screaming kids and their parents that would have driven him out of the building in a hurry on any other day.

He even had fun. Which, he recognized, was because

Kate was there with him having fun, laughing at herself as she almost went nose-first down the lane with the ball, applauding him, applauding Ben, interacting with the other adults with cheerful ease, more relaxed and carefree than he had ever seen her.

And beautiful. Don't forget beautiful.

It was sometime between bowling and dinner, which the three of them had together at Rotolo's, a little Italian restaurant Tom knew, that he accepted the fact that there was no maybe about it: He *was* stupid. He'd fallen hard for this woman, and her kid as well, which meant his heart was hanging out there, vulnerable, just like he'd sworn he would never let it be again. But this thing between him and Kate had snuck up on him, and it was now too late to do anything about it. He was along for the ride, wherever it went.

It was upon leaving Rotolo's that they ran into his mother. Of course. The day had been going too smoothly not to have a bump in it.

Not that his mother was a bump, exactly. But she was definitely nosy, definitely more than interested in his love life, and if he'd had a choice, he would have kept Kate and her son out of her orbit for a good long while to come. He was following Ben and Kate, and as soon as he stepped out the door of the restaurant he saw his mother there on the sidewalk, waiting to walk in. Their eyes widened in mutual recognition – actually, hers widened in mutual recognition and delight, his in mutual recognition and horror – and then she said 'Tommy!' with a huge smile on her face, and he saw Natalia and her husband, Dean, and their two kids behind his mother the instant before she engulfed him in a Shalimar-infused hug. Then his nephew and niece threw themselves at him and he'd had to hug them and his sister and shake his brother-in-law's hand.

And then five pairs of interested eyes turned as one to Kate and Ben, who were standing together a little way away, obviously waiting for him.

So he caught Kate's hand, pulled her over, and performed the introductions, knowing even as he did it that the family gossip network would go into overdrive about this. While Kate was interrogated by his mother – 'What do you do?' 'Where are you from?' 'Oh, a widow, so sad' – Natalia looked her over from head to toe with speculative interest. Then, as he caught his sister's eye to frown at her, Natalia gave him a look of such wide-eyed glee that he'd known she was onto him, known she'd guessed that Kate was someone special, known that she was practically bursting with excitement at the prospect and ready to spill her take on the relationship to all family members not present as soon as he was out of the way and she could get to her phone.

God save me from my family, he thought sourly, and as soon as he decently could, he ended the gabfest by announcing that they had to go.

'She's a nice girl. I like this one,' his mother whispered in his ear as she hugged him good-bye. Then, to Kate, she added, 'We have lunch every

Sunday. The whole family. Lots of good food. You and your son should come.' Then she looked at him again. 'Tommy, you bring them.'

Tom made some kind of noncommittal reply, then, catching Kate's hand again, beat a hasty retreat, conscious of being followed by his mother's and sister's eyes until he and Kate and Ben rounded the corner into the parking lot and were out of sight. It was night now, and cold, and he was wearing a white shirt, which he wore untucked to hide his gun, and jeans with no coat. Still, he felt surprisingly hot, and unwillingly acknowledged that it just might be with embarrassment.

'Sorry about that,' he said, shooting Kate a sideways look. Smiling, with her hair waving down around her shoulders and her eyes sparkling with amusement, she looked young and gorgeous and happy. No wonder the group had been eyeing her like a trout spotting a fly.

And then there was Ben. They knew Tom well enough to guess that no way would he be just casually dating a woman with a son.

Think Superman and kryptonite.

Therefore, they would assume that this was something serious.

Which maybe it was.

'Are you kidding? They were wonderful. Your mother is so nice. And your sister looks just like you.' Her eyes twinkled at him. 'Tommy.'

He responded to that with a smile.

'How many people are in your family?' Ben asked as they piled into the Civic, which was what they were driving since Tom had not yet had a chance to retrieve his car from the Roundhouse. 'It seems like a lot.'

'There are a lot.' Tom pulled out of the parking lot and hung a right on Chisholm, which would take them to the expressway and then to Kate's house, where, he and Kate had agreed in a very adult, logistics-of-the-relationship kind of discussion before they picked up Ben, they would spend the night. Another part of the agreement had involved their behavior around Ben – no kissing, no overt displays of affection, no sleeping together while Ben was under the same roof. Tom doubted that he would have been allowed to stay over, now that things between him and Kate were personal, if Kate had been totally sure whoever killed the guy in her garage wasn't coming back. But since he actually admired her efforts to protect her son, Tom found he didn't have a problem with the restrictions she laid down. Besides, the kid went to school, he and Kate both had lunch hours, and there were always nooners. And babysitters. 'Nineteen, at last count.'

'Wow.' Ben sounded impressed. To this only child of a single mother, the thought of so many relatives was mind-boggling. 'How do they all fit in one house?'

'It's a squeeze,' Tom admitted with a laugh.

Kate hadn't been back to her house since he had taken her out of there the night before, and Tom could tell she was a little uneasy as they turned onto her street, which was dark except for lights burning from a few windows along the way. With what he considered truly praiseworthy sensitivity to her feelings, he parked in her driveway. No need to use the garage tonight, or at all until he'd done a visual inspection to make sure that the crime scene had been completely cleaned up, as he'd made arrangements for it to be. The only other visible signs of what had happened were a few tire tracks in the front yard. Otherwise, the house looked just as it always did.

Just to be on the safe side, though, Tom went in first, turning on the lights and conducting a quick – and, he hoped, unnoticed by Ben – search of the house. It was clean.

He nodded at Kate to tell her so when he returned to the living room.

It was almost eight o'clock by that time, and he was starting to feel the effects of almost a whole week with very little sleep. He eyed the couch with disfavor. But there was no way he was leaving these two alone until he was sure they would be safe, and Kate had nixed the idea of sleeping over at his house again, because she didn't want Ben to get the wrong idea (or was it the right idea?) about their relationship. Since her third bedroom was unfurnished, it was either the couch or her bed, and it had already been made clear to him that her bed wasn't an option with her son in the house.

So it looked like his only alternative was to learn to love the couch.

He and Ben shot a little ball – the kid was getting

better every time, although he remained gloomy about his prospects for not sucking the following week in gym – and then the three of them settled in to watch a movie on TV, with him and Ben side by side on the couch and Kate sitting primly all by herself in the gold chair. Tom didn't realize he'd dozed off until his phone, which was in the pocket of his jeans, started vibrating like crazy and woke him up.

The end credits of the movie were scrolling across the screen, and both Kate and Ben were on their feet, looking at him, when his eyes popped open and he reached for his pocket like he was going for a gun before he remembered who was who and what was what.

The caller was Fish.

'Just wanted to let you know that they found your girlfriend's car.'

That woke him up. He sat up, blinking. 'What? Where?'

'About a block from her house. Mulberry Street. They towed it in. It's at the impound lot.'

'Oh, yeah?' Clearly hoping to keep Ben from over-hearing things he shouldn't, Kate was already shooing the kid toward the stairs. Tom stood up and walked into the dark kitchen. 'Anything I should know?'

'Dead guy's fingerprints are all over it. I'd say it's a sure bet that he drove it over there. Probably walked the rest of the way to her house. How he got into the garage, though, is still up in the air. No sign of breaking and entering.'

'Maybe he was able to activate the garage door opener.' *Or* – and Tom hated the fact that the thought even ran through his mind – *maybe somebody let him in.*

'Maybe.'

'Any leads on who might have shot him?'

'Not yet.' There was a pause. 'Where are you?'

'Kate's house.'

'Why doesn't that surprise me, I wonder?' Tom could almost see Fish's grimace. 'Stay objective, man.'

Tom recognized a warning when he heard one.

Kate came into the kitchen then. The light from the living room backlit her blond hair and slender shape. Just watching the movements of her long legs and swaying hips as she walked toward him turned him on. Leaning back against the counter near the sink, Tom settled in to enjoy the effect.

Think she's told you everything? Not a chance. You still don't know what she's been lying about. You still don't know what's been scaring her. And for all she told you about her past, she hasn't said a word – not one – about what caused her to leave Baltimore.

'I'll call you if I hear anything else,' Fish said.

'Yeah. Thanks.' Tom disconnected, stuck the phone back in his pocket, and said to Kate, 'They found your car.'

She stopped in front of him. 'Where?'

'A few streets over.' With the kitchen dark and the light behind her, he couldn't read her expression. The fact that he felt he needed to was a problem.

He was crazy about her, no doubt about it. But that didn't mean he was totally brain-dead. The lady wasn't playing straight with him, and he knew it.

Even if he hated to face the fact.

'Are my things still in there? My briefcase? My phone?'

'Fish didn't say. If they were, it'll probably be a few days before you can get them back.'

'I really need my briefcase. I was able to get duplicates of the case files, but I need my notes.'

'I'll see what I can do to speed things up.'

She smiled at him. 'Thanks.'

His eyes slid over her face. 'Where's Ben?'

'Taking a bath.'

She might be playing him. He prayed she was not. But the niggling doubt was enough to make him just a little rougher than he needed to be when he put a hand behind her neck and angled her mouth up to his and kissed her hard, then picked her up and swung her around to perch her on the counter, still with his tongue deep in her mouth. She wrapped her arms around his neck and wrapped her legs around his waist and kissed him back for all she was worth, and he was instantly so hot for her that he was surprised steam wasn't pouring out of his ears.

'Mom!'

She stiffened and pulled her mouth from his. Reluctantly, he let her go.

Sliding off the counter, she made an apologetic face at him as she went to read Ben to sleep.

Such were the realities of life with a kid.

With that, he could deal.

In the end, because Natalia called and begged; because Vicky and Tina got on the phone and said how disappointed their mom would be if he didn't; because Charlie, fresh out of the hospital, was going to be there; and because Kate didn't object and Ben actively wanted to, they ended up going to his mother's for Sunday dinner. It was everything Tom had thought it would be – his relatives swarming around Kate and Ben – but the chicken parmigiana was out of this world, as usual, and he had missed it, and, if he was honest, he'd missed his family, too. And he kind of enjoyed watching Kate, demure in a knee-length black skirt and pale blue sweater set that she'd actually been nervous enough about to ask him if he thought it was 'suitable' for the gathering, fielding questions and making conversation and in general interacting with the zoo that was his family.

'She's hot, bro,' Charlie told him in a congratulatory tone after they'd finished eating. It was probably four o'clock by that time, and the late-afternoon sun was causing the trio of fat spruces that dominated the yard to cast long shadows toward where he and Tom sat on the small patio behind the house. Tom was kicked back in a lawn chair, sipping a beer. Charlie sat beside him in the wheelchair to which he gloomily expected to be confined for the next few weeks, likewise sipping a beer. The women were in the house. The brothers-in-law were grabbing beers of their own, and would be joining them on the patio momentarily. The kids were running all over the backyard, playing some kind of game that involved a lot of screaming. Ben, Tom was happy to see, seemed to be joining in and having a good time. And he was interested to discover that he was pleased about that.

'Yeah,' Tom agreed.

'She a keeper?'

Tom shrugged.

Charlie grinned. 'Mom's over the moon. She thinks you've found The One.'

'Jesus,' Tom said, revolted, but before he could add anything to that the brothers-in-law came out and the conversation got instantly general.

By the time they got home, they were too tired and stuffed to do more than finish homework (Ben) and watch TV (Tom, and Ben when his homework was finished). Kate did a couple of loads of laundry and some stuff upstairs before heading into her office to, as she told them, go over some files for tomorrow. Stretched out in the gold chair with Ben curled up on the couch, Tom was just reflecting on how normal this was starting to feel when Ben looked over at him.

'There were a lot of kids there today.'

'Yeah, there were.'

'We played some games that were really fun.'

'Looked like it.'

'So, are you my mom's boyfriend now or what?'

That got Tom's full attention. He sat up a little straighter and gave Ben a considering look. Clearly, the kid was no dummy, but he wasn't sure how Kate would feel about the two of them having this conversation.

'You'll have to ask her that.'

'She won't tell me anything about stuff like that. You know how she is. Overprotective.' Ben shook his head in transparent disgust.

That was actually true. And kind of funny, coming from a nine-year-old. But the thing was, Ben was asking, and Tom didn't want to be anything but straight-up with him.

'I guess I am her boyfriend now. Do you mind?'

Ben shook his head. 'It'll be a relief to have someone else to help take care of her. She can be a lot of trouble, you know.'

Tom had to grin. 'Yeah, I know. Maybe we can help each other out with that.'

About that time Kate came out of her office, and they must have both looked guilty as hell because she said, 'What's up?' and gave them a sharp look. But Tom wasn't telling, and if Ben did, Tom didn't hear about it, not then and not later, when Kate came back down to do one more thing and wound up sitting on his lap kissing him good night. After that things between them got so hot they ended up getting it on in the little bathroom under the stairs, with the door locked, in absolute silence because Kate was afraid that Ben (who was sound asleep) might hear something. But then she went off to her own bed to sleep, and he sacked out on the couch, where he tossed and turned, and so her rule about not sleeping in the same bed together when Ben was in the house was preserved.

The next day started out just fine. The weather was cold but clear and sunny, blue skies all around. He and Kate dropped Ben off at school, and the rest of the way to work she fretted about how Ben was going to fare in gym, and Tom tried to reassure her that the kid would survive no matter how the basketball thing went. He dropped her off in front of her office – this was another agreement they had going: no more half-empty parking garages for her for the time being – and drove on to the Roundhouse, where he arranged to have the Civic picked up by the rental car agency and Kate's car released from the impound lot. Fish made a few off-color jokes and shook his head at Tom a few times over Kate, but Tom was busy and paid no attention. There were a thousand things needing his attention, and he methodically tried to work through the pile. He was checking out known associates of the two men in the burned-out U-Haul, having confirmed their identities earlier, when Kirchoff, blond and preppy, looking like he had just stepped out of a J.Crew catalog, stopped by his desk.

Tom looked up inquiringly.

'I just wanted to let you know that we've got an ID on that dead guy in Mrs. White's garage.'

'Oh, yeah?'

Kirchoff's telling him was a courtesy thing, because Tom had been there in Kate's house and obviously had an interest in what was going on. But it was

Kirchoff and his partner's case, technically nothing to do with Tom at all.

'It's all right here.' Kirchoff tapped the manila folder he was carrying.

'Can I have a look?'

Kirchoff handed it over. Tom flipped it open.

'Guy's name was Mario Castellanos,' Kirchoff continued. 'Just got out of the detention center a few days ago. Rap sheet a mile long. So far, no idea what he was doing in that garage.'

Tom had no idea, either, not even when he finished checking the guy out. But he did have lots of ideas about lots of other things.

Like some of the things Kate had been lying to him about.

26

When Tom walked through the door to her office, Kate had just returned from a makeshift courtroom in City Hall – the Justice Center was still closed – where she had argued that a motion to suppress evidence in an upcoming armed-robbery trial was unjustified, and won. Kate was at that moment on the phone, relaying this news to Bryan, whose case it technically was, although she was handling it as one of the residual cases they were both assigned to before she went totally solo. Bryan had just called to ask about its resolution, interrupting Mona, who had dropped by to offer Kate what she promised was a totally to-die-for slinky black evening gown to wear to the upcoming fund-raiser for Jim Wolff, the very thought of which was enough to make Kate groan.

'. . . look fantastic,' Mona mouthed over her shoulder as she headed out the door, only to say, 'Oh, hello,' out loud, and in a tone that made Kate, who was still talking to Bryan, look up.

Then Tom walked in, his usual tall, dark, and hot self, and Mona, behind him, made big eyes at Kate and gave a speaking little wave of her manicured fingers before disappearing. He didn't look any too happy, but that didn't stop Kate's heart from radiating a warm little glow at the sight of him.

Where he was concerned, she still didn't regret a thing.

She smiled at him.

He didn't smile back. In fact, he looked downright grim.

Kate began to feel the first stirring of unease.

Finishing up with Bryan as quickly as she could, she hung up the phone.

'What?' she asked without preamble, because it was clear from Tom's expression that there was something wrong.

'Come for a walk with me.' There was absolutely no intonation at all to his voice. His eyes were darker than usual and impossible to read. His cop eyes. His cop face. Kate glanced at the clock. It was thirteen minutes until five. Her eyes flew back to his. Her heart began to beat faster.

'Where to?' she asked. Then, because something in his expression told her that this was very, very bad, her mind immediately went to the worst thing she could think of, and she started to her feet. 'Is it Ben? Has something happened?'

His eyes narrowed. 'Ben's fine, as far as I know.' His gaze swept past her, to the coatrack in the corner. 'Get your coat.'

Because it had been cold this morning, and because she'd known she would be walking to and from City

Hall, she had worn her black felt overcoat, complete with a long, gray crocheted scarf, over her favorite black pantsuit and white tee, with her black flats. Puzzled but obedient, she fetched it from the rack and put it on, looping the scarf around her neck.

'What is it?' she asked again, as she joined him. He wasn't wearing an overcoat. His charcoal blazer, black slacks, white shirt, and red tie were what he'd left the house in that morning.

He shook his head as he immediately started walking toward the door. Without touching her, yet.

Her unease started to turn into real anxiety.

'I don't want to talk about this here,' he said.

So they didn't talk, not one word, at least not to each other. Kate told Mona, whose head popped out of her office as they passed, that she had to run an errand. She waved at Cindy and exchanged a few remarks with other people she knew on the way out of the building. But Tom, beside her, remained silent as the Sphinx.

Finally, once they were on the sidewalk moving at a brisk pace away from the building, she tugged at his sleeve.

'Would you please tell me what's going on? You're scaring me to death,' she said, exasperated.

Tom cut his eyes at her, then glanced around at the jostling crowd they were in the midst of, at the dozens of pedestrians waiting to cross with them when the signal changed, at the bumper-to-bumper traffic. Dozens of chattering voices combined with the sounds of the traffic and the *whoosh* of wind through the concrete canyon into a low roar. The smell of car exhaust was strong. Sunlight glittered off the cantilevered tops of the skyscrapers, limning them with gold.

'In a minute,' he said, and caught her elbow to propel her through the intersection as the signal changed. His grip wasn't gentle. It was hard – and purposeful.

Two blocks later they were in the paved center courtyard of the Masonic Temple, a circa-1873 architectural treasure that was actually a series of meeting halls with various courtyards and its own museum. Only steps away from the busy street, the parklike square was all but deserted. Surrounded on three sides by ornate stone walls complete with arched leaded windows and fantastical carvings, the courtyard boasted fountains, statues, and benches. A flock of cooing pigeons pecked placidly at some crumbs that had found their way into cracks among the paving stones. The scent of burning candles from the nearby chapel wafted through the air. The autumn sun, apricot-colored this late in the day, hung just above one of the Gothic towers. The sky, which earlier had been a clear, pale blue, was just starting to turn pink to the west. It was warmer than it had been that morning, and there was no wind in this secluded enclave, but Kate was still glad of her coat.

Tom stopped walking near the base of a large bronze statue of a man on horseback and swung her around to face him. A few tourists were climbing the steps of the temple across the way, but no one was nearby. If he'd been seeking privacy here in this crowded part of the city, this was probably as good as it was going to get.

'So, *what*?' Kate demanded.

Jamming his hands into the front pockets of his pants, he seemed to be studying her face.

'Does the name Mario Castellanos mean anything to you?'

Kate felt a sudden constriction in her chest. Little curls of panic swirled like ice shavings through her bloodstream.

'Why?'

Tom's lips compressed. 'That's the name of the man who was found shot in your garage.'

Kate didn't say anything. She couldn't. She couldn't bear to lie anymore, especially not to Tom. But she couldn't tell the truth, either. She pressed her lips together with what she hoped looked like firm resolve, and stood her ground.

'I checked him out,' Tom continued, when she didn't answer. 'He's got a rap sheet stretching all the way back to when he was a kid in Baltimore. You know what's funny about that? He lived in Baltimore at the same time you did. Same general area, too.'

He paused, obviously waiting for her to reply. His face was tight with tension.

Kate said nothing. Her stomach was in the process of tying itself into knots, and the constriction in her chest had spread to her throat. She could feel her heart thumping against her breastbone.

His jaw tightened when it became obvious she wasn't going to say anything.

'Okay, how about we go for another coincidence? He was in the Criminal Justice Center Monday to testify in a trial. They lost track of him in all the confusion, but when they found him again as they were evacuating the building, he was in a holding cell all by his lonesome on the second floor.' He smiled at her, but it wasn't a nice smile. 'Oh, and you want to hear something else funny? Castellanos was left-handed.'

Kate suddenly found it impossible to breathe. She felt like she'd just taken a blow to the stomach, one that had knocked all the wind out of her. Mutely, she looked at him. His jaw was set now. His mouth was a thin, straight line, with white triangles of tension at the corners. His eyes bored into hers.

'Say something, damn it.' His mouth twisted violently, and he reached out and caught her by her upper arms. Kate jumped. She could feel the strength of his fingers through the layers of her coat and jacket. He didn't shake her, didn't hurt her, but he pulled her closer and loomed over her, his eyes blazing angrily down into hers.

'What do you want me to say?' She was surprised at how cold and clear her voice sounded. He glared at her. Dark color had risen to stain his cheekbones. His face could have been carved from stone.

'I want you to tell me the truth. Did you know Mario Castellanos?'

The thing about being a lawyer was, it had taught her one important rule: When the going gets tough, keep your damned mouth shut. She had to stay mute. He was on the trail of her terrible secret, although he clearly didn't know anything for sure, or yet have an inkling of the worst of it. But knowing something and proving it in a court of law were two very different things. They might be involved, she might have spent a good part of the weekend in his bed and in his arms, but when it came right down to it, he was a cop. With that in mind, she had to remember that she was once again fighting for her life.

'Get your hands off me.' She tried to pull her arms free, but he only tightened his grip.

'I take that as a great big *yes*.'

'You can take it any way you want. Let *go* of me.'

He ignored that. 'Castellanos was the second man Charlie saw back there in the secure corridor, wasn't he? You knew him, he was back there in that corridor with you, and I'm willing to bet anything you want he's the one who shot Rodriguez.' Kate felt the color leaching out of her face. Tom's face tightened with anger. His voice turned harsh with it. His eyes glittered like pieces of jet. 'Goddamn it, Kate, tell me you didn't have anything to do with getting those guns in there, or setting up that escape attempt.'

'I already told you that.'

'Yeah, and I believed you, too, like the damned fool I am.'

He let go of her suddenly, walked a few steps away,

ran his fingers through his hair, and turned back to look at her.

'Look, do you think I'm the only one who's going to be asking you these questions? I just put it together quicker than anybody else because I have access to the files from Castellanos's murder and the murders at the Justice Center. And I know something about your background. But I can't keep it a secret. *I can't fucking keep this a secret.*'

'So why did you bring me out here? To warn me?'

His eyes flashed at her. 'You want the truth? I was hoping I was wrong. I was hoping there was an explanation. I was hoping you would deny everything.' He laughed bitterly. 'But I'm right on the money. I can see it in your goddamned face.'

Kate's fists clenched. She felt dizzy, sick to her stomach, faint.

'Did you shoot him? Castellanos?' Tom's voice was sharp.

That was so unexpected she was startled into replying: '*No.*'

He stared at her. It was the first of his new questions that she had answered. Apparently, he realized it, too, because his eyes took on a hard, cold intensity.

'Ah,' he said. 'So we've finally got a *no.*'

'Go to hell.' Furious at herself, Kate turned and started walking toward the street. 'And stay away from me,' she threw back at him over her shoulder. 'You want to ask me any more questions, I'll get you the name of my lawyer.'

She half expected him to come after her, but he didn't. He let her walk away without another word. Which was a good thing, Kate thought fiercely. She should never have allowed herself to get involved with any man, much less a cop.

She could feel tears starting at the back of her eyes. Her heart pounded. She felt an aching in her chest, too, that she hated. But she knew, and there was no denying it: It was her poor, fragile heart breaking in two.

She should have known better. She had known better. But she had walked right into this disaster anyway.

It was because he'd had a son who had died. That's what had done it. When she had learned that about him, the hard little shell that she'd grown around her heart had cracked.

And let Tom in.

Now she was having to wrench him out again. And it hurt, badly, just like she deserved.

That little bit of happiness she'd had with him had just been a setup for today's crash and burn. Just like she'd feared. Just like she'd known.

Now she got to pay the price, and the price was pain. Tears blurred her eyes by the time she reached the street, but she determinedly blinked them back.

I'll be damned if I'm going to cry over him.

Knowing that what they'd had was over hurt so much, though, that she had trouble pushing it aside to focus on the rest of her problem: what Tom knew.

If he managed to put a few more puzzle pieces together, or even if he didn't, she was likely to find herself in legal jeopardy very soon. On the face of it, the prospect was terrifying. The thing was, though, he didn't know about David Brady, and with Mario dead there was no way that she could see for him or anyone else to find out. That was the charge that would ruin her. That was the charge that would stick.

Because in the eyes of the law it was true.

Of all the rest, she was innocent.

She just had to keep that firmly fixed in her mind.

So maybe she could weather this. Maybe she could get through it with her job and her life intact.

Maybe she could end up making Tom look like the suspicious jackass he was.

But that still wouldn't bring him, or what they'd had this past weekend, back.

Damn it, she was crying. Right in the crowded middle of Kennedy Boulevard. She could feel the tears spilling over to course hot and wet down her cheeks. Glancing around self-consciously to discover that she was already the object of curiosity for a couple of passersby, she discreetly swiped at the tears with her knuckles.

They kept falling.

Damn it.

Ducking into the nearest alley, she turned her back to the street and gave a mighty sniff and scrubbed at her cheeks with both hands.

She couldn't go back to work like . . .

The thought was interrupted as a big black SUV nosed into the alley beside her.

She glanced at it in surprise at about the same time that something hard slammed into the back of her head.

Her eyes went wide, and then she crumpled without a sound.

27

By the time Tom reached the street, Kate was nowhere in sight. He was still furious enough to chew nails, still cursing under his breath, still calling himself ten kinds of an idiot for getting involved with her, for getting, as he suspected, played, but the bottom line was that no matter how many damned lies she told him, her life might still be in danger, and that wasn't something that he was prepared to take a chance on.

Castellanos had been killed with a single gunshot to the middle of the forehead. Just like the two guys in the burned-out U-Haul. And all of them were connected to the attempted escape from the Criminal Justice Center. It didn't require genius to deduce that maybe the same killer – or killers – had taken them all out. The questions were who and why, and what was the connection to Kate?

Until he knew for sure who was who and what was what, he was going to follow Kate around like a damned puppy dog unless she was actually at work, where he figured, in the midst of so many people, she was fairly safe.

And to hell with whether she liked it or not.

That Castellanos was the other man in the secure corridor, whom Charlie still wasn't one hundred percent positive he had seen, had been Tom's guess, although exactly how he had gotten himself out of the holding cell he'd been placed in and back in again would require some working out. But the more he'd tried fitting the puzzle pieces he knew with the puzzle pieces he didn't know, the more convinced he had become of it. Castellanos as Rodriguez's killer made a hell of a lot more sense than Kate in the role. But he still didn't have proof positive of it – except for Kate's face. Watching it as he spelled his theory out for her was better than a stack of sworn affidavits as far as he was concerned. Her eyes had flickered, and then she had gone white as a ghost.

Bingo.

The thing was, like he'd told Kate, so far he was the only one who had put it together. Maybe none of the others ever would. It was possible that, if he had forensics double-check Charlie's gun, the one with which Kate supposedly had killed Rodriguez, they would find a partial print, some DNA, something, belonging to Castellanos on it, and there would be the physical proof he needed. He should be on the phone right now, calling for those tests. But he wasn't. He was out on the damned street doing his best to pry secrets out of a woman whom he should be clapping handcuffs on and hauling off to jail about now. He wasn't briefing Fish, or Stella, or Kirchoff, on his newly gleaned insights, either. What he was doing was racking his damned brain to try to come up with some way, any way, to avoid doing just that. Given that Kate knew Castellanos; Castellanos had been part of the escape attempt and had, in fact, killed Rodriguez; and Kate had been in the secure corridor with Rodriguez and Castellanos when all this had gone down, the probability that she was involved in the escape attempt in some way seemed high. Add the fact that she had lied repeatedly to him and to everyone else about this, and the probability turned into a near certainty. The most obvious assistance she could have rendered the would-be escapees would have been to smuggle in the guns, which would make her, best-case scenario, an accessory to Murder One.

Worst-case scenario was something he didn't even want to think about.

But she had told him she hadn't had anything to do with any of that, and, God help him, he still – almost – believed her.

So then why was she lying? What was she scared of? What, exactly, was her connection to Castellanos? And what the hell had happened back there in that secure corridor? Because now that he thought about it, the terrified woman whose eyes had held his as she was dragged back in there was, in some indefinable way, different from the one who had come out.

Until he got more of a handle on exactly what Kate was hiding, he knew he wasn't going to put the puzzle pieces together for anyone else. Despite what he'd told her.

By keeping what he knew to himself, he was compromising his integrity, compromising the investigation, compromising his job. He made himself party to whatever the hell she was involved in. In all his years as a cop, he had never so much as been tempted to step over the line. Unlike some others in the department, his reputation was sterling. He was seen as – and he was, goddamn it – incorruptible.

That he was ready to blow all that for Kate both appalled and infuriated him.

But he was.

Because he'd been damned stupid enough to let himself fall in love with her.

'Ms. White?' The voice was a man's. It was soft and raspy, with a menacing undertone that made Kate shiver even as she hovered on the brink of regaining full consciousness. 'Can you hear me? Ms. White?'

Something cold touching the back of her neck made her jump. It shocked her back to full awareness. Her eyes popped open – to total blackness.

The cold thing was withdrawn. It had felt hard and metallic – like a gun.

Her heart lurched. Her pulse skyrocketed. She could see nothing – absolutely nothing at all. And it was the most terrifying thing in the world.

'You're awake.' There was satisfaction in the voice.

Something – a cloth, smooth and dry, its texture like that of a sheet or pillowcase – was wrapped around her eyes, covering them. That was why it was so black.

My God, had there been an accident? Was her head bandaged? There was a painful throbbing behind her right ear, and she remembered being hit on the head. She reached up instinctively, meaning to push the bandage out of the way, wanting to see, needing to see, only to discover that her hands were handcuffed together behind her back.

The hair rose on the back of her neck as she realized that what was covering her eyes wasn't a bandage but a blindfold.

'Who's there?' The question was meant to be sharp. Instead, it came out wobbly. At the same time she became aware that she was sitting on a cushiony leather or vinyl seat. There were people seated on either side of her: She could feel their bodies crowding against her, feel their heat, smell cologne or body spray and maybe garlic, hear their breathing – but the voice talking to her didn't belong to either of them. It was in front of her. She was conscious of being in motion, of certain sounds – a humming, a whooshing – and realized that she was in a vehicle of some sort. Seated in the rear, on a bench seat. The speaker, she felt, was in the front passenger seat.

All at once she remembered the black SUV that had pulled into the alley beside her.

'Let's just say we're friends of Mario's.'

Oh my God. She broke out in a cold sweat.

'What do you want?'

A chuckle. It made her skin crawl.

'Before I get to that, there's something you should

know: Mario was a big talker. We know all about you and how you shot that cop at that convenience store in Baltimore.'

Oh, no.

Her lungs seemed to have constricted, making it hard to breathe. Her heart hammered. Her pulse raced. She felt suddenly clammy as more cold sweat broke over her in a wave. A denial rose instantly to her lips, but she choked it back and didn't say a word. Whoever this was, whatever they wanted, pleading her innocence was clearly a waste of time. Anyway, even a denial confirmed that she at least knew what they were talking about, which could be a mistake. Best to say nothing.

'I'm sure you remember.' There was a rustle of movement from the front seat, and one of her minders – or so she was beginning to think of the men (she was almost sure they were men) on either side of her – shifted in his seat, jostling her. 'There's something else, too.'

She heard a small metallic sound and instinctively flinched. But the weapon they were threatening her with wasn't a gun: It was a tape recorder.

Kate listened with a sense of shock. It was the phone conversation she had had with Mario. The one where she'd asked him to meet her at her house on the night he was killed.

'We also have the gun that was used to kill Mario,' she said. 'It has your fingerprints all over it. We made sure of it while you were unconscious just now. You're a prosecutor. You do the math.'

Kate suddenly felt nauseated. Her head swam. Her heart pounded in sickening strokes. As a prosecutor, she knew very well she could take those vital pieces of evidence and run with them. To say nothing of what she could do with the murder of David Brady.

'Is there a point to this?' Her voice was surprisingly steady.

'Yeah, there's a point: Mario doesn't own you anymore. We do. And we want you to do us a favor.'

Kate's breath caught. 'What favor?'

Another chuckle. 'Don't worry, when the time comes, we'll let you know. For now, just remember we're around.'

The vehicle stopped. Kate's heart pounded so loudly that she could feel her pulse thudding against her eardrums. Her mouth went dry. What was happening now? Why were they stopping? The man on her right pushed her forward roughly, then reached behind her and unlocked the handcuffs.

'Tell anybody about this, and you're dead,' the voice said, and there was something in his tone that made Kate believe him. Then the handcuffs were pulled away, the blindfold was ripped off, and Kate was shoved out the door, which slammed shut behind her. She hit the ground on her hands and knees, hard. Tires squealed as the vehicle took off. It was the black SUV, but that was all she got. The license plate was impossible to read in the dark.

Because she *was* in the dark. While she'd been in the SUV, night had fallen. They had pushed her out, into the alley between her office and the parking garage where she usually left her car. Only today she hadn't. Someone had been going to drive it over from the impound lot and drop the keys off with security. The deal had been that Tom would meet her in her office at six, then walk her out to her car and follow her home.

It made her cold all over to think that the thugs in the SUV knew where she habitually parked her car.

And it made her cold in a different way to know that Tom wouldn't have been there anyway. They were over. History. He was too much the cop. And she had too much to hide.

Her whole life had blown up on her one more time. But she still had Ben to pick up. She still needed to get home.

Ignoring her aching head and stinging knees, she went inside to security and got the keys and location of her car from the guard on duty. Since it was already almost six-thirty and the place had pretty much emptied out, he offered to walk her to her car, which was on the second level. Sparing a fleeting thought for her briefcase, which was still in her office – she wasn't up to fetching it and possibly facing whichever of her colleagues remained on the ninth floor – she accepted. Of course, that was pretty much like closing the barn door after the horse had run off, but still, there was always the chance those thugs might come back.

She shivered at the thought.

As soon as the elevator doors opened and she and her big, burly bodyguard – Bob, by name – stepped out onto the second level, she saw Tom. Her eyes widened. Her heart lurched. For a moment, merely a split second, she was so glad to see him that it was like a burst of warmth inside her. Then she remembered all the reasons why she wasn't glad to see him, and she frowned. He was pacing in front of her Camry, clearly agitated, running a hand through his hair as he talked on his cell phone. Then he turned, saw her, and stopped dead. Watching her walk toward him, he said something into the phone, then snapped it shut. His eyes stayed glued on her. His expression could best be described as savage.

'Is this gentleman a problem, Ms. White?' Bob asked, sounding worried, as her spine stiffened and her head came up in response to the glare Tom was focusing on her. Bob was already reaching for the two-way radio clipped to his belt as he spoke.

'No.'

'Are you sure? Because he looks—' Bob's voice broke off because they were within earshot of Tom. Kate knew what he was going to say, anyway: furiously angry. On the verge of losing it. Dangerous.

'Where the hell have you been?' Tom burst out when she was close enough. He came toward her, his eyes blasting her. He barely spared Bob a glance, which was another indication of how truly upset he was. 'You scared the absolute shit out of me.'

'Hey, buddy, you want to watch your mouth

around—' Bob began, walking a little faster so that he was a pace or so ahead of her, putting himself between her and Tom. Tom snapped out his badge and flashed it at him, skewering him with his eyes at the same time, which had the effect that had undoubtedly been intended: Bob shut up and quit walking.

'It's okay,' Kate said over her shoulder to Bob as she passed him. 'I know him. Thanks for walking me to my car.'

Looking unhappy, Bob faded away.

'Where'd you go?' Tom was breathing fire at her. 'I've been up to your office multiple times. I've searched every damned floor of that building. I've walked every route I could think of between here and the temple. It was like you dropped off the face of the earth.'

The good thing about Tom being so worked up was that any signs she might be exhibiting of her recent ordeal went right over his head.

As she reached him, she was absolutely cool and proud of herself for it. His car was parked next to hers, she saw.

When she continued walking past him, he caught her arm. 'Wait a minute. I've been going out of my mind for a fucking hour and a half, and you're not even going to tell me where you've been?'

'It's none of your business.' Kate pulled her arm free and glared at him. 'Remember that whole call-my-lawyer conversation we had earlier? In case you couldn't tell, that was you getting dumped.'

For a moment he simply looked at her as if he couldn't believe what he was hearing. And she used that moment to slide into her car and power-lock all the doors.

'Goddamn it, Kate.' Glaring at her through the windshield, he slammed a hand down on her hood in frustration as she started the ignition. Then, as she put the transmission into drive, he got out of the way.

Smart man.

He followed her all the way to the Perrys'. Which was fine. By the time she reached Ben's babysitter's, she had a plan. She was going to take Ben and run.

She didn't know exactly who those goons in the SUV were. What she did know was they scared her. Worse than Mario ever had. Because she didn't think they were street punks. There was a deadlier, more organized, more polished feel to them. Like they were professionals. Like they were Mob.

Were the Black Dragons associated with the Mob? Who the hell knew? Who the hell cared? A few days from now, it wasn't going to matter to her anymore.

Because this was too big and too dangerous for her to deal with. Taking on Mario was one thing. Taking on a group like this – she knew as well as she knew her name that she couldn't win. She knew how these people worked from bitter experience. She would end up doing their bidding forevermore, or she would end up dead. It was as simple and as terrible as that.

She and Ben couldn't go tonight, because she didn't have any money except the few dollars stuffed in her pocket. If they were going to head for California – or maybe Oregon or Washington, somewhere as far away as she could get – she needed every dime she could scrape together. All that was in her bank account was her most recent paycheck. Could she afford to wait for another one? The more she could get together, the better off they would be, but the problem was, she didn't know how much time she had.

The creeps in the car wanted a 'favor.' But she had no idea what the favor was, or when they would cash it in.

Waiting around to find out was probably not a good idea.

She could clean out her 401(k), which had maybe a thousand dollars in it. There were things she could pawn. Her wedding ring, which she never wore but kept carefully to give to Ben one day. A video camera. Probably other things if she looked around. Getting money that way was quick and easy – she'd done it plenty of times before. It wouldn't be a lot, but added to her paycheck, it would have to do, because she didn't think she could take more than a week max to get ready. At least the money would get them a place to stay for a month or so, and she could waitress if necessary until she could find another job.

Just thinking of leaving behind everything she had worked so hard for made her sick. The house, the furniture – she was going to have to abandon it all, except for what she could carry in her car. Backing a U-Haul up to the door and loading it up with all their things would not, she was sure, be wise. Because they might be watching her.

The thought made her heart start tap-dancing in her chest.

She had things going on at work, too. Hearings. Depositions. Trials. The idea of just walking out on them was staggering. But there just wasn't any other way that she could see to keep herself and Ben safe.

At this point, if they left, she didn't think the goons would come looking for them. She was no threat to them, not like she had been to Mario. If she lit out now, before she got in any deeper, she didn't see any reason why they wouldn't just let her go.

So that was the plan.

Even if every time she thought about it she felt like she was bleeding to death inside.

It was hard putting on a happy face for the Perrys, for Ben, apologizing for being late and pretending all was well and things were going to go on this way forever, world without end. As quickly as she could get things together, they would be gone.

Ben would be sad.

She would be sad.

But what choice did she have?

'Are you okay, Mom?' Ben asked, as they pulled into the driveway. Tonight she was using the garage, and to hell with any bad karma from Mario's ghost, because she wanted to load a few things in the car to pawn tomorrow, and she didn't want to go outside to do it. It was far-fetched, she knew, to think that the goons might be watching her twenty-four-seven, but still . . .

Pressing the button for the garage door – God, she was even going to miss the damned glacier-slow door – she looked over at Ben.

'I'm fine. Why?'

'Because I told you I made a basket in gym, and all you said was *mm-hmm*.'

'You made a basket? *Wow*.' Despite everything, Kate's face lit up. For the first time since she had picked him up, she really focused on her son. He nodded and grinned at her.

'It was a fluke, though. I just kind of threw it up there and it hit the edge of the backboard and rolled in.'

'That works. What did the rest of—?' The door was up, and she was just getting ready to pull forward when Ben interrupted her.

'I got to go tell Tom.' Grabbing the door handle, he opened the door and burst out of the car like a mini-explosion.

Looking in the rearview mirror, Kate saw that the Taurus was pulling in behind her.

28

Kate drove on into the garage and parked. As she got out, she saw that Tom had parked in the driveway. He was standing beside his car, and Ben, practically vibrating with excitement, was standing in front of him, no doubt telling him all about the basket he'd made.

Tom was smiling down at Ben.

Kate's heart clenched. Her stomach turned over.

The hardest thing about leaving was going to be Tom.

As much as she knew that getting involved with him had been an error, as surely as she knew that ending it was the only possible course of action she could take, leaving Tom behind when she ran was going to hurt like nothing she had ever felt.

Gritting her teeth, she walked toward the pair of them.

'Sweetie, why don't you run on in?' she said to Ben when she reached them. Tom looked at her over Ben's head. His smile was gone. The drive had apparently cooled his temper, because he was no longer obviously seething. But there was a glint in his eyes as he met her gaze that told her the underlying anger was still there.

'You want to talk to Tom, huh?' Speculation was plain in Ben's face as he glanced from one to the other of them.

So much for trying to keep stuff from Ben.

'Yeah, I do. So would you please get out of here?'

He made a face at her, glanced at Tom, who responded with a sympathetic grimace, and then obediently headed through the garage for the house.

'You can go ahead and get started on your homework,' Kate called after him out of habit. Although, of course, (a) he wasn't going to, and (b) homework for this school didn't really matter anymore. In a week or two, he would be starting over somewhere new.

'I want you to leave,' Kate said without preamble when Ben disappeared inside the house. 'We took a chance, we had fun, but it's over.'

Tom leaned a hip against the side of his car and looked at her consideringly. The light from the garage was behind her, which kept her face in shadow. His she could see. His expression was grim.

'Look, I know you're lying to me. I know you've been lying to me from the first. I admit, I don't quite have a handle on what you're hiding, but I will figure it out, unless you want to make this easier on both of us and just tell me.'

Okay, at least his bulldoglike tenacity was making this less painful than it could have been for her.

She turned away. 'Good-bye, Tom.'

'They're professional hits, Kate. The two guys in the U-Haul, and Castellanos in your garage. I'm willing to stake my badge on it. What's scaring the life out of me here is the thought that you could be next. Think about it: Everybody we know of who was in any way involved in that escape attempt is now dead – except you.'

That stopped her in her tracks. She closed her eyes for an instant – her back was to him so he couldn't see – as an icy finger of fear ran down her spine. Her hands clenched into fists. What if the guys in the SUV came back, only this time with murder in mind? What if they weren't the only ones out there? The possibilities were endless – and terrifying.

'I keep telling you, I wasn't involved in it.' But she turned back to face him. Her heart was racing. She had to force herself to breathe normally.

'And I take your word for that.' He straightened away from the car. His eyes were intent on her face. 'You don't want to continue our personal relationship? That's fine. Not a problem. Consider it over. But I don't like the idea of you and Ben being alone here at night. Even with the new locks and the alarm system, you're too easy a target. All somebody has to do is kick in the door, pump off a few bullets, and get out before the cops show up. Piece of cake, especially for a professional.'

Kate felt her throat dry up. She had never thought of it that way before. She wished she wasn't thinking of it that way now.

'If you go telling everyone down at the PPD your personal theory of what happened in the security corridor, I won't have to worry about it, will I? According to you, I'll be in jail.'

His face tightened. 'I'm not planning on telling anybody just yet. Except for me and Fish, you're not on anyone's radar screen yet. What I've got so far is exactly what you said – theory, but no proof.'

Kate understood what he was telling her: Despite what he'd said earlier, he was going to keep what he knew, and what he suspected, to himself.

For now, at least.

'Okay, fine, you can stay.' Her tone was less than gracious. A moment later she added, almost gruffly, 'Thank you.'

And she wasn't just talking about his offer to stay the night.

His eyes were dark and unreadable as they met hers. 'You're welcome.'

Turning away again, she headed for the house. Having him stay over until she could get things together and take off with Ben was only smart. As many unknowns as there were in this, it just might keep them alive.

But at the same time it was going to be hard on her heart.

Tom followed her in without another word.

Two days later, Kate acknowledged the truth: She was stalling. Even while she was making preparations to run, she kept putting off actually leaving. During the day, she continued to handle her normal workload while also going over her schedule for the next few weeks, postponing and handing off what she could without rousing suspicion, and making copious notes about other things she was working on so whoever took over for her – probably Bryan, at least at first – would know what was going on. She amassed as much cash as she could. She packed suitcases in secret and stored them in the Camry's trunk. Their most prized possessions – Ben's baby book, the few things she had of his father's, precious mementos and photographs that couldn't be replaced – she tucked away in the trunk, too. If her heart ached when Bryan called her for an update on a case, or when Mona brought in her long black dress and sparkly earrings and insisted Kate try them on, or when a hundred other ordinary, everyday workplace happenings went down, well, she could deal.

She was having a much harder time dealing with the idea of leaving Tom.

Not that there was anything going on there anymore. He met her at work and followed her home; he ate supper with them (ordering pizza once, and helping with the cleanup each night); he played ball with Ben (who had yet to make another basket in gym, but who seemed philosophical about it); he watched TV and slept on the couch. He didn't grill her, didn't ask her any questions at all, as a matter of fact, and spoke to her very little. Their relationship could best be described as polite but guarded. In fact, Ben asked her in private if they'd had a fight, and when Kate responded with an 'of course not,' he gave her a look that said, *Yeah, right.* The bottom line was, he was there as a protector only, and she did her best to stay out of his way. She had the feeling he was doing the same thing with her. Nevertheless, just from living under the same roof with him, she learned certain things: that he was prone to being grumpy and taciturn in the mornings before he had his coffee. At night he was cheerful with Ben, less so with her, though occasionally she would catch him following her with his eyes. That he left dishes in the sink and the toilet seat up.

The thing was, though, she loved having him in the house.

She should never have let him stay.

Because more than ever now, she didn't want to leave.

Mid-morning Thursday, she got the wake-up call she needed. She went to the ladies' room during a break in an evidentiary hearing at the Criminal Justice Center, which was once again open for business. The restroom was empty when she went in, and she ducked into a stall, meaning to make it a quick in and out because the judge had given them only a ten-minute break. She was in the stall, actually sitting on the toilet, when something made her glance to her right.

There, just visible beneath the wall of the stall next door, was a man's leg, which she could see from just above the ankle down, in black trousers and a black wingtip shoe.

Her eyes went wide. Her heart leaped. Her pulse surged.

'Hello, Ms. White.' He spoke before she could move or suck in enough air for a scream. As she realized who it was, her heart started beating very fast. 'It's almost time for you to do us that favor. Answer if you can hear me.'

She went cold all over. But what could she do? Clap her hands over her ears? Pretend to be deaf? Jump up and run?

Play the game out.

'I can hear you,' she said.

'Good. Tomorrow night, you're going to a fund-raiser for Jim Wolff at the Trocadero Theatre. We'll call you while you're there with further instructions. Please repeat what I just said.'

Kate's hands clenched into fists on her lap.

'You'll call me with instructions while I'm at the fund-raiser for Jim Wolff.'

'That's right. You go to the fund-raiser, stay there until we call, do what we tell you then, and we're square. We leave you alone. You screw up, or tell anybody about this, and we kill you. Got it?'

'Yes.'

'Good.'

There was the sound of the stall door opening, a quick footfall, and then he was gone.

Kate, on the other hand, sat there shivering for so long that she was late for the rest of the hearing.

What could they possibly want her to do?

Short answer: nothing good.

Maybe she was supposed to deliver a message. Or steal something. Or rob someone. Or . . .

The possibilities took on hellishly sinister overtones the more she thought about them. Jim Wolff was a highly controversial figure. A former vice president. The clear front-runner for his party's nomination. Quite possibly the next President of the United States. He had heavy security around him at all times. Access to the fund-raiser was tightly controlled. Already, she'd had to turn in the name of her planned escort for the evening – Tom, whom she had asked over the weekend when things between them were different, although the date was clearly not going to happen now – to be vetted by the FBI or the Secret Service or whoever vetted those things.

The thought hit her like a two-by-four – was it possible they thought they could blackmail her into helping with an assassination attempt?

But then, it wasn't going to happen. Nothing was going to happen. Because she wasn't going to be there for it to happen to.

Time's up. We have to go.

Even though it broke her heart to leave.

But she knew she had to be careful. They had known where she parked her car. They had cornered her in the alley Monday. They found her in the restroom today.

They *were* watching. And the really terrible thing about it was, she didn't have a clue who *they* were.

Anyone – colleagues, juror, people in the system, passersby – could be one of them. They could be watching at any time, and she wouldn't even know. Kate shivered at the thought.

They couldn't be allowed to guess that she was going to run away.

She didn't know what the consequences would be, but she was confident they would be bad.

With that in mind, she made sure to keep the rest of the day as normal-seeming as she could. Luckily, because she was so anxious she could barely think, the highlight of the afternoon was a deposition, which she could do in her sleep. She put her office in order, got her briefcase – the money was stashed in there – and her coat. With all her heart she wanted to say good-bye to Mona, to Bryan, to Cindy, and to the entire rest of the ninth floor. She'd been so proud to work there, so proud to be one of them, so proud of the life she had made for herself and Ben. But in the end she didn't say a word to anyone, because she couldn't. The whole key was to make this look, to any possible observer, like any other day. Forty-five minutes early – not too early to be suspicious but early enough to avoid Tom – she walked out of the building for the last time.

She had a huge lump in her throat as she drove away.

The plan was, she was going to meet Tom at the back door of the building at six. Tom would wait for a while, she knew. He would call her cell phone. He would go up to her office. He would look around the building. First, he would be scared when he didn't find her. Then, when he saw that her car was gone and figured out that she had left without him, he would be livid.

She couldn't let him just wonder what had happened to her. Once she had Ben, once she was safely out of the city, she would call him and let him know she was leaving.

Although, of course, she couldn't tell him why.

Dangerous as it probably was, she made one final swing by her house. Her heart was in her throat as she ran inside, but there were still a few last things she couldn't leave behind. Ben's teddy bear, which he loved. A few of his favorite stuffed animals. The book he was reading. The damned beginner basketball.

That was what finally made her cry.

As she pulled out of her house for the last time, tears were streaming down her face, and it was all because of that stupid basketball.

Forever after, every time she looked at it, she would think of Tom.

And her heart would break.

When had she fallen in love with him? She didn't know – but she had.

Getting Ben was quick. Of course, not knowing that he would never see them again, he left the Perrys with a nonchalant 'bye,' which she just as nonchalantly – she hoped – echoed.

When he got in the car she had a bad moment,

because there was no way he was going to miss the stuff piled in the front passenger seat. Even though she had been very careful to cover it with her coat.

'What's all that?' he asked, right on schedule, frowning at the mound.

'Oh, just some things I picked up today.' She had been debating when to tell him the truth for most of the afternoon, but she wanted to hold off for as long as she could. Even if he begged not to go, she couldn't change her mind, and that would upset both of them. If he cried, she would cry, too. It was all she could do to keep her composure now. 'How did school go?'

As far as distractions went, that worked. He told her, and she nodded and made what she hoped were the appropriate responses as she turned, not toward home but toward the expressway. He would see they weren't headed home soon and ask . . .

Twilight had fallen, and her automatic headlights were now on. The twin beams arced over a stand of near-leafless trees, a closed-up-tight metal garage, and an empty lot as they left the residential neighborhood behind. Stopping at the stop sign just before the ramp to the expressway, she saw that it was ten minutes past six o'clock. Tom would be getting impatient by now. He probably wasn't too worried about her yet, but he soon would be.

Oh, God, she didn't want to leave. Her heart felt like a giant hand was squeezing it dry.

'Who's that?' Ben gasped, startling her out of her reverie.

It was the only warning she received before the window behind her smashed with a boom. Little beads of glass hit her in the back of the head as she jumped and her head whipped around toward the sound.

'Mom!' Ben screamed in terror.

With a single all-encompassing glance, she saw that his window had been broken out and someone – a man, dressed in black, black gloves, black coat – had an arm in the opening, reaching down to open his door.

'No!' she screamed.

A car squealed to a halt in front of her, blocking them in, blocking her from stomping the gas and rocketing away. A man jumped out of the car, but all she saw of him was a blur as she turned in her seat, frantically seeking another way out. Behind her a second vehicle slammed on its brakes, stopping her from going in reverse. Screaming, shoving the transmission into park, adrenaline exploding like a bomb inside her, Kate surged partway through the opening between the front seats to grab her son, to keep him inside the car, to fight off the man who had wrenched the door open and, impossibly, unbelievably, was yanking Ben out.

'Let him go!'

'Mom!'

She couldn't hold him. His blue jacket was satiny, slippery.

'Ben!' she shrieked as he was pulled from her grasp, then turned and catapulted from the car through the driver's door to go to his rescue. 'Help! Help!'

But they were alone at the stop sign, and it was almost dark, and the world was gray and full of shadows so no one could see, even if there had been anyone nearby. But there wasn't, this particular spot was light industrial, with small businesses in warehouses and pole buildings that seemed to be deserted. No cars in the gravel parking lots, no cars on the street . . .

There is no help.

'Mom! *Mom!*'

'Let him go!'

Even as she threw herself after him, something slammed hard into the back of her head. The pain was blinding. Kate dropped to her knees and saw stars, and no doubt would have blacked out had she not been so riveted on saving her son. As the world swam around her, her eyes never left him. Kicking and fighting for all he was worth, Ben was being carried away, screaming, in the grip of a large man in black with a ski mask over his face.

Toward the white panel van that was blocking in the Camry from behind.

'Mom!'

'Ben!' It was a choked cry uttered as she struggled to get to her feet.

She didn't even see the man who punched her in the stomach until the blow landed. It felt like a train ramming into her just below her belly button. Folding forward, sick with pain, her breath exploding from her body, she collapsed to her knees again and at the same time caught a glimpse of her attacker – but only as a quickly moving shape. Then he was behind her, grabbing her around the neck in a choke hold as she held her midsection and gasped for breath.

'You shouldn't've tried to run,' he said, as he yanked her upright. It was the same man as before, the voice from the restroom and the SUV.

'Mom!' Ben's terrified voice pierced her like a spear. 'Mom! Mom!'

Hauled to her feet, shaking, her knees barely able to support her weight, Kate gagged and choked and fought, straining against the arms locked around her neck and waist as Ben, screaming, was thrust into the back of the van. The door rattled shut.

Ben.

But she screamed it only inside her head, because the arm around her throat was now too tight for any cries to escape.

Ben, she screamed silently again as the van reversed and then, with a squeal of tires, shot forward again, driving around them, disappearing into the dark.

'Ms. White, you need to listen closely,' the man holding her said. 'You didn't do what we told you once already, and now, see, you've put your son in danger. Tonight and tomorrow, you act normal, like nothing's wrong. Tomorrow night, you go to that fundraiser and you wait for us to call you and you do what we say.' He paused, and his arm around her neck loosened just enough so that she could suck in air. 'You do that, you get your son back. You go to the cops or anybody with this, or you don't answer the phone, or you don't do what we tell you when we call, and your boy's dead. You understand?'

'Ben,' Kate choked out, her eyes straining desperately in the direction the van had taken.

'*You understand?*' His arm forced her head up.

'Yes. *Yes.*'

He let go. Her knees gave way, and she collapsed onto the ground.

29

They would kill him. The fear filled Kate with an icy dread, causing her heart to pound in slow, sickening strokes, making her pull over twice to vomit during the short drive back to her house. She was deathly afraid she knew how these people worked: Now that they had Ben, they would kill him no matter what she did. Oh, God, would they even wait until tomorrow? Or was he already . . .

She went dizzy at the thought.

Stop, she ordered herself fiercely as her mind reeled from visions of her terrified little boy being hurt, being . . .

Shuddering, she had to force the hideous images away. If Ben was to have any chance at all, she had to get and keep a clear head.

Dear God, please keep him safe.

As she pulled into her garage, she felt a wave of nausea so strong that she nearly didn't make it into the house in time.

I shouldn't have waited. I should have left yesterday, or the day before . . .

She'd stayed to get more money. She'd stayed

because she hated to leave. She'd stayed for Tom.

Tom.

The thought of him steadied her. There was someone she could run screaming to, someone she could turn to for help, someone on her side, after all.

You go to the cops or anybody with this . . . and your boy's dead.

He was dead if she didn't: She was convinced of it.

I have to be careful. They might be watching.

Okay. Make this look real. I'm home, doing exactly what they want.

Quickly, she went through the downstairs, closing the curtains, making sure the panels met at the center so that no one could see inside, turning on lights as she went. She went up to her bedroom – she couldn't even look at Ben's open door without tears streaming from her eyes – and closed those curtains and turned on that light, too. Then she called Tom.

'Where the hell are you?' he exploded at her over the phone when she said his name. 'Damn it, Kate—'

'Tom, listen.'

He must have heard the distress in her voice, because he broke off in mid-tirade.

'What's wrong?'

She took a deep breath. The idea that they were watching, listening, with eyes and ears everywhere, unnerved her. If she thought that by doing what they wanted tomorrow, they would release Ben unharmed, she would have done anything. But she didn't. And so this was the only choice she could make.

Making it terrified her.

'Something's happened.' Her voice sounded raspy to her own ears.

She heard him inhale. 'I'm on my way.'

'No! No.' She tried to think. 'Don't come to the house. Go to the corner of Spruce and Mulberry' – two blocks away – 'and wait for me there.'

'What the hell?'

'Tom, please. How long will it take you to get there?'

'Fifteen minutes, max.'

'Park. Stay in the car. I'll come to you.'

'Jesus, Kate, what the hell is going on?'

'I'll tell you when I see you,' she said, and disconnected.

She was already wearing her black pantsuit and flats, which was good because she wanted to blend into the night. She went out to the car to retrieve her black coat, doing her best not to look at Ben's things that lay beneath as she uncovered them. Putting on the coat, buttoning it up to her neck, she wrapped the gray wool scarf around her head to hide her bright hair. Then she turned on the TV in the living room, just to make it look even more like she was still home in case anyone was watching and could tell about things like whether or not the TV was on. Then she went into the kitchen. Turning off the kitchen light, she waited a moment. Then, taking a deep breath, she opened the door and slipped outside into the dark.

There was a full moon, but it was still low in the sky and pasty white, and the light it gave off was faint. The night was cold and breezy, which was good because it helped clear her head. Heart pounding, casting furtive glances everywhere, keeping to the deepest of the shadows, she made her way to the intersection, watching for Tom, keeping carefully out of sight. Tom pulled up just a few minutes after she got there. Before he had time to park, she ran across the sidewalk and tapped smartly on the passenger window. The door unlocked with an audible *click,* and she slipped into his car.

The brief illumination of the interior light terrified her. What if they were nearby and saw her in Tom's car? Her heart pounded. Her pulse raced. She glanced desperately all around. If they saw her they would kill Ben – but who would be watching here?

Please, God, let no one be watching here.

'What the hell is going on with you?'

The light faded. Kate sank down in the seat, wrapping her arms around herself, shivering, feeling as if all her bones had turned to jelly.

'Don't sit here. Drive. Get us out of this neighborhood.' She sucked in air as, without asking any more questions, he did as she said. The car turned the corner, heading toward the entrance to the subdivision. 'Oh my God, Tom, they took Ben.'

'*What?*' He stood on the brakes.

'*Keep driving.*' She was frantic. 'If they see—'

'Who? If who sees? Who took Ben?' But the Taurus

was once again moving. His hands were clamped tightly around the wheel. His face had gone hard and tense. But his voice had gone the other way, maximum calm and cool, and she was instantly reminded of the cop who had tried to talk Rodriguez down in courtroom 207.

'I don't know.' Her voice was unsteady. 'Mob, I think. Or maybe – I don't know. Everything you suspected about me – it's true. I have been lying. About all of it. I . . . They said they'd kill him if I went to the police or anybody. But I think they'll kill him anyway. You have to help me figure out what to do.'

She was shaking so hard her teeth chattered by the time she finished.

'O-kay.' She heard him exhale. 'When did they take Ben?'

His steady self-control helped her get hold of herself. She couldn't lose it. Ben's life was at stake.

'Half an hour ago, maybe.'

'Where did this happen?'

'At the entrance to the Perrys' subdivision. I was at a stop sign, getting ready to turn onto the expressway, and . . . they dragged him out of my car.' Her stomach twisted. Tears stung her eyes.

'Who dragged him out of your car?'

'I told you, I don't know. I saw two men – they were wearing ski masks. One hit me, one grabbed Ben. There had to be more, though, in the van and the car.'

Tom swore under his breath. But when he spoke

again, it was in that same controlled voice. 'Can you give me any more of a description of the vehicles than that? It helps a lot to be specific when you're putting out an APB.'

'It was a white van, a paneled van like workers use. And a dark car. A sedan. Four-door.' Then it hit her, and terror shot through her. 'You can't put out an APB. They told me not to call the police. They told me to go home and act like nothing had happened. I turned on the lights and the TV so they'll think I'm still in there.' She took a deep breath. 'They want me to do something for them. Tomorrow night at that fund-raiser for Jim Wolff. They said they would call and tell me what it is they want me to do once I was there. And if I do it they'll let Ben go, and if I don't they'll kill him.'

'Jesus.' For a moment, naked emotion came through in his voice. Then Tom cut his eyes at her. 'Kate, listen: I need to put an APB out on those vehicles right now.' The steadiness was back. 'And I need to call Rick Stuart on the Major Case Squad – they've got the expertise in kidnapping. And I need to call Mac Willets at the FBI.'

'No.' Kate rocked back and forth in her seat, staring unseeingly out at the dark streets surrounding them. Panic rose like bile in her throat. 'You can't. They've been following me. They know things about me. What if they're listening to police scanners to see if I called the police? What if one of them's a cop?'

Tom was silent for a beat.

'You're being paranoid.'

'No,' Kate said. 'No, I'm not. You don't know.'

'All right. Then you need to tell me.' He seemed to think for a moment. 'We're going to my place, and you're going to tell me the whole thing, and then we'll decide what's best to do.'

Kate didn't object. It was the closest to a plan she could come up with.

He made a right, and a few minutes later they were on the expressway. Fifteen minutes after that, they were walking into his living room, having, at Kate's insistence, parked on a side street and entered through the back door.

In case someone knew that she'd been seeing Tom and was watching his place, too.

'Damn it to hell and back anyway,' he said when he flipped on the light and got his first good look at her. 'Are you hurt? You said they hit you. Where?'

Kate had no idea what she looked like, but it was easy to guess that it was bad. She was shivering and sweating and nauseated and light-headed all at the same time. Her head ached and her stomach churned. Her eyes felt swollen and grainy. Her lips and mouth were dry. She had no doubt she was deathly pale.

'It doesn't matter.' Her eyes met his. Her voice shook. 'I'm so scared they'll hurt Ben.'

'Yeah, I know.' He pulled her into his arms without another word, holding her tightly, offering her wordless comfort. Kate wrapped her arms around his waist and pressed her face into his chest and breathed in the familiar scent of him. He was wearing his gray corduroy jacket. It felt cool and soft against her cheek. Beneath it she could feel the solid shape of his shoulder holster and the sturdy warmth of his body. If she hadn't had him to turn to, she didn't know what she would have done. He was so solid, so strong, and she trusted him absolutely, something she had rarely done before in her life. But she allowed herself only a moment of weakness before she pulled out of his embrace.

He let her go.

Clasping her hands together, she looked at him anxiously. 'I need to tell you what happened. We need to decide what to do.'

'You're not hurt anywhere? You're sure?'

'I'm sure.'

'Then start talking.' He unwound the scarf from her hair, then undid the two buttons that fastened her coat. She slid out of it, and he threw it and her scarf over a small rocking chair beside the fireplace. 'Sit down first. You look like you're going to pass out.'

She felt like it, too, and so she sank down on the couch and drank the Jack Daniel's and Coke – heavy on the Jack – he brought her and quickly told him the whole story: her early history with Mario; David Brady's murder; Mario's recognition of her in the secure corridor and his subsequent shooting of Rodriguez and attempt to blackmail her into getting him out of jail; the visits to her house by Mario's henchmen, which Tom fortunately had interrupted; that it was Mario in the back of her car and that he had been taking her to meet his 'friends' when she escaped; about her decision to deal with (okay, kill) Mario on her own and how she had called Mario to set up a meeting at her house and how she had thought the whole nightmare was finally, blessedly, over when he had wound up dead in her garage, courtesy of someone else. Then she told him about being snatched off the street by Mario's 'friends,' and how they had threatened her and told her she was going to do them a favor or else, and about the man who had followed her into the ladies' room at the Criminal Justice Center earlier that day. And finally she told him about Ben being snatched away.

By the time she finished, tears brimmed in her eyes, and she closed them to try to keep them from spilling over. But she could feel them seeping out, trickling down her cheeks, sliding hot and wet over her skin.

'Hey,' he said. He'd been standing over her, his face hardening, as he listened intently to every word. Now he took the nearly empty glass from her hand, and as she opened her eyes in response she saw him set it on the table/box beside the couch. He still had his cop face on, but as she looked up at him and their eyes met, his expression softened slightly. He bent, scooping her up in his arms, and sat down in the shabby green armchair next to the couch with her in his lap. 'Don't cry. It's going to be okay.'

'It doesn't matter about me.' Her voice was fierce as she tightened her arms around his neck and buried her face in his shoulder and sobbed and shook and let her tears soak into his jacket. 'It's Ben. We've got to find Ben.'

'We'll find him.' His voice was soothing. His arms around her were comforting and strong. 'It sounds like we've got some time. Whoever took him would be stupid to hurt him before they've got what they want out of you.' His hand was on her nape, long-fingered and warm, and then it gently burrowed beneath her hair. In the course of her narrative, Kate had told him how they had hit her in the back of the head, and now she winced as he found the bump. 'How bad does that hurt?'

'It's just a bump. I'll live.' Impatient, she brushed it off. Her minor physical injuries were nothing compared to the constant, grinding torture of Ben's loss. Sniffling, gritting her teeth, fighting to control her emotions with every bit of determination she had, she lifted her head from his shoulder and looked at him steadily. 'Do you think, if I do what they tell me tomorrow night, there's any way they might just let him go?'

Tears still stung her eyes, and her voice was thick with anguish, but she was fighting hard to get her distress under control. Her fear for Ben oozed like some terrible icy poison along her nerve endings, through her veins, and into every organ of her body. She prayed for his safety with every breath she drew.

'No.'

Okay. At least he was honest. She didn't think so, either.

'We have to find out who took him. Mario was a Black Dragon. They're a gang . . .'

'I know all about Castellanos and the Black Dragons. I've been looking into his background pretty thoroughly these last few days, believe me. I know you visited him at the detention center, for instance.'

'Oh, yeah?' Had she really thought he had stopped investigating her? Well, at least now he was saved the effort. She had handed herself over to him on a platter, and the legal consequences were still to come. But she didn't care. All she cared about now was saving Ben. Whatever it took.

'Did you forge Judge Hardy's signature on the release order that got Castellanos sprung from jail?'

'What?' Kate sat up in his lap, dashing the last of the tears from her eyes with both hands as she spoke. 'Somebody forged the release order? It wasn't me.'

Tom returned her gaze steadily. 'There's a security tape from the clerk's office showing the order being filed. I haven't looked at it yet. I wasn't sure I wanted to know.'

'I swear I didn't,' she said. 'I'm finished telling lies, I promise.'

The slight inclination of his head accepted that.

'Somebody did. I'd say identifying that somebody is our first step, because it seems pretty clear to me that Castellanos was signed out of jail to take you to his "friends," whoever they are. Otherwise, why get him out? And why kill him? Right now, I'm thinking he was killed so whoever this is would have sole control over you.'

'I was going to check on who signed the order to get Mario out,' Kate said. 'But I never got around to it. It didn't seem that important.'

'Well, now it is.' He stood up with her without warning, lifting her easily, depositing her back on the couch. Straightening, he pulled his cell phone out of his jacket pocket.

'Tom—' The sight of it alarmed her.

'I need to call the people I told you about, Rick Stuart with Major Cases and Mac Willets with the FBI. And I want to bring Fish in on this. We need help, and I know those guys personally and I trust them. It won't go beyond them until we put together some kind of plan.'

The idea of telling anyone else sent cold shivers up and down Kate's spine, but she trusted Tom and he said he trusted them, so she nodded.

He picked up the phone and walked away from her and placed the calls. By the time he returned, phone nowhere in sight, Kate was shaking again.

'They're on their way,' he told her. She was huddled in a corner of the couch, and he stopped in front of her. Doing her best to control the long shudders that racked her, she met his gaze in mute inquiry. 'Willets thinks like you do, that this may be part of a conspiracy to murder Jim Wolff. If so, this is big. Even if it turns out to be wrong, it still gives us enough leverage to swing a deal.'

'What kind of deal?'

'In return for your full cooperation, we can offer immunity from prosecution for any crimes you may have committed, including the murder of that security guard. We'll get it in writing when everyone gets here.'

Kate took a deep breath. The idea of no longer having that hanging over her head was dazzling – or it would have been were it not for Ben.

'I don't care,' she said, in a voice she kept carefully steady. 'Just as long as I get Ben back.'

'Well, I do care.' Tom caught one of her hands and pulled her to her feet. 'We'll get the immunity deal done. And we'll save Ben, too. Why don't you go wash your face while I make some coffee? It's going to be a long night.'

As far as Kate was concerned, the rest of the night and most of the following day went by in a blur. The reinforcements Tom had summoned arrived, and after that, things seemed to happen at warp speed. Certain moments stood out, such as when she signed the immunity deal Tom and Special Agent Mac Willets had hammered out and knew that she was finally free of the threat of prosecution for David Brady's death – although the death itself would forever stain her soul. And when she sat with Tom and Fish in the kitchen, watching on a monitor Fish brought the replay of the security tape showing a Caucasian male in maybe his late thirties to mid-forties wearing a gray business suit handing Mario's release order across the counter to the clerk. The quality of the tape was not good, and the angle was never right to get a view of the subject's face. All they could glean from it was a general description that could have fit hundreds of people. But watching the subject walk to the counter – which she did at least three dozen times – Kate was struck by the niggling sense that he was somehow familiar. Try as she did, though, she couldn't come up with even a tentative ID. Their next hope for uncovering his identity was running a fingerprint and DNA check on the document itself, which was ordinarily a process that could take several weeks. A favor was called in, and the results were promised for the next day. Which meant the timing was going to be way too close for them to count on it as a means of tightening the net around whoever was holding Ben.

Who'd had no supper. Who might be cold, or exposed to the elements. Who was certainly terrified.

Thinking of those things made Kate want to climb the walls with panic, so she tried not to think about them. But she couldn't sleep, although Tom urged her to lie down for a few hours. And she couldn't eat, although he tried to get her to. All she could do was down coffee and assist every way she could in trying to unravel the web that would lead to Ben.

Before dawn, it was agreed that Kate needed to go back to her house, so that she could leave from it the next day as if she had spent the night there. She would go to work, trying to behave as normally as possible. Then she would go home again, where Tom would pick her up at seven for the fund-raiser. At the fund-raiser, she would go through the motions until the phone call came through. What couldn't happen was for the conspirators to suspect anything had gone wrong with their plan.

Even if Ben was rescued before then – and Kate prayed that the fingerprint or DNA evidence would come through from that release order, or the description she'd given of the van and car would cause one of them to be spotted, or that an investigation of the Black Dragons might lead to something that would lead to Ben – going to the fund-raiser and waiting for the phone call were part of the deal she'd made to get immunity.

At the idea that Ben might still be missing by tomorrow night, Kate felt cold to her bone marrow.

Tom took her home at about five A.M., walking her through the dark backyards, sneaking into her kitchen with her. As far as she could tell, no one was watching. The house was just as she had left it, with some lights on and the curtains drawn tightly. She took a shower, changed her clothes, drank coffee, and took a single bite of the toast Tom had made. It made her stomach heave, so she didn't eat anything else.

At shortly after seven, when it was time for her to leave for work, he walked her to her car in the dark garage.

'A car will follow you in,' he told her as she unlocked her door with a beep of her keys. 'You may not see them, but there'll be somebody on you all day.'

They had agreed that it would be best if he stayed away from her until he picked her up that night.

'Okay.' Kate opened her door. The Camry's interior light flashed on, making her cringe instinctively. But of course they were in the windowless garage. No one could possibly see inside.

'What's all that?' Tom was looking at the pile of Ben's most precious possessions that was still heaped in the passenger seat. The sight of Ben's teddy bear alone was enough to make Kate's throat close up. So she didn't look at it, turning instead to look at Tom, who stood right behind her, a tall, dark figure in the gloom just beyond the reach of the car's light.

'Ben's things.' Her reply was as brief as she could make it, because it hurt so much to talk about. 'Stuff I couldn't leave behind.'

'Were you really going to just leave without a word?' There was something in his voice that made her gaze sharpen and focus on his face.

'At the time, it didn't seem like I had any choice.'

'You would've broken my heart, you know.' The smallest of wry smiles curved his mouth, but his eyes were dark and serious as they held hers. 'Just for the record, I think you ought to know that I'm crazy in love with you.'

Kate stood there absorbing the look in his eyes while, despite everything, her heart began to pound and her breathing grew ragged. His hand slid warm and smooth against her cheek and he leaned forward, clearly meaning to kiss her. Before their mouths made contact, she stopped him with a hand pressed flat against his chest.

'I'm in love with you, too,' she told him.

His smile widened. 'I thought you might be,' he said, and kissed her, a quick, hard, but nevertheless infinitely satisfying kiss that ended when he put her in the car.

Then he vanished back into the house while she punched the button to open the garage door.

The next fourteen hours were the longest of Kate's life. By nine o'clock Friday night, as she left the stage in Mona's slinky black dress and rhinestone earrings, clutching the Shining Star award (a gold-colored plastic trophy in the shape of a star on a pedestal) that the mayor had just presented her with to thunderous applause, it was all she could do not to give in to blind terror. No word had been heard from the kidnappers. Some progress – via the unraveling of the Black Dragons' ties to the Mob – had been made on possibly identifying them, but not enough. Jim Wolff had left the building. After making nice with the big donors in attendance, he had been whisked away by his security detail, which had been notified of the possible assassination attempt in progress and declined to take the risk of leaving him in place even to possibly save the life of a little boy. Ever resourceful, the team working to save Ben had substituted a ringer – a man in a business suit with the same general height, build, and coloring – who was now supposedly in a back-room meeting with more potential big donors, which in reality were a gaggle of FBI agents. During the brief time he'd been present, Wolff had been covered by all the local TV stations, and no one knew of the ringer except their own small group, which was sworn to secrecy about the entire operation. But Kate was sick with fear at the thought that somehow the kidnappers had found out.

As the minutes crawled past with no phone call, she became increasingly convinced of it. Her heart pounded in great, panic-stricken strokes.

She rejoined Tom – so handsome in his tux that she would have melted looking at him under any other conditions – at their table just as his phone rang. The sound startled her so much she almost fell out of her chair.

He excused himself to answer, and she excused herself to follow. If he was taking a call now, it had to be about Ben. Had the kidnappers somehow gotten hold of his number? Had Ben been found? Had . . .

Her wild speculation ended when he disconnected and looked at her. They were standing in a little hall along the east side of the building by this time. Inside the main event room, she could just glimpse the stage, where the mayor was introducing someone else, and one of the huge gilded arches that girded the ceiling.

'We got an ID on the man on the security tape,' Tom said. 'Edward Curry. He was the PD in court-room 207 that day, remember. It looks like he forged the judge's name and filed the order himself. Plus, one of his fingerprints matches one on the gun Soto used to kill Judge Moran, so we got him on planting the weapons, too.'

Ed Curry. Kate was momentarily staggered. 'Have they picked him up? Has he said anything?'

She meant about Ben. Her entire focus was on Ben.

Tom shook his head. 'They don't want to pick him up yet. In case that should somehow tip off whoever's got Ben that you went to the cops. They're watching him, and he'll be picked up later.'

He meant if there was no other hope for finding Ben.

'Oh my God.' Kate felt a terrible sinking sensation in her stomach. 'What happens if—'

Her phone began to ring.

30

Casting a single petrified look at Tom, Kate snatched her phone out of Mona's borrowed evening bag. The ID line read *Unknown caller*, she saw as she answered.

'Hello.'

'Hello, Ms. White.' It was him. *It was him.* Kate nodded wildly at Tom, who stiffened and picked up the two-way radio he had clipped to his belt, then moved away as he started talking quickly into it.

'Where's my son?' Kate demanded. Her hands shook, and her legs felt about as stable as Slinky toys. Her heart did flip-flops in her chest.

'I'll tell you – as soon as you do that favor for us.' He was on a cell phone, she thought, because there seemed to be a lot of static. She could hear a low hum punctuated by a faint *click-click-click* sound that wasn't coming from her end. 'Are you listening?'

'Yes.'

'I want you to go into the ladies' restroom in the back hallway near the kitchen and unlock the window.' *Hum. Click-click-click.*

So someone could enter through it? A gunman, perhaps?

Tom was back beside her. He had his cop face on. His eyes were fastened on her face. He made a motion with his hand that meant she should keep the conversation going as long as possible. They were, she knew, trying to trace the call.

'Did you hear me?' the voice asked.

'I want to speak to Ben first,' Kate said, as she had been instructed to do. 'I'm not doing anything until I talk to my son. How do I know he's even still alive?'

'Ms. White . . .' *Hum. Click-click-click.*

'I mean it. I want to talk to Ben. I won't do it until I talk to Ben.' Her voice climbed dangerously near the edge of hysteria.

It must have convinced him, because he said, 'Wait.' Except for the static, there was silence. Kate could hear muffled voices in the background, as if two people were quickly conferring. Then he was back. 'Hold on.'

A moment later Ben said, 'Mom?'

'Ben?' Kate's heart lurched. She nearly crumpled to the floor with relief. 'Are you all right?'

''Member when I had that nightmare about the tyrannosaurus?' Ben's voice was shaky, but there was a note in it that made her brows contract. Her hand tightened on the phone until her knuckles hurt. 'I had another one last night.'

There was a scuffling sound, followed by a thud and a muffled *'Ow'* from Ben.

'Ben,' Kate said desperately, knowing he could no longer hear her as she called to him. *'Ben.'*

Except for the static, there was nothing on the other end.

'Ben,' she begged, going weak all over as she held the phone to her ear. Her breathing came fast and shallow. She felt as if she might faint. Her pulse raced.

Don't lose it. She had to keep it together for Ben.

'Go unlock the window, Ms. White.' The man was back.

'Did you hurt him?' Her voice was fierce. She shook with reaction and fear and anger. 'If you hurt him—'

She broke off because he disconnected. She knew instantly, because the static was gone. Her lips parted as she sucked in air. Her eyes flew to Tom.

'Tom—' She couldn't bear to close the phone.

Tom's eyes stayed on her face as he spoke into the two-way. 'Did you get it?'

Kate knew he was talking to whoever was trying to trace the call. His grimace told her the answer even before he shook his head in response to her pleading look. Leaning against the wall, using it as a crutch to aid her untrustworthy knees, she saw that their handpicked squad of police and FBI agents was converging on them from various directions like an army of ants, including the female agent in the blond wig and slinky black dress whose assignment was to take her place in carrying out the caller's request. Ignoring them, Kate grabbed Tom's arm.

'I think I know where he is,' she said, dry-mouthed.

'What?' Tom lowered the radio to stare at her.

'Last summer I took him to the navy yard to look at the ships. There was a billboard with a picture of a tyrannosaurus attacking another dinosaur on it. It was advertising one of the museum exhibits. He had a nightmare about it that night. On the phone just now he said, "'Member when I had that nightmare about the tyrannosaurus? I had another one last night." He's somewhere where he can see that billboard. He was trying to tell me where he is.'

'Jesus,' Tom said, as the infantry engulfed them. 'Smart kid.'

The Philadelphia navy yard was located down at the end of South Broad Street, with the smooth, dark waters of the Chesapeake Bay stretching seemingly endlessly beyond. Strung out along the waterfront were three miles of floating docks for visiting or anchored or dry-docked battleships and aircraft carriers and gunboats and the occasional submarine, as well as barges and freighters from all around the world, plus a small flotilla of commercial fishing vessels. There were cruise ships, too, docked at their own small, relatively upscale area off to one end. Dozens of identical gray and blue metal warehouses lined up in rows behind the docks. Huge metal shipping containers waited beside the warehouses to be moved either into the warehouses or onto ships. Forklifts, cranes, and winches sat idle, waiting for the coming of day. Narrow concrete roads ran between the warehouses and parallel to the docks. Gravel pocked with scrub grass covered everything else. Big halogen lights lit the area near the docks, although farther out, the shipyard, which covered hundreds of acres, was dark. A single security guard in a small guardhouse controlled the entrance to the cruise-ship compound. A couple more security guards patrolled the areas in front of the commercial vessels. Except for maybe half a dozen dockhands still laboring to unload one of the freighters, the rest of the compound appeared deserted.

Six cars, moving in single file, pulled slowly and as silently as possible onto one of the roads in the middle of the shipyard. Two of them were police cruisers, black-and-whites, with the sirens off. Two more were unmarked cars. The final two belonged to the FBI. Altogether, there were twenty law-enforcement officers in the six cars. With time so short, more reinforcements had been called in, and other cars and officers were at that moment setting up a perimeter around the shipyard. Radio silence was being strictly enforced, in case the kidnappers had access to a police scanner.

'This place is going to be a bitch to search.' Fish sounded grim. He was in the backseat of Tom's car. Tom was driving, and Kate was in the front passenger seat. She was looking out through the windshield at a billboard just beyond the northern edge of the property. Positioned so that it could be seen from the nearby expressway, raised three stories high on rusty metal legs, it was the tyrannosaurus sign Kate remembered, advertising a display at the Seaport Museum. Well-lit, it was impossible to miss.

It could be seen from everywhere in the shipyard. And probably for a quarter-mile in three directions beyond. As well as by every car zooming past on the expressway.

Her stomach dropped as she realized the enormous scale of the task before them. If they didn't have some way to zero in on a specific location within view of that sign, hunting for Ben still would be like looking for the proverbial needle in the haystack. Fearfully, she scanned the area.

Ben, where are you?

'Why do you think nothing's happened at the fund-raiser yet?' Kate asked, trying to keep the fear out of her voice. Tom had just gotten off the phone with one of the cops who had remained behind at the Troc. The agent had unlocked the window, as Kate had been instructed to do, and a contingent of FBI agents were standing by to take down anyone who came within a mile of it.

So far, no one had.

'The plan was for Wolff to exit through the hall that goes past that restroom,' Tom said. 'Maybe whatever they're planning is supposed to happen as he leaves. And he was scheduled to leave at ten, which is in about twenty minutes. There's no need to think anything's gone wrong yet.'

'They're still trying to get a lock on the cell phone that called yours,' Fish said. 'It had to bounce off a tower somewhere, and by checking all calls that came through in this area at that exact time and then triangulating it between towers, they may be able to find it.'

What he didn't say was that such a search would take time, if it even succeeded. And time, Kate feared, was exactly what they didn't have.

It had been only maybe ten minutes since she had talked to Ben, but in this situation, ten minutes was a lifetime.

Do they know their plan's been exposed yet? Do they think they don't need Ben any longer?

Both thoughts made her feel like all the air was being sucked out of the car.

The cars in front of them were stopping. Tom parked the Taurus, and they got out. The night was cold, and her bare feet in the sexy silver stiletto sandals Mona – whose feet were the same size as hers – had loaned her to go with the dress were freezing. Kate was glad to have her coat, which she had worn over the evening dress despite the fact that it was definitely not evening wear and thus didn't match at all. It was overcast, no moon or stars visible at all, and would have been dark as pitch had it not been for the glow of the halogen lights. The wind blowing in off the bay smelled of the sea, and of the coming rain. The surging of the tide against the shore was a constant murmur in the background.

Closer at hand was the sound of briskly approaching footsteps.

'Whatever happens, you stay with me,' Tom said to her as Willets and his partner, who as Feds were nominally in charge of the operation, came toward them. 'I'd leave you in the car, but too much could go wrong. Anyway, I don't trust you to stay there.'

'Is that the sign?' Willets asked as he reached them, nodding toward the tyrannosaurus. Willets was about six feet tall and well-built, with thick, short tobacco-brown hair and a handsome, square-jawed face. Like the rest of the federal agents and Fish, he was immaculately dressed in a suit and tie.

'Yes,' Kate said.

Willets turned in a full circle, hands on hips, looking all around, and gave a dismayed little whistle. 'You can probably see it from every square inch of this place.'

'Hurry,' Kate breathed. Willets glanced at her and nodded.

Five minutes later they had divided the area into grids and were searching it systematically, warehouse by warehouse, being as quiet as possible in hope of not alerting their prey to their presence. Only she and Tom were left by the cars. She because, as a civilian, she was not allowed to join in the search, and Tom because he refused to leave her.

'Can we at least walk around?' Shivering, Kate thrust her hands deep into her pockets. She was so cold, freezing, but she knew it had little to do with the chilly weather. It was the bone-deep cold of abject fear. If she was wrong about this, if Ben wasn't here . . . She couldn't even finish the thought. 'I can't stand this.'

Tom glanced around. The searchers had fanned out from their location in the middle of the shipyard. From where he and Kate stood by the cars, they could see dark figures slipping into narrow side doors and brief bursts of light as flashlights were judiciously employed. Occasionally, a whole warehouse would light up, although not all of them had working lights.

'Come on.' Tom slid a hand around her elbow, and together they walked down the line of parked cars. The narrow ends of the three-story warehouses were maybe six feet from them on either side. The dark metal buildings blended into the night, faceless and anonymous. The idea that her son might be imprisoned inside one made Kate want to run among them, shrieking his name. Only the thought that if his captors were alerted to their presence they might kill him on the spot kept her quiet. By ten o'clock, though, whoever was holding Ben was going to know that something had gone wrong. Time was running out.

Every time she remembered that, terror ran cold and thick through her veins.

Kate stopped and clenched her fists and closed her eyes.

Please, God, keep Ben safe.

'What?' Tom's voice was low.

'Shh. I just want to see if I can feel him.' Maybe it was stupid, maybe it wasn't. But her whole life since his birth had been about Ben. She loved him with every fiber of her being, and he loved her back. She could almost feel the bond between them like an invisible cable stretching out through the darkness, connecting her to him. She'd never been one to believe in psychics or anything like that, but this was different. This was Ben, and her love for him was so strong that she hoped it would act as a beacon drawing her toward him.

Ben. Where are you, Ben?

There was something – something tugging at the edges of her mind. Not knowing quite what it was but obeying her instincts, she turned her head to the left, then started walking that way, down the path between the long sides of two of the warehouses, frowning. Drawn by *something*. Her heels plunged unevenly through the gravel, making walking precarious.

Ben. Are you there?

'Kate . . .' Tom was beside her, his hand curling around her arm.

'Shh.' She shook her head at him. She didn't know where she was going, or what was pulling her, but it felt important somehow. They reached the end of that row of warehouses, crossed another of the narrow roads, and walked between more warehouses. The farther they got from the lights, the darker it grew, and Kate could feel Tom growing restive beside her. The crunch of their footsteps in the gravel was loud. She didn't know if this area had already been searched or not, but none of the searchers was in sight. She was peripherally aware that, beside her, Tom had drawn his gun.

Then she heard it. Or, more likely, she'd been

hearing it all along, but as the sound grew more distinct, her mind finally made the connection.

Hum. Click-click-click.

It was the sound she'd heard over the phone, which she had thought was static.

Her heart leaped. Her head turned sharply in the direction of the sound. It seemed to be coming from inside the warehouse to her left, which had a sliding, garage-size door in its side. The door was open about three feet, just about the width of an ordinary door, revealing a glimpse of almost impenetrable blackness inside. Except for, a few feet beyond the entrance, a dull silver gleam. Eyes widening, Kate realized as the shape took on form and substance against the more amorphous background that what she was seeing was a car's bumper.

A black SUV's bumper, to be precise.

'Tom.' She grabbed his arm to alert him, turning to look at him through the thick shadows. Their eyes connected, and he started to say something. Then his gaze moved beyond her and he froze.

'Mom.'

Kate was still in the process of following Tom's gaze to see what had so transfixed him when she heard Ben's voice. For one brief, shining instant it was the most welcome sound she had ever heard – until she registered how quiet it was, and how shaky.

Then she saw what Tom was staring at: Ben stood just inside the open warehouse door. The reason she was able to see him so well was that somebody off to one side was shining a flashlight on his face. As well as on the thick, black-clad arm around his neck, and the businesslike black gun pressed to his temple.

She felt all the color drain out of her face. The sudden lump that formed in her throat was hard, cold fear.

'Ben.' Instinctively, Kate started toward him. Tom grabbed her arm to keep her in place.

'Don't move. Don't make a sound. Or the kid's dead.' The voice spoke out of the darkness just behind Tom. Kate jumped, glancing around, her eyes widening with horror as she realized that while they had been focused on Ben, someone – the man on the phone, the man in the ladies' room, the man who'd done all the talking in the SUV, the man who'd punched her, it was his voice – had crept up behind them. He was a big, burly shape in the dark – with a gun pointed straight at them.

'Ike?' There was no mistaking the disbelief in Tom's voice. Clearly, this was someone he knew. A cop? Had her instincts been right?

'Put the gun down, Tom. Nice and slow. And Ms. White – I wouldn't move if I were you. That's your kid over there. He wouldn't be so cute with a hole in his head.'

Kate froze. Her stomach plunged. Her heart stopped.

'We got twenty people within a hundred yards of you,' Tom said. 'Plus, there's a perimeter set up around the edge of the property. There's no way you're getting out of here.'

'You underestimate the value of being a police sergeant. We could shoot you all three right now, and then get in the car and drive on out there like we've come to help in the search and nobody would question it. Now put your gun on the ground. Don't make me off the kid.'

The man holding Ben must have tightened his grip or done something else to cause him pain, because Ben made a little sound of distress.

'*Ben.*' Kate's stomach turned inside out. She was breathing way too fast, and her heart pounded like she had been running for miles. All she wanted in the world was to rush to him – but she couldn't. She didn't have a single doubt that these men would kill them with the least provocation. And there was still a gun to Ben's head.

Letting go of her arm, Tom bent and put his gun on the ground.

'Now back off,' Ike said. 'And keep your hands where I can see them.'

Tom took a couple of steps toward Kate. Ike scooped Tom's gun off the ground.

'Why?' Tom asked.

'Some of us need to supplement our income.' Ike's tone was the verbal equivalent of a shrug. 'I've been on Genovese's' – Kate recognized the name as that of an organized-crime boss in the area – 'payroll for a while. Wolff pissed him off, and Genovese put a million-dollar price tag on his head. Long as it couldn't be traced back to him. We had a guy going in the window dressed like a waiter. Wolff always drinks a cup of hot tea before he hits the road at the end of these things. Our guy was going to put poison in it.'

'Poison?' Kate asked, before she could stop herself.

'See, you shoot somebody, they're on top of you right there. You basically got no chance of getting away with it. Poison, it takes a little longer to act and it's not so easy to trace. Plus, it makes a statement, which is what Genovese wanted to do.'

'What about Ed Curry?' Tom asked. 'Is he on Genovese's payroll, too?'

'Nah. He's just somebody we had something on, like Ms. White here. He does what we tell him. When we tell him.'

'Not anymore. He's being picked up as we speak.'

'Shit.' Ike sounded genuinely concerned, and Kate guessed he was worried about what Curry might spill. Then his tone changed. 'Or you're full of shit. And I'm betting you're full of shit.'

'I'm not. We got Curry. But it's not too late for you to make a deal,' Tom said. 'Go state's evidence against Genovese.'

'I don't think so. Pissing Genovese off is not a smart thing to do.' He gestured with his gun. 'No more talk. You think I don't know what you're trying to do? Walk into the warehouse. And don't get between her and the gun, Tom. I'll shoot you right now if you do.'

From that Kate deduced that Tom had been moving into a position to block her from Ike's gun with his own body, probably hoping that she would make a break for it. But there was no way in hell she was leaving Ben. Her eyes found her son's face. Still wearing the jeans and blue jacket he'd had on when he'd been pulled from her car, he looked pale and small and tired and scared to death.

Kate knew how he felt.

Please, God, let Fish or Willets or somebody realize we're missing and come looking for us. We're right over here . . .

The man holding Ben pulled him back out of the way as Kate stepped through the door.

'Mom,' Ben whimpered as she neared him.

'It's going to be okay, sweetie,' she lied. Kate would have gone straight to him then, but someone grabbed her arm, yanking her the rest of the way inside, causing her to stumble in her unfamiliar shoes, twisting her arm up behind her back so that she cried out in pain. By the shifting beam of the flashlight her captor held in his other hand – he was clearly the one who had been shining the light on Ben – Kate saw that she was in a cavernous space with a peaked, corrugated ceiling, metal rafters, metal walls, and an earthen floor. Tall stacks of wooden crates formed a wall about twenty feet in. Farther than that she could not see. Closer at hand were two plastic lawn chairs, a sleeping bag, and a kerosene heater. As soon as Kate saw the heater, she knew that this was the source of the sound she had heard: the steady hum of its operation, and the *click-click-click* as it oscillated back and forth.

She saw, too, that the man holding Ben had loosened

his grip. Ben was no longer being held quite so tightly against him, and he no longer had a gun to his head. His eyes were on her, wide and terrified.

Despite the fact that she was sweating bullets and her arm was breaking and she was so frightened she felt like the blood was draining from her head, she smiled at him.

Then Tom walked through the opening, hands up, closely followed by Ike. Kate was sure that they were going to die, all three of them, in probably a matter of minutes. Tom knew them, and Ben and she could identify them. There was no way in hell any of them was going to be left alive.

'Goddamn it, Ike, are you going to kill a woman and a little kid?' Tom demanded as the flashlight swung toward him.

The man holding Ben screamed.

'Ow! He bit me! The little shit bit me!'

Unbelievably, Ben was free, exploding toward the opening, screaming like a fire engine.

'Shit!'

'Grab him!

'Catch him!'

'Go, kid! Go!'

'Run, Ben!' As her captor's grip on her arm slackened with surprise, Kate slammed her stiletto heel back into his knee with every bit of strength she possessed. He yelped, and she was able to jerk free. But the doorway was blocked and she couldn't get out, so all she could do was scream like a steam whistle and dodge her captor, who came after her with a roar, as she sought a way out. Then she realized that it was Tom in the doorway, Tom struggling with Ike and the man who'd been holding Ben, keeping them from going after her son, whose screams as he raced away echoed her own. Blows were falling thick and fast. The sickening thud of fists on flesh filled the air. As Kate, darting around the wooden crates with her captor in hot pursuit, glanced back in horror, Tom doubled over as if he'd taken a fist to the stomach.

Crack. Crack.

'Ahh!'

The gunfire was just a few feet away, definitely inside the warehouse. The sound was so loud that Kate felt her ears ring. The cry was hoarse, pain-filled, sounding like someone had been shot – was it Tom? Her heart exploded with fear for him, her pulse leaped into overdrive, and for a moment the world seemed to slow down as she tried to see just who was down.

All the noise was sure to bring help, but would it be in time?

Please, God, please . . .

Then she heard the most welcome sound she had ever heard: Willets's voice shouting, 'Freeze, FBI!'

Moments later, when the lights had been turned on and the bad guys had been cuffed and Kate was standing next to Tom, who wasn't wounded but had managed to wrest away Ike's gun and put a bullet into his leg to boot, Ben came trotting in with Fish. He still looked pale and small and tired, but the fear had left his face. He ran to her, Kate wrapped her arms around him, and they hugged as if they would never let go.

'You were so brave,' Kate told him when he pulled out of her arms at last. 'I can't believe you bit that guy.'

'Somebody had to do something or we were all gonna die.' Ben looked at Tom. 'Okay, I've done my part. I saved her life. Now it's over to you for a while.'

Tom looked surprised. Then he grinned and ruffled Ben's hair.

'Fair enough,' he said, and wrapped both Ben and his mother up in a hug.

31

Eight months later, Tom stood in the front of Our Lady of the Sorrows Church and watched his bride walk up the aisle toward him. Charlie, his best man, stood at his side. Fish and the brothers-in-law (no way was he getting away without including them) were ranged beside Charlie. Already having walked down the aisle in front of Kate, his sisters and sister-in-law plus Mona wore lacy lavender dresses and were lined up on the other side of the altar.

His mother was blotting her eyes and beaming at him from the front pew.

And the church was filled to overflowing with every relative, friend, acquaintance, or associate of all of the above, approximately five hundred strong.

The thing was, all he and Kate had wanted was a civil ceremony. Second wedding for both and all that. Go to the courthouse, get married. No fuss, no frills.

And this was how it had worked out.

Not that, right at the moment, he minded.

Because Kate, looking beautiful in a long, white dress, was smiling at him. And Ben, who was walking her up the aisle and looking surprisingly grown-up in a black tux just like the one Tom was wearing, was grinning at him, too.

In about half an hour, give or take a long-winded speech or two by the priest, whom he had known all his life, they would be a family.

Every once in a while, you just get lucky.

KAREN ROBARDS

Obsession

Katharine Lawrence has just survived a nightmare.

She remembers the vicious burglars who shot her best friend, the
terror she felt the night she nearly died.

But there are things she doesn't remember at all. Like her lover's
voice on the phone. Like her clothes in her luxurious Washington
townhouse. Like the face in her mirror. Everything in her life
feels utterly wrong, as if the trauma has given her some kind of
amnesia.

As Katharine acts on her instincts and runs for her life, she's rescued
by Dan Howard, the handsome doctor who lives next door. She
thinks she can trust him, but she will have to decide fast.

Because the killers are back.

HODDER

KAREN ROBARDS

Vanished

Seven years ago, five-year-old Lexie Mason vanished and her mother Sarah was left to pick up the pieces of her shattered life.

Then one hot August night Sarah picks up the telephone to hear a child's terrified voice whispering, 'Mommy, help, come and get me . . .' The call is cut off, but not before Sarah's heart soars. The voice belongs to Lexie.

Sarah goes to the police, the FBI, friends and her co-workers at the Beaufort County, South Carolina Prosecutor's Office, but none of them can help. Desperate, she turns to Jake Hogan, her closest friend in the world, the man who has stood by her throughout the long years of searching. Jake is now a private investigator and though he is sceptical – convinced that someone is deliberately tormenting the grief-stricken mother – the attraction he feels for Sara makes him join her search.

Lexie may still be alive – and they may be able to rescue her.

HODDER